KOSHER KILL

STERLING ANTHONY

In dedication to all survivors, whatever their challenges might be.

1.

   Matthew Kent had filled both cups to the brim, a mistake on the one that was to be his, so he took hurried sips, enduring the scorching cocoa, until the level was down enough to add rum. He'd considered using mugs but cups and saucers seemed more likely to impress, especially being bone china. From their bag, he pulled a handful of miniature marshmallows, dropped them one-by-one into the cups, and grinned contently when the count turned out even. He took a cup and saucer in each hand, made a mental note of which cup was spiked, and headed out the kitchen en route to the living room.

From a CD player, Nat King Cole was crooning his seasonal classic. That, in addition to the redolence of pine intermingled with those of peppermint candy canes, nutmeg, and cinnamon, told the time of year as reliably as any calendar—not that the decorations, alone, didn't say it all.

In the spirit and tipsy, Kent dared some slow choreography, a few back-and-forth steps, then a step-around, never spilling a drop. Kent might not have been feeling his age but his wrists were. They began to quiver under the weights, causing the cups and saucers to jingle-jangle, like bells on that one-horse open sleigh carolers sing about.

The quivering caused the marshmallows to bob, like that horse's head might do, and the steam from the cocoa to wisp and swirl, like that horse's wintry breath might do.

Succumbing to discomfort, Kent stopped the dallying and quickened his steps. Upon turning the corner, he saw that the living room was empty, a mystery soon solved when he noticed the closed bathroom door and the light showing from underneath. In front of a plush sofa was a marble-top coffee table, on it a tray of still-warm-from-the-oven cookies in the shapes of Santas, snowmen, and toy soldiers, the tasty assortment untouched.

Kent's wrists were close to giving out, yet he vacillated over which cup to place down first, silly indecision due to bottled holiday cheer. He chose simultaneous placement. While he was carefully gliding the cups down, and before he could land them, he was ambushed from behind, the assailant's right arm clamping around Kent's neck.

For an insane instant, Kent tried to keep the shaking china level, tried to keep the cocoa from spilling. The china clattered like two skeletons wrestling and the marshmallows splashed about steamy surfaces like flotsam in choppy, fog-blanketed waters. Survival instincts prevailed and Kent let the cocoa fall and then clutched his freed hands around his assailant's arm.

The assailant silently cursed Kent for being bald. An Afro, ponytail, braids, dreadlocks–anything to grab from the back and pull, exposing the target–would have been appreciated, would have made matters easier, cleaner.

"What the—" Kent began, but the assailant's arm jerked tighter, chopping off the rest of that desperate query.

Next came a dervish dance, out of step with the background music, Kent leading with spinning, twisting, lurching moves.

Kent yanked at the arm, but the assailant's left hand locked onto the right wrist for added resistance. The assailant wore a thick sweater and had donned gloves, safeguards against having a clutching, scratching Kent getting DNA under his fingernails.

Kent bent forward sharply, lifting the assailant off the floor. The load was too much for his frail frame and he had to straighten. Then he tried flinging the assailant over his shoulder with a corking motion. His spine wasn't up to it, the lumbar pain so sharp that it made him bolt upright.

That's when the assailant wedged a forearm under Kent's chin and pried upward, trying to force Kent's head backward. Kent, feeling choked, turned his head to the right, nestling his chin within the crook of the assailant's elbow. The maneuver relieved some pressure off Kent's Adam's apple.

It also served the assailant's intention. Starting at Kent's left ear, the assailant traced a crescent across the neck, ending just past the right ear.

"Although it's been said, many times, many ways," sang Nat, as the assailant released Kent and took a step back, both to avoid the gush and to observe.

Kent wobbled in place, unable to control his head movements; however, the hand he clamped around his throat was meant not as a steadying device but as a tourniquet. The hand became wet, warm, sticky, and as blazingly red as any of the yuletide decorations adorning the room.

The assailant rushed forward and gave Kent a stiff shove in the back, meaning to send him to the floor. *Drop and die, already. Don't suffer unnecessarily.*

But Kent remained on stumbling feet that were incapable of beating a path of escape, feet that only could manage several steps into the adjoining family room. There, he collapsed. On the way down, he wildly clawed at air before grabbing a branch of the Christmas tree. Needles folded umbrella-fashion and the branch slipped from his grip as the tree toppled. Ornaments popped loose, falling to a carpet too thick to cause them to break.

Kent, facedown, dusted with artificial snow from the tree, couldn't get up, couldn't turn over, couldn't even rotate his head. He had to rely upon his fading peripheral vision to glimpse his assailant. It was confirmation not discovery; for, who else could it have been?

Coldness was coursing through Kent, despite the warmth radiating merrily from crackling logs in the fireplace. Kent's life force was like a helium balloon tugging against a loose slip-knot, and after it pulled free and floated off, Kent's eyes remained opened in puzzlement, the *who* having been answered, but not the *why*.

The assailant crept close for an inspection, wishing that there could have been some way to have clocked the whole thing. The elapsed time couldn't have been long in the absolute sense; still, it was too long. All that trashing about was uncalled for; so, if Kent suffered, even mentally, prior to the coup de grâce, he only had himself to blame for resisting. Then again, maybe his resistance quickened matters—raised the heartbeat, made the heart pump faster and the blood spurt stronger.

Such rationalizing was meant to counter the dissonance being experienced by the assailant, who'd been lectured innumerably about the humaneness of swift, precise technique. Having taken up the mission—more than that, having dispensed with the first target—now was not the time for doubts nor misgivings.

Looking for anything incriminating, the assailant's eyes darted about, before fixing on the slightly opened curtains of a side window. How could they have been overlooked? Turned out they hadn't. The curtains were being held open by a branch of the fallen tree. A quick, worried peek though the curtains was reassuring. A thicket of shrubs, bare and strung with holiday lights that flickered like multicolored fireflies, ran along that side of the house. Only someone with a determined motive would brave the thorns to look in the window; more so, the lack of footprints in the snow indicated that no one had.

The curtains were an unnerving reminder of the necessity to attend to details. Accept whatever good luck befalls, but it's no substitute for competence. Good and lucky: a difficult combination to beat.

While the assailant still was peering through the curtains, it started to snow. These flakes weren't the downy, moist variety descending uniformly. These flakes, from a charcoal, constipated night sky, were scrawny, dry, and scattering fitfully, like dandruff in a wind tunnel. As for the actual wind, it was blowing fiercely and could be heard as it went about its business of slashing to the bone people who were inadequately layered, seemingly bragging to the assailant about how a true pro does it.

And whereas most people would take the wind's gelid howl as a warning to stay hunkered down indoors, to the assailant it was a reminder that it was time to venture back into the chapping cold, prompting the thought, *Too bad about the cocoa because I could use something to warm my insides.*

2.

Mary Cunningham, naked, freshly-showered, and smelling of apricot, lay supine across the king-size bed. Her left arm was bent and her head rested in her left palm. Her eyes were closed. "Firmer, Cliff," she directed. "A little firmer."

Cliff, flustered, lifted his hand off her breast.

But Mary quickly pressed it back in place, applying the desired pressure, saying, "Like this."

Cliff, in boxers, resignedly said, "I'll try again."

She removed her hand from his but cautioned, "Just like I showed you."

With three fingertips, he pressed in circles, starting at the perimeter and working toward the center. "Too hard?"

Eyes still closed, trying to concentrate and relax at the same time, she answered, "No." Once again, she had assigned the task to husband, Cliff, distrustful of her own ability to distinguish between the real thing and the product of fearful imaginings.

Dutifully, Cliff continued. He felt around the nipple and then trapped it between his thumb and index. He squeezed it experimentally a few seconds and then released

it. He repeated the sequence before reporting, "No dis-
charge."

"Good."

Cliff rested his palm flat against her breast and following a burdened sigh asked, "Can I stop now?"

Mary opened her eyes and then narrowed them in
displeasure. She pushed away his hand and with attitude
declared, "Since it's such a burden, I won't ask you again."

"That's not fair," he protested. "I did as you asked.
Went through the entire procedure. Twice. Both breasts."
He might have been better served if he hadn't added, "And
you only have two."

Mary shot back, "Yeah, for now," but wasn't implying the
possibility of growing a third.

"Be reasonable. This is the third time in less than a
month."

"Well, excuse me for wanting to live."

"Drop the sarcasm, will you, please?" implored Cliff.
"I understand your worries, I do, but you must try to keep
them in reasonable check."

"So, what you're saying is that I'm not trying to your
satisfaction."

Put on defense, Cliff said, "Like the other week, during
foreplay. I'm sucking your nipples, caressing your breasts,
when out of nowhere you ask if I feel any lumps."

She gave the biting reminder, "It didn't cause you to
lose your hard-on, so I guess you weren't too distracted,
were you?" With that, she sprang her 5'6", 150 pounds from
the bed and hastened to the armchair where rested the

clothes she'd laid out to wear to work. She snatched the white cotton panties, plowed one leg through, then the other, and jerked them up by the waistband. She snatched the matching bra then loaded the 36-B cups. "Mind fastening me, or is that also asking too much?"

Cliff gave what he hoped was a disarming smile. "Turn around."

After being fastened, Mary dryly said, "Thanks." She pulled her head back so that Cliff's attempted kiss to her cheek only made brushing contact. In quick order, she donned gray slacks, pink shirt, black socks, and black winter boots. Then she strapped on the shoulder holster containing a 9 mm. Glock semi-automatic and hung her I.D. around her neck. Last to go on was a black blazer, a pink ribbon pinned to the lapel.

Cliff had stood in silence, scratching his mustache, his dark-complexioned face somber. Knowing that Mary soon would be leaving the house, he said, "We agreed long ago not to go to bed angry and not to part company angry."

She gave a, "Humph," yet claimed, "I'm not angry. What gave you that idea? Hurt, yeah, that I can't ask my own husband for a small favor."

"Small or large, there's nothing I wouldn't do for you. And you know that."

She broke eye-contact and then said, "At this moment, I'm wondering."

"No, you aren't. You're stressed and scared, and since I'm the closest at hand, you're taking it out on me."

"Oh, poor, poor, you."

Quickly and sharply, Cliff said, "That's enough." He closed in, until they were almost nose-to-nose, and offered, "Since you seem to want a punching bag, is this distance close enough?" When the response wasn't immediate, he added, "This also is a distance suited for embracing. What's your choice, Sweetheart?"

Mary felt a nasal stinging sensation as her eyes began to water. She pursed her lips but that didn't stop them from quivering. When Cliff took her in his arms, she pressed her face into his bare chest and blubbered, the outburst a needed catharsis. Her first attempt to speak was an unintelligible garble of sobs and syllables, before she offered a, "I'm sorry."

"Shhh," sounded Cliff, not needing an apology. He kissed her forehead then massaged the back of her neck. "You are not alone." Then he held her by the shoulders, better to peer into her eyes, and guaranteed, "I'll be here for you the entire way."

Mary's head bobbled knowingly, before she said, "I never truly doubted you." She paused and then admitted, "I knew I was saying things uncalled for and I wanted to stop, but...I don't know. Hard to explain."

"No explanation needed."

"I love you for being so damn understanding," she said and guiltily added, "but by comparison, I come off like a spoiled brat."

Cliff placed a finger under her chin and lifted her head. "But you're my spoiled brat."

"You're not supposed to agree with me," she said in mock reprimand. "I still can make you that punching bag." She made a fist, threw a roundhouse at his face, but missed by the proverbial mile, as intended.

The Cunninghams shared a solidly-middle class house in Detroit's New Center Area. They were empty-nesters, her daughter and his son from previous marriages now grown and living on their own.

From across the room, Mary glimpsed herself in the vanity mirror and assessed, "I look a holy fright." She walked to the mirror and leaned forward, frowning, as she turned her head at varying angles. "Eyes all bloodshot, and shit. Nose runny. Ugly."

"You might not be looking your best right now, but you're never ugly," contended Cliff. "Plus, you have inner beauty."

"Inner beauty is nice," she conceded, all the while patting her short, graying-at-the temples-afro into place, primping. "And outer beauty might be only skin deep but I want it on my skin." In that pursuit, she started for the bathroom but then halted. "Cliff?"

"Yes?"

"When you mentioned inner beauty..." Mary was wrestling with how to pose the question. "Were you saying... did you mean..."

He sensed where she might be headed and therefore said, "It was nothing more than an honest compliment."

On the next try, Mary spit it out, sort of. "What if I had to have a mastectomy?"

"Whoa!" pleaded Cliff. "Let's not get way ahead of ourselves."

Mary pressed the issue. "Would you look at me the same way after a mastectomy? Love me just as much?"

"Absolutely," insisted the English professor, who had once written an ode to her breasts, describing them as scoops of caramel ice cream, topped with chocolate spills, capped with licorice gum drops. "I can't deny that I love your breasts, Honey, but the same goes for everything about you."

Her "Un-huh," was lukewarm, meant to invite more convincing.

Cliff went to her and began a touch-and-tell recital. "I love your apple-shaped ass," he said, and squeezed it, "your big, fine legs," he said, and rubbed them, "and, your hairy, tight coochie," he said, and cupped it. "It's synergy, the total greater than the sum of the parts."

Mary's smile was ear-to-ear, making the childhood scar above her mouth flatten. "I'm sold."

"That's my Baby." Sounding as sure as an Alaskan weatherman predicting cold temperatures in January, Cliff said, "You're going to have a very long life." But he wasn't through. "And I want to spend the rest of mine with you."

"Oh, how I needed to hear that." Mary then changed her focus. "I have to go splash some water on my face and get out of here."

"Okay."

"First, you have to let go of me."

Cliff's hand was still cupped between her legs. "Oh, right." He released her, in a slow, pressing, upward motion.

Mary read his eyes, knew his thoughts. "Stay put, Baby Boy. I'll be back in a minute."

3.

Once sweet and spongy, the marshmallows now lay bloated and hard, resembling faceless dice, which Mary was rolling back and forth with her foot. It wasn't for any forensic purposes; she was idling, playing scenarios in her head, theorizing about how Kent had met his demise.

A couple of hours earlier, she'd floated into the precinct, aglow from the quickie she'd had with Cliff, in makeup of their tiff over breast examinations; however, she wasn't able to bask long before being dispatched to the house in Detroit's Boston-Edison District.

From upstairs came the rumblings made by others who were processing the crime scene. She'd made a quick canvas of the upstairs, basement too, after which, she decided to limit her attention to the downstairs living quarters.

"I wish I kept such a clean house," admitted Dora Craig, who was descending the stairs. A recently divorced suburbanite and fitness devotee, Craig had been a homicide detective for three years. "The only dust in this place is what the techs are laying down for prints."

"Cleaner than my house, too," confessed Mary, not given to small talk at a crime scene.

Craig, who was, said, "Neat-and-tidy crime scenes are the best to investigate, in my opinion. Easier to notice when something seems out of place."

"For all the good this one is doing us." Mary's comment reflected the fact that, with the glaring exceptions of the toppled tree, spilled cocoa, and blood, nothing seemed out of place. As for the dead body that would belong in that category, Kent had been taken to the Wayne County morgue.

"What do you figure happened?" asked Craig.

"Ambush. The victim was carrying the cups and dropped them. A struggle took place from the spill to where the body was found. I say the whole thing went down quick."

"I agree," said Craig. "The killer cuts the victim's throat, the victim drops the cups, tries to escape, falls, and dies."

"You have the sequence wrong," said Mary. "Look at the blood, where it starts, where it trails, where it pools." Pointing, she continued, "No blood where the cups spilled. That means they were dropped first, at the beginning of the attack. Then came the struggle, which ended when the victim's throat was cut."

Craig accepted the correction in stride and came back with, "The two knew each other, obviously."

"That, they did." Mary removed her latex gloves, stuffed them into her pants pocket, and gave an order delivered as a question. "Ready to go, Dora?"

"If you feel there's no reason to hang around."

"Then, let's make like shepherds and get the flock out of here," said Mary, safe from being told that the line was corny.

"Lead the way."

Mary had driven the two of them to the crime scene but they were not partners. Mary had not had a partner, formally, for years.

Craig's coat was draped around the back of a dining room chair. After she donned the hooded, bulky, down-filled garment, there was no doubting that she took Michigan winters seriously.

Mary, on the other hand, had not removed her calf-length overcoat, and only had to button it in preparation for their departure.

"What do you think the odds are of solving this one?" asked Craig, walking toward the door.

A knitted cap had been sitting high on Mary's head and she pulled it down and tight. "One-hundred percent. That's always my thinking, unless and until I'm proven wrong."

4.

The director shouted, "Cut!"

Myron Shuster, in pantomime, wrapped an imaginary rope around his neck then made a yanking upward motion. His neck fell to the side, a faked suicide for once again having flubbed his lines.

Mary had never seen the filming of a television commercial. She'd been directed to this location, north of Detroit, by Shuster's secretary. This being the first break in the filming since her arrival, she took the opportunity to identify herself. She approached, held out her I.D. for a second, and then let it fall back in place around her neck. "Mary Cunningham, Detroit homicide. I'd like to ask you some questions, Mr. Shuster."

Shuster was about to send an email on his BlackBerry. He slowly returned the device to its belt clip. "I'm guessing this is about Matt."

"If you mean Matthew Kent, yes."

"When I heard about him on the news, it was like a mule kicked me in the belly." Shuster wore elevator shoes because he believed that taller salespeople were more successful, although his pudginess subtracted from the vertical effect. He was early-sixties and his mop of grey-streaked hair included bangs that cascaded to his eyebrows. He wore a garish plaid sports coat, a size too large. It was all costume, that of the nerdy pitchman for his successful chain of appliance stores.

"Is there somewhere we can talk in private?" asked Mary.

"I'll clear the place." Speaking loud enough to be heard across the set, Shuster said, "Jerry, you and the crew take early lunch," a directive that immediately was obeyed.

Privacy achieved, Mary began the interview. "According to Mr. Kent's appointment book, you were to meet with him yesterday morning. Ten o'clock. Tell me about that."

"Went to his home. Rang the doorbell a number of times. No answer. Called both of his phones. No answer. So I left. I had no idea he was in there, dead." Shuster shrugged, a punctuation that signaled that there was nothing else to tell.

Mary felt otherwise. "What was the reason for your visit?"

Shuster leaned against a washing machine, actually a prop, as were the other appliances arranged in simulation of one of his stores. "You might say charity. More or less."

"Let's go for precisely or exactly."

"Then, here're the details," announced Shuster. "Matt and I have worked together for more than ten years. I'm chairman of the southeast Michigan branch of the Jewish Elves. Maybe you've heard of the organization."

"I'm not sure. Tell me about it."

"Jewish volunteers substitute for Christians who'd otherwise have to work Christmas Eve and Christmas, job requirements permitting, of course. For example, can't have someone without medical training substitute for a nurse." As an afterthought, he said, "Law enforcement is excluded for the same reasoning."

"Don't rub it in," Mary said. "How was Mr. Kent involved?"

"He was a coordinator who matched volunteers with beneficiaries. Yesterday, I came over to give him his latest list of volunteers. I also had appointments that day with some other coordinators. I can give you their names, to check, in case I'm a suspect."

Mary scratched behind an ear. "Suspect? I hope I haven't given you that impression." But she barely paused before saying, "But since you offered, I'll take you up on those names."

"As you wish." Out came his BlackBerry and he scrolled the contacts, calling out names and numbers as Mary jotted, and then asked, "Anything else?"

"Yes. Did you think about calling the police after learning of Mr. Kent's death?"

"I thought about it," said Shuster, unfazed, "but didn't because I felt I had nothing to contribute." He stood erect, giving up the support of the prop. "Let me be emphatic. I have no knowledge of what happened. Saw nothing. Even with the answers I've given you, I can't see how I've supplied anything of worth."

"Let me be the judge of that."

"Gladly." Shuster got in a question of his own. "Is it true what's been reported about how his body was discovered?"

"I don't know. What's been reported?"

"That his security alarm was blasting all night before complaining neighbors got the authorities out there."

"Thanks for that information," said Mary, with a straight face. She wasn't about to share her theory that the killer, not knowing the code, triggered the alarm upon leaving. "Let's see if you can be even more informative. Why didn't you put the list in the mail slot?"

"Because I knew, at least I thought I knew, that I'd be seeing Matt soon, anyway. He and I had to schedule the publicity."

"What publicity?"

"We get coverage from the media. Interviews and the like. And, of all the coordinators, Matt was the best with that sort of thing."

"Was your association with Kent limited to the Jewish Elves?"

"Strictly." Shuster held back for some moments before adding, "It couldn't have been otherwise."

"Why?"

"Matt was gay. And he wasn't that closeted about it. I'm sure your investigation would have revealed that, if it already hasn't."

It hadn't, but Mary didn't say so. "Do you have something against gays?"

"Don't have a discriminating bone in my body. I was merely speaking from a birds-of-a -feather perspective."

"Do you know the names of any of his associates, whatever their orientation?"

Shuster's mouth turned downward and he shook his head while saying, "Can't help you there. I've seen a few at his house."

"Anyone particular you recall?"

"Nope, just younger guys."

"What race?"

"Some white, some black."

"Ever witness any friction between Mr. Kent and any of them?"

"No."

"I suppose you don't know whether Mr. Kent was having problems with any particular person, regardless of relationship."

"You suppose correctly."

"And, you had no reason to kill him, did you?" asked Mary, for thoroughness.

Shuster rubbed his palms together. "That's quite a question to put to someone who's not a suspect."

"I never said you were or weren't."

His palms came together in a single clap. "I stand corrected." In a sudden digression, he asked, "Does your interrogation room have that single light bulb hanging low from the ceiling, or is that just a movie stereotype?"

"Please answer the question."

His attempt at levity having bombed, Shuster said,
"I will, although I would have thought that my previous
answers would have made that question unnecessary." He
went on to remark, "I'll say it as unequivocally as I know
how. I had no reason to kill Matt. I did not kill Matt. I
don't know who did."

"Noted. Thanks for your time."

5.

Dr. Laura Wright, a beanpole with a mouth full of large, pearly, perfectly aligned teeth, was standing with her left forearm against her abdomen and her chin resting on her right fist. She was a practicing oncologist and a medical professor at the University of Michigan Medical School. "I hope I didn't confuse you, Mrs. Cunningham."

"Somewhat," admitted Mary, seated at a table, but in truth, parts of the presentation had caused her blood-shot eyes to glaze over. Her knowledge of DNA almost exclusively was limited to police work, and even then, she knew little—and didn't care to know more—about the science and laboratory procedures behind its forensic applications. No two individuals shared the same DNA, with the exception of identical twins; therefore, its presence at a crime scene, depending on circumstances, can be damning evidence. How much more does a homicide cop, with a high-school education, need to know? What she'd just sat through, however, had nothing to do with crime-solving and everything to do with a supremely personal matter.

Standing beside Wright and better at laymen explanations was Dr. Sheila Finney, a radiation oncologist, as attractive as any lead character on a medical drama series. "All cells contain DNA. Cells grow by dividing. DNA is copied to the new cells. But things can go wrong and some cells end up with damaged DNA." Finney sought feedback, asking, "Are you with me so far?"

"Yes," answered Mary.

"Fine," said Finney. "Cells usually repair their damaged DNA but sometimes the damage is too great to repair and under those circumstances the cells are supposed to self-destruct."

"Supposed to," repeated Mary, grasping the significance of that qualifier.

"But they don't always," resumed Finney. "Sometimes those DNA-damaged cells that don't self-destruct start dividing abnormally fast. When that happens, the result is cancer."

The interior of the Jonas Cancer Center was colorful, not the monotonous, sterile, whiteness common to such clinics. This meeting room, like the others in the facility, contained hardy plants, some blooming, in contrast to the slumbering outdoors, it being February. Even the framed wall hangings were consistently of the enjoyment of life, everything from dancing to skydiving. Still, ambiance, no matter how cheerful, doesn't undo the impact of the C-word.

"Cancer." The utterance shrunk Mary just a little. She had a headache that would give a pair of aspirin a real go of it. Betrayal rang in her voice, as she said, "What's the use of eating right, exercising, doing the things you're supposed to do, if—"

"All of those things are good to do," interrupted Wright, "but, there are no guarantees against breast cancer. One in every eight women will contract it. And, I'm among those health professionals who believe that the odds for contracting it increase with age."

Finney added, "But a woman need not be up in age." Then, she confided, "I'm a breast cancer survivor. Going into my fourth year."

"I never would have suspected," said Mary. "I wish you the best."

"Thank you," said Finney.

"Even though this facility specializes in the treatment of cancer," said Wright, "there is much we simply don't know." She ran her hand up and down her arm a few times, like she was soothing a sunburn under her lab coat. "That goes for breast cancer and any other form of the disease." Sounding a positive note, she said, "But there is one thing that's known and on which the medical community agrees. The best prospects for survival derive from early detection and treatment."

"Which brings us to the discussion of the file," said Finney. "Early detection wasn't made due to missed opportunities." She walked to a wall. There, she flicked a switch, illuminating a board, on which hung a row of x-rays— mammograms, to be exact.

"These are arranged in a timeline," said Wright, now also at the board.

"This mammogram is from three years ago." Finney picked up a pointer from the ledge. "Those white spots are calcifications, more specifically, micro-calcifications."

"As opposed to the other type, macro-calcifications," added Wright, "which pose no danger." Wright walked to the table. The file that Wright had left in front of Mary was as thick as a suburban phone book and along the edge were yellow Post-it flags that Wright had placed for navigational purposes. Wright flipped to a particular page and placed a finger on the part that she was about to reference. "Right here is where they wrote that it was macro-calcifications."

"But the size, shape, and pattern of these spots," said Finney, using the pointer, "should have led them to diagnose it as micro. I consulted with several other specialists at our clinic and all agree."

"And you're about to tell me that micro is a bad thing," deduced Mary.

"It often is," said Finney. "Micro-calcifications can be residue from rapid cell growth, and therefore, can signal cancer."

Wright reentered the conversation, saying, "It's only fair to state that the diagnosis between micro and macro is not always clear cut and easy to make."

Finney quickly said, "Yes, but when the call is close, the proper thing to do is perform a localized biopsy."

Wright nodded in agreement. She turned to another page of the file and then said, "You can see, Mrs. Cunningham, by this entry, that all they did was recommend a follow-up mammogram for the next year."

Finney tapped the pointer on the second x-ray. "Here is that follow-up mammogram. Microcalcification here, too.

Not only that, now some of it is in clusters. I don't know how they could have misread it."

"What would you have done?" asked Mary.

"Taken enlarged-view mammograms to see whether there were smaller calcifications clustered within these visible clusters," answered Finney. "If there were, the chances of malignancy would have been very high."

"This is depressing," lamented Mary.

"I understand your feelings," said Finney. "This follow-up mammogram was also misdiagnosed as macro."

"That's not all," said Wright, as she turned pages, stopping at an illustrating notation. "It reads here that patient reported no lesions from self-exams. Unfortunately, they used that fact to corroborate what was a misdiagnosis. What the mammograms indicated should have been given more weight than the reported results of self-exams. Here, too, a biopsy should have been performed."

Finney took a half-step along the board. "This third mammogram is from the following year. By that time, self-exams had revealed a lesion." Again, she used the pointer. "That's this white area."

"They said it was a cyst," remembered Mary.

Wright located the corresponding entry in the file and read aloud. "Lesion in left upper quadrant of left breast, approximately 2.0 cm., regular in shape, not hard, moves under tactile pressure. Consistent with cyst."

Finney said, "At least, they were consistent, misdiagnosing at every turn. It was inexcusable, given they could have made sure whether it was a cyst."

Mary, more downcast by the minute, asked, "How?"

"FNA," answered Wright. "Fine needle aspiration."

Finney jumped in as translator. "Aspiration is a fancy word that means to draw out, or extract, and fine refers to the narrowness of the needle. A hollow needle is attached to a syringe. Then the needle is inserted into the lesion. If it extracts fluid, it's a cyst, unless the fluid is bloody or colored, which might signal cancer. But if it extracts just cells, it's not a cyst and likely a tumor."

"Tumor it definitely was," said Wright. "It's almost beyond belief that they were still misdiagnosing when the cancer reached Stage IIIB."

"At Stage IIIB, the cancer has spread throughout the breast and into the lymph nodes," said Finney. "In this case, it worsened into inflammatory breast cancer, which is very aggressive. Indicators are breast redness and skin texture that resembles orange peel, which they also misdiagnosed."

"As an infection. I remember, all too well," said Mary, saving Wright the trouble of showing her the entry.

Finney slowly laid down the pointer. "Mrs. Cunningham," she said solemnly, "Dr. Wright and I could continue detailing all the things done wrong, but that only would delay giving you our conclusion."

Mary, not waiting for a wave of wooziness to subside, said, "I know what you are going to say."

Finney said it, anyway, genuine sadness etched on her face. "Now, it's Stage IV. I couldn't be sorrier."

"I, neither," said Wright.

Mary closed her eyes and pressed fingertips against throbbing temples. When she opened her eyes, she asked, "How much time?"

"It can't be predicted with precision," hedged Finney. "Treatments can slow the progression. Even so, survival rates are discouraging when the cancer is this advanced."

"I'm going to leave now," said Mary, and rose shakily to her feet.

"Mrs. Cunningham?" said, Wright.

"Yes?"

"In all my career, I can't remember a worse case of medical malpractice." Wright paused, more like hesitated, knowing that doctors seldom give the advice she was about to offer. "You should retain an attorney."

6.

Mary's torso heaved, expanding and contracting, as if the tip of a bellows were inserted down her throat, fanning the flames of her rage. Her breathing was audible. Her teeth softly chattered. The tears welling in her eyes made the room blurry. The pause was the latest of several wherein she suspended her narrative until she could collect herself. It had been an ordeal, but, she had chronicled and detailed her tale of woe, even repeating herself at times, and now, she felt she could summarize. "The bottom line is that the clinic repeatedly fucked up." Then, remembering that certain others were in the room, she said, "I apologize. I shouldn't have cursed."

Lisa Rose, dressed office-casual and seated at the head of her conference table, finished her notes with a few underlining slashes. She rested her pen on the legal pad. She struck a pose, left elbow bent upward on an armrest, a thumb and index finger forming an L under her chin and against the side of her face. For most of the appointment, she'd been the silent listener, except for a few clarifying questions and offers of refreshments.

Mary, awaiting a response, felt nervous, anxious, like someone who had auditioned in front of a lone, unreadable judge. Stiffening for possible disappointment, she asked, "Well, what do you say?"

Rose readjusted herself in the high-back, leather swivel chair and declared, "I'll take the case."

"Wonderful!" proclaimed Mary, beaming, but otherwise maintaining decorum.

"This is going to have to start out as a medical malpractice case," said Rose.

Squinting in confusion, Mary asked, "What do you mean by start out?"

"Malpractice cases can take years to come to trial. I don't mean to sound insensitive, but..."

Mary, finishing the thought, said, "A plaintiff that's Stage IV might not live to see the trial."

"Sadly, yes. I file malpractice now, knowing that later it might have to be amended to wrongful death."

Death. The word finally had been invoked. Mary had alluded to it, danced around it, as if voicing it had the power of summons. Now that it was in the open, it imparted a liberating aspect to the discussion.

Rose showed sensitivity and addressed Mary's mother directly. "My deepest regrets, Mrs. Kingsley."

Sophie Kingsley was seated at the table, husband Joe's hand resting on top of hers. The left side of the sweater she was wearing lay flat. She no longer wore a wig, and what little hair had grown back resembled white lamb's wool. The complexion that once glowed shinny-dark, like the skin of a ripe plum, was ashen. Former laugh lines had deepened into grief crevices.

For Mary's part, her mother's impending death carried the added specter of heredity. When Mary was a girl, a great-aunt died from breast cancer, a remote memory recently thrust to the forefront. More recently, a first cousin succumbed to the disease. Did it run in the family?

Throughout the years, Mary had followed the recommended procedures: annual mammograms, annual clinical exams, and monthly self-exams. Regarding self-exams, specifically, since Sophie's diagnosis, thirty days seemed so riskily long, although Mary now could take a shower, walk pass a mirror, but resist the compulsion to feel on her breasts. Additionally, she hadn't recruited Cliff's participation since their heart-to-heart discussion, months earlier.

"I appreciate your kind words, Ms. Rose," said Sophie, the cancer having stolen some of the richness from her voice. "Whatever money comes out of this won't do me no good. But I'm gratified that it will go to my family."

"To your estate, actually," Rose said, "but your wishes can be carried out through a last will and testament. Do you have one?"

"I do."

"I'd like to review it, if I may, to make sure that everything is in order."

"Please do," said Sophie.

"I'll drop it off tomorrow," volunteered Mary.

Rose, middle-age, a tad taller than average, and fit, wished for more curves and a shorter face. Were she to let the perm wear out, her shoulder-length hair would revert to crinkled; and, thanks to chemistry, she was starlet blond.

Building on her earlier comment, she said, "A wrongful death case is bought on behalf of the estate. Who's going to be the estate representative? You, Mr. Kingsley?"

Joe, a retired cop, gave a startled jerk of the head, like he'd been drafted to run for President. He waved a hand in refusal or at least as a plea to be spared responsibilities that he considered beyond his talents. A big guy, his flannel shirt had him resembling an urban lumberjack. "I don't have the understanding for it," he demurred. "I say make Mary the representative. You agree, Sophie?"

"Yes." In fiat-accompli fashion, Sophie proclaimed, "Mary will be the representative, Ms. Rose."

"I guess you never get too old to have parents make decisions for you," Mary said, but wasn't complaining. She turned to Rose and asked, "What will I have to do?"

"Basically, be the one I keep informed about the case, especially any settlement offers, because you'll have to okay them."

There came two raps on the door, it opened, and in walked Rose's secretary. The bifocals and the silver hair gave her a matronly aspect; furthermore, by the designer knit dress, silk neck-scarf, and gold bracelets, she could pass for someone who had her own secretary. "Excuse the inter- ruption, folks," she said to the visitors. To her boss she said, "You wanted these to go out in the afternoon mail," referring to the stapled sets of documents she was carrying.

The secretary already had each set turned to the sig- nature page. The secretary laid down a set, Rose signed, the secretary picked up the set. Four times this sequence played out, to the drone of a copying machine that could be heard through the opened door. Her purpose fulfilled, the secretary left the room.

Rose resumed, saying, "I can't guarantee it, but maybe the other side will want to settle the malpractice and not face wrongful death later."

With guarded hopefulness, Mary said, "That would be ideal. That way, my mother does not leave this Earth without the satisfaction of knowing that those low-lives did not get away scot-free."

Rose got up and walked to her new client. She sandwiched Sophie's hands in hers. "In my opinion, Mrs. Kingsley, what they did was criminal and they deserve prison. But, I'm not a prosecutor who can bring charges. In a civil suit, the law only provides for money damages."

"I understand," said Sophie.

Rose released Sophie's hand and to Joe, said, "Be strong, Mr. Kingsley."

"I'll do my best," pledged Joe.

"I'll have the papers drawn up in a day or two. But before I file them, I'm calling a news conference. I want each of you there. In fact, have as many family members there as you can arrange. Let's make it a week from today. Nine in the morning."

"Alright," said Mary.

Rose gingerly pulled Sophie's chair away from the table. Joe stood and helped his wife to her feet. Mary was the last to rise.

"That'll do it for now," said Rose. "I'll see you good people to the door."

Mary, giving a pumping handshake, said, "I'm grateful to you, Lisa."

Rose smiled warmly, so as to take the edge off of how she was about to respond. "Save the gratitude until I've produced results."

7.

From a distance, it could be mistaken for a giant dictionary, the type kept opened on a lectern, in a well-appointed study, next to a giant globe. But this was no pampered tome. It was kept unceremoniously on a metal table, in the back, against a side wall. Its cloth cover, once the color of cheese mold, was faded, coffee-stained, and threadbare at two corners. Open it too quickly and strongly, and a page or two flies away and crisscrosses down to a scuffed tile floor. There's no inscribed title to denote its purpose, but its users refer to it simply as, the Ledger.

As Mary recorded her latest entry, she printed, as always. To her, printing demonstrated respect. It annoyed her that some of the chicken-scratch entries probably couldn't be decoded by a pharmacist. She equally was resentful that some entries were in pencil, as though the basic truth being recorded is not permanent or is erasable. And don't even mention the assholes responsible for those felt pen entries that bleed together or onto other entries, obliterating them.

"What are you entering, Mary?" Brian Rutgers had just come in and was putting his parker on a hanger. His rock salt-stained shoes had laid a trail of wet, dirty tracks. The calendar-start of spring was near, but in Michigan, winter often overstays, like a deadbeat in-law.

"Caught a justifiable today," Mary explained, meaning a case of justifiable homicide. "Boyfriend violates restraining order taken out by girlfriend. While he's bouncing her off the walls, he gets his skull bashed in with a poker by girlfriend's son."

"How old was he?" asked Rutgers, several years from retirement, who considered himself close enough to shore to wade the rest of the way.

"The boyfriend or the son?"

"The son."

"Twelve."

Rutgers went to his desk but remained standing. There were two sheets in his in-box. He summarily filed them into the trash can. "Twelve and killed somebody." He cynically added, "Might not be the first time that kid has killed. They start young. And might not be his last. Anyway, one less scumbag boyfriend."

Mary sensed that Rutgers was about to preach his philosophy that some homicides are gifts to society. She decided to head him off. "So what had you out today, Brian?"

Because of a horrific toupee, Rutgers and a big-breasted woman could have an hour-long conversation and never once look one another in the eye. "The daughter's getting married this summer." He smiled proudly. "I was out there paying the deposit on the reception hall."

I should have known it had nothing to do with work. The last time you closed a case, Model-T's were rolling the streets. "How nice. Your youngest, isn't she?"

"Yep. You and her got the same name, remember?"

"You don't forget something like that." Mary hoped that would be the end of the conversation. The two other cops in the room were seated at their desks, one on the phone, the other immersed in a real estate course that he'd bought through an infomercial, neither interested in bailing out Mary.

Rutgers sat on the edge of his desk top and shook a lecturing finger at Mary. "A hard-working cop like you deserves a justifiable now and then. Shoes aren't cheap. Save all the sole leather that you can. I wish you more of the easy ones."

Easy or not, they all have to be recorded, thought Mary. After making the entry, consisting of a name and a date, she remained at the Ledger, battling an ambivalent urge. She gave in and started scanning backwards through the entries, noting those she had made. The stroll down mortuary lane produced slam flashbacks, like in the movies, of the faces of the dearly-departed: Opal Stokeley, Calvin Lipinski, Roman Jackson. All were of the current year and closed cases.

Police consider a case closed when a suspect has been identified and charged, regardless of how the suspect fairs in court. Mary had the best closure rate within the homicide unit, considerably better than the unit's overall .500 batting average; but, she never had learned how to wear a helmet of professional detachment to the plate, so she took every strikeout personally. She was determined to never be a going-through-the-motions type, like Rutgers, even if she remained on the force until she had to take her lunch through a straw.

Mary knew where to stop thumbing through the Ledger to avoid the reminder, but she kept going...until, there it was, her last unsolved case from last year. The entry might as well have been highlighted, the way it leapt at her, as neatly spaced and aligned as an engraving on a headstone: Matthew Kent.

The investigation into Kent's background and his last twenty-four hours had produced leads that fizzled out like an Alka-Seltzer dropped into a lake. Myron Shuster had been cleared, as had others with known recent dealings. Kent's gay lifestyle hadn't produced a single substantive lead. The case had proceeded slowly and tediously, like passengers moving through airline security, but without the occasional beep from a metal detector to break the monotony.

Couldn't scrounge up a decent motive, neither. Kent had a brief and childless marriage, and his ex-wife was deceased. He didn't have life insurance, and most of his estate had been bequeathed to charity. No individual was in line for a financial windfall resulting from his death. Not that money is always the motive, but investigations into other list-toppers, such as jealousy, revenge, silencing, robbery-gone-bad, and so forth, also had led nowhere.

Was the murder scene as forensically sterile as she had conceded? No unaccounted-for prints. No fibers. No trace evidence, and most unfortunate, no DNA. Jurors want DNA in every crime that's more serious than jaywalking. Yet, it wasn't an ethereal spirit, materializing out of nothingness and escaping back into same, who had opened Kent's throat.

She'd deduced that the killer had to have been an acquaintance. So what. And the blood evidence revealed the path Kent took from the start of the attack to his collapse. Big deal. Even Brian Rutgers, allergic as he is to work, would have reached those conclusions.

She was dissatisfied with herself, gnawed by certain unanswered questions. Why one clean cut? Whatever the particular weapon, why that choice? And most nagging, why hadn't she made better progress?

On that last question, Mary had considered the possible role of timing. Last winter, she'd been knocked down and run over by the news of Sophie's condition. Crime-scene tape is the equator that encircles Mary's world, separating it into hemispheres: personal and professional. But sometimes they overlap. Had that been the case during the early stages of the investigation, especially the first forty-eight hours? Had she been thrown off stride by personal matters such that she hadn't been as sharp as usual?

Prospects for solving a murder cool almost as fast as the corpse. It takes a hot suspect to keep a case warm. By the laws of thermodynamics that govern homicide work, Kent was a cold case.

Rutgers wasn't the only one of Mary's fellow detectives who by now would have dropped the Kent folder into the cold case filing cabinet known as the Fridge. Besides, new cases intrude, necessitating attention, else they, too, go cold.

Weeks ago, Mary, the Kent folder in hand, made a trip to the Fridge, pointlessly, as it turned out; because, the hand wouldn't let go, sticking to the folder like a tongue on frozen metal. She ended up carrying the folder back to her desk and stashing it into a drawer. Thus hidden, it wasn't a visible reminder of her failure; yet, it remained within convenient reach, should she catch a lucky break. Right.

Don't forget that five grand, she'd reminded herself. Once, at lunchtime, at the Greektown Casino a few blocks from Police Headquarters, she hit for that amount on a slot machine. On the first pull, no less. Never mind that she'd since lost it all back, plus some. It's not an encouraging sign when a pep talk refers to a one-in-a-million event.

Nonetheless, die-hard Mary was undeterred. *Not just yet,* was the thought she'd directed at the Fridge. *Your name makes no sense, anyway. A fridge keeps its contents cold. Your contents keep you cold. They should have named your ass, the Icebox.*

8.

Lisa Rose, seated center, stood out, like the white sheep of a family that's posing for a photo. Actually, there were cameras present, but those shoulder-mounted Cyclopes that television crews lug around. Microphones were present, too, some in the hands of reporters, others strapped to booms and extended overhead by technicians. The most important microphone rested on a stand, on the conference table, in front of Rose. A single tap on the microphone showed that it was live and she began with, "My client, Mrs. Sophie Kinsley, here, has Stage IV breast cancer because of the malpractice and cover-up committed by the Franklin Clinic."

To Rose's right sat Sophie and Joe, to her left Mary and Cliff. Among the relatives standing two-rows deep were Gazelle, Mary's biological daughter, and Kyle, Cliff's biological son. Gazelle, a Michigan State University graduate, lived in Chicago. Kyle had graduated from Morehouse College and lived in San Diego.

"Outrageous!" decried Rose. "There's no other way to describe the behavior of the so-called doctors at that clinic. For years, they misinterpreted Mrs. Kingsley's mammograms. Even when they finally, and I do mean finally, realized the presence of cancer, they misdiagnosed the severity. So, naturally, they prescribed the wrong treatment. If ever there was a case of compounded medical malpractice, this is it."

As Rose paused, pens scratching notes on paper were the dominant sound. Two cameramen moved forward, adjusting their lens for a close-up of Sophie.

"And," resumed Rose, with a sharpness that caused the cameramen to pan to her, "they should be held accountable." She slapped the desk and revised her words to, "They will,"—emphasizing that last word—"be held accountable."

For the next several minutes, Rose berated the deeds of the clinic, twice placing a hand on Sophie's shoulder. Upon concluding, Rose drew her microphone even closer and then placed her hands palms-down, fingers interlaced, on the table. "I'll take your questions."

A reporter from ABC affiliate Channel 7 was first. "About the cover-up, could you give additional facts?"

"Sure. Mrs. Kingsley's condition worsened, and under the urging of her family, she changed clinics. Franklin forwarded her medical records, certain parts falsified. I won't go into all of the specifics, but suffice it to say that the cover-up was amateurish and obvious to the new medical team."

A reporter from Fox affiliate Channel 2 took a turn. "What type of money damages are you seeking?"

"It's not the money that should be our focus. Mrs. Kingsley has been damaged beyond any amount's capability to make her whole." Rose continued, "That fact understood, the monumental malpractice warrants sizable compensatory damages. The only other thing I'll say regarding money is that I'll be going for punitive damages, also."

A reporter from the Detroit News raised his pen to be called upon, but another television reporter began a question.

Rose raised her palm in interruption and said, "Hold on a second, Jeneen." Then she told the News reporter, "You're next, Fred."

And Fred asked, "Do you know of any other patients that were misdiagnosed by the Franklin Clinic?"

"Not at this time. But we're in the earliest stages of discovery. Having said that, it wouldn't surprise me if there are others, including some who are deceased. My exclusive concern presently, however, is Mrs. Kingsley."

"Naturally," said Fred. "I was just wondering whether you're going to allege that misdiagnosis and cover-up by Franklin is an established pattern of behavior."

"Listen to you, tossing around legal terms," ribbed Rose. "Another wannabe lawyer."

It drew scattered laughter from a few reporters, short-lived, however, as the chucklers remembered the solemnity of the occasion.

Rose, having not forgotten the reporter that she had placed on hold, said, "Let's have your question, Jeneen."

"Why did you accept this particular case?" Jeneen asked, in unspoken acknowledgement of Rose's celebrity.

"A fair enough question," began Rose. "It's well known that I don't accept all, nor even most, cases brought to me. But as to my reasons for taking this one..." She fell silent, staring outward, at no one in particular, mulling, but only for a few seconds. She retrained her sight on the reporter and then answered the question with a question. "What if it had been your mother?"

9.

Mary hurried up the walkway and onto the porch, the morning edition of the Detroit Free Press her umbrella against April sprinkles. Battling a cold, she hacked and sneezed. She contracted colds more frequently of late, perhaps due to an immune system compromised by the stress from watching Sophie deteriorate.

As she rang the doorbell, she noticed that affixed to the front of the house was a mezuzah. The religious symbol measured six by three by one inches and was made of iron, stained glass, colored acrylic, and gold leaf, assembled in a lattice design. At its center was a sterling silver tube that contained printed parchment. This was a fancy mezuzah, to be sure, since some are no more than wood boxes.

There came the sound of the unlocking of a deadbolt. The entrance door opened and standing there was Warren Newberry. He turned the latch on the security door, swung it open, and held it in that position, out of impatience not chivalry. "Get in here," he barked.

"Good morning to you, too, Inspector," greeted Mary, in cheerful sarcasm. No sooner had she stepped inside that she held out a straight arm to maintain distance, turned her head to the side, and underwent a spasm of sneezes.

Upon its conclusion, watery-eyed, she said, "I should have called in sick."

"Looks like you're trying to get sicker, running around under that soaked newspaper. Give it here."

Mary did, saying, "Nice of you to be concerned about my health."

"Yeah, a regular Florence Nightingale, that's me." Newberry snapped open the newspaper, tearing some of it in the process, and quickly flipped to the sports section. He grouched, "Those blankety-blank Pistons lost again." When he refolded the newspaper it tore further. He shoved the soggy, worse-for-wear edition at Mary. "Take your paper."

"I should have known better," she said, before snatching it.

Newberry locked the security door; in so doing, he again saw the two cops in raincoats guarding the front gate against on-lookers. Then he closed the entrance door. Without another word, he walked away, leaving Mary standing in the vestibule.

Luckily, in a corner was an umbrella holder, an appropriate enough receptacle, in which she stuffed the tattered, water-logged paper. Then she set out in the direction that Newberry had gone. The vestibule led into the living room. Rather than venturing farther in, she stood at the perimeter, taking in the scene and its cast of characters.

Newberry was waiting for Dr. Morris Lee to finish speaking into a portable tape recorder. When Lee turned off the machine, Newberry put a hand on his shoulder, leaned in, and spoke briefly. Then, Newberry called across the room,

"Over here, Mary." When she made it a trio, Newberry told her, "You might have questions for the doctor." Then, Newberry did a disappearing act.

"How are you, Doctor Lee?"

Lee, Chinese-American and boyish-looking, nodded in the direction of the dead body. "Well, Mary, I'm doing better than he's doing."

The deceased was fifty-three year old Allan Winkler, outlined in tape, laying face-up at the foot of the stairs. He was dressed in tan trousers, white shirt, and a print tie.

"How did he die?" asked Mary.

"Two gunshots into his back. Both shots exited the body."

"How long has he been dead?"

"From the time he was shot," said Lee, who'd worked in the Wayne County Medical Examiner's office for under a year. Reacting to Mary's facial expression, he quickly said, "Sorry. I thought homicide cops liked gallows humor." Reclaiming a professional demeanor he said, "From all signs, I'd say several hours, tops."

Luther, an evidence technician, came bounding down the stairs, carrying a paper bag and announcing its contents to all within earshot. "Hey, y'all, I found a firearm upstairs."

Mary commented, "Could be the murder weapon. Let's have a look-see."

"It's not the murder weapon," said Luther. "Tell you that, right now." He opened the bag with the eagerness of a trick-o-treater. "This is a snub nose .38 caliber. Too small to make those holes in the victim."

"Where'd you find it?" asked Mary.

"In the nightstand in the master bedroom."

"Alright," responded Mary, about to resume with Lee.

But, Luther wasn't through. "Tell you what, though, the victim might have been running to get it when he got shot on the stairs."

"So, now you're a detective, Luther?" asked a reappeared Newberry.

"No, uh-uh," denied Luther, unnerved by a man inches shorter. "I'll stick with collecting evidence."

"Damn good idea," said Newberry, his glare sending Luther slinking away. Then he asked Mary, "How's the briefing going?"

"Fine." She turned to Lee and asked, "Can I touch the body, Doctor?"

"Yes," consented, Lee, who had to give permission before cops could handle the body. "I've announced him dead. And I've examined him as much as I can until I get him to the morgue."

"Hold off on that, Mary," instructed Newberry. "First, I want to go over some things with you." His presence at a scene meant that this was a homicide that had community ramifications. It wasn't that he didn't trust his people; he liked an occasional escape from the administrative humdrum that came with being a member of the brass. "No signs of forced entry. The victim might have let the killer in. We found on the victim his wallet containing cash, credit cards, and I.D. He also was wearing a nice watch and a gold wedding band. Though that doesn't rule out robbery."

Mary responded to the information by nodding her head. She raised a wait-a -second finger as her nostrils tingled. In preparation of the oncoming sneeze, she stepped away from Lee and Newberry and dug into her pants pocket. She pulled out tissue just in time.

"Gesundheit!" wished Lee.

Through the tissue, Mary returned a nasal, "Thanks." She finished wiping her nose and then stuffed the tissue into the pocket of her trench coat. "Can I bum a pair of gloves, Doctor?" she asked, ready to examine the body and thinking Newberry had finished reciting.

"Sure thing," said Lee. "They're in my bag."

But Newberry said, "I wasn't through, Mary. You have a hot date, or something? You'll get to examine the body, soon enough. For now, pay attention." He stepped around the body and climbed to the fifth step, careful not to step in blood. Having positioned himself so that his back was against the wall opposite the banister, he pointed to the step upon which he stood. "He was shot in the back somewhere around here."

Next, Newberry pointed up and ahead, to the wall in front of the landing where the steps made a 90-degree turn. A hole had been circled. "The bullet lodged there. The killer fired in an upward angle, likely from the foot of the stairs. The victim fell forward, and either slide down or was pulled."

Newberry came back down the stairs and continued his narrative. "Underneath the body is the second bullet lodged in the carpet. The killer stood over the victim and fired into his back."

Mary knew that a wound's shape and size don't necessarily tell all, but that's not why she said, "By your account, Inspector, the wounds in the victim's chest are exit wounds."

"Obviously. And what's with the confused look? You see any stippling on his chest?"

"No," she answered, in reference to the freckled pattern of gunshot residue that surrounds an entrance wound made at close-to-intermediate distance.

"The wounds on the back are stippled," said Newberry, concluding his argument.

Lee joined in with, "The Inspector saw the back wounds when I rolled the body onto its side. I returned the body to the face-up position that it was in when officers arrived."

Mary sniffed, had to clear her throat. "I'm guessing that the left-center wound is through the heart. A person doesn't roll onto his back after that."

"That occurred to me, too," said Newberry. "No mystery. The killer must have turned the victim."

"Why?" Mary was quick to ask.

"Good question," conceded Newberry. "Give me your take on it."

"Maybe for the satisfaction of looking at the victim's face, even speaking something to the corpse."

"You're talking a killer with a personal motive," interpreted Newberry.

"Could be." Mary twitched her nose, trying to ward off a sneeze. She then took up a previously broached scenario. "If the victim let the killer in, when did the victim realize he was in danger?"

"Whenever it was," said Newberry, "he might have tried to defend himself with a knife."

Mary's eyebrows lifted. "What knife?"

"It's been bagged as evidence. It was next to the body and there was blood on it. It came from a butcher block set that's on the kitchen counter."

Now Mary was trying to ward off a sneeze by rubbing the bridge of her nose with the back of her hand. "Hmmm," she mused. "I'm having difficulty with that one. Who runs for a knife when the other person has a gun?"

"I'm with you," said Newberry, "but maybe, the victim went for the knife when it became clear that his life was in danger. Maybe the killer said something. Threatened the victim. Before the gun came into play."

Busy envisioning it, Mary repeated, "Before the gun came into play."

"Right. And when the killer pulls the gun, the victim tries to make it up the stairs, probably to get his own gun."

"And takes the first bullet to the back," said Mary, in part conclusion, part question. Her brow was furrowed. "Could have gone down that way," she allowed, but her tone lacked conviction.

"I know my theory isn't rock-solid," disclaimed Newberry, "so don't patronize me."

"I wasn't." And as if in proof, Mary said, "At this point, we don't know whose blood it is."

Lee had stepped to the side and had resumed speaking into his tape recorder. He stopped recording and said,

"DNA analysis will at least tell whether the blood is the victim's." Then he declared, "I don't think I'm needed here any longer. I'm leaving."

By that time, something had caught Mary's attention. "The gloves, Doctor," she said, in reminder, as she extended her arm, palm up, fingers wiggling to signal her hurry, all the while keeping her sight on the victim.

"You see something?" Newberry wanted to know.

"His belt is unbuckled, pants unzipped."

"You're not just now noticing that, I hope," said Newberry.

"No." Mary's vision was locked on what resembled a fold on the inner-thigh of the left pant leg, about six inches above the knee. She felt Lee slap the gloves in her palm and she had them on in a jiffy. Under the watchful and curious gazes of Newberry and Lee, she bent down and touched the fold with an index finger, gingerly, before giving it a poke. She quickly straightened to a standing position and then stared some seconds at the area.

"What's the deal?" asked Newberry.

"There's something in the pants leg." Mary then looked at Lee and requested, "Take it out."

"I will, at the morgue."

"Now," insisted Mary. "Please."

Lee, who'd taken off his gloves, got another pair out of his bag. He put them on, in textbook surgical fashion, stretching each tightly over the fingers, before releasing the bottom, for that signature snap against the wrist. He lowered to one knee, hesitant, uncertain whether to fish blindly or to pull down the pants. To do the latter might allow trace evidence to fall out, so he pulled back the waistband and stuck his hand down the pant leg. And retrieved something. When he saw what it was, he winced.

Mary's eyes widened, even though her suspicion had been confirmed.

Newberry gave no outward reaction, but did say, "That answers whether this was personal." He asked Mary, "How did you know the man's penis had been severed?"

"It was so far down his leg, that it was either severed or he was one for the medical books."

"Whose blood in on the knife seems less a mystery now," said Lee, "although testing will have to confirm it."

Further conversation was interrupted by the sound of the front door banging open, followed by a woman's shouts. "Out of my way! Out of my way, I say!"

A uniformed officer also had come inside. He had stopped at the end of the vestibule, using its walls to contain the woman and his own large frame to block her view. Shifting back and forth laterally to prevent the woman's passage, he hurriedly explained the situation. "Excuse me, Inspector. She has keys and insisted on letting herself in."

Suspecting the woman's identity, Newberry said, "That'll do officer. Return to your post."

The woman, indignant over her treatment, but no longer obstructed, nonetheless did not advance, but spoke from that distance. "I deserve to know what has happened," said the wife of the murdered rabbi.

10.

Debra Winkler downed the water in bird-like sips until she emptied the glass. "Thank you. I was so parched," she said, seated on her living room sofa, knees held tightly together.

"Can I get you anything else?" asked Newberry, as though he were hosting in his own home rather than conducting official business in this house in the University District, so called for its proximity to the University of Detroit-Mercy.

"No."

"Then, would you be up to answering some questions, Mrs. Winkler?"

"Yes." Winkler was thin and petite. The skin of her slender neck was loose and ringed with a few engraved winkles, in contrast to the nipped-and-tucked tightness of her face. Her auburn hair was streak-highlighted. Over-all, though, she was plain, and designer jeans, cashmere sweater, and diamond pendant earrings only went so far.

"Good." Newberry, who'd already introduced himself, said, "This is Lieutenant Mary Cunningham."

"And I'm Detective Ross Brogan," said the ex-Marine, middle-age and burly, with a crew cut. He loved his nickname, G.I. Joe.

Mary, Newberry, and Brogan remained after the rabbi's body had been taken to the morgue and the rest of the crime-scene investigators had left. Newberry's game plan was for Mary to conduct the questioning, figuring a woman-to-woman approach might place Mrs. Winkler more at ease. Of the three cops, Mary was the most sensitive, despite her nickname, Bloody Mary, which she loathed.

Mary sat next to Winkler, at a distance calculated for scrutiny without invasiveness, although she explained it as, "Don't want to get too close. I have a nasty cold."

Winkler's top lip curled. "I hope that's all it is and not the flu of some strain or another."

"Just a cold."

Winkler placed a palm on the seat cushion and pushed, although there were only inches in which she could slide farther away. "Colds are contagious. You shouldn't be around people."

Mary cut Newberry a look that said, *I don't need this,* but voiced to Winkler, "If it were up to me, I wouldn't be."

Winkler, aware that the distance maintained between Newberry and Brogan made it difficult to monitor them simultaneously, said, "You gentlemen are free to take seats."

"We don't mind standing," said Newberry.

Beset with headache, stuffiness, and sinus drain, Mary plowed to the heart of the matter. "Mrs. Winkler, do you have any idea who killed your husband?"

Winkler flattened her palm against an almost-as-flat chest, so shocked by the mere notion. "None whatsoever. People loved the rabbi."

"When did you last see him alive?"

"He was in bed this morning when I left for work."

"And...and what..." To avoid the embarrassment of a runny nose, Mary snatched tissue from a box on the coffee table. Talking through the tissue, she said, "Excuse me," then blew.

"Chicken soup," said Winkler. "That's what will help your cold."

"I'll remember that," Mary said, and helped herself to a few more sheets, just to have them at the ready. "And what time did you leave?"

"7:00 a.m., thereabout."

"Where do you work?"

"I own Milk 'n Honey, a delicatessen and catering business in West Bloomfield." Winkler's eyes followed Brogan, as he stepped away and rested an elbow on the fireplace mantle. Those eyes then made a quick, furtive inspection of the room, finding it neatly arranged and reflecting well on her decorating tastes.

"That's about, what, a thirty-minute drive?" Mary asked, in reference to the swank northern suburb.

"Depending on driving conditions, yes."

"Do you always leave for work about the same time?"

"Mostly."

"Can anyone account for your arrival time this morning?"

"My assistant manager and two cooks. They'll be at work until 4:00 p.m." Winkler leaned to the side and from a back pocket took out a business card holder. She handed a card to Mary.

"Do you usually know your husband's schedule?"

"No. It's all I can do to manage my own schedule." Winkler had perfect diction, but whenever she spoke at length, her voice was exposed as squeaky, not in the rubber duck sense, but enough to grate on a listener. "I know my husband was to give a speech this morning at Cobo Hall, only because I received calls asking if I knew why he hadn't showed. I called home, his cell, and his office. I became concerned and requested that a squad car pay a visit."

"Without knowing that something was wrong," clarified Mary.

"Intuition," said Winkler. "I'm sure you've acted upon it from time to time."

"That, I have."

Meaning to ingratiate herself with present company, Winkler said, "I know the precinct captain quite well. I made the request and that's all it took."

"Had your husband spoken of threats or problems with anyone?"

"None." She looked at Newberry and said, "Inspector, my religion requires burial within twenty-four hours, if at all possible. Will it be?"

Newberry straightened his posture and responded, "No. Not with the autopsy that has to be performed. But your husband's body will be released as soon as possible."

"That would be greatly appreciated."

"Excuse me, again," Mary said, then blew her nose.

Winkler leaned away. "I have soup in the refrigerator. You can take some with you."

"Thanks, Mrs. Winkler."

"The least I can do. You're a walking epidemic, if I do say so, myself."

Mary let the comment pass. "A gun was found in the main bedroom. How many guns are kept in the house?"

"Just that one. I don't like guns. Never fired one in my life."

"So you were against having a gun in the house," presumed Mary.

"No. The rabbi was." Realizing the need to clarify, Winkler added, "I told the rabbi that we needed the protection. I don't like guns but I'm a realist, nonetheless. The rabbi, on the other hand, often was at home with the security alarm off. I don't mind saying that I didn't approve."

"Thanks," said Mary, "for clearing that up."

"Of course." Winkler folded her arms and resentfully said, "It was a complete waste of your time testing my hands for gunpowder residue."

"Routine, Mrs. Winkler," said Mary, explaining, not apologizing. "Just like the testing we'll have to perform on the clothes you're wearing. We'll have to take them with us."

"If you must, you must."

"What do you make of the dismemberment? Does it suggest anything to you?"

"A deviant, perverted mind."

"Did your husband have any unconventional sexual tastes?"

Thinking that the question was a follow-up to her last response, Winkler said, "I wasn't referring to my husband."

"I didn't think that you were."

Assured, Winkler asked, "What do you mean by unconventional?"

"However you wish to define it."

"Under any other circumstance, I'd consider that an impertinent question. I don't know what other couples engage in," Winkler said, controlling the urge to squirm, "but what the rabbi and I did in the privacy of our bedroom was between consenting adults and nothing that I consider unconventional."

Mary imagined Winkler's tiny hands clamped around the handle of a high-power weapon, squeezing the trigger, being rocked back by the recoil. *Possible. Possible. Could have done it before leaving that morning. Could have sneaked back and done it. Means, opportunity, but what motive?* "Describe your marriage, Mrs. Winkler."

Winkler raised her head a prideful notch. "Functional. That is to say, it worked. Had for twenty-nine years."

"And, by functional—"

But Winkler had more to say. "We raised three successful children. They've given us five grandchildren. Only, don't get me started. The youngest grandson, a music prodigy, that kid. You wouldn't believe how he plays. Already, he can—"

"Functional," interrupted Mary, "what did you mean by that?"

In an undertone that bespoke offense, Winkler rhetorically asked, "What kind of person doesn't want to hear about grandchildren?" Then she redirected herself. "I meant that passion can wane, Lieutenant, leaving a couple to decide whether there remains enough to sustain the marriage. With us, there was."

"So no one was talking divorce, consulting lawyers?"

"Correct."

"No calls to police on domestic violence?"

"Certainly not."

"Any extra-marital affairs?"

Winkler smiled faintly. "My, how subtlety suffers in these matters." Then the smile vanished. "I, personally, have had no affairs. The rabbi was handsome, intelligent, and eloquent. Women were attracted to him, sure, but, I've never had any proof of an affair."

It sounded technical to Mary. "What about suspicions of an affair?"

"Your work is based on suspicions, Lieutenant Cunningham, and, of course, I understand why. But, a marriage based on suspicions is something that I don't believe in."

"Any new life insurance policies on your husband, or increases in old ones?"

"Not to my knowledge and not of my doing."

Mary always looks early and hard at those who were closest to the victim, while remaining aware of the thin line that separates aggressiveness and insensitivity. Winkler might be a killer. She also might be an innocent, grieving widow. "That does it for me," announced Mary, dabbing a watery eye. "Inspector Newberry, Ross, any questions?"

Brogan raised both arms into a stretch, lowered them, and said, "I got none."

"We'll get back to you, Mrs. Winkler, if there's reason," said Newberry.

Winkler nodded consent.

Shortly thereafter, Mary waited outside a bathroom. Inside, Winkler bagged the clothes and then emerged wearing shirt and slacks. The women rejoined Newberry and Brogan in the living room.

As the cops gathered their coats, Winkler proclaimed, "Oh, you mustn't leave just yet," spun, then rushed toward the kitchen, promising, "Back in a minute." Almost to the second, she reappeared carrying a quart glass jar filled with chicken soup. She walked to Mary. "Here you are, my Dear."

Mary took it and held it eye-level, peering into the concoction. "Looks rich," she said of the color and chunkiness.

Winkler boasted, "Campbell's can't hold a spoon to it." She instructed, "Warm it over medium heat, but not to a boil. And don't microwave. It destroys nutrients."

Brogan, forever macho, wanted to get out of there before the women started swapping cookie recipes. He was standing next to an embroidered cloth mizrach, mounted

on the wall to show east—the direction toward Jerusalem—
which Jews face when praying. In boredom, but with no
intended disrespect, he strummed a finger along the tassels
at the bottom.

Winkler sternly said, "Please don't touch that."

Brogan stepped away, offering, "Sorry."

Winkler didn't want his apology, but his exit. "This has
been the worst day of my life. Forgive me for asking you to
see yourselves out."

"Quite all right," said, Mary.

Winkler said, "Oh," suddenly remembering. She quick-
stepped to the coffee table, grabbed the box of tissues, and
gave it to Mary. "With my compliments."

"Thanks," accepted Mary, immediately.

After all, it wasn't as though Winkler would miss the
box; for, since the time she burst into the house, she hadn't
shed a tear.

11.

Lisa Rose was gazing through a smudged glass window. The paint on the window frame was blistered and nippy air was entering through gaps in the caulking. The window ledge was dirty and dotted with the dried-out shells of insects that had dropped from spider webs. "Are you ever going to move out of this rat hole, Fritz?"

Fritz Mueller, 72 year-old son of German immigrants, was in the kitchen, stirring a pot on the stove. "What for? It's cozy," he said of his one-bedroom apartment above a bike repair shop in Ferndale, just north of Detroit. He was as thin as a reed but not tall enough for lanky; nonetheless, he had disproportionately broad shoulders, always held square, like those of a general. Bald, spindly neck, prominent Adam's apple, and hooked nose, he resembled a vulture. His most vibrant feature was piercing blue eyes, far recessed in their sockets.

Rose arched back her head, opened her mouth wide, and emptied the last pistachios from a vending machine package. A few dropped and rolled along the wood-plank floor. She might have picked them up to discard them properly, but why bother, given the overall condition of the place. "Know something? The only job more impossible than being your attorney would be being your cleaning woman."

Taking no offence, Mueller said, "I'm grateful you chose law over cleaning, otherwise, we might never have met." Still having not emerged from the kitchen, he extended an invitation. "Please stay for lunch, Ms. Rose. Today's special is beef stew."

She scornfully said, "You know that I don't eat meat."

"I must have forgotten," he lied. "It's just that a tigress that abstains from meat seems such the anomaly."

Rose walked to a spot that allowed her to see into the cramped kitchen. The refrigerator's door handle was held by duct tape and the burners on the stove were encrusted. "You're not getting under my skin," she said. "You can forget it."

He knew her whereabouts from her voice. He grabbed the empty beef stew can and dropped it into the paper grocery bag that served as a garbage pail. "I was complimenting you."

"I don't need your compliments, thank you very much. What you better do is tell me why I'm here, or I'm leaving."

"Don't overlook that I offered to come to your office."

"What? And set rumors flying?"

"Small minds will find something to fixate on, regardless." He turned off the flame and lifted the pot. He moseyed into the kitchen nook. There, he poured his lunch into a plastic bowl that sat on a wiggly dinette table. None of the four chairs matched. He extended a different invitation. "If you won't dine with me, at least have a seat."

Rose accepted. The seat was vinyl and at its center was a puncture, spiking up like tiny spears into her bottom, causing her to shift and supplying her with another reason to regret being there. From where she sat, she had too good a view of the bowl's contents. "Even if I were a meat-eater, I wouldn't touch that slop. It looks like chopped turds floating in vomit and smells worse."

Mueller, now seated, smiled good-heartedly and scooped a tablespoon of stew and brought it to his lips, first saying, "You do have a talent for phrasing, Ms. Rose," before downing his first swallow.

"Get to the point," demanded Rose, who hadn't been able to get him to state his business over the phone. "But if it turns out that you've—"

"I haven't," preempted Mueller.

Dialing up the sternness in her voice, Rose warned, "Because, if you violate our agreement, I'll sever all relations."

He made a few lazy stirs in the stew and then let the spoon rest within the bowl. He reached into a bag of white bread, pulled out a slice, and sopped it into the stew. The bread became mushy; yet, he chomped down on it and snapped his head to the side, as if he were tearing into a piece of jerky. When his throat was clear, he asked, "Why do you get so riled at me?"

Rose took a deep, silent breath so that she would sound collected and credible. "Don't flatter yourself, buddy boy. I have buttons that you wouldn't begin to know how to push. For the last time, get to the point."

"I will. It's about the press conference you held a while back. The one with the woman with advanced breast cancer."

"Kingsley," said Rose.

"Kingsley."

"What business is that of yours?"

"I'm angry at myself for not coming up with the idea instantly." Mueller ran his tongue across his teeth, sounding a smack, and then said, "I can help you with the case."

"And how might that be, fool that I am for asking."

"As your expert."

Rose stared incredulously for a few seconds. "You can't be serious."

"Dead serious. I'm eminently qualified, plus I'll do it for free."

Rose waved dismissingly. "Most things that are free turn out to be worth the price."

"Well, if that's a problem, donate my fees to charity. But I won't accept money directly. We're a team, you and I."

Batman and Robin? Butch and Sundance? Or maybe, Dr. Frankenstein and the monster, except, who created whom? The saga of Rose and Mueller had begun nine years prior. Back then, she was a rising star at the Wayne County Prosecutor's Office, having never lost in court. When she learned that criminal charges had been brought against Mueller and that she had been assigned the case, she not only resigned but became his lawyer. Amid international coverage, she won his acquittal. Since then, she'd won acquittals for him in three similar cases.

"This conversation is a laugher," described Rose, "starting with the fact that you are not an oncologist."

"You'll also need an expert in medical ethics. I envision that role."

"What you envision is irrelevant. I decide case strategy, and there's no place in it for you. Besides, you've been stripped of your medical license, or had you forgotten that little detail?"

Always disdainful of legalities with which he disagreed, Mueller said, "Doesn't matter. Serving as an expert is not the same as practicing."

"True. But, I can't image a judge qualifying you as an expert."

"There's not a judge around who can challenge my credentials."

"Allow reality to intrude for a second. No judge is going to put his head on the chopping block for you."

Unimpressed, Mueller said, "You've found ways around roadblocks before. If you don't want my help, have the balls to say so."

Rose didn't dignify the reference to anatomy. "I'll gladly say it flat-out. I don't want your help."

"Why on Earth not?"

Rose whistled a few notes, riding out the frustration. "You mention Earth like you live there. It's not just the judge, you extra-terrestrial. My client wouldn't accept you."

"You're sure of that?"

"Positive."

Mueller asked, "What if the decision were totally yours, Ms. Rose?"

"A ridiculous hypothetical, but I'll answer it anyway. I wouldn't entertain the thought. My answer would be, no. My answer is, no."

"Then it's a dead issue," he said, as acceptingly as if he never truly expected any other response.

Rose became aware that she was sitting akimbo, her hands clamping her waist with corset tightness, although she didn't know for how long she'd been in that posture. She dropped her arms to her sides and took a deep breath. "This has been a total waste of time," she declared.

"Stay seated, please, long enough to hear my other offer."

"Be quick."

"Here it is, then. There's another type of service that I can provide to Mrs. Kingsley, down the road, when her suffering becomes unbearable."

Rose slammed her fist on the table. A geyser of stew flew up, some landed back into the bowl, some on the table. Her lips contorted into a snarl. "You've crossed the line, just by letting something so ridiculous escape your mouth," she said.

Mueller used the napkin with which he'd been dabbing his mouth to wipe up the splash. "I'm surprised and confused by your response. You and I each have a specialty. They don't conflict. The same person can have need for both."

Rejecting the comparison, her anger evident, Rose said, "You should be licking the soles of my shoes in apology. Instead, you continue with your asinine comments. I've had it with you. You're not worth it. I'm bowing out, as of now."

"You don't mean that. You're speaking in the heat of the moment."

Through gritted teeth, Rose said, "You are so damn condescending."

Mueller didn't sound frustrated when he said, "I seem to be making bad matters worse, so probably the wise choice is for me to get your jacket." He got up and walked to the closet.

Rose followed, close enough to practically speak into his ear. "You stay clear of my client? Oh, and in case you didn't know, the daughter's a cop, homicide, in fact."

"So happens that I do know that. Read it somewhere, I think." Mueller opened the closet door and retrieved her jacket. He held it gallantly for her to slip into.

Instead, Rose snatched it and stormed out of the apartment, slamming the door, but not before having glimpsed something on the closet floor, something so makeshift that no self-respecting fifth-grader would have it as a science-fair project.

Mueller had named it the Morpheus Machine, after the mythical god of dreams. Detractors, however, were less given to whimsical names for the contraption used in the assisted-suicides performed by Fritz Mueller, a.k.a Dr. Deceased.

12.

Luther, the technician, already had collected the laptop.

"Take the desk computer, too," instructed Mary.

"Just the hard drive or the whole hookup?"

"Hard drive."

Mary had told him that there was no need to dust for prints. It was just as well because the office inside Temple Beth El was small enough to induce claustrophobia and dusting might set off respiratory distress. The store-front synagogue on Wyoming Street was the lone holdout in what used to be a Jewish area, there, in northwest Detroit. Now, the Nubian Hair Braiding & Nails Salon next door was symbolic of the metamorphosis the area had undergone.

Mary, in waiting mode, was facing a floor-to-ceiling bookshelf that was built into the wall and that was crammed to capacity. Many of the books were of a religious bent, others secular, dealing with psychology, sociology, philosophy, and the like. Mary's gaze was drawn to an eye-level corner section containing several titles from the *Chicken Soup for the Soul* collection. "Know what, Ross?"

"What?"

"Mrs. Winkler's chicken soup helped."

Brogan didn't disguise his skepticism. "If you're feeling better, Cunningham, it's because the cold is running its course."

"Yeah, well, I suggest that you give it a try next time you have a cold."

"I'm sticking with hot toddies, heavy on the booze. If it doesn't help, it still helps, if you know what I mean. So spare me the girlie remedies, if that's not too much to ask."

"Why are you being so surly?"

"I'm not."

"Yes, you are, and I know why."

"Then please enlighten me, O wise one."

"You have what I call irritable bowing syndrome. Irritable over bowing to a woman, or at least that's how you see it."

"Hear that, Luther?" Brogan flicked a hitchhiker's thumb and said, "Cunningham, here, has appointed herself my shrink, though we've never worked together before yesterday."

Luther raised both hands in surrender and pleaded, "Don't drag me into this."

"Your shrink, no," denied Mary. "But, I've heard your views about women in the workplace."

Brogan, ignoring Luther's plea, said." Now, I'm being called a sexist."

"That's one way of putting it," Mary said. "But it need not be a problem."

Knowing what was being implied, this time Brogan addressed her directly, saying, "As long as I don't forget who's heading the investigation, that's what you mean, right," and ending with a stretched out, "Lieutenant?"

"Cool out, Ross," advised Luther.

"Thought you wanted to stay out of this," said Brogan.

"There shouldn't be anything to stay out of, fella. I've worked with Mary plenty times and can tell you she's not the type who pulls rank."

"Not unless I'm forced to." She was nipping potential problems in the bud, not that Brogan had given her any real grief; then again, yesterday, after interviewing Mrs. Winkler, she and Brogan had separately canvassed the neighborhood. Hard to get on one another's nerves from blocks apart. Neither she nor Brogan had been able to scare up a viable lead, though.

The next-door neighbors on either side had performed their routines that morning: leaving for work, shuttling kids to school. They said they'd heard no gunshots. Ditto for neighbors farther away. Neighbors also disclosed that it was customary for the rabbi to have visitors with no set pattern, that he had various community involvements, and that he frequently conducted business at home.

Back at the synagogue, Brogan looked at his watch and put on a frown of impatience. "Where is that guy? No one can get lost in this matchbox."

As if in confirmation, David Pearl, shaggy, plump, and thickly-bespectacled, came jingling into the office, carrying a big ring of keys. "Sorry for the wait. There were a few calls I had to take. The phone has rung non-stop with people wanting to know about Rabbi Winkler."

"Hardly noticed you'd left," Brogan said.

"The keys for all locks in the synagogue are on this ring." Sounding nervous and apologetic, Pearl, the Assistant Rabbi, said, "I have no idea which one unlocks the rabbi's desk."

The desk had a center drawer and to the right a column of three drawers. All four were locked. Pearl began the trial-and-error testing with the center drawer. Unsurprisingly, the first try was a bust.

"Did the rabbi act different in the days just before his death?" Mary asked.

"Not by me." Pearl tried a key that inserted but wouldn't turn. He extracted it.

Mary asked, "Did you two associate outside of the synagogue?"

Pearl's pattern was beginning to suggest that he couldn't try keys and answer at the same time. The key ring fell silent as he spoke. "I wouldn't say so. I should add that I was hired four months ago, straight out of rabbinical school. My predecessor left for Rochester Hills. I was still getting to know Rabbi Winkler professionally. We didn't associate socially."

Mary's next question was, "Has the synagogue experienced any problems lately?"

Pearl had tried a few keys in between questions. "Anti-Semitism?"

"Or otherwise."

"No."

"Why did your predecessor leave?"

"Promotion. Not that I knew him, but that's my understanding. He went from assistant rabbi to rabbi."

"As you hope to do someday, I suppose," said Mary.

"True, but for the interim, I like where I am." Pearl's cherubic face brightened in recall as he said, "Rabbi Winkler was fond of saying that Temple Beth El is homely, but no matter how beautiful a synagogue may be, there are Jews somewhere who swear they wouldn't be caught dead in it."

"Still no open drawers, huh?" asked Brogan.

The not-so-subtle prod got Pearl to resume trying keys.

Brogan joined the interview. "What about trouble from outside the neighborhood? You got your hate groups out there. And there's the Jew-Arab thing, too."

"When I said no problems with anti-Semitism, it covered those possibilities, too."

"What denomination is your synagogue?" asked Brogan.

"Our movement," Pearl said in correction, "is Conservative."

The now educated Brogan asked, "Was there any bad blood with members from other movements?"

Pearl's face turned quizzical. "What do you mean?"

"No offense, but don't Jews argue a lot among themselves?" asked Brogan, who had served in the Marine Corps, never the Diplomatic Corps. "I mean, if that's just a stereotype, let me know."

Mary's jaw tightened over Brogan's jackboot style, but she held her tongue.

Meanwhile, Pearl again had paused with the keys. This time, he stared fixedly at Brogan. His facial expression was gentle, but his delivery was assertive. "We Jews have our differences, as do other religions. But, I'm betting that you never worked a homicide where the victim had been argued to death."

Mary stifled a smile and jumped back in with, "Who else within the synagogue would know how the rabbi was spending his time?"

A quick study, Pearl had learned to talk and try keys at the same time. "Richard Spiegel, president of the congregation, probably had the most dealings with the rabbi professionally. Hmmm, and Sally Abrams would know most about his appointments. She's the administrator and secretary combined. In a small synagogue, it's not unusual for people to wear more than one hat." He tapped his skull cap and added, "Or more than one kippah."

A key turned, sounding a click. The center drawer now was unlocked.

Pearl stepped aside but remained in the room.

Mary pulled out the drawer. With one hand, she slid the contents around. Nothing notable: pens, pencils, a stapler, cellophane tape, AAA batteries, lottery tickets, Detroit post cards, and breath mints. She closed the drawer and then said, "Let's try the others."

"Right away," said Pearl. He extracted the key from the center drawer and unlocked the other three.

Mary examined the contents of the top drawer. Nothing of substance. Same for the middle drawer. The bottom drawer, the largest, was a file drawer. She took a seat in the chair and began to finger through some folders, mostly reading the tabs. She reached the back of the drawer without having pulled out any papers. Bending forward, she noticed something at the very back. It wasn't paper, wasn't filed. More like hidden. She sat erect and made a single slap against a knee, deliberating. Then, she bent down and looked again. Then, from the center drawer, she took a pencil and with it snared what was at the back of the file drawer. She raised her catch slowly, it dangling precariously on the pencil.

Pearl started biting a fingernail.

Mary moved the pencil toward Luther, causing its load to sway. "Take them off the pencil."

Luther hurriedly put on gloves and then did as requested.

Mary said, "Hold them out, like they're hanging on a clothesline."

And that's what Luther did, using thumbs and index fingers like clothespins.

Mary made a silent guess before walking over to read the label. She'd been spot-on. Size 10. The Victoria's Secret satin lace panties, black with gold trim, were too large to belong to the petite Mrs. Winkler.

13.

"Be still," requested Mary.

Sophie stopped shifting her weight and stood erect in front of the bathroom mirror. She was wearing the pants to some silk pajamas. She was naked waist-up.

Where Sophie's left breast used to be, Mary placed a wad of gauze, then held it in place with a gloved hand and waited as Sophie tore strips of medical tape. One at a time, Sophie handed the strips to Mary, who used them to carefully secure the gauze. This was a twice-a-day procedure: irrigating the area with sterile water, applying topical antiseptic, and dressing it with gauze.

Mary stepped behind Sophie, squared her in front of the mirror, and asked, "Did I do a good job?"

"An excellent job. I just hate being a bother to anybody."

"No bother. I keep telling you that." Mary took Sophie's pajama top off the door knob. She held the garment as Sophie inserted one arm and then the other. Mary pulled it up onto Sophie's shoulders.

Sophie arched her back and grimaced. "Ouch!" The mere brush of the light-weight, almost frictionless silk against her skin was painful. The surface of her torso was pocked with tumors, malignant clumps resembling blackened cauliflower and smelling of rotting hamburger. As much as anything else, they were torturously sensitive and given to bleeding.

Mary's stomach knotted. "Sorry. I'm so sorry."

Sophie calmingly said, "It's okay." She went on to gingerly button her pajama top, enduring the settling fabric without outcry, all to spare Mary further alarm.

But Mary's eyes already had begun to water, and her mouth quivered, as she proclaimed, "It's not fair. You don't deserve this cancer."

Sophie shook her head, but not in self-pity. "No one deserves cancer, so fairness has nothing to do with it." She sensed that her daughter knew that, so she asked, "What's actually bothering you, Mary?"

Pressed, Mary admitted, "It's about the pain and suffering. I can't bear the thought."

"Don't dwell on it."

"I can't help it."

"You can and must. All the fretting in the world is not going to change what's in store. It's a terrible disease and likely to take me through a wringer, but mercifully, the end is not far off."

The forthrightness of that last comment caused Mary to momentarily close her eyes. She opened them and said, "You'd think working homicide, I could handle this better. But seeing death after the fact is different than seeing it on the approach, especially with my own mother."

"I understand," assured Sophie, "but I don't want you to put your life on hold. You have a good husband and great children. Don't shortchange them."

"It's just that I feel so useless. Like there's nothing I can do."

"To a certain extent, there isn't. You need to accept that." Sophie patted her daughter's cheek, kissed the other, and said, "But one thing's for sure, I'm blessed to have you around."

Mary's eyes took on wattage and her spirits levitated, and all she could say was, "I love you so much, Mama."

"I know. And it means the world to me." Sophie then returned to the subject of Mary's torment. "The doctors will do what they can to minimize the pain and suffering. Beyond that, I'll try to endure. I've led a Christian life and I'm counting on going to Heaven. It remains to be seen what type of Hell I'll have to go through, first."

14.

Mary flashed her badge and asked, "Are you Alison Petrocelli?"

The woman, dripping sweat, held her bottom lip in a salty overbite while chewing on what she'd been asked, as though it had been a trick question. Eventually, she responded, "Why?"

"We're investigating the murder of Rabbi Allan Winkler. I'll ask again, are you Alison Petrocelli?"

"Yes."

"We have some questions for you," said Mary.

"You have a warrant?"

Curtly, Brogan said, "Don't need one to ask questions. You going to talk to us or not?"

"Not now. You caught me in the middle of something."

"Police have a knack for catching people in the middle of something," said Brogan.

Petrocelli didn't like his phrasing, considered it innuendo. A thick vein running up her toned neck pulsed, as she said, "I can't imagine why you would think I can help your investigation."

"Rest your imagination," advised Brogan. "The questions won't require it."

Mary was still adapting to Brogan's style, but long experience made her nimble at playing off any partner. She needed to contrast his sarcasm. "And the sooner we can ask them, Ms. Petrocelli, the sooner we can be on our way. May we step inside, please?"

Petrocelli wiped her face with one end of the towel that was draped over her shoulders. Displeasure evident in her voice, she said, "Alright." She unlashed the door.

The constant hum that they heard upon stepping inside was coming from a treadmill, churning at a moderate clip. It was in the living room and could be seen from where they stood.

"Nice piece of equipment," commented Brogan. "Mind if I take a closer look?"

"I do. This is as far as you go. Ask your questions."

"Sure," said Mary.

"But let me say this, real quick," said Brogan, "looks like you work out regularly."

Had the setting been different, Petrocelli might not have frowned at the compliment. "I exercise to keep down stress." Her last eighth of a mile on the treadmill had been run during the relentless ringing of the doorbell. Finally, it had blown her runner's high so completely that she hopped off in anger to confront whoever it was who had more persistence than sense. Even off the machine and standing still, she personified motion, curves running recklessly all over her tall frame. Her pink tank suit hugged like it had been applied with a spray can.

"Let's start with the last time you saw Rabbi Winkler," said Mary.

"I don't remember."

"Give it your best," urged Brogan.

Petrocelli said, "Maybe it'll come to me. In the meanwhile, what's your next question?"

"How long," continued Mary, "did you know him?"

"Little more than a year."

Brogan asked, "How'd you meet?"

"Wait here," asked Petrocelli, as she stepped away to the treadmill and took the water bottle from its slot. She squeezed a long stream into her mouth. She returned, hydrated and having decided how she was going to answer the question. "Business."

"Be more specific," said Mary.

"I'm in public relations. A client of mine introduced us."

"Did the rabbi become a client?" Brogan, again.

"Yes."

Snidely, Brogan asked, "How personal were those services that you provided?"

Petrocelli, growing less and less fond of Brogan's phrasing, answered, "I worked with him on community outreach programs." She ran the towel across her head, the hair short, curly, raven, and still wet from the workout.

Mary knew something about exercise herself. After the warm up, you kick into gear. "When did you and Rabbi Winkler become lovers?"

Petrocelli's taut abominable muscles tightened further. "Excuse me? Ours was a business relationship." Her mind raced speculatively and she said, "Yes, we've conducted business at his home and workplace, but—"

"Save it," interrupted Brogan. "We have his computers. Deleting something doesn't erase it from the hard drive. The lab boys recovered all those steamy e-mails."

"And I'm not going to ask your undergarment size," said Mary, "seeing that we have a man present. But if I had to guess, I'd say you're a size 10."

Petrocelli's jaw muscles twitched. She haughtily said, "So, we had an affair. Ever hear of consenting adults?"

"I certainly have," said Mary, "but that doesn't justify lying during a murder investigation."

Explaining herself, Petrocelli said, "I was just trying to keep a good man's reputation from being dragged through the mud, that's all."

"Very considerate of you," said Brogan. But, he doubled back with, "When did you see him last? You never did answer that question."

Underarms clammy, her antiperspirant that had endured the treadmill now surrendering, Petrocelli blurted, "I'm not answering anything else without my lawyer."

"Which is your right," said Mary.

But Brogan said, "Just one more thing."

Emphatically, Petrocelli declared, "I said I'm done with your questions."

"This one is harmless. And I'm out of here afterwards. Scout's honor."

"I'm not promising an answer." However, in hopes of quickening his departure, Petrocelli said, "But go ahead and ask."

"Is Petrocelli your married name?"

"Yes. I'm divorced."

True to his word, Brogan followed Mary out the door. As they walked to the car, he spoke loud enough for Petrocelli to hear. "You know, Cunningham, I figured it was her married name. First thing I said to myself when I saw her was that she don't look Italian."

Instantly, Petrocelli's eyes became locked and loaded. If only they were weapons that she could fire. What she wanted to shout at him, she instead kept as a thought. *Kiss my black ass.*

15.

Mary had just risen from her desk when she spotted the woman sashaying toward her. *Damn! Of all people.* She dropped back into her seat, flung open the folder that was lying on her desk, and pretended to be absorbed with its contents, hoping to look too occupied to be interrupted.

Linda Goings, dolled up in a short, tight skirt, low-cut blouse, fishnet stockings, and strawberry-blond wig, rapped her knuckles on the desktop, announcing her presence. "Yoo-hoo, anybody home?"

Mary looked up. "Oh, hello, Linda. I'm so busy, I didn't see you."

Goings didn't budge. "Girl, what's this I hear about your mother having breast cancer? Stage IV, too. Is it true?"

"Yes. Now, I have to get back to work."

But Goings already had flopped down into the chair in front of the desk and was scooting it nosily along the floor to Mary's side. "I know what you must be going through. Couple of summers ago, my sister had fibroids removed. Before that, she bled a river every month. I was crazy with worry before the surgery. She made it through, thank God."

Ordinarily, Mary was more tolerant when Goings came to worship; but, this visit proved vexing. First, Mary didn't need to be reminded of Sophie's condition. Second, Mary was testy over having made a particular decision. Third, Mary, to ward off what Goings was about to do, had to say, "I'd appreciate it if you didn't smoke around me, Linda."

Goings snatched the cigarette from her lips and tucked it back behind the ear from which she'd retrieved it. "No problem. I need to be around you all the more, if that'll help me quit."

That last statement also was the last thing that Mary wanted to hear. "Look, Linda, don't take this the wrong way, but I have things to do."

"Say no more. If there's anybody that can identify with being busy, it's me. Last week I had backlog farther up than a tampon."

"Glad you understand."

Goings stood up from the chair, craning her neck to steal a glimpse at the opened file. In a scattered pile lay some photos, the top one jumping out at her. She recoiled and pressed a palm against her abdomen. "Snap! Somebody really did a job on him."

Mary closed the file to prevent further comment. That didn't work, either.

Still making no move toward the door, Goings asked, "You ever regret leaving vice for homicide?"

"No."

"Me, I can't take looking at dead people."

Not caring if it sounded sarcastic, Mary said, "If you can't take looking at blood, don't become a surgeon. If you can't take looking at dead people, don't join homicide."

"Touché," conceded Goings, lingering like acid reflux. "Because that photo gives me the heebie-jeebies. I'll stay with decoy work," she said, of masquerading as a prostitute to snare unsuspecting johns.

"Each to her own calling, Linda."

Goings continued prattling. "No sooner than I joined vice, I started hearing stories about you. And I'm thinking, I've got to meet this Mary Cunningham. Pick her brain."

"It's slim pickings today, believe me."

Goings, dressed as her street alias, Honey Child, was in full regalia: caked foundation, lashes as long as rakes, and raccoonish eye-shadow. Hoochie Mama personified, and it worked for her. She had a respectable arrest rate. "Mary, on your worse day, I could learn loads from you. Be nice and send me on my way with some advice."

Wanting to send Goings a-stepping, Mary said, "Alright. Never let your guard down. There's no such thing as safe police work. Any situation can turn dangerous."

Goings became giddy. "Advice from someone who's been there. But, I'm glad I haven't had to kill anyone. Tell me, girl, what's it like?"

Mary stood. She took Goings by the elbow. "Let's go."

Taken aback, Goings asked, "Did I say something wrong?"

"You? Never." Mary held on to Goings' elbow all the while that she escorted her to the door.

Speaking fast, Goings said, "Got to get back to work, do you?"

Mary said nothing.

"We'll talk some other time, then, when you're not so busy."

Continued silence from Mary.

"And if you ever need someone to talk to about your mother, remember, I'm always here for you."

Mary held the door open and with a guiding push sent Goings on her way. Then, she marched dutifully back to her desk, blocking out the other people and noises in the room. Still standing, she picked up the folder and placed it under her arm, protectively, as a diplomat might treat an important dossier.

Mary walked to a certain file cabinet. That was what she'd been on her way to do when Goings entered. It was a deed overdue, one that Mary stubbornly had resisted for months. She pulled out a drawer and all but thought that she felt a rush of cold air brush her face. Into the Fridge she placed the folder of Matthew Kent.

16.

Brogan didn't want to stand a second time. He turned his knees toward the aisle and motioned Mary to squeeze past him.

Mary, having returned from the restroom, was put off by the discourtesy, but didn't contest. As she attempted to return to the middle seat, the guy in front of Brogan chose that time to recline his seat. She lost her balance and landed forward on Brogan. Their faces were momentarily close enough for her to smell the sour breath lingering from his nap.

"Hey, hey," he protested, his arms warding off Mary. "If I wanted a lap dance, you wouldn't be my choice."

Mary regained her footing, stepped sideways, turned, and sat. Since the window seat next to her was occupied— by a grandma type—Mary leaned toward Brogan to confidentially deliver the response. "And if I wanted to give one, you damn sure wouldn't be my choice."

"Loosen up, will you, Cunningham? I was pulling your chain, that's all. Don't always be so quick to bare the claws."

"They're retractable, you know. And if you don't want them out in the first place, don't give me cause."

"Whatever." Brogan shielded a yawn with the back of his hand and then asked, "Where in Backwoods, U.S.A. is Crowley?"

"Somewhere west of—" then, in a panic, Mary clutched her armrests. "What was that?"

Brogan, entertained by her reaction, snickered and said, "Relax. We hit an air pocket, that's all."

Mary was embarrassed upon receiving a reassuring pat on the hand from the grandma, who hadn't so much as flinched. "I hate flying," she grumbled, before finishing her answer. "Somewhere west of Baton Rouge."

"I'll drive. Women have no sense of direction. I let you behind the wheel and we'll end up in a swamp full of alligators."

"The car I've reserved has GPS," informed Mary. "But keep it up with the bonehead comments. Just don't complain when the claws come out."

"I didn't mean anything by it. If I was really out to piss you off, I'd call you that name you hate."

"Which you never have, at least never to my face, and I appreciate that."

"But I'm still driving."

The lab results were in: the DNA from the panties and from a certain second source both had come from the same person. But Alison Petrocelli? That can't be determined until a sample is obtained from her for comparison.

Having obtained a search warrant, required for obtaining DNA from a non-volunteering suspect, Mary and Brogan returned to Petrocelli's home to grab her and take her downtown. A full mailbox and a week's worth of newspapers suggested that, this time, her not answering the door wasn't because she was in there hoofing on the treadmill. The two cops went back to the judge, this time swearing out an arrest warrant, making Petrocelli a suspect and person of interest. Against the possibility that Petrocelli might have crossed state lines, they enlisted the help of the FBI. The Baton Rouge office was among those notified, after some background checking into Petrocelli's family roots. A stake-out of a cousin's shanty, out in the sticks, yielded results.

After being apprehended, Petrocelli was taken to the nearest lockup, which was in Crowley. She had chosen not to fight extradition. More interestingly, she had demanded to talk by phone to Mary.

"What's this crap about Petrocelli needing police protection?" asked Brogan.

"I don't know. That's what she claimed over the phone. She said her life is in danger."

"How?"

"Said she'd supply the details in person."

"It's a scam, if you ask me."

"Maybe. But her story isn't our first order of business."

"She'll get her police protection," said Brogan, "up 'til when the judge sentences her to life."

They suspended their conversation when the beverage cart rolled up.

The stewardess chimed, "And what would you like to drink?"

"Diet soda," said Mary. "Doesn't matter what kind."

"How long before meal service?" asked Brogan.

The stewardess answered, "About twenty minutes."

"I'll tough it out," said Brogan.

"On second thought," said Mary to the stewardess, "I'll have water."

After the cart had rolled passed, Brogan asked, "How far is Crawfish from the airport?"

"That's Crowley, and I was told a hundred miles, more or less."

"The less the better."

"There you go starting up with me again," she accused.

"I wasn't referring to your company. Your problem, Cunningham, is that you think you're on everybody's mind."

With feigned astonishment, Mary asked, "You mean, I'm not?"

"What I was referring to is that a lot of the drive probably is back roads. That, or highway dotted with speed traps manned by good ol' boys."

Mary said, "If we get pulled over, I'll let you do the talking."

"Smart," said Brogan. "I'm getting some more shuteye. Need to be rested, if I'm going to baby-sit you." Soon thereafter, he was snoring.

Mary, nervous from being in an airplane, would have preferred his conversation. She considered awaking him on some pretense, but didn't. Meanwhile, the grandma had taken out some needlepoint, and that's simply too Americana to disturb. No, Mary would have to endure in silence

and hope for an uneventful flight. Those prospects, however, were threatened when she felt the plane bump once,
then again. She stiffened, not caring that grandma didn't
miss a stitch.

The captain's voice came over the address system.
"Folks, I've turned on the seat belt sign. Looks like we're
in for some turbulence."

Mary dropped her head resignedly. She pressed fingertips on the sides of her face and slid them upward and
around until they met in the middle of her forehead, and
in reference to the captain's announcement, said under her
breath, "In my case, that's something that can be taken
more than one way."

17.

Newberry knew who was at his office door by the knock: the dun-dunna-dun-dun...but no finish. "Get in here, Mary."

She did, along with Brogan, who reported, "We're back from the trenches, Inspector."

Newberry didn't turn to look at them. His gaze was fixed on an area of the carpet, as he incredulously asked himself, "How did I misread that break?"

Mary sized up the situation differently. "At least it came close."

"Closeness counts in horseshoes and darts." Newberry, putter in hand, paced off a distance and set down a golf ball. He tapped the ball. It rolled rather straight, until it reached the area of interest, broke to the left, and went into the hole—actually, a paper cup lying on its side. He extended his prominent bottom lip and made the fist pump that he and countless others had shamelessly stolen from Tiger Woods.

"Nice," said Brogan.

"Thanks. You golf, Ross?"

"Nope. Not physical enough for me. No offense."

"None taken."

Mary wanted to trade talk of golf for talk of what had transpired in Louisiana. She and Brogan had flown back and had come straight to headquarters, Petrocelli in tow. "Ready to be briefed?" she suggestingly asked.

"I'm listening." Newberry retrieved the ball. With one foot then the other, he started sweeping random patterns in the carpet. He attributed his low handicap to this unconventional practice. Learn to judge ball travel on a mussed carpet and reading a putt on a green is like reading the first line on an eye chart.

"The Prosecutor's Office is not bringing murder charges at this time," Mary said.

Newberry took the news nonchalantly, only asking, "Whose call?"

Mary answered, "Gerald Lewis."

Newberry, having readied the next putt, asked, "No fugitive charges, either?" Club taps ball, ball travels, ends up in cup.

Brogan reentered the conversation. "No, because she left before the arrest warrant was issued."

"Plus," said Mary, "she hadn't been ordered not to leave town."

Knowing that a suspect who hasn't been charged can be kept in custody, although not indefinitely, Newberry asked, "Does Lewis want her held anyway?"

"Negative," answered Brogan.

"I'm not going to concern myself with how Lewis does his job," said Newberry. "Get to the part about Petrocelli's safety."

"The story goes," said Mary, "that Petrocelli's life is in danger from an ex-boyfriend. Supposedly, she got interested in Rabbi Winkler and kicked the boyfriend to the curb. The boyfriend got mad and threatened to give, quote, that Jew motherfucker a second circumcision, unquote."

The implication obvious to Newberry, he asked, "Did she specifically mention dismemberment?" knowing that such information had not been divulged to the public.

"No," said Mary, "and we didn't tell her about it."

"So what?" countered Brogan. "If she's the murderer, she wouldn't have to be told. She's lying about the so-called ex-boyfriend to shift our focus elsewhere."

Newberry had crossed his legs and was leaning to the side, the putter supporting him like a cane. "I can't see Lewis freeing her on that story. He might be stringing her along until her DNA results come back."

Brogan, however, said, "The lab people took DNA samples from Petrocelli, but her lawyer is cutting our knees from under us with admissions. He says that Petrocelli admits having an affair with the rabbi and that explains the panties with her DNA in the rabbi's desk. He says that she admits having had sex with the rabbi in his house the morning he was killed and that explains her DNA on his severed pecker."

Now, Newberry lifted the putter and twirled it slowly like a baton, half-frowning. "Shortly ago, you said that she hadn't spoken about the dismemberment and hadn't been told about it."

"Actually," said Mary, about to set matters straight, "her lawyer said she admits to sex with the rabbi in his house the morning he was killed and that it explains any of her DNA that we might have found in the house or on the rabbi."

With just enough sternness in his voice to get the point across, Newberry said, "You're in here to report, Ross, and I expect it to be done accurately."

"Understood," said Brogan.

The putter now tucked under an arm, Newberry, addressing both his detectives, said, "What else about this ex-boyfriend."

Mary said, "Petrocelli claims that he had been stalking her."

"She's scamming," accused Brogan, "wanting us to believe that he murdered the rabbi after she left the Winkler residence."

"Maybe," conceded Newberry, "but I'm sure that Lewis isn't taking her claims on faith. Did Petrocelli say the stalking continued after the murder?"

"She said that he came by uninvited the day after the murder and told her that the investigation would uncover her affair and told her not to talk to the police without a lawyer."

"Nothing criminal about that advice," said Newberry.

"No," agreed Mary, "but she said he warned her not to mention his name and that she'd be more than sorry if she did. According to her, he's capable of making good on that threat."

Brogan waved a hand in rejection. "She left Michigan because she feared what her ex might do to silence her? Too convenient, if you ask me. I don't buy it."

"That's what Petrocelli told you, Ross?" asked Newberry.

"Mary told me, in Louisiana. Petrocelli wouldn't talk in my presence."

"Losing your charm with the ladies?" needled Newberry.

"Even your greatest hitters strike-out, now and then," said Brogan.

"You two collect your thoughts for a minute," Newberry said, then walked to the cup, retrieved the ball, backed up a few paces, and dropped the ball onto the carpet. His trusty putter back in position, he performed his pre-putt ritual before settling into his stance over the ball and sending it on its way. The route was bumpy, the break sharp. The ball contacted the lip, pushing the cup aside. "Catching the edge like that, it might have dropped under actual play," he rationalized.

"Let me try that stick," requested Brogan.

Newberry offered the putter, grip-first. "Be my guest, but you might want to start with a bunny," he advised, meaning a short, easy putt.

"No need." Brogan picked up the ball, placed it at a distance similar to Newberry's last, said, "Prepare to be impressed," and without ritual, struck the ball.

After the ball rolled to a stop, Newberry's analysis was merciless. "That was fucked-up. You lifted your head. You flicked your wrists. You muscled it. It's a wonder that the ball didn't take flight."

Brogan wasn't peeved as much by Newberry's taunts as by Mary's reaction. He thrust the putter challengingly to her. "Here. You're standing there giggling, like you're on the pro circuit. You try it."

"No thanks. I'm not in here for that."

"Mary's right," admitted Newberry, although he was en route to the ball. Heavy-handedly, he remarked, "I take it that you two are on your way to check out the ex-boyfriend."

Brogan responded, "We left our rooms at four this morning and have been on the go since." He hesitated momentarily. "There's been no mention that the guy is a flight risk, so—"

"Never thought I'd see the day," interrupted Newberry. "G.I. Joe admitting to battle fatigue."

"I wasn't speaking about myself, but Cunningham. She probably wants to go home, take a nap, freshen-up. You know how women are."

"Since you're such the expert on women, Ross, you know that we love to run our mouths," Mary said, with a combination of sarcasm and payback. "I'm ready to go interview me somebody."

"Then it's settled," declared Newberry. "So, go, already." With that dismissal, he got into his putting posture.

Her hand on the doorknob, Mary said, "You'd never guess who Petrocelli says is the ex-boyfriend, Inspector."

Newberry kept his head down, focusing on the ball. "Lucky for me that I don't have to guess."

Having gotten the message, Mary said the name, which, up until that time, she even had not shared with Brogan.

Newberry had been midway into his stroke when he heard the name. He flubbed the putt, and the ball veered crazily wide of the cup.

18.

For four decades, Fritz Mueller had owned the same telephone, a relic: desk model, black, rotary dial, heavy enough to be a murder weapon. Its most modern feature was that it didn't require cranking. Age, however, had not diminished the strength by which it announced a call. Its ring was as jolting and foreboding as the alarm in a fire station.

Mueller lifted the receiver and ever so cordially greeted, "Hello? May I help you?" The initial silence on the other end didn't annoy him since he'd come to expect that from certain callers. It gave him hope.

"May I...may I please speak with Dr. Fritz Mueller?"

Muller made note that the caller's voice was weak, hesitant. "This is he."

"My name is Thomas Duval."

"How may I be of service, Tom?"

"I think I want to die."

"I see. Tell me more. Start wherever you wish." Mueller was seated on his couch which had so lost its springiness that its cushion sank under his modest weight. In front, stretched his combination coffee table and workbench: a picnic tabletop on milk crates. It was spread with newspaper on which stood a mound of modeling clay. To free both hands to sculpt, he placed the receiver on his shoulder and clamped it there with his ear. "You have my full attention, Tom."

Duval said, "I can't stand the indignity. I'm a proud man. All I am is a burden to my family."

Wanting to know about potential obstructionists, Mueller asked, "By family, whom are we talking about, Tom?"

"I have three grown children."

Mueller's hobby was sculpting figurines. The gargoyle he was presently crafting had too much of a pot belly. He slenderized it with one deft slice with a scalpel. He didn't believe in spending money on handicraft tools if he didn't have to. "Wife?"

"I'm divorced."

"Do the children know of your decision?"

"I haven't made a decision. They know nothing about what I've been thinking, if that's what you mean."

"What would be their reaction if you told them?" Mueller had sliced too much from the belly. The wings were causing his creation to slump. He pinched some clay from the mound and applied it. Bad posture corrected.

"Most likely, they'd try to talk me out of it."

The response prompted Mueller to lay down the scalpel and take the receiver in hand. "Not surprising. And certainly they would be well-meaning. But they aren't the ones suffering. You are."

"And I am suffering."

"I believe you, Tom. It's you who must decide what to do about it. Naturally, you consider the opinions of your loved ones, but the decision has to be yours."

"I was hoping you could help me decide."

The crisis seemingly weathered, Mueller repositioned the receiver on his shoulder. Using just the tip of the scalpel, he drew a tiny skull on the bottom of the figurine's foot. It was his signature, his trademark, found on all his artwork. Then, by silent fiat, he declared his latest creation completed. "What's your medical condition, Tom?"

"I have chronic fatigue syndrome and fibromyalgia. The first keeps me too tired to do anything and the second keeps me in constant pain. Basically, all I do is sit and ache."

"How long have you been suffering?" Mueller placed the figurine next to the other two he'd created that day. He had use of a kiln at a nearby ceramic tile factory. The kiln reminded him of a crematory and he took satisfaction that he used this oven to bestow life. It was always gratifying to reverse the order of things, flout the status quo.

"Three years, and I don't think I can take anymore. Plus, I'm depressed all the time."

"How old are you, Tom?"

"Forty-six."

"That's young."

"With the energy of a dead battery," said Duval.

"The pain. Describe the pain."

"It's like I've been dismembered at every joint then glued back together."

Mueller started rubbing clay from his fingers. All his figurines were demons, monsters, and boogey-men. Whether that was contrived or simply consistent with his psyche, it was marketing magic. His artwork stayed in demand by collectors. "CFS and fibromyalgia are difficult to diagnose. The symptoms can mimic other ailments. But let's assume, for the sake of discussion, an accurate diagnosis. What treatment has been prescribed?"

"At one time or another, it's been anti-viral drugs, vitamins, supplements, special diets. I could go on but you get the picture. None of it has helped." Duval's voice had trailed at the end of his last sentence, and he paused, apparently to catch his breath. "For the pain, I started with ibuprofen. Now, they have me on acetaminophen with codeine. In between, it's been Percocet, Vicodin, you name it, I've had it. They might as well have been jelly beans."

"Have you received psychological counseling, Tom?"

Duval's tone became defensive. "Why? You think it's all in my head?"

Trying to sound more pleading than demanding, Mueller said, "Please don't put words in my mouth, Tom."

"I've read up on my condition and know that some shrinks say it can be psychosomatic. I'm not imagining this suffering."

An instigator's smile played on Mueller's face. "If you ask me, psychobabble is the most frequent form of medical malpractice."

"And thrust me, Dr. Mueller, my imagination is not strong enough to produce this degree of pain and suffering."

Mueller inspected his palms. Clean enough. He flipped them to check the nails. Loose, wrinkled skin covered the backs of his hands, blue veins and liver spots their only coloration. The fingers were long and bony, yet ever so nimble, as evidenced by how he still could wield a scalpel. In his hands, it might as well have been a Swiss army knife, so many uses could he make of it. It became a grooming device, as he began scraping clay from under his finger-nails. "You mentioned depression."

"I'm on a combination of Prozac and Elavil. But how can they work when what I'm depressed about never lets up?"

Modulating his voice to sound thoughtful and sincere, Mueller said, "Tom, it would be unethical for me not to mention that your ailments are not terminal."

"I wish they were. At least then, I could look forward to eventual relief. Dr. Mueller, I think you know that there are things worse than death."

"Indeed. What is your line of work, Tom?"

"I used to be a forest ranger, here, in northern Califor-nia. All my life, I've been an outdoorsman and sportsman." Another one of those pauses. "I...I'm confined to a wheel-chair, Doctor. My independence is shot." He became nasal when he added, "My children plan to put me in a nursing home."

"But, you'd rather die?"

"I believe so."

It was because he was developing a crick in his neck that Mueller took the receiver in hand. "The service I can provide you, Tom," continued the salesman, "is to assist you in carrying out your choice, in a dignified and pain-free manner."

"Pain-free. Those are beautiful words. No more suffering."

The ABCs of selling: Always Be Closing. "Let's talk logistics, then. All of my out-of-town clients come to Michigan. How soon can you make your travel arrangements, Tom?" The ensuing pause was the longest, and Mueller sensed that it bespoke indecision, so he emphasized, "It would mean the end of the pain, Tom. The end of all your suffering."

"Yes, but I'm not one-hundred-percent sure of the decision at this point. It's not that I'm trying to waste your time."

"It could never be a waste of time speaking with you, Tom. What does the decision hinge on?"

"No one factor above all others, but the message it might send to my children is high on the list."

"The message should be that a person has the right to die in dignity when living becomes unbearable," responded Mueller. "I've never married and have no children. That doesn't disqualify me from saying that it would be selfish for loved ones to put their wishes over your suffering."

"Another thing is that I'm Catholic. I'm sure that you are aware that Catholicism considers suicide to be a mortal sin."

"Ah, sweet religion. All religions owe their existence to suffering. For matters that he can't endure, can't understand, man turns to religion, to a God who's all-enduring and all-knowing. So man permits himself to be told how to suffer and how to die, presumably by an entity who's not subject to either." If, at this point, discretion whispered to Mueller that he had said enough about this potentially volatile topic, he ignored the warning, enthralled by his own eloquence. "I'm a scientist, Tom, not a theologian. But, unlike religion, I've never failed those who have turned to me for help."

"God doesn't fail, either," insisted Duval, with newly-found assertiveness. "I've decided not to go through with it."

A defeated chess Grand Master mentally replays every move, even as he shakes the victor's hand. Likewise, Mueller already had admitted to himself where he had blundered. He resolved to henceforth keep God out of the conversation, at least out of his half. "Then, I must respect your decision, Tom."

"You promised me your full attention, Dr. Mueller, and you gave it."

"I could do no less."

"And I thank you. Good-bye."

"Good-bye, Tom."

The dial tone hummed tauntingly.

Mueller hung up. He snapped his skeletal fingers once, but not from a sudden recall. This was a snap of self-annoyance, from a fisherman who'd allowed a catch to escape. But he disallowed himself further emotion and returned his attention to his little darlings on the table. Moping about the one that got away is for amateur anglers. The professionals concern themselves with keeping the tackle box stocked and at the ready, because there are always other fish in the sea.

19.

Brogan, driving the unmarked police car, turned sharply into the parking space and then came to the proverbial screeching halt. Eager to get out and attend to matters, he threw the transmission into park, killed the ignition, pulled down the door latch, and pushed the door open with his shoulder. A few seconds later, with a sweep of his arm, he slammed the door closed.

Mary's seatbelt had restrained her from hitting her head on the dashboard from the forward inertia; however, Renard Cruise, the uniformed officer in the backseat, had been forced to extend an arm against the back of the front seat. After they exited, Cruise easily closed his door, but Mary's door had a bum hitch that caught halfway. She pulled upward on the handle while bumping against the door, trying to close it.

Brogan, standing on the opposite side, grabbed his waistband and twisted it back and forth a few times—a habit when he was gung-ho—and while walking away, said, "Leave it ajar if it's too complicated for you, Cunningham."

Mary ignored the comment and administered another bump, which did the trick.

"When should I start shooting?" asked Cruise, fortunately referring to the video camera he was carrying. The young Latino added, "Want me to get you going in?"

"No. After we're inside." Mary then jogged, to catch up with Brogan, who was well ahead of them.

Inside, as the three were walking down a hallway, Brogan, said, "Come on, admit it, Cunningham. You hate the guy."

"No, I don't."

Brogan said, "Well, I don't mind admitting I can't stand him. What about you, Renard?"

Cruise smacked on chewing gum a few times before answering, "To tell you the truth, I don't have an opinion, one way or the other."

Up ahead, two children shoved each other at a water fountain. They were attendees at a youth program being held at the New Mission Baptist Church, a stone-and-mortar structure dwarfing the surrounding homes in a northwest Detroit neighborhood. The girl bullied her way to drinking first, only to have the boy push down her head, causing water to shoot up her nose.

"You, butt-face," said the girl, getting ready to deal with the prankster.

But he sprinted, with her in pursuit. When they spotted Mary, Brogan, and Cruise, they slid to a stop. Each child flipped a switch that turned on a radiant smile and stood erect and well-behaved. But they'd already been busted.

"You two get to wherever you're supposed to be and stop the running and the horseplay," demanded Mary, the mother and cop in her converging. "Understand?"

The girl angelically answered, "Yes."

So too, did the boy.

The children took the stairs to the cavernous basement, after which, the fading sounds of giggles and racing footsteps told that their halos had been discarded.

But, all along, there had been other sounds, and they were getting stronger, as the cops neared the end of the hallway. Rousing sounds. Joyous sounds. Voices. Music. Upon reaching the source, Mary swung open the doors of the auditorium and the three of them stepped just within. They gazed across the theater-capacity seating to the front of the room.

Choir rehearsal continued, not a note missed, as the choir director, a frail young man, continued to slice the air with his arms. He did, however, maintain a worried watch on the trio, having recognized Mary and Brogan from their prior visit.

"Now," signaled Mary to Cruise.

She and Brogan started walking toward the front, Cruise following closely, filming. They stopped a short distance behind a man standing in evaluation of the rehearsal.

He was massive, by height, width, and weight. Eyes closed, smiling blissfully, and outwardly absorbed in the choir, he nonetheless was aware of his visitors, though he kept his back turned. Even after Brogan made one of those announcing coughs, the man-mountain remained facing forward. He did, however, start clapping in approval of the choir. "Bravo. Rehearsal is now over."

Without hesitation, director and choir hurriedly filed out.

The large man chose that time to turn and face his guests. He was wearing a black jogging suit, and draped around his stump of a neck was a thick chain attached to a huge platinum, diamond-studded cross. His eyeglasses were tinted lens within a bejeweled frame. He spoke, the voice serene. "Back again, Lieutenant? You're becoming such the visitor that you might as well become a member."

"I already belong to a church."

"The invitation goes for you, too, Detective Brogan. We have white members."

Brogan patronizingly said, "I'll get back to you."

"Same for you, Son. What's your name?"

Cruise didn't respond, just kept filming.

Not bothered by the snub, the big fellow said, "The young man is single-minded in the performance of his task. That's a good thing, right, Lieutenant?" But before receiving a response, he contritely added, "Shame on me, standing on ceremony, referring to you by title, when we're old friends. I'll drop the formalities, okay, Bloody Mary?"

Mary showed that there's a time and place for titles and formalities, saying, "Reverend Pastor Jeeter McArthur, you're under arrest for the murder of Rabbi Allan Winkler."

20.

Gerald Lewis, Wayne County Prosecutor, was watching like an eagle with binoculars as the Reverend Jeeter McArthur was being booked at police headquarters. Lewis had ordered that the booking be videotaped as he had for the arrest. The tapings were insurance against anticipated accusations that law enforcement was exacting revenge against McArthur and was not according him all his rights. Lewis even was blinking with less frequency than normal, so determined was he not to miss anything; and, for good reason, because he himself was going to try the case against McArthur.

Hand it over, Tiny, thought Lewis, as McArthur removed the cross and chain and then gave them to a booking officer. *All of it.*

McArthur pulled diamond rings off fingers the size of hot dogs, then parted with the Rolex. All the bling went into a personal property envelope.

Without diverting his gaze from the proceedings, Lewis cocked his head toward Mary and in a hushed voice asked, "You sure everything went okay at the arrest?"

Mary had answered his question several times already and this time said, "If you don't count when we stopped taping while we worked him over with brass knuckles. Satisfied?"

Bitch. Lewis couldn't say that aloud, but did say, "The reason that donkeys are denied an education is that nobody likes a smart-ass."

"Ha!" exclaimed Brogan.

Lewis considered Mary a liability given her history with McArthur, but his lobbying to get her removed from the case had been unsuccessful. "We're stuck with each other, like it or not," said Lewis, eyes still fixed on McArthur. "Let's be professional."

"Let's," Mary said.

"Cunningham's a team player," vouched Brogan.

"I never suggested differently." Lewis' desire to be the Republican nominee for State Attorney General was an open secret. Accomplished, tall and toned, with rugged features, he was a self-described upholder of family values and the rule of law. Others have gotten elected on less.

Mary had advised Lewis to postpone charging McArthur so that she could build a tighter case. Lewis considered it meddling, her job being to provide the evidence, his to decide whether it's good enough. He had made his decision and didn't care whether she agreed.

Lewis was even less concerned about Wanda Bush, McArthur's personal attorney. Bush was no criminal attorney, which she'd proven with her clueless counsel during the several times that the cops interrogated her client during the weeks leading up to his arrest.

So, why hadn't Bush been dumped? Lewis believed the answer was that McArthur considered himself a master at beating the authorities and only needed a robot to program. Okay with Lewis, because it would be as if McArthur were defending himself, and as the saying goes: Anyone who's his own attorney has a fool for a client.

A booking officer said, "Please step over here, Reverend McArthur."

McArthur graciously complied and was handed the license-plate-size placard that contained his arrest case number. He held the placard in front, just below the chin. The height chart in the background showed him to be six feet, six inches.

Another booking officer snapped the frontal mug shot. "Now, kindly turn and give us your right profile, Reverend."

Click.

"Now the left, please, Reverend."

You forgot, pretty please with a cherry on top, thought Lewis, who had told the booking team to be respectful to McArthur in front of the camera but believed that they were overdoing it.

Click.

"Now, please step on the scale, Reverend."

McArthur obliged, all three hundred, forty-four pounds of him.

The phone rang and was answered by one of the booking officers, who announced, "Your attorney has arrived, Reverend, and is being sent up."

Lewis thought, *Bush, the robot, has come to be programmed.*

"You're officially booked, Reverend," said the officer who had worked the scale. "Sorry, but next we gotta cuff you."

After the handcuffing, McArthur was flanked by two officers, whose duty was to take him to his cell. Although themselves beefy, they would have had difficulty restraining McArthur, had he not been the model of cooperation. They left the booking room, followed closely by Lewis, Brogan, and Mary; and, upon exiting, all became audience to an authoritative greeting.

"Excuse me. I'm here to consult with my client."

Immediate surprise flickered in Mary's, Lewis', and Brogan's eyes—darting eyes exchanging glances that asked whether anyone had prior knowledge of this development. And McArthur himself, who throughout the booking had been unflappable, seemed flummoxed by the sight of Lisa Rose.

21.

Raymond Gibson held the hose and turned on the faucet, aiming into the Rubbermaid wringer bucket. The sight and sound of running water had the power of suggestion and they pushed his full bladder pass the tipping point.

Turn off the faucet or leave it running? Lock the door behind himself or was there time? Rush down the hall to the men's room, simultaneously getting the key ready? He found his suddenly-presented predicament too complex for immediate sorting. Meanwhile, seconds took on the effect of minutes. No time to even move the bucket out of the way. Franticly, he started fumbling with his zipper. No sooner had he extracted himself than his stream gushed forward, spiraling up in an arc then splashing down into the bucket, frothing with the cleaning solution. He kept his eyes closed, savoring the relief, up until the final drops and the two shakes.

Gibson's added ingredient was not detectable above the lemony scent of the cleaning solution, but, out of guilt, he poured a couple more gulps into the bucket. He grabbed the handle of the wringer and pushed the bucket out of the janitor's closet.

"Opps!" he exclaimed, upon realizing his dick was dangling out of his pants. He tucked it in, then zipped the pants of his gray uniform.

Gibson was on the top floor of a ten-story office building in Detroit's Cultural Center, where he worked cleaning restrooms. His routine was to start at the top and work down.

The left front wheel on the bucket wobbled, necessitating that Gibson steer as well as push, as he made his way down the hall to the men's restroom.

"I keep forgetting to let them know about that wheel." Gibson talked to himself a lot.

There, where he had parked it along the wall outside the men's restroom was his cleaning cart. It carried cleaning supplies, toilet paper, paper towels, and liquid soap refill. Hanging on side hooks was a wastepaper hamper.

Gibson rapped on the door with ebony knuckles. "Janitor," he announced, to no response. From his front pocket, he pulled out a key ring on a chain clipped to a belt loop. There were only three keys: the one with the blue cap was for the men's restroom; the one crowned in pink was for the women's restroom; and, the one without coloring was for the janitor's room. His supervisor made things simple for him.

Gibson unlocked the door and propped it open with a wedge. He gathered his supplies in his arms and went in. All the men's restrooms housed two urinals and two stalls.

He made quick work of the urinals, squirting the caustic solution from a squeeze bottle, swabbing each receptacle with brisk strokes, and wearing neither rubber gloves nor goggles. Masters of their craft can play loose with safety, if they so choose.

The cleaning of the first toilet went quick and easy; however, when he swung open the second stall, he was met with the bane of the business. The inside of the bowl had been splattered by diarrhea. He lifted the seat, finding its underside and the bowl's rim similarly mucked.

"Doctors that cut people open deal with worse," Gibson reasoned aloud.

"They sure do. So let's get at it." Gibson also was in the habit of holding conversations with himself.

First, he aimed and squeezed the bottle, ringing the toilet bowl. The thick, milky stuff ran slowly down, but not for long, because he swished it about, dipping the swab in the water, stirring a sudsy sea. In quick sequence, he attended to the rim and the underside of the seat. He flushed, slapping the swab back and forth against the sides of the bowl, in the escaping water. As the bowl refilled, he shot some cleaner dead center and used the new solution to do the top of the seat and the outside of the bowl. By the time he finished, the overhead light was glistening off the sanitized porcelain.

In due course, the sink was left spotless and the faucets shinning. The counter was wiped and dried. The mirror was so clean that it squeaked during the finishing wipes. Paper and soap were replenished as needed. The wastepaper was emptied. All that was left to do was to mop the floor.

Gibson sent the mop through wide sweeps. He had thick, heavily veined wrists and forearms, more powerful than the average man of his advanced years. As he mopped, he was revisited by guilt over having urinated in the water. "The cleaning liquid will kill the pee," he rationalized. "No different than when somebody's aim is bad and they get pee on the floor." But his other self was more contrite. "Come back and do a quick once-over after you change the water," he advised, referring to the change he always made midway through his shift. Gibson regarded his job as important, and he couldn't have been more dedicated had the restrooms been in the White House. "People want a clean place to do their business," he often told himself.

Having finished the men's restroom, he turned his thoughts to the women's restroom at the opposite end of the floor. As he traveled down the hall, pushing the cart with his left hand and the bucket with his right, the wobbly wheel on the bucket kept turning perpendicular. The required coordination threatened to confound him. "First thing at lunch, I'm telling them about this wheel."

When he reached the women's restroom, he announced, "Janitor," after having knocked extra times for courtesy. He went on to whip it into guestroom shape.

Matters went routinely for a couple more floors, down to the women's restroom on the seventh. He let himself in and wedged the door. He was aligning his supplies along the counter when he heard a creaking. Just before he spun around, he caught a glimpse in the mirror of a woman exiting the stall. His mind went straight to panic. *Please don't scream, lady,* was his dominant thought. When he found his voice, he stammered, "I, I didn't know, didn't know, you were in there."

"No harm."

"I knocked and called out."

"I said, no harm. Relax."

Her reaction put him a little at ease, although he thought he remembered glancing at the bottom of the stall and not seeing feet. "I'll wait outside until you come out."

"Don't be silly. I'm just going to wash my hands. Go on about your work."

"No disrespect, but that's against rules. I can't work with you in here."

"If you have to leave, leave."

Gibson scurried out of there, avoiding eye contact. He removed the wedge and the door closed. For added measure, he stepped a distance away from the door and then leaned against the wall.

Shortly thereafter, the door opened and the woman stuck out her head. "Step here a minute."

"Me?"

"No, the invisible man next to you. Of course you."

Gibson came timidly. "What is it?"

"You must have tightened the faucet handles too tight. I can't budge them."

"Wasn't me, 'cause I didn't get to them yet."

"Well, somebody did. I'm going to be mad if I break a fingernail."

The threat sounded formidable to Gibson. "I'll try to undo them."

"Well, what are you waiting for?" she asked, after some seconds.

"First, you have to come out."

"For crying out loud! Do I frighten you?"

"It's the rules."

"Of all the…" Seeming to have given in, she said, "I don't want to make a night of this." She stepped out but held the door open, saying, "Technically, I'm standing outside. Undo the handles. Run out. And I'll step back in."

Gibson felt that he was outmatched. Rather than debate, he would attend to the sink and be done with it. At the sink, he gripped both handles at the same time and yanked. Because the handles were never stuck, the water rushed out, full-blast and splattering. He hurriedly turned off the faucets.

But, by then, Lisa Rose had closed in from behind.

22.

Brian Rutgers came strutting into homicide on a Monday at 11:06 a.m. "How's everybody doing?"

Mary was standing at her desk watering her African violet and was the only one to respond with more than a wave or grunt. "So, Brian, which is it? Coming in early for the afternoon shift or late for the morning?"

"It's my first day back after weeks working afternoons. Can't reset the internal clock as quick as I used to. Blame it on old age. You'll be there one day yourself, Mary. Cut me some slack."

"You had the weekend to get reset," said Mary, not that there was much difference between his absence and presence, as far as solving cases.

Rutgers went to his desk and sat on its edge, a habit. To sit in the chair might result in work, and why take reckless chances. "Mary, you know I light up this place. You should be welcoming me instead of busting my balls."

"Forget I opened my mouth."

"Forgotten." Rutgers reached inside his sports jacket, pulled out a packet, and said, "Come over here, you guys, and get a load of my daughter's wedding pictures."

"When was it?" asked Mary.

"Saturday. I got these printed this morning."

"While you were resetting?"

"I'm beginning to feel my balls in that vice again," complained Rutgers.

"Okay, I promise to leave you alone." Mary walked to him, saying, "Let's see those pictures."

Three others in the room accepted Rutgers' invitation. One was Ross Brogan, which surprised Mary, because she couldn't imagine him getting weepy over wedding pictures.

Brogan proved true to his nature. "I see you splurged on a disposable camera. There are professional photographers who do weddings, you know."

Same old Ross, thought Mary, reassured. She and Brogan were of the same opinion that Rutgers was a lazy investigator, although they showed different levels of tolerance toward Rutgers.

"We hired a photographer, you clown. And I'll have you know I took these with a digital camera." Rutgers took the photos out of the packet. He reshuffled them to his liking while remaining seated on his desk. "This is me walking the lovely bride down the aisle."

"And lovely, she is," said Mary, genuinely.

"Thank you." Rutgers pointed and said, "You can tell by my face that I was as proud as a peacock. Or, maybe I should say, proud as a penguin. The tuxedo. Get it?"

Brogan got it, alright. Got fed up. No way was he going to suffer through the rest of the photos. Without excuse or apology, he went back to his desk.

Mary wanted to speed up matters but disguised it by sounding eager. "Stop holding out," she said, slapping him lightly on the shoulder. "Let's see the rest."

Rutgers proceeded picture-by-picture, dragging out the process with his narratives. Mary, in the words of Ross Brogan, would tough it out, would let the old guy brag on his daughter. Mary kept her eyes from glazing over by thinking of her daughter, Gazelle, who was of marrying age. Gazelle, someday a blushing bride? And, sometime thereafter, Grandma Mary? The idea of grandchildren was appealing enough, but Mary wasn't quite comfortable with what it implied about stage-of-life. Grandmothers are old, aren't they?

"That's the last one," Rutgers eventually said.

Mary's eyelids suddenly felt lighter. "Give my congratulations to the newlyweds."

"Mine too," said one of the others.

"Will do." Infused with camaraderie, Rutgers said, "When the professional photos come back, I'll bring them in, too, to share with you."

Give me a day's notice, so I won't be here. "Congratulations to you, too, Brian. New father-in-law, and all." Mary headed back to her desk.

"Thanks." Rutgers reached over to the edge of his desk and grabbed a folder.

When Mary turned to sit, she noticed that Rutgers had gone to the Fridge. *Again? If it were a real refrigerator, you would have burned out the light.* "Filing something, Brian?"

"A case I investigated when I was on afternoons." He dropped the folder on top of the Fridge and pulled out a drawer.

"What happened?" asked Mary.

"Oh, some geezer got his throat slashed." Rutgers then picked up the folder.

That description immediately triggered Mary's interest. "No, wait. Don't file it yet."

Surprised and feeling challenged, Rutgers asked, "Why?"

Mary didn't answer but hurried toward him with her own question. "Where did it happen?"

"In some office building in the Cultural Center. I worked the case thoroughly. It's cold, I tell you."

"If you don't mind," Mary said, easing the folder out of his hand. She went straight for the crime scene photos, rifling through them. After moments, she told Rutgers, "I'm going to hold on to this folder, for now. I have my reasons. No reflection on you, of course."

"No skin off my nose," stated Rutgers, but his pouting face showed that he felt otherwise. He hadn't offered any details while she'd studied the photos. After all, they weren't of his daughter's wedding. He sulked from the room without having closed the drawer.

The discourtesy was fine with Mary because it made it easy for her to reach into the Fridge and retrieve the folder of Matthew Kent.

23.

Bernie Rosenberg was seated under a gazebo that was encircled by towering palm trees, their leaves stirred by saline breezes. His poor vision notwithstanding, he could see the visitor approaching from a distance.

It was Lisa Rose who was stepping lively across the meticulously mowed grounds. She was hiding something behind her back, in her right hand. While still feet away, she caught a whiff of Bernie's aftershave from his daily dousing. *Skunk In a Bottle would be a good name for it*, she thought. She stopped in front of him. "So, how do you feel?"

Bernie ran his fingers through his wavy white hair and then fussed, "How am I supposed to feel? I'm old, for God's sake."

"By one year. Happy birthday."

Bernie looked away, arms crossed, the body language deafening. "Better I should never have lived to see this day."

"That's no way to talk," Rose said, as she suddenly brought her hidden hand from behind her back. "Here. For you."

He deigned to glance at the offering but didn't reach for it. "Pretty wrapping. The prettier the wrapping, the more the guilt."

"Yours or mine?" asked Rose behind the darkest of sunglasses.

"I have nothing to be guilty about."

Realizing that her hopes for a pleasant visit were foolish, Rose thrust the package, stopping just short of Bernie's nose. Neck muscles tense, teeth almost clenched, in irritated slowness, she said, "Take the bleeping gift."

"You watch your mouth." He snatched the package. "What is it?"

"The idea is to open it."

He held the package to his ear and shook it. Unceremoniously, he tossed it on the table. "Whatever's in there, you can afford it."

Rose, in white linen slacks, a beige cotton shirt knotted at the midriff, and blue boat shoes, said, "You're a miserable, hateful old man."

"Miserable, I'll grant you. An animal shouldn't suffer like I'm suffering. Uprooted and replanted in this concentration camp."

"Concentration camp, you say?" Rose's head did a quick series of short nods, but she wasn't signaling agreement. She turned her head to one side then the other viewing the surroundings and then sarcastically said, "Some concentration camp, this is."

Bernie lived in southeast Florida, at the Shalom Senior Community, in its assisted living residence, a 12-story structure, with balconies and resort amenities. The other buildings, widely spaced on sprawling acres of campus, were a synagogue, a nursing home, an adult day care center, an Alzheimer care village, and a rehabilitation center.

The gazebo where Rose and Bernie were having such pleasant exchanges rested on a slight rise, several steps up. From their vantage point, they could see seniors in a variety of activities. Some moved sprightly, others less so, including those using canes and walkers. There were those who steered around in wheelchairs, motored and manual. Yet others sat together on benches or at tables, chattering, or playing cards or board games. And there were those who sat alone, drawing from the deep well of thoughts and memories to which only oldsters have buckets.

Rose exhaled audibly. "Mind if I ask you something?"

"As if I could stop you."

"Why won't you socialize? Every time I come here, you're off to yourself. Try making friends."

"I had plenty friends back in Michigan."

"We both know that's not true." Rose then tried to lighten the conversation. "If I didn't know you, I'd mistake you for a true Floridian. I mean, is there a state law that says old Jewish men have to wear high-waist polyester pants? Try natural fabrics. Polyester can't breathe. Your pants have asthma." Playfully, she pinched a leg of his pants and pulled upward, stretching the fabric.

Bernie shooed her hand, just as he'd do a pesky fly, but she was too quick and had already released. He smoothed out the peak left by her pull. Then he tugged the ends of his Havana shirt, all to communicate that he was satisfied with his fashion statement. "I want to go back to Michigan."

"Why? You were always kvetching about cold weather settling in your hip and neighbors you couldn't stand. Have I left anything out?"

Bernie was short, brawny, and walked with a noticeable limp, owed to a crushed right pelvis suffered decades prior. He sharply said, "They weren't my kind of neighbors. I make no apologies for that." Then, with added sharpness, came, "And I don't need you, of all people, to say anything about my hip." He got up and hobbled off a few paces, signaling that he didn't want to be close to her.

"I didn't fly down here to argue with you."

"I didn't send for you. Most likely, you came down to stay at your fancy-shmancy house," he railed, referring to her estate in nearby Palm Beach.

"Why do you resent my success so much?"

"What's not to resent, considering what it's built on."

"Meaning?"

"We could start with that murdering Nazi, Mueller."

"He's no Nazi. No murderer, either. I'd expect you to be a supporter. Or are you only against the suffering of animals?"

Bernie didn't answer, just kept attacking. "And God forbid we mention rabbi killers."

"I assume you're referring to Jeeter McArthur."

"If that's his name."

"Seems someone's been keeping up with my work. I'm flattered."

"Don't be. I only know about the case because I saw you on television but wasn't quick enough in changing the channel."

"That aside," said Rose, masking the sting, "Jeeter McArthur is innocent until proven guilty."

"Of course, you'd say that." Then, he hurled the accusation, "You schvartze-lover, you!"

"They prefer to be called Afro-American. Black will do, too."

"I say schvartze, so schvartze it is," he shouted, waving his arm in emphasis and accidentally knocking off his glasses. He bent down after them.

But Rose was quicker in picking up the specs. She examined them for damage and finding none, held them in front of her eyes and looked through the lens. "Where'd you get the prescription filled, at a Coke bottling plant?"

He snatched the glasses. "Again, with the jokes. You're nobody's comedian."

"So you've said many times."

"Then stop making a fool of yourself. You shame the art."

"Keep being ornery," warned Rose, "and I'll take back the gift." Enticingly, she revealed, "It just so happens to be a boxed collection of DVD's of comedians from the Borscht Belt era. Classic stuff."

Now aware of the contents, Bernie reached for the tossed box and positioned it upright on the table. "I suppose you expect a thank you. Well, thank you." But it was more of a sendoff than a show of gratitude, for he said, "Now leave me to my concentration camp."

Rose bit her lip to keep from saying it but then said it, anyway. "You dishonor all who actually spent time in one."

Knowing what was being insinuated, Bernie shook his fist and said, "Don't you bring up my wife. She was a saint, that woman."

"Would have been nice had you told her that while she was alive."

"Oh, now you're the authority, Ms. Never-Been-Married? Just as well. You'd probably reject a husband's name, too. But know this, a Rose by any other name is still a Rosenberg."

"I'll say it again, you're a miserable, hateful old man."

"Whom do I hate?"

"To answer that, I'd be here until your next birthday."

"I don't hate, but even if I do, at least I'm not a self-hating Jew. And that's more than I can say for you."

That was a new one and it stunned her, and that took some doing, given how accustomed she was to his put-downs. She was still recovering as she slowly removed her sunglasses. She threw back her head, shaking her dyed tresses. She stepped closer and to the side of his good ear; for, she didn't want him to miss a syllable. "If," she said, emphasizing the hypothetical, "I hate myself, dear Grand-father, it has nothing to do with being a Jew, and far more to do with you."

24.

Faye Ferguson, seated in a finely upholstered lounge chair, recited the name three times slowly, to no avail, before admitting, "Can't say that I have. Sorry."

"What about a shortened version, like Matt, even Mattie?" asked Mary.

"No. To the best of my memory, my father never mentioned that name."

Faye, forty-two, was squat and chocolaty. Had she been a brand of candy she would have been a Chunky.

Standing with his hands buried in his pockets was husband, Ernie Ferguson. Had he been a brand of candy he would have been a Tootsie Roll. "I never heard him mention the name, either."

Faye and Ernie lived in the Chandler Park district on Detroit's eastside. They owned a realtor franchise.

"I'm going to show you a photo," Mary said, reaching inside her tangerine blazer. Mercifully, the photo showed a live person, about whom she asked, "Do you recognize this man?"

Ernie said, "I don't."

Faye said, "Me neither. Is that Matthew Kent?"

"Yes," Mary said and re-pocketed the photo.

In a wondering tone, Faye said, "Detective Rutgers didn't ask us about him."

"He didn't have a reason to at the time," said Mary.

Faye squared her shoulders, bracing for the answer to, "Do you suspect that this Matthew Kent killed my father?"

"No. That's not why I asked you about him."

"Then, what's the connection?" asked Ernie.

"There might not be one." Mary was a staunch believer in dispensing information on a need-to-know basis, even to a victim's family. Loose lips sink ships, and many a S.S. Investigation has met a watery grave due to torpedoes fired from a loaded mouth.

Faye slumped and sighed. "It still seems like a nightmare, except that I awaken to it instead of out of it."

"Did your dad have known enemies? Was he feuding with anyone? Had he complained of threats?"

"No, none of that. My father got along with everyone."

Mary, who'd investigated her share of murders of people who didn't have an enemy in the world, asked, "How often would you have contact with your dad?"

"Regularly. A lot by phone, and we'd have him over now and then. Sometimes, I'd drop by his place to look in on him."

"And up to the end, he seemed normal?"

"Normal for him," said Faye. "My father was college educated. When I was little, he was in a car accident and suffered brain damage. It affected his I.Q. as well as erased some memories. He improved with therapy, but never beyond being able to do certain work."

"Like janitorial," added Mary.

"Yes, although he didn't have to work at all. Could have just drawn his SSI payments. But he was a proud man who placed family obligations first. He always contributed to my support while I was a minor."

"Where is your mother?"

"Houston. Been there for at least a dozen years."

"More like fifteen," said Ernie.

"Lives with her second husband. She divorced my father a few years after his accident. She didn't attend his funeral."

"You're an only child?"

"Yes."

"Who's the next closest of kin?"

"I have two uncles. Both younger than my father. My father's parents are deceased. There's other family scattered around, but we aren't close."

"What about your dad's possessions? I understand that he lived in a house that you own."

"Correct. We let him stay there for free. He kept it spotless. He didn't own much materially. He did keep an old trunk full of mementos, though. When I find the strength, I'll sort through his possessions."

"I'd like to have a look through the house before you dispose of anything," requested Mary.

There came the sound of the kitchen screen door opening then banging shut. It was followed by the sounds of the opening then closing of a refrigerator, cabinets, and drawers, simultaneously enough to suggest that more than one person was doing the rummaging.

Reminded by the sounds, misty-eyed Faye said, "One more thing about my father, he loved his grandchildren."

"Hey, Mom!" shouted someone unseen. "Can Ivan come over for dinner?"

A second disembodied voice shouted, "Sean drank out of the milk carton again, Mom."

Looking sheepish and wishing to spare herself further embarrassment, Faye called out, "We have company, boys. Behave."

Ernie, who'd hit upon a solution, called out, "In fact, come in here and get some money, so you can walk to McDonald's."

The boys raced in, shoving each other.

Ernie gave them a drill-sergeant's stare that put them at attention. Reaching for his wallet, he said, "Boys, this is Lieutenant Mary Cunningham, of the police."

Sean, nine years old, enthusiastically said, "A lady policeman!"

"Policewoman," corrected Mary, always sensitive to gender-bias language.

"Awesome!" Sean was lean, like his dad, and had the mischievous face of a kid who broke things for a living. He accepted a five-dollar bill in his unwashed hand.

Ernie Jr., a fourteen-year-old jock, wearing glasses with head-straps, received the same amount. Then he turned to Mary, and on a guess, asked, "Are you here about my grandfather?"

"Yes, I am."

Sean, his facial expression sober and hopeful, asked, "Are you going to catch who killed my grandfather?"

"I'll do my best."

Sean gladdened, as though he'd been given an iron-clad guarantee. "Then you'll put him in jail?"

"Then I'll put him in jail." After an instant's reflection, Mary amended, "Him or her." But it was just that sensitivity to gender-bias language kicking in again.

25.

Lisa Rose had ignored the first round of buzzes to finish reviewing a document and on the second round she pressed the flashing button and lifted the receiver.

"Lieutenant Mary Cunningham here to see you," informed the receptionist.

"Send her up."

Rose gathered the pages, tapped their edges against the desktop for alignment, stapled them, and cast them into the out-box. She did some quick tidying of her desk, first scooping up two Chinese food containers and tossing them into the wastebasket.

Her custom-designed desk was mammoth, its top extending beyond its base, like the deck of an aircraft carrier. Two black leather chairs sat in front of the desk and matched the couch across the room. The office had its own restroom. To the right of the desk was a wall-length window. When its maroon, brocade curtains were opened, the view below was of Jefferson Avenue, a downtown main artery that ran parallel to the Detroit River.

The rest of the second floor consisted of individual offices for Rose's secretary and paralegal, another restroom,

the conference room, and a library. The offices of her partners, Jacob Miller and Howard Greene, were on the first
floor, as were those of the associates and the other secretar-
ies and paralegals.

Mary entered and marched straight to the desk. "Lisa
Rose, you're under arrest. You have the right to remain
silent—"

"Slow down, Roadrunner," Rose interjected, before
Mary could finish the spiel. "You've left out why I'm under
arrest."

"Oh, that's right." Mary contemplated a bit, slowly strok-
ing her chin, before coming up with, "For being so good at
what you do, that it's criminal."

"Then, I'm as good as convicted. I'll go quietly." Rose
raised her arms in surrender. She pushed against the carpet with her heels, and her chair wheeled away from the
desk.

Both women broke out laughing.

Abandoning the nonsense, Mary said, "I don't know
what brought on that silly mood."

"Don't apologize. Other times in here you've been so
downcast."

"Hard not to be."

"I know. Have a seat," said Rose, grabbing the edge of
the desk and pulling herself forward. "I asked you to come
by because the other side has been extending feelers."

"Like what?"

"A hypothetical or two. They're trying to gauge your
openness to an out-of-court settlement."

"What have you told them?"

"That we'll only respond to a firm offer." In justification, Rose said, "Responding to things that aren't officially on the table is bad negotiating."

"Makes sense."

"Keep in mind that I'm bond by law to present all offers to you," Rose said, in preamble. She leaned forward, rested folded arms on the desk, looked away and then back at Mary, before asking, "But, is there a particular figure or range that you have in mind?"

Mary understood the practicality of the question but it didn't diminish its disturbing impact. "I can't…" she began to say, before falling silent a few seconds. "I wish you hadn't asked."

Rose came to the rescue with, "Forget I did. It's useful information but I can work without it."

Still fighting conflicting emotions, Mary said, "I'd rather face the money decision when there's a decision to make."

"Say no more."

But, Mary did. "At that time, I know you'll give me the best advice."

Rose, seeing how much her client's mood had gone downhill from the earlier foolishness, tried to reverse it. She grinned broadly and bragged, "Like, when have I ever given advice that wasn't the best?"

Mary grinned broadly herself and said, "One of these days, you're going to inflate your chest so much that it's going to explode before you can thump it."

Rose leaned her head back in wishful imagination. "I, with boobs big enough to explode? I can only wish."

The comment caught Mary off guard, for she hadn't meant it that way. "They...you know... yours look okay."

"Thanks for that ringing endorsement," said Rose, with mock hurt.

"I wasn't being patronizing."

"It's okay. After all, I'm not a vampire who can't cast a reflection in a mirror. I see myself everyday and know what I have, or I should say, what I don't have." Then Rose shared, "I once answered a classified ad for a topless dancer, but the bar owner took one look at me and said that he hadn't meant it literally."

Mary laughed, and not just because she was sure that the story was bogus.

It encouraged Rose. "But you never had that problem, Mary. In our heydays, if you and I had been a pair of soap operas, you would have been The Bold and the Beautiful, and I would have been The Young and the Breastless."

Chuckling and talking simultaneously, Mary said, "You need to stop."

"You know that I'm telling the truth."

"What I know is that you'd make a good stand-up comedian. And now that you've tried your material out on me, is there anything else we need to discuss?"

"I guess not." Rose consulted her watch and said, "I don't mean to rush you out, but I'm pressing up against my next appointment."

Mary stood and lightheartedly said, "I can take a hint. Don't bother getting up."

"I'll keep you posted." Rose started reading another document.

A police siren wailed, a cross between rusty bagpipes and a cat getting its tail smashed. As it faded, it was evident that the car was headed east on Jefferson, maybe to the bridge to Belle Isle, the sylvan park jewel in the middle of the Detroit River, or maybe just to some trouble spot on the east side.

Moving ever so slowly toward the door, Mary said of her unseen colleagues, "The city's finest on the job. I hope it's not a homicide."

Not looking up, Rose said, "If it is, the killer better pray that you don't end up with the case."

"What's this we have going, a mutual admiration society?"

"Nothing wrong with that," said Rose. "You and I are sisters in the struggle, in careers dominated by men. We ought to support one another."

"Well said." Still having not reached the door, Mary detoured to a wall adorned with plaques and framed photos, the latter signed by the pictured dignitaries. "Every time I'm here, there's a new addition to the wall."

Rose made a checkmark on the document and then looked up. "Let's have out with it, Mary."

"What are you talking about?"

"Why are you still here?"

"I was on my way out."

"You've been on your way out for a while. You keep find-ing excuses to extend your exit. Why?"

"Okay, I'll come clean. It's the name on the note there on your desk. Couldn't help but notice. Is it who I think it is?"

"So now I'm a mind-reader?" But Rose confirmed the identity by saying, "There's only one."

Mary didn't care if it sounded like pleading. "Let me stay until she arrives. Just so I can say that I was in the same room with her."

Rose understood. "I don't see how it would hurt."

"Thanks so much."

Rose reared back and laced her fingers at the back of her head. "Let's use the time to face something we've been tiptoeing around."

Mary gave an apprehensive look and walked to the desk. "What?"

"It's clumsy, I know, our being on opposite sides of the Jeeter McArthur case. I want to get it out in the open that working with you on your mother's case and against you on his won't pose any conflicts with me. I'll do whatever I have to in each, without regard to the other."

"So will I."

Rose stood and extended a handshake. "Allies and adversaries?"

Mary shook hands. "Allies and adversaries."

The phone rang.

After Rose hung up, she said, "She's on the elevator."

Mary became anxious. She wished she were dressed more presentably. She ran her hands down the front of her pants, although there wasn't a single wrinkle, mainly because of the few pounds she'd gained over the last year.

When the knock came, Rose granted Mary the privilege. "Open the door."

Two people entered.

"Hello, Mrs. Grace Emanuel," greeted Mary. "I'm on my way out, but allow me to say what an honor it is to meet you."

"Thank you, young lady," returned Grace, age having weakened her voice, having bent her slim frame.

"Sit wherever you choose, Mrs. Emanuel," instructed Rose.

"The sofa will do just fine," said Grace.

"And nice to see you, Congressman," said Mary.

Andrew Galliger, accustomed to speaking to people he didn't know, said, "Nice to see you, too," as he slowly escorted Grace.

"I'm Mary Cunningham."

Grace responded with a glance backward and a smile.

Galliger said, "Hello, Mary Cunningham."

And Rose said, "Goodbye, Mary Cunningham."

26.

"I found Ray right here, face-down, in front of the sink," said Christopher Post, sporter of a shaved head and a handlebar mustache that seemed to elongate his face and give him droopy eyes. His teeth betrayed his fondness for chewing tobacco. "In front, but sort of to the left."

"What did you do first?" asked Mary. She'd already interviewed the other janitors during the weeks that Post had been on vacation.

"Kicked open the stall doors. When I seen we were alone I turned him face-up to see if there was anything I could do. I could tell from his face, the color of it, that he was gone. Even without that, I knew he was dead. Nobody survives losing that much blood."

Mary, in jeans, lowered to one knee and began inspecting under the sink.

"What you looking for?"

"Whatever there is to be found."

"This place been cleaned lots of times since poor Ray was killed. If you could see atoms, wouldn't help you none."

"Doesn't seem to be an atom in sight," Mary conceded, as she got up, her knee popping, causing the thought, *Face it girl, you're getting old.*

Post wiped the back of his hand across his mouth before saying, "Then again, the place don't get much use, not since the word got out about what happened in here. My guess is, most who know go elsewhere in the building. Can't say I blame them. What gal could sit and relax with those thoughts on her mind?"

Mary wasn't having anything to do with that discussion. "Why did you look for him that night?"

"The crew takes lunch on the third floor where there's a vending machine room with tables. Ray didn't show and that was unusual. I didn't make too big of a deal out of it, right then. But when he didn't punch out at the end of the shift I knew something was up." Post rubbed together his calloused palms, like he was warming them before a fire while asking, "Seen enough?"

Mary wouldn't be rushed. "Not yet." Investigating, she went into the stall, letting the door close behind her. Then she came out. "The door creaks when opened and closed."

"I heard it," said Post, seeing no relevance.

"You personally looked for Gibson after he didn't punch out?"

"Sure did. Started at the top and worked down. On each floor I looked to see if his cart was in the hall since he's not supposed to take it into the john. I ended back on the first floor without spotting his cart. I go back to the top, only this time, I look in the johns. Needless to say, the search ended here."

"A person has to have a key to get into this restroom, right?"

"All the public johns in this building require a key."

"The cart was in here too?"

"Sure was. The door should have been wedged, like I got it now, but I don't have to be no detective to guess who must've closed the door."

"Anything else against procedure?"

"The mop bucket was in here. Ray wouldn't have rolled it in until he finished all the other cleaning. You mop last."

Killer didn't want to leave anything in the hallway to point to the victim's whereabouts. "Mopping is last. Got it. Run through the entire sequence for me."

Pointing around the room as he spoke, Post said, "You do the toilets first. Second, the sink. Then the counter. Then the mirror. Then you empty the paper. Then you restock. And, like I said, you mop last."

"As best you know, did Gibson always follow procedure?"

"Let me put it this way, the man probably farted the same time every day. Ray always did what he was supposed to do, how he was supposed to do it, when he was supposed to do it. Workers with his limitations usually do."

"That night, did you notice how much had been cleaned in here?"

"I don't believe he got around to anything, really."

"Why do you say that?"

"Cleaning supplies were on the counter, true enough, but he hadn't used them. I say that because—and I don't mind admitting this—once I turned him over and saw his neck, that plus the blood made me sick to my stomach. I ran to the toilet to upchuck and it hadn't been cleaned. Might be a weird thing to remember, but, hey, I pay attention to details. I'm the supervisor."

"Back to the keys. Where are they kept?"

"Each office has two. One for the men's and one for the women's. Some of the fancier offices have their own restrooms."

"Are there different keys for each floor?"

"No. One key fits all the women's restrooms. Another for the men's." Post scratched his stubble and said, "You ask more questions than that first detective who was out here."

"But nothing that you haven't been able to answer," charmed Mary.

"If it has to do with janitorial work around here, if I can't answer it, it can't be answered."

Prove it. "What time would Gibson have gotten to this floor?"

"Let's see. The shift starts at six, he worked his way down to this floor, finished the men's room, so, I'd say around seven-thirty, there or about."

"Who would be in the building at that time?"

"Most of the offices are nine-to-five, though some people work late. But you can't get into the building after six without signing in downstairs at the security desk. That other detective had security make him a copy of the sign-in sheet."

Although there's nothing in the folder that shows he interviewed anyone on the sheet. "How often do you have to replace keys that are not returned?"

"Not that often. Who steals restroom keys? When one goes missing, most times it's because somebody left it in the restroom or accidentally took it with 'em. Every key is attached to something that has the name of the office it came from, so returning it is easy. That was one of my ideas."

"Was a key left in here the night of the murder?"

"I sure didn't find one."

Mary took a different approach. "Around the time of the murder, did you have to replace a women's restroom key?"

"It's not like you're asking me something that happened yesterday, you know."

"Yes, but you did say that if you can't answer—"

"And I meant it. I got a memory for this kind of thing." He tapped an index finger on his chin, supposedly thinking, and then said, "Can't give dates, but two come to mind."

Mary indulged him his dramatic pause, after which, she asked, "And?"

"One time was for a tax firm on the second floor. The other time was for a law office on this floor."

27.

Lisa Rose and her clients sat at the plaintiff's table. Her locked briefcase sat on the floor beside her.

The two defense attorneys had their briefcases opened on their table. They'd arrived before Rose and were taking turns whispering to their client, who resembled an aging surfer bum, despite the custom-tailored suit. And in a way that seemed choreographed, the attorneys were taking turns shifting in their seats.

Either their Preparation H has quit or they're nervous, maybe scared, thought Rose.

"All rise," ordered the deputy.

Judge Bertram Yardley lumbered through the door that connected his chambers with his courtroom, there in the Federal Courthouse in Detroit. He had a blotchy complexion plus a ridiculous comb-over that started just above his left ear but didn't make it completely across the top. After taking the bench, he announced, "You may be seated."

Shortly thereafter, the courtroom was standing again, this time for the entry of the jury. They filed into the box and sat, stone-faced and motionless, as if shielding against being preempted by mind-readers.

Yardley said, "Madame Foreperson, I understand that the jury has reached a verdict."

A woman in her early fifties stood, hair pulled back in a bun. "Yes, we have, Your Honor."

"Please hand it to my deputy."

The deputy stepped to the jury box and accepted a folded sheet of paper. He transferred it to Yardley, who read it silently. Yardley gave the paper back to the deputy, who returned it to the foreperson.

"Madame Foreperson," said Yardley, "you may now read your verdict."

The moment was the culmination of what had begun three years earlier with the murder of sixteen-year-old Austin Holbrook. Austin had been gunned down because the killer, himself a teen, wanted Austin's brand-new basketball sneakers. The killer was apprehended, tried, and convicted of first-degree murder.

Rose, however, contacted the parents and proposed a civil suit against the Titan Corporation, the multi-billion dollar manufacturer of the shoes. The Complaint alleged that predatory pricing and exploitive advertising featuring street-credibility themes combined for foreseeable violence and that Austin was not the first victim to die for Titan-brand shoes.

The defense basically argued that shoes don't kill people, people kill people, and that sad examples abound of youths being killed for a variety of other possessions, some less pricy than basketball shoes.

The trial had lasted six days. A lot to digest; yet, it was as if the jury room had a revolving door, so quickly had the duly-sworn dozen returned.

The foreperson held the verdict sheet in slightly trembling hands, and peering through cat-eye glasses, read, "In the matter of Holbrook versus Titan, we find the defendant liable." She cleared her throat before adding, "We assess compensatory damages in the amount of one million dollars."

Rose twisted her hand out of Mrs. Holbrook's grip and pressed it on the client's shoulder to calm her. There was yet another decision to be announced. Although any amount with the word, million, after it seemed staggering to the Holbrooks, those at the defense table seemed unmoved; for, in relative terms, the amount wasn't even a slap on the wrist. More like a kiss on the back of the hand.

"We further assess punitive damages," resumed the foreperson. She looked up from the sheet. She knew the amount and wanted to announce it while looking at the defense table.

The amount might still have been vibrating off the foreperson's vocal cords, so soon did the courtroom break into noisy reaction, prompting Yardley to pound his gavel. Mr. Holbrook's eyes were bucked, for to close them might confirm that he was dreaming. Mrs. Holbrook was pressing both palms forcefully against her chest, less her heart leap through. Rose sat inscrutable, her turn to confound would-be mind-readers.

Not so with lead defense attorney, Tillman Dozier, patrician, silver-haired, who had catapulted to his feet and was shouting to be heard over the din. "Your Honor, this verdict is a travesty and an extreme example of a runaway jury. In the interest of justice, you must set aside this obscene verdict."

Yardley declined, saying, "Take it up with the Appeals Court, Mr. Dozier. That's what it's there for." He succinctly thanked the jury for its service then slammed the gavel and declared, "Court is adjourned."

28.

Mary entered through the kitchen door, having just returned from shopping at Farmer's Market—or Eastern Market—as most Detroiters call that congregation of stores and outdoor stands. "Hey, sleepy-head."

Cliff, still in pajamas, was seated at the table finishing a bowl of granola and reading the Saturday newspaper. "Hey, yourself."

"You want to get the stuff out of the car?"

"Sure thing." And out the door he went.

"And set the flats of flowers on the driveway," she called after him, planning to plant them later that day.

Minutes later, Cliff had brought in the bags and immediately started peeking inside them like a curious kid, especially liking the assortment of fresh fruit. "We should be good for smoothies for a little while."

"You're too smooth, as it is." From the cabinet, Mary retrieved a large glass bowl and set it on the counter. Suddenly, she exclaimed, "Don't do that!"

Startled, Cliff missed the strawberry that he had tossed into the air to catch in his mouth. "What? What?"

"They haven't been rinsed. You don't know what's on them." Mary dumped the strawberries into a colander and rinsed them. "I swear," she muttered, her smile giving her away, "you can be worse than a kid." She held up a lusciously large berry and said, "Open up."

Cliff bit down, slicing it in half. Juice trickled out the side of his mouth.

"Be still," Mary said, and licked the juice with the tip of her tongue. "Sugar sweet."

"That's me, not the fruit," claimed Cliff.

"No arguments from me." Mary placed some berries on a sheet of paper towel. "Take these and stay out my way." As he turned to head back to the table, she slapped his butt.

Back at the table, Cliff didn't sit. He rotated the newspaper so that the printing read right-side up. "Your girl did it again."

Mary, still at the sink, asked, "Who is my girl supposed to be?"

"Lisa Rose. She's in the paper."

Mary made the connection and stopped arranging fruit in the bowl. With eyebrows raised in interest, she turned. "The basketball shoe case? Did the jury come back? What happened?" Last night, she and Cliff had gone ballroom dancing, their specialty being the Tango, and had missed both the early-evening and late-evening news telecasts.

"Check out the headline for yourself," said Cliff.

She did, but of course, it didn't tell the whole story, so she asked, "What was the award?"

"Try and guess the amount," challenged Cliff.

Smiling, but annoyed just the same, she responded, "Are you a game show host? I don't want to guess." Conflicted and reluctant, she sidled closer but not enough to be able to read the smaller print.

"It's not a snake that will bite you, Mary." He handed her the paper.

She began reading, silently, lips moving, eyes barely blinking. When she finished, she said, "Wow! Lisa's done it again."

"The other side probably will appeal," Cliff predicted, "but whatever's finally paid will have lots of zero's behind it."

"Heck, if we do anywhere near as well with Mama's case," began Mary, before suddenly falling silent and sullen.

"What's the matter?"

Mary's face registered shame. "I got hyped over money, forgetting that it comes with Mama's death."

"Come on," urged Cliff. "You didn't mean it like that."

"Don't defend me. I don't deserve it. Just as bad, I lost sight that a youngster died and that his parents would gladly trade the money to have him back." She stared blankly in painful introspection.

Cliff pulled her into an embrace and softly rocked her. "Don't torture yourself like this. You're a good person and no one knows that more than I."

Posture slack and head hung, she mumbled, "Maybe that was my reason for choosing Lisa Rose. Her reputation for big awards." She looked up and asked, "What is my real priority? Money? Justice?"

"You can't separate the two. Not in a civil case. Anyone in the same situation would have sought the best attorney available."

Halfheartedly, Mary said, "I guess."

Shortly ago, you claimed you didn't want to guess. But Cliff knew better than to voice it.

29.

Mary fired rounds until the slide on her semi-automatic locked open, indicating an empty magazine. She laid the gun on the ledge in front of her. She activated the target carrier, and the contraption resembling a mechanized clothesline whirred toward her. She unpinned the target and studied it for something positive but her pained expression told the tale. She removed her ear-protection headgear, allowing it to ring her neck like a horseshoe.

Ross Brogan, in the booth to the left, also had removed his headgear. "Apparently, you're practicing the fine art of nicking somebody," was his critique.

By way of seeing the glass mostly empty instead of completely empty, Mary said, "One shot hit center, kind of."

"You could have closed your eyes and done as well." Brogan snatched the target. Seeing it up close only increased his disgust. With both hands, he mashed the target into a tight ball and threw it down. "Pathetic."

"Did it ever occur to you," said Mary, "that I have feelings?"

"Then, what you should be feeling is time running out on you. You choose. You want me to baby you or get you ready for certification?"

Mary had not taken a certification test on the firing range for years, even though departmental policy required that it be done annually. Prior to this day, the last time she'd fired her weapon had been in self-defense, killing an armed assailant. The incident further contributed to the legend of Bloody Mary. Now, her years of excuses, promises, and avoidance had caught up with her. The powers-that-be had notified her that either she gets certified or gets stripped of her authority to carry a weapon.

"The test hasn't changed since the last time you took it and passed, Cunningham. The requirements aren't that tough."

"I know that."

"Then stop obsessing like you're testing for S.W.A.T."

"Alright, already. Stop beating me up."

"Put your ear protection back on," said Brogan as he did the same. "Now, look and learn."

He pinned a target to the carrier and sent it down the lane. He unsnapped his shoulder holster and drew his weapon. He assumed a two-handed firing stance and in rapid succession shot five times, all striking center-chest. He admired the tight spacing for a few seconds before suddenly raising his weapon and blowing a hole through the head.

The firing range was an indoor facility, its airflow system faulty, as evidenced by wafting gunsmoke. It stung

Mary's nostrils, causing her to wiggle her nose, in a manner somewhere between that of a rabbit and Samantha of the classic TV series, Bewitched. When the nose stilled, the mouth went into motion. "You're a big showoff. There's no denying it." Years ago, she would have applauded such marksmanship; now, she had almost an aversion to firearms.

Brogan stuck his gun back into its holster and again removed his ear protection. "You keep your weapon in operating condition?"

"Yes," she answered, also having removed her ear protection.

"When was the last time you disassembled and cleaned it?"

Mary diverted her glance guiltily and made the closed-mouth, sing-song, I-don't-know grunt; but, under Brogan's glare, admitted, "I'm not certain, but it wasn't so long ago."

"Hand me the gun." He worked the slide back and forth, tested the trigger resistance, held the gun up to firing position, and looked down the barrel at the sight. He gave it back. "Seems fine to me. The problem must be you. For one thing, you didn't shoot like you meant it. A gun can almost sense when that's the case. Firm your wrist, smooth out the trigger pull."

Mary sighed heavily and then said, "I'll keep that in mind."

"And stop shooting like a girl."

"Just can't suppress that sexist streak in you for long, can you?"

"Just being straight with you. If that pisses you off, take it out on the target. Imagine it's me."

Smiling wickedly, she said, "That's what I call motivation," although she was being facetious. In recent times, she had come to trust Brogan, even confide in him. She ejected the 15-shot magazine and began loading it from a box of ammo, her arthritic fingers stiff from having repeatedly pulled the trigger.

While waiting, Brogan restarted an earlier conversation. "You really think there's a woman going around saving the government some social security payments?"

"You're hopeless," Mary said, in response to his insensitive phrasing. "It's just a theory. I hit on it after the second victim. Killed in a women's restroom."

"Doesn't mean it was by a woman," countered Ross.

"True. Can't rule out the possibility, though."

"Odds favor a man," said Brogan, playing dual roles of sounding board and devil's advocate.

"True, again, if you're referring to the fact that men kill more often than women. But a man waiting in a women's restroom is taking a big risk. A woman might come in at any time. The woman is going to remember him."

"I once was in a restroom when a woman brought in her young son," recalled Brogan. "Every guy in there stared and could have given a description of her. She should have taken the kid to the women's restroom. I think she was hoping to see something hanging, if you know what I mean."

Mary, pushing the last bullet into the magazine, said, "You sure know how to take a conversation downhill."

"That was a true story, but back to your theory. A man could have come in, hid in a stall, and waited."

"Doesn't change the risk of being seen going in and coming out. Besides, hiding and waiting for whom?"

"Any woman who enters. Look, the guy could have been a pervert."

"It was a man who was attacked and killed, remember?"

"Easily explained. The guy wasn't counting on a janitor coming in. The janitor discovers him, words fly, there's a confrontation, the janitor is killed."

"No confrontation. The janitor was attacked from behind and was facing the sink. If your guy was lying in wait for a woman, why would he ambush the janitor?"

"To keep from being identified or being retained."

"You talk like your guy was facing thirty-to-life if caught in a women's restroom. He could have walked out. I researched for area cases of women being attacked in restrooms. Nothing. That further shoots down the fear-of-being-identified motive."

"Well, I'll think about it some more," said Brogan.

"And while you're at it, keep in mind that your guy could not have accidentally walked in on the janitor. The cleaning cart parked outside the door and the door wedged open tell passers-by that a janitor is inside."

"I got something for you," said Brogan. "He could have walked in thinking the janitor was a woman."

"And discovering different, could have made a turna-round. Although, I haven't come up with an explanation

of why Gibson was at the sink when it wasn't time to clean
it."

"How do you know that?"

"Gibson's supervisor told me that the restrooms are
cleaned in a certain sequence."

Brogan was determined to serve up something, no matter how small, that she couldn't make into Swiss cheese.
"Every detail doesn't have to be relevant. Gibson could have
been washing his hands."

"Why would he turn his back knowing that another
man was in the room? If he didn't know, why would the
other man attack, instead of—"

"Getting the hell out of there," finished Brogan.

"Exactly."

Brogan put his thumbs in his waistband and rubbed his
index fingers together, like they were sticks and he was starting a fire, before desperately coming up with, "The killer
could be a man trying to throw suspicion on a woman."

"I don't buy that," said Mary, then reminded, "It didn't
work on you."

"In other words, the killer figured on an investigator
smarter than me?" bristled Brogan.

"Contain your ego, Ross. And don't distort my words."

Pouting, Brogan remarked, "If you were half as good
at putting holes in a target as you are putting holes in my
theories, you wouldn't be such a lousy shot."

Mary had long ago come to believe that it's the rooster
whose feathers are the most easily ruffled. She reached
across and placed a hand on Brogan's shoulder. "Ross, I

appreciate your help on the firing range. I also appreciate your theories."

"Alright, already," said Brogan, repeating Mary's earlier plea. He pulled a target from the top of the pile and gave it to her, saying, "Here you go." Looking straight ahead and almost speaking out of the corner of his mouth, he said, "Man, woman, or hermaphrodite, the two murders don't have to be related."

Mary hung the target then sent it on its way. She picked up her gun. With a palm heel, she pushed the magazine into the handle. But instead of proceeding to fire, she put the gun in the holster. She first wanted something understood. "They're related. Of that, I'm sure." She repeated, slowly and emphatically, "They're related."

"Have it your way. They're related. But since you've said that the first murder involved a struggle, I suppose you'll be looking for an Amazon who overpowers men."

"An ambush and a slit throat can give the advantage even to a child. Both victims were seniors, although Kent was frailer than Gibson."

"What about a man disguised as a woman? You think of that?"

"For a second. Too left-field."

"Thanks for the compliment."

This time, Mary didn't try to smooth feathers. "That the cases are related strengthens my suspicion of a woman."

Brogan's eyes rolled upward, figuratively searching a shelf for something useful, but finding it bare, asked, "Why?"

"I say related cases because the victims are similar. Similar victims spell targeted victims. Gibson's killer was not hunting for a female. And, if Gibson was the target all along, why choose a women's restroom instead of a men's? I think the answer lies with the killer's gender."

Brogan's eyes returned to the shelf, with the same result, so he said, "Not bad, Cunningham. Not saying I agree with all of it, but you make a logical argument."

Mary snidely added, "For a woman."

"You said it, not me."

"But you were thinking it."

Without denying her claim, Brogan, in a challenging tone, said, "You haven't spoken one word about motive."

Mary placed her hands on her waist and sighed resignedly. "I haven't come up with one."

Having at last posted a point on the scoreboard, Brogan said, "From the looks of it, these won't be the easy cases Rutgers is always wishing on everybody."

"You're telling me."

"What's your next move?"

"Follow some leads on women's restroom keys. The supervisor remembered replacing a couple not long before the murder."

"A killer, possibly a woman, steals a key, to kill the victim, at his job. That's your theory, Cunningham?"

"Until something better comes along, yes."

"If I mention that a man could have stolen the key," said Brogan, "we'll end up going back-and-forth like we already have."

"Yes, we would."

"In that case, I'll just wait and see what you turn up." Then Brogan asked, "You going to get back to target practice, or what?"

"Yes, but one more thing. I learned from the supervisor that the same key unlocks every women's restroom, regardless of which floor it's on."

"So what?"

"Maybe, just maybe, the killer didn't know that and assumed that each floor had its own key."

"I know where you're going with that. You think that the killer might have gotten the key from the same floor that the murder took place."

"Right. And guess what? The supervisor said that he replaced a key for an office on that very floor."

"But you haven't interviewed that office?"

"Not yet." In explanation, Mary said, "it's been catch-as-catch-can with these two investigations. I use whatever free time I have between new cases."

"So what you're hoping is that the killer made a wrong assumption."

Mary reached across and again placed a hand on Brogan's shoulder. In a lecturing delivery, she said, "Ross, my friend, one mistaken assumption can be a killer's undoing, even a smart one. Murder is not that killer's full-time profession. But catching killers is mine. Don't ever count me out."

"Cocky." Brogan attempted to take her down a peg, by saying, "You better hope that cracking the cases won't require you to shoot at anything smaller than the side of a mountain."

The dig produced the opposite effect, for Mary experienced a surging, a reawakening. She stared steely-eyed down the lane, took out her weapon, aimed, and fired six rounds. She reeled in the target. "Well?"

Eyeing the results, Brogan crowed, "I'm one helluva good instructor."

30.

Gale Norman considered it a dopey question. "I couldn't tell you who used the key yesterday, let alone the time you're talking about." Norman was late-twenties, medium-complexioned, long-legged, and firm-bodied. A tattoo ran up one side of her neck but her style of dress was conservative.

"I can understand why that would be," said Mary, "but try hard to remember."

"I have and my answer is the same." Norman placed her palms on the armrests, in readiness to stand, but knew to ask, "Will that be all, Mr. Sloan?"

Dennis Sloan, seated at his desk, wearing a custom-tailored suit and a colorful bowtie, said, "That's up to the lieutenant." Before having summoned Norman from her receptionist's desk, he had given Mary a description of the firm. "We're basically a glorified sweatshop," he'd confided. "You have to be, when you specialize in workers' compensation. Since the attorney fees are limited by law, we have to rely on volume. We survive on hustle. We have to constantly be out there gathering cases and settling them quickly. The hours can be insane. There might be one of us in the office at any hour of the night."

Mary had told him, "I'll think of you, the next time I feel like complaining about my hours."

Then Sloan, who looked older than his forty-four years, had said, "We're diversifying into other areas of the law. In the meantime, the bills have to be paid."

In the present, Mary said to Norman, "I have a few more questions."

A look of annoyance flashed across Norman's face. She slid her hands off the armrests and pressed her spine into the back of the chair. She crossed her arms at the wrists and rested them in her lap. The body language was outwardly relaxed but the aura radiated uneasiness. Some people just don't like talking to police.

"The key never was recovered?"

Norman answered, "I said that."

"When did you discover that the key was missing?"

"All I remember is that a client asked for it and it wasn't there. I let her use our office restroom. Later, I sent the head janitor a note that we needed a replacement. We received one. End of story."

"I take it," said Mary, "that you don't remember the last person to have the key before it went missing."

"Not in the least," said Norman, with borderline attitude. Anticipating, she said, "I don't know how long it had been missing, either."

Mary's theory that the killer might have had a key was going nowhere, slowly. And although Sloan had allowed her to review his appointment book and those of the other attorneys, nothing stood out. Sloan's partners were in court, and the lone associate was in the office but had been of no help to Mary's investigation. Everything documented within the months prior to Gibson's murder seemed within the routine course of business.

Standing there, the stubbornness of the case increasing at every turn, Mary battled discouragement. Why couldn't she be more like other homicide investigators—though never as bad as Brian Rutgers—and bow to statistics? You can't win 'em all, didn't become a cliché for nothing. Some crimes simply go unsolved. Get over it.

Through the years, she'd tried to become more impersonal, more dispassionate. Tried and failed. Her father, Joe, retired cop, of whom she never knew to have taken a sick day, was a factor. Definitely a factor was her older brother, Junior, whose murder by a rogue cop, she'd witnessed as a girl. Change her obsessive devotion to her job? Easier to change her gender.

Still, there comes a time when one has to stop drilling a dry hole, if only to prevent choking on the dust. It was time to wrap up the inquiry about the key because it wasn't unlocking a damn thing. And not that it had anything to do with solving the case, at least the receptionist at the tax firm had been more pleasant than the snooty Gale Norman.

"Last question," promised Mary. "Where is the key kept?" It was mostly a fluff question, meant only to pave the way for a face-saving exit.

Norman's palms returned to the armrests and this time she stood. "On a hook, on the side of my desk. That way, I never have to touch it. Just point." Explaining, she said, "After all, it is a restroom key." She loftily added, "I don't believe in touching anything that's unclean."

Envious, Mary thought, *What a luxury.*

31.

One morning, at breakfast, the then six-year-old Lisa Rosenberg, head hung, shoulders drooped, speared a morsel with her fork but slid it around aimlessly on the plate. She released the fork. It fell, clinking onto the plate, its handle getting wet in syrup. She let the fork lie and began to cry.

Yetta Rosenberg had been washing dishes, singing. She hustled from the sink, drying her hands on her apron, and then hugged her granddaughter about the shoulders. Yetta, barely five-feet tall and plump as a dumpling, didn't have to bend far to smother Lisa's forehead with quick, worried kisses, cooing, "My Bubeleh, my precious little Bubeleh. Why start such a beautiful summer morning in so sad a way?"

Lisa's crying tapered to sniffling, interspersed with panting. Her voice cracking from apprehension, she asked, "How much longer before Grandfather comes home?"

"That's for the doctors to tell us. For now, the best place for him is in the hospital." Yetta picked up the fork, rinsed it, and then placed it in Lisa's hand. "Eat, my child. Eat the happy face, and it will shine through," she claimed, of the big, round potato latke, the eyes dollops of sour cream with raisin pupils, the nose a slice of strawberry, and the smiling mouth a split of banana.

The piquant scent in the kitchen was from the onions that had gone into the latkes, but depending on the day and time, the pungent steam from boiling cabbage, the savory trail from a baking rhubarb pie, or the appetite-whetting whiff from a roasting chicken would swirl about the kitchen. There always were smells, fiercely territorial, throughout the Rosenberg domicile, a four-bedroom brick house on LaSalle Street in central Detroit. Yetta's and Bernie's bedroom broadcast cedar mixed with mothballs. The living room stayed redolent with air freshener, the since discontinued kind, with the scent diffusing from a saturated wick pulled up from the glass container. Even so, never absent was the chemical trace of the vinyl that covered the furniture and preserved it like museum pieces, vinyl that screeched each time a butt slid along it and in the summer stuck against bare skin like flypaper.

Despite Yetta's enticement, Lisa laid the fork down, her appetite a casualty of frazzled nerves and a nervous stomach. "He is going to blame me."

"He will not. It was an accident." Yetta had come to the U.S. as a teenager after World War II, and the outermost layers of her eastern European accent had peeled away; however, a remnant was her tendency to pronounce "w" as "v."

Lisa meekly said, "He didn't like me, even before it happened."

Yetta shivered and her spirit nosedived upon hearing those words from someone so helpless, so dependent, so innocent, and sternly instructed, "Do not utter those words again, Lisa. He loves you."

"I want him to love me, Grandmother."

"How could he not? You are flesh of his flesh and you've been our sunshine from the first time that we laid eyes on you. Now, you eat." As incentive, she said, "There's no meat."

Lisa picked up the fork and with it smeared away the food's happy face. Mechanically, she cut a wedge and inserted it into her mouth. She chased it with a swallow of milk. "It tastes good, Grandmother."

Yetta was heartened by the prospect that Lisa might finish a meal. She rubbed the top of the girl's head. "Mrs. Joan Kellerman and Mrs. Selma Cohen are having their grandchildren for the weekend. The three of us have planned some fun for you children. That's something to look forward to, isn't it?"

Lisa gave a weak, "Yes."

"So, eat, my child. Eat, and be strong and healthy."

But, as had become the pattern, Lisa soon thereafter declared herself finished, although plenty remained on the plate. "May I be excused, please?"

"Yes, little angel."

"Thank you, Grandmother." Lisa hopped from the chair, bolted out of the kitchen, and bounded up the stairs to her room.

Yetta was grateful for the hasty exit; otherwise, Lisa would have seen the tears now wetting her face. Summoning resolve, she dried her eyes with her palm, a move that thrust an up-close look at the numbers permanently inked on her inner forearm. She was committed to being strong for Lisa. She was the girl's guardian and protector, roles to which she devoted her all, even while keeping her own health challenges secret from the child. If having lived all those years with Bernie hadn't taught her what to expect upon his return, having visited him in the hospital certainly had. In the meantime, her hopes that she and Lisa would be able to make the best of his absence weren't panning out.

32.

The white and tan Volkswagen bus clunked westward along I-94. The morning traffic was sparse, yet, the VW labored below the posted minimum speed, hacking and emitting soot. Vehicles barreling alone in the same lane switched to pass on the left. Some motorists cast glances of annoyance, others of amusement, at the rolling relic.

The VW seldom saw the expressway, since it had a tendency of popping out of gear at higher accelerations. That wasn't all that subtracted from its road worthiness. Compression across the four cylinders was uneven. Front-end misalignment had caused its present set of tires to go prematurely bald, a hazard exacerbated by brakes that squealed like piglets. Shock absorbers had become shock amplifiers. The engine couldn't hold a tune-up and would lose a quart between oil changes. Those ills were consistent with the condition of the vehicle's body: creased, dented, dinged, and in some spots rusted through.

As such vehicles are commonly labeled, this was a death-trap, an appropriate enough description, considering the owner. The vehicle was being maintained on life-support, long after it should have been mercifully put out of its misery. Again, considering the owner, that was pure irony, if not outright contradiction.

Fritz Mueller watched the scenery unfold through the dirty windshield that had a crack running across the top like a uni-brow and an arc on the passenger's side engraved by a bladeless wiper. He saw a Delta Airlines passenger jet in its landing approach, the sun reflecting off a silvery wing. The airport was two exits away.

His radio didn't work, but if it did, he would not have had it on, busy as he was reminiscing about the past year. There'd been that call to a features editor at *USA Today*.

"Who shall I say is calling?" the secretary had asked.

"Fritz Mueller."

"I'm sorry. Would you repeat the last name?"

"Mueller. I'm Fritz Mueller."

"Hold, please, Mr. Miller."

"That's Mue—" but he didn't get a chance to finish the correction. It made the wait all the more perturbing.

Eventually, came, "Lyric Albert, speaking."

"Ms. Albert, good morning. Fritz Mueller, here."

With neither reverence nor excitement, Albert asked, "As in Dr. Deceased?"

"If you insist."

"What do I owe the pleasure?"

What followed was a pitch that was journalistic gold, guaranteed to captivate readers across the nation.

"Yes, I see." But Albert proved that she didn't, by saying, "It's not news, Doctor. I mean, you've said it before. It's been printed before. I'd love to toss around new angles with you, but I'm running late for a meeting. Tell you what, I'm switching you to my voice mail. Leave a number and I'll call you back. Gotta go."

"...at the sound of the beep..."

Mueller had interrupted his seething long enough to leave name and number. He never received a return call. This disrespect from someone, who the week prior, had done a by-line on rapper, Eminem. What historical crusade had Eminem ever championed?

After the *USA Today* debacle, Mueller had decided to grant the scoop to the magazine industry. There would be a sacrifice in immediacy but compensated for by permanence. Magazines can lie around for years; in that respect, salons and medical waiting rooms are time capsules. Yes, magazines were a good Plan B. *Time* and *Newsweek* both declined his generosity.

But there are other letters in the alphabet. His next plan had been to go local. Sometimes you scale down. He knew reporters in the metro-Detroit media, both print and electronic. They were in his debt for past interviews, even exclusives. They showed themselves, however, to be ingrates.

But, et tu, Lisa Rose?! As was said concerning that other Caesar, this was the unkindest cut of all. Where would she be, if not for him? Probably chasing ambulances. He never would have believed that she could be so traitorous. That's not biting the hand; that's cannibalism.

Yes, there had been the spat over that Sophie Kingsley woman, but he hadn't taken seriously Rose's threat to sever relations with him. She just needed time to cool and regain her perspective. After what should have been more than enough time for her to do so, he came to her office, unannounced, bearing a bouquet of flowers as a peace offering. At first, Rose had refused to see him, but it's a woman's prerogative to play hard to get. She relented after being told by the receptionist that he was chatting up visitors in the lobby.

"Those must be artificial flowers," Rose had commented, "otherwise, they would have swiveled and died in your grip."

To show they were real, Mueller started plucking pedals. "You love me. You love me not."

"Not, doesn't do justice. I told you that I'm through with you, so why are you here?"

"We must patch things up, Ms. Rose. Our cause is too important to be jeopardized by squabbles."

"We? Our? This is no partnership. Whatever you choose to call it, it consisted of my keeping you out of prison, without, I'm quick to add, much help from you. Do us both a favor. Do what's expected of men your age and go feed pigeons."

Ordinarily, Mueller was a steel-plated armadillo who could gambol through verbal briar patches, never pricked by thorns; however, his losing streak had made him more thin-skinned and more conciliatory. "Maybe not a partnership, but certainly a team. I know you believe in the cause. You've said so from the beginning."

"I believe that people should be spared a painful, lingering death," edited Rose.

"My sentiments, exactly. People who are dying and suffering should have the right to decide when enough is enough. Animals die better than humans, thanks to the Humane Society, the American Society for the Prevention of Cruelty to Animals, and who knows how many individual laws. Someone needs to speak for humans."

"Initially, you did. Now, I think not."

"Then, what am I doing?"

"Ego-tripping. Grandstanding. You've put yourself above the cause."

Mueller, refusing to bow to the apparent, asked, "Are you truly bailing out on me?"

"If that's how you want to describe it. I have other things on my plate."

"Such as?"

"You don't want to know, believe me. Now take your flowers and go. Our dance is over."

Oh, but the music will, indeed, play on, now thought Mueller, as he ended his reminiscing and redirected his thoughts to current matters.

The exit sign over the expressway announced, *Detroit Metro Airport/ Merriman Road.* Mueller pressed down his right-turn signal. Well, it had been working fine yesterday. Within the exit ramp, he eased off the accelerator, but the engine threatened to stall, so he fed it more gas.

Upon coming to the fork in the exit ramp, he veered to the right, the opposite way from the airport. He obeyed the stop sign, then proceeded north on Merriman Road. Already, he saw his destination up ahead. After traveling the two blocks, he applied the complaining brakes, waited for oncoming traffic to clear, and then turned left into the parking lot.

The VW crept stealthily, Mueller eyeing the numbers on the parade of doors, until he saw room 137. He was at the Dakota Motel, accommodations for the budget-minded. Definitely, fate was along for the ride, judging by the empty parking space exactly in front of the room. Mueller cut the ignition and waited the few seconds while the motor wheezed until it died. He rolled up the windows, entrapping the rankness of the interior.

VW buses once were a symbol for an entire generation and for an entire social mindset. Mueller, however, despite the bouquet brought to Rose, was no flower child, unless the topic was funeral wreaths or pushing up daisies. And, he wore no peace medallion, he, the guru of rest-in-peace.

A blue-collar type of guy, Mueller was brown bagging it, his lunch atop a pile of items cluttering the front passenger seat. Originally, the bus seated eight; but, years ago, he removed the back seats, more room for a passenger to stretch out. Literally stretch out.

Fate understood that Fritz Mueller was too great to be relegated to feeding pigeons ammo with which to bomb statues. He tingled with anticipation. He would have experienced an erection, except that he'd long since lost that ability.

There was etiquette to observe, introductions and the like; therefore, it was best not to walk in lugging the equipment. That might seem too forward. His plan was to dispense with the chit-chat as quickly as possible, good bedside manner allowing, and then bee-line it back to the bus to grab what he needed.

Mueller glanced over his shoulder into the back of the bus at the Morpheus Machine. His face exuded reassurance, as if his thoughts were, *Don't you fret, now. Daddy won't be long.*

33.

Joe Kingsley was at Detroit Receiving Hospital, a world-class trauma facility among a cluster of hospitals forming the city's Medical Center. He was standing outside a curtained section, visibly wrought.

When Mary spotted him, she rushed to his side, asking on the way, "What happened, Daddy?"

"Your mother had a bad nosebleed. Started out of nowhere. I squeezed her nostrils. It did no good. I ran to the bathroom and got a wet facecloth and held it against her nose. That didn't help either. She was getting faint. I called 911." Joe looked defeated. Blood stained his shirt, pants, and the top of his shoes.

"You did all you could. Did the paramedics stop the bleeding?"

"No. They packed her nostrils with gauze and brought her here." Joe laced his fingers and tapped his thumb tips together. His gaze was downward.

Against a soundtrack of occasional moans and groans, Mary asked, "There's something else on your mind, isn't there?"

Joe's first attempt to answer was delayed by a single, dry cough, before he said, "She's gotten worse lately."

It wasn't unexpected news; nonetheless it hit hard. Mary absorbed the jolt and then asked, "In what way?"

"The pain. She never sleeps through the night anymore. Her appetite is next to nothing. And the other day her legs went from under her and she fell."

"I wish I'd known," said Mary.

"She told me not to tell you. Didn't want you worrying."

"But, I was just over yesterday."

"Your mother puts on a good face when you come around."

But Mary wouldn't allow herself that convenient out and self-accusingly asked, "Did she fool me, or did I choose to be fooled?"

A nurse emerged through the curtains, which hung on hooks that ran along an overhead U-shaped track. She acknowledged Mary and Joe only with a smile and nod before hurrying off.

Next, a doctor came out. While looking forward, he reached back and pulled the curtains together, like a master-of-ceremonies does upon taking the stage. "You can see your wife now, Mr. Kingsley."

"Thank God. Doctor, this is my daughter, Mary."

Dr. Peter Burlington, in scrubs, stethoscope hooked around his young neck, shook hands while saying, "Nice meeting you." He turned and parted the curtains to let Mary and Joe precede him.

Mary tucked her arms tightly to contain a shiver. Her mother lay motionless, on her back, eyes closed, too similar to being...to being.... But she wasn't. She was warm to the touch when Mary took her hand, when she kissed her forehead.

"She's sedated," said Burlington, explaining Sophie's non-response.

"But conscious?" asked Mary.

"More like asleep," said Burlington.

Mary asked, "What's your diagnosis?"

"Epistaxis, medical-speak for nosebleed," explained Burlington, "which can flow quite freely with advanced-stage cancer patients." In reference to a bag hanging from a bedside pole, a tube connecting it to the needle in Sophie's left arm, he said, "As you can see, she's being given blood. She'll be given two pints."

"What can be done to prevent this from happening again?" asked Mary.

"Nothing. The cancer makes her susceptible. Nosebleeds sometimes signal impending heart failure or blood clotting problems. High blood pressure can play a role, but your mom's numbers are good. Is she on any blood-thinning drugs?"

"No," said Joe, man of few words, although this day, he probably had used up his quota for the week.

"I ask because that can be a factor, too." Then, Burlington said, "You folks are welcome to visit for as long as you wish, but do you mind stepping outside with me to discuss a few matters?"

"Okay," said Mary.

Once outside, Burlington said, "Even when someone is sedated, you never know what might filter through. That's why I thought it best to speak outside her earshot."

"Whatever it is, Doctor," said Mary, readying herself, "give it to us straight."

Burlington placed his clipboard against his chest and held it there with crossed arms. "She is beyond cure, so the only aid medical science can provide is palliative, in other words, pain management. While we'll certainly do that for as long as she's here, we can only keep her for a couple of days, at the most."

"There are others who can make better use of a bed, is what you're saying," translated Mary.

"It's not my call," said Burlington. "Hospital policy."

Conceding the point, Mary said, "I understand."

"I hope that you do, too, Mr. Kingsley."

"I do."

"Mrs. Kingsley will be given a room upstairs," said Burlington. "She'll receive our best care."

"I appreciate that, Doctor," said Mary, "and I wasn't accusing you of being uncaring."

"And I hope you still don't after I bring up another unpleasant subject," Burlington said, and lowered his clipboard to his side. "Mrs. Kingsley might have to be rushed to emergency in the future and need resuscitation." He hesitated, before saying, "There might come a time when resuscitation won't necessarily be a humane option."

Trying to contain her discomfort, Mary asked, "Are you telling us to put in a do-not-resuscitate order?"

Burlington was quick to say, "I wouldn't presume to tell you what to do. It's the most personal of decisions."

"And not to be made on the spot," said Mary. "This emergency has brought it to the forefront, that's for sure. The family will discuss it."

"In that regard," said Burlington, "it's helpful to know the patient's wishes. Often, it's the patient who brings the most realistic perspective."

Mary reflected on that comment, then responded, "A patient might be ready to die, even when the family isn't ready to let go. That's what you're talking about."

"Yes. It's human nature to want to hold on to a dying family member. One more thing that should be decided is whether Mrs. Kingsley is to die in a hospital or at home. Do you know about Hospice?"

"Yes," answered Mary. Then, to Joe, she asked, "Ready to go back in?"

"Ready."

An intern, in a white lab coat, came running. The souls of his sneakers squeaked as he came to a halt. He was wired about something. His gaze zipped from Joe to Mary and back to Burlington, as he contemplated how to interrupt. "Uh...Pete, can I speak to you for a second?"

"Sure." But even then, Burlington was staring away, at a far wall, the top of which was glass. He could see hospital personnel scurrying, some of them performing broken-field running, trying to get to the front of the rush. "What's with them, I wonder."

"That's what I came to tell you," said the intern. "Dr. Deceased made a drop-off."

34.

Fritz Mueller was seated at a table, slouched and smiling, silent, too, but only because he'd been told to shut-up long enough to be informed that he was under arrest. He restarted, saying, "Now that we're done with that little formality, may I continue?"

"It's your funeral," Mary said, standing directly in front of him. She'd converted a hospital conference room into an interrogation room. She'd also borrowed a tape recorder from the hospital. She pressed the play button and made introductory remarks, citing time, place, that Mueller had been given his Miranda rights, and that the recording was being made with his knowledge and permission.

Looking around at present company, Mueller asked, "Where did I leave off? Somebody please jog my memory."

Mary uncooperatively told him, "Dig your own grave."

Mueller gave a condescending laugh and said, "Funeral, grave. How many more witty references to death do you have?"

"I'm fresh out." Mary took in a long, steadying breath, like a person who suspected an ordeal ahead. The intake filled her lungs with hospital smells— medicinal, antiseptic, with a hint of bleach—but since the room was a distance away from the wards, the smell might have been residual within her nostrils.

Upon learning that Mueller had delivered a body like it was a pizza, Mary rushed to detain him. Her backup was two uniformed officers recruited from elsewhere in the hospital. Cops are commonly at Receiving Hospital, interviewing victims of crime, bringing in injured arrestees, guarding the rooms of suspects and prisoners, etc. These two were standing on opposite sides of the sinewy Mueller, but not for restraint, because Mueller was tickled to be there. Their role was as witnesses.

"Murder is a serious charge," was Mueller's understatement. "One that I've faced before, but each time, a jury sided with me."

Mary stepped away, flicked her wrist dismissively, and mocked, "Everything's about you. It gets boring."

"Really?" Muller shrugged and said, "I bet you'd rather hear about the deceased." He paused for confirmation, but not receiving it, volunteered, "His name is Thomas Duval."

With Mueller dangling information like a string of yarn, Mary had no choice but to be the kitten and paw at it, hoping he wouldn't yank it out of reach. "And how did Thomas Duval die?"

"Excellent question." Smugly, Mueller answered, "Like all people die. Heart stops beating. Brain waves cease. Dead." He studied his fingernails and asked, "Anyone have a nail file?"

I ought to drop kick your old ass straight out that chair, thought Mary. But what accounted for her unraveling patience, her mounting anger? She'd dealt unemotionally with many egotists, handled them by letting them think that they were the puppeteers controlling the strings. Why was Mueller getting to her? She concluded that it was because she'd had to rush off to Mueller before she'd had the chance to speak with her mother. That had to be it: simple resentment. Must keep personal and professional matters separate; besides, it was early afternoon, and having rushed from work after Joe's phone call, she was still on the clock. "With your medical background, you can be more exact than that," she coaxed.

"Thomas Duval committed suicide."

"You were present at the suicide?" Mary asked.

"Yes."

"Did you participate?"

"How could I have?" Mueller's tongue, purple on the underside, wiped back and forth across the front of his teeth. Amused, he said, "Had I participated in suicide, I'd be dead."

One of the uniformed cops shook his head in pity at the juvenile nonsense, while the other chewed on a tooth pick and monitored Mary for her reaction.

She wanted to curse at Mueller but reminded herself that it was worry over her mother that was weakening her tolerance. The smile of embarrassment was phony. "You got me there," she admitted, and ingratiatingly added, "Doctor," knowing that he no longer was licensed. She revised the question. "Did you assist in Mr. Duval's suicide?"

"Yes. Assisted suicide is the service that I provide to society."

"How did you provide the service to Mr. Duval?"

"Same as with all the others. The name Morpheus Machine came from the media. I just call it my invention."

"So you hooked him up to your invention?"

"More humane than hooking him up to artificial life support like they do in a hospital. That's perpetuating suffering. I end it."

"Where did you assist Mr. Duval in his suicide?"

Mueller cocked his elbow on the armrest and struck a heads-up version of The Thinker. The reels of the tape recorder made rotation after rotation, capturing silence. Then his eyebrows peaked, and he said, "I'm going to withhold that detail for now."

"Because?"

"Not the right time."

Mary relented, confident that the information would be known soon enough. For the present, she would let Mueller orchestrate. "Was there anyone else present?"

"Yes. His daughter."

"Where is she now?"

"Around. And at the appropriate time, she will speak publicly."

The cop with the toothpick intervened. "Look here, guy, this is no game." He was quieted by a butt-out look from Mary.

Mueller ignored the cop's remark, seizing the occasion to stretch and yawn. "Back to the question about where

Tom died. Wayne County. It'll be up to Gerald Lewis on whether he'll waste the county's money on another trial."

"You're picking a fight with Lewis," interpreted Mary. "You actually want to go to trial."

"I'm willing," corrected Mueller, "to go to trial. There's a difference."

"What was the date and time of Mr. Duval's death?" *I should have asked that earlier.*

"This morning at ten forty-two." Mueller's voice was animated and his face took on color, as he grinned and said, "I wonder if he's up for another go?"

Lost, Mary asked, "Who?"

Mueller tried to look apologetic but the sentiment wouldn't stick to his face. "Sorry," he claimed, anyway. "My mind wandered. It happens when you get my age. I was thinking out loud, referring to Mr. Lewis."

Mary wasn't fooled by his feigned senility; yet, had she been at her sharpest, she might have made the connection. Covering up, she said, "You don't seem worried about Lewis."

"No reason to be. Michigan has no laws against assisted suicide." Mueller smirked. His eyes danced. "Mr. Lewis has nothing on his side...unless... there's something different about this one."

"Was there something different?"

"Let's let Mr. Lewis make that determination, shall we?"

The doorknob jiggled noisily, followed by rapid knocking. One of the uniformed officers opened the door and in walked Ross Brogan. He didn't bother with greetings. He pointed to the door through which he'd entered and said to Mary, "Got something to tell you."

She nodded. She stated on tape that the interrogation was being suspended and gave the time. She shut off the recorder and left the room with Brogan. "What is it?"

"Inspector Newberry wants Mueller brought downtown."

"My cell phone works. He didn't have to send you."

"I volunteered."

"Message received, then." Mary placed a hand on the doorknob, about to reenter the room.

Brogan gently grabbed her arm. "I'm not here as a messenger. I'm here to take Mueller in so that you can stay and be with your mother."

"That's so thoughtful," said Mary, who knew not to get too sentimental, less she embarrass Mr. Macho. What she didn't mention was that she was relieved to suspend the interrogation. Mueller had affected her in a manner and to a degree with which she had not yet come to terms.

And, Mueller tried to build upon it as soon as she reentered. "I hope that you weren't talking about me behind my back. That would be rude."

"You are going to be taken downtown," said Mary.

"Splendid. Ready when you are."

Mary then said, "He's all yours, Ross."

Brogan told the cops, "You guys can take off." He stepped toward Mueller and gestured him to stand.

Mueller complied, but asked Mary, "Are you and I parting company?"

Mary fluttered her eyelashes flirtingly and claimed, "I'm brokenhearted over it."

Shrugging his square shoulders again, Mueller said, "Just when you and I were establishing such rapport." To Brogan he said, "Take good care of my bus for me."

"Do I look like valet parking?" Brogan pulled out the handcuffs and ordered, "Hands behind your back."

"Your bus will be impounded," said Mary.

"Thank you," said Mueller. "Not many of them around anymore."

"Let's go, Gramps," said Brogan. "A comfy holding cell awaits."

"I won't be there long," Mueller promised. "I'll be afforded a phone call when we get there, won't I?"

"I've heard that's how it's done," said Brogan.

"I'll be calling my lawyer." Talk first and then contact the lawyer. Backwards for most people but typical for Mueller.

"I'm leaving," announced Mary.

Even Brogan's huff exterior couldn't filter out the sincerity in his voice, as he said, "My regards to your mother, Cunningham."

Mueller took note, his response instant, almost Pavlovian. Had he not been cuffed, he would have pointed jabbingly, good manners be damned. "I know who you are, now," he proclaimed in epiphany. "You're the officer whose mother is dying of breast cancer." He took her silence as confession. In divining Mary's identity, he had belied the ruse that he'd tried to perpetrate earlier, that he was an absent-minded, doddering old man. Still, he shook his head and tried to look embarrassed. "This is the second time that I've been asleep at the switch, slow to connect the dots, concerning your mother."

Mary's heart rate shot north. *Second time? What the fuck is he talking about?* she wondered, not knowing about his offer to Lisa Rose. She wanted to ask—no, demand—that he explain. But to do so would confirm that he was playing her like a radio. Believing that any utterance would be ill-advised, she pressed her lips tightly.

Mueller, nearly psychic in matters of death and dying, said, "Your mother must be here. That's how you showed up so quickly. You already were here visiting her."

Brogan interceded, saying, "You don't have to listen to another word from him, Cunningham. Leave now, if you want."

Mueller said to Brogan, "Allow me a minute for some parting words with my new acquaintance."

"What about it, Cunningham?" asked Brogan.

"It better be quick," said Mary.

Mueller, nonetheless, did not quicken his delivery, telling Mary, "Many times I've witnessed the effects of advanced, incurable cancer. I know the indescribable pain and suffering it can bring. There'll come a time when she'll beg for it to end."

"That's enough," Mary abruptly declared and then told Brogan, "Get him out of here."

But even while Mueller was being marched toward the door he was looking backward at Mary, talking. "Our paths crossing like this, yours and mine. It's like it was predestined."

As Mary watched Mueller exiting, he transformed before her eyes—rather her mind's eye—into what she perceived him to be: Death, as much as if he had been wearing a black, hooded, ground-dragging robe, and carrying a scythe. It was a perception that she had tried to suppress during the interview but it had distracted her and thrown her off stride. Mueller's being at the same hospital, same time, as Sophie, was too foreboding. *Alright, girl. Shake it off. You'll probably never have to deal with that ghoul again,* she told herself. The thought didn't produce the settling effect that she sought, and she felt like a person who was whistling pass the graveyard.

35.

On a morning several weeks before young Lisa would let the happy-face potato latke breakfast go to waste, she awakened to the realization that the world was out of kilter. First, she'd been roused out of sleep, and not by gentle pokes from Yetta but by firm jostling from Bernie. Lisa, though, had not overslept; the dawn cast her bedroom in an illumination that was eerie and disquieting. Furthermore, it was summer, no school.

Nonetheless, Bernie's stern instructions had been stronger than her urge to pull the bedcovers over her head and wait for normalcy to return. She got out of bed and turned on the light. If only there were a switch that could shed light on what was afoot.

Most disturbing, there were no signs of Yetta, and Lisa wasn't relying only on voice. She knew the sound of Yetta's footsteps, which, at that time of day, would have been house slippers shuffling along hardwood floors. And, there was neither sound nor smell emanating from the kitchen, although it would be unthinkable that Bernie, master and breadwinner, would be denied his breakfast.

And it was from the kitchen that Bernie bellowed, "If you know what's good for you, Lisa, you'll be down here soon."

As threatening as that command might have sounded, Lisa had never known physical discipline, let alone physical abuse. But there are other types, as hurtful and more lasting. Duly motivated, she speedily tied her remaining shoe, getting a finger trapped in the loop. "Coming, Grandfather."

"My patience is not without limits."

Lisa came downstairs wearing a pink jumper, her face meticulously scrubbed, even behind the ears. She wanted to look every bit the loveable young lady. As an accessory, she put on her sweetest, most innocent smile and asked, "Where is Grandmother, Grandfather?"

"Not where she should be. And I'm not in the mood for your questions, so keep that in mind." Had he not been who he is, he might have told her, in a tone to minimize trauma, that Yetta was in the hospital.

The night before, en route to going upstairs to bed, Yetta collapsed. When she regained consciousness, she found herself looking up at Bernie, her face wet from having been doused with a glass of water. She asked him to call an ambulance because she still felt disoriented, but asking turned to pleading before he acquiesced. Even as she was being taken out, she told him that if the hospital keeps her to take Lisa to Joan Kellerman in the morning.

Bernie did not wait for morning. Immediately after Yetta was taken, he got on the phone. It turned out, however, that Kellerman wasn't the picture of health, herself. For the past day, the flu, a stomach virus—whatever it was— had her in its grip. She wouldn't risk passing it to Lisa.

Undeterred but desperate, Bernie then dialed Selma Cohen, whom he did not know as well as he did Kellerman, but whom he disliked just as much. He sucked up, complimenting her granddaughter. Cohen agreed to baby-sit, but wouldn't be available until after her late-morning appointment at the hair-dresser.

Better than nothing, but it forced upon Bernie a choice: either nursemaid Lisa and miss a half-day's work or take her with him and get her to Cohen at lunchtime. He chose the latter, as any dedicated professional would have done.

Lisa, barred from asking further questions, could only hope that Bernie would be forthcoming on his own. Meanwhile, she would demonstrate just how little of a bother she could be by preparing her own breakfast. She used a footstool to get a box of cereal from the cabinet. Before she could step down, however, the box flew from her hand.

"What do you think you're doing?" Bernie asked, holding the snatched box high. "A man works all his life, making a way for his family to eat well, and this is his thanks?"

Taken aback, Lisa cowered and said, "I'm sorry, Grandfather." She loved cereal, but had forgotten that Bernie considered it an improper breakfast food and that she and Yetta had conspired to smuggle in the offending box.

Bernie slammed the box into the garbage pail. He went to the refrigerator and took out something wrapped in brown paper and tied with twine. He undid the package, revealing a pair of steaks. He turned a knob on the stove, there was a *poof,* and then he adjusted the flame to medium. On it, he placed a cast iron skillet, added a little oil, and in due time tenderly added the meat.

"May I please have some orange juice, Grandfather?"

"I have but two hands. Get it yourself."

As Lisa later sat downing her juice and watching Bernie at the stove preparing breakfast, she wanted to believe that he was being nurturing. At the same time, seeing him playing chef was a reminder that it should have been Yetta at the stove and that she still didn't know Yetta's whereabouts. And if that was Lisa's first worry, uncertainty about Bernie's plans for the day ran a close second.

36.

The rusty groan of the door sliding open awakened Mueller. He sat up from the wooden bench and blinked his eyes into focus. He grinned inanely, as the door closed with an authoritative slam. "I hope you don't take offense, there stranger, but you have a dangerous look about you," he told the newcomer. "What are you in for?"

"Cut the crap," said Rose. "I had half a mind not to come."

"But the other half told you that you had to." Mueller scooted closer to the end of the bench, clearing space, and then said, "Have a seat."

"I'd rather sit bare-assed in an outhouse on a toilet seat that hasn't been lifted in a year." The bench was spotted and stained. Some areas of the floor were sticky. And the cell smelled like an unwashed armpit. Rose was even careful not to lean against the bars.

"Seated or standing," said Mueller, "you're still a vision of loveliness."

"I told you to cut the crap. I asked them to let me talk to you while the release papers are being readied."

"I never doubted that you would come through."

"I didn't do anything," admitted Rose. "The victim's daughter came forth and said that it was assisted suicide."

"You said, victim." Mueller testily claimed, "Thomas Duval was a client."

"Client, then."

"Thank you."

"Gerald Lewis released a statement that he wasn't going to prosecute without a law to back him up."

"That's disappointing," complained Mueller. On the bench, in a corner, was his dinner: a baloney sandwich on a paper plate, a bag of chips, and a carton of belly-wash. He brushed them to the floor and took their place, knees up, arms folded.

Rose gritted her teeth and shook her head. "It's because of that very attitude that I can't represent you any longer."

Mueller buried his face in his palms for a second before clasping them in prayer position. Then, he opened them, beseechingly. "What? A person can't express disappointment?"

"Over not being prosecuted? Get real. It proves that you're driven by ego, man."

"You couldn't be more wrong. With me, it's all about the cause."

"Save it. You want a media circus starring yourself. And what's my role? Sideshow attraction, like a bearded lady?"

"It pains me to see you so upset. It truly does." He stood. He stepped toward her, his outstretched arm on its way to wrapping around her shoulder.

Rose knocked it away. "Don't touch me!"

Mueller, wide-eyed, said, "Take it easy. Look, I'm sitting back down."

"You are beyond redemption." Rose turned to face the bars, about to call for the guard.

"No, wait." Still seated, Mueller leaned against the wall and slightly bumped his head, before asking, "What can I do to save our relationship?"

"It's too late. At first, the authorities came after you. Now, you come after the authorities."

"I don't know what you mean."

"Liar. You're all about sensationalizing. What you provide is not my idea of a dignified death."

"I disagree, but that's not what's important. I'm willing to do whatever it takes to change your mind."

"I gave you a chance. You agreed not to perform any more assisted suicides without first giving me the heads-up. And that you'd supply me information about the person, so I can determine, before the fact, whether there's protection under the law."

"Yes, that was the agreement. But there were extenuating circumstances with Tom Duval."

The disbelief obvious by her tone, Rose said, "Yeah, like what?"

"Tom called the night before, saying he'd decided and wanted it over immediately."

"That's a lame excuse. I've learned that he came from California. You talk like he drove cross-town. You had time to notify me."

Speculatively, Mueller asked, "Are you up in the air over the fact that Tom wasn't terminal?"

Her displeasure having increased, Rose said, "I didn't know that. And it underscores how you kept me uninformed."

"A person doesn't have to be terminal to suffer unbearably."

"I never claimed otherwise, but that's not the point. There are other considerations, such as compos mentis and being of legal age." Rose went on to vent, "It's the assisted suicide, itself, that's all-important with you and you wouldn't think twice about administering to, say, a disturbed teenager."

"I had no idea that your opinion of me was so low."

"Oh, come off it, will you. You wanted to use my own client for headlines."

"The woman dying of breast cancer?"

"You know damn well whom I'm talking about."

"Now, whose ego is running amok? Just because she's your client shouldn't mean she can't end her suffering."

"Tell the truth. You see her as a trophy."

Mueller hung his head, like he'd been shot through the heart, but only for a moment. "Nothing of the sort. Unfortunately, you stormed out of my apartment that time and didn't give me a chance to clarify. Actually, it's because she's your client that I don't want to see her suffer beyond help."

"But that's up to her."

"Totally."

"She'll never call you."

"And maybe she will."

Rose knew that they'd played this conversational ping-pong before, yet returned the ball a last time, saying, "She won't."

"You're probably right," was Mueller's nonchalant concession. He raised his arms into a stretch and held it for several seconds. His eyes were prone to irritation, lacking some of the natural moisture they once had. He closed them and with the heel of his palm massaged one socket then the other. And when he opened them, his cobalt irises lay against a pinkish background, color-mismatched orbs that he now retrained on his irate visitor. "In fact, our paths, I'm talking about Mrs. Kingsley's and mine, probably won't cross again, after today."

Rose understood that she was being led and equally understood that she was ill-positioned to resist. "What are you talking about?"

Mueller's brows arched theatrically. "You didn't know that she was at the hospital when I delivered Tom?"

"No, I didn't."

"Well, she was."

"Did you have the indecency to say something to her?" Rose dropped her arms to her sides and made fists. "Because if you did..."

"I didn't even see her." Adding to the mystery, Mueller said, "But I know she was there, just as I know it was under emergency conditions. I need not remind you of her affliction, do I?"

"I refuse to be jerked around like this. Take your secrets and shove them."

"At least let me finish telling you about Mrs. Kingsley."

"No need. If you and Mrs. Kingsley were at the hospital at the same time, it was mere happenstance."

"Happenstance? Some other explanation might be in order. At the hospital, I was interrogated by Mrs. Kingsley's daughter, who was there visiting her."

Rose did not have the arrest report nor had she known of Mary's involvement. "Whoppty-do. I still say happenstance."

"I'm a man of science, ruled by intellect, and therefore inclined to agree that it was happenstance. But my instincts argue otherwise. I believe yours do, too."

"What you believe is of no concern to me."

Mueller repositioned himself, such that one leg was stretched along the bench, the other bent, fingers interlaced around that knee. "I wish I could have watched the press conference you held with her family, but after broadcasting went digital, I was slow in getting a converter box."

"I suppose there's a point to this."

"There is. If I'd been able to see the press conference, instead of having to read about it, I would have sensed a link with that family. Don't ask me how."

"Don't worry. I won't."

"You don't seem to understand. At some point, Mrs. Kingsley's suffering will cause her to think of me. Why? Because you are her attorney and to think of you is to think of me."

"You're delusional."

"And you're in denial. If you weren't, you'd admit that we made one another and that we're forever linked in society's consciousness."

"Being the man of science as you claim, not to mention one with medical training, you can appreciate what I'm about to say."

Mueller sat up erect and asked, "What might that be?"

"Even Siamese twins can be separated." Smiling proudly and feeling liberated, Rose pulled her purse strap higher on her shoulder, turned, and yelled, "Guard! I'm ready to leave."

37.

"Yes, what is it?" asked Cliff, after having been summoned to the family room.

"Come watch this with me," requested Mary, relaxed on the couch in a nightshirt.

"Baby, I love you, but no Home and Garden Channel for me tonight."

"It's not Home and Garden. Sit down." Her wide-set brown eyes looking Bambi-like, she implored, "Please?" stretching the word into two syllables.

"Aww, okay," agreed Cliff, caving in like thin ice under a Sumo skater. He plopped down next to his wife then instinctively picked up the remote control.

"Oh, no you don't." She extended an open palm. "Hand it over."

"I was only going to adjust the volume."

"The volume's fine. Sit back and behave." She took the remote then smacked a kiss on his lips.

At the end of the commercial break, Clarice Rutherford was back on camera, anchor desk style, head and torso only. "Welcome back," she greeted. Then, in her folksy, southern manner, she announced, "On live hook-up from the Motor

City, we have none other than famed attorney, Lisa Rose. Howdy-do, Lisa."

Cameras gave a split screen, Rutherford on the left, Rose on the right.

"Good evening, Clarice," said Rose, in a red polo shirt.

"You're looking fit," observed Rutherford. "Been hitting the gym?"

"Jim, who?" toyed Rose.

"That's g-y-m, though there's probably an opposing attorney or two named Jim, whom you've hit, make that clobbered."

"I don't remember any Jim's offhand. But we lawyers aren't as adversarial toward one another as commonly believed."

"You're not here to sing Cumbaya, Lisa Rose, so let's get this interview off on the right footing. It would rise to malpractice if I didn't ask about your most notorious client, Fritz Mueller, Dr. Deceased, himself. How is he?"

"Fine, I hope."

"I can't let you get off that easy. Is the report true that following his last arrest, you visited his cell and was overheard fussing at him?"

"Attorney-client discussions are privileged."

"So, you are still his attorney?"

"He and I know the answer, and right now, that's all who need to know."

"Hey, you know me. I can take rejection but don't punish the viewers out there who have tuned in to hear the latest about Dr. Deceased."

"Invite him on your show," Rose suggested.

"For sure. Though it's not technically correct to refer to him as Dr. Deceased anymore since his medical license was yanked. Not to worry, I've coined him another name. Mr. Mortality. Tell him he can use it. Just send me my royalties."

Rose's delivery was friendly but matter-of-fact. "I'll let you tell him. Cut out the middleman, and all that."

Rutherford had big, round, expressive eyes that often spoke in place of her thin, painted lips, eyes that now batted in frustration. "If this is going to be like pulling hen's teeth, Lisa Rose, I'll just change the subject. How's that?"

"It's your show."

"Tell us about your reverend-kills-rabbi case. Sounds like a doozie." Rutherford immediately added, "For the benefit of viewers unfamiliar with the case, Lisa represents the defendant, a Reverend Jeeter McArthur." True to the irreverent asides that she was known for, she said, "Boy, with a name like that, I wonder what his parents had against him." Then she said, "Okay, Lisa, I'm all ears."

It was Mary who used the remote to notch up the volume and then said, "Yeah, me, too." She then folded her legs to the side on the couch, and the nightshirt rode up her thigh, betraying that she was wearing nothing underneath.

"My client is innocent and is looking forward to his day in court."

"If I ever hear anything different from a defense attorney," declared Rutherford, "the shock will kill me." She continued, "Alas, some of us former prosecutors chose something honorable, like broadcasting, while others chose defense work. And speaking of prosecutors, you're going up against a dandy in Gerald Lewis, who has charged your client not only with first-degree murder, but a hate crime. What say you about that?"

Cliff started to say, "I didn't know—"

"Hush," said Mary, emphasizing with a harmless slap on his shoulder. "Let me hear this."

Rose said, "Mr. Lewis wants to be State Attorney General, ironic when you consider that he either doesn't know when he's misapplying a law or doesn't care. The Michigan Hate Crime Law has no sway in a first-degree murder case because upon conviction, the sentence is automatically life without parole, regardless of the presence or absence of hate."

"Fine and dandy," said Rutherford. "So, exactly what's this law supposed to address?"

"Criminal intimidation, which the penal code establishes as a felony and defines as the specific intent to intimidate or harass a person because of that person's race, color, religion, gender, sexual orientation, or national origin. It covers personal injury and property damage, and sets penalties of imprisonment of up to two years, fines up to five million dollars, or both."

Impressed with the recitation, Rutherford said, "Either you've memorized the law, chapter and verse, or you have a teleprompter there in the studio with you."

"And," said Rose, in gear, "even a first-year law student knows that no one should be charged under a law that neither applies to the guilt nor penalty phase of a trial."

"I should mention," said Rutherford, "that Gerald Lewis declined our invitation to appear on tonight's show, but if he were with us, I'm sure he'd have a different take."

"Needless to say," said Rose.

"Lewis' take might be, and I'm speculating, that if the rabbi realized that his attacker was motivated by ethnicity, then it constituted a hate crime, separate from the murder. In other words, the rabbi was ethnically intimidated before he was killed. What say you to that, Lisa Rose?"

"I say, whatever Mr. Lewis' theories are, the courtroom is the forum in which I'll respond."

"I heard of keeping things close to the vest," said, Rutherford, "but yours must be lined with pockets, to spare." She then said, "But let's move along."

"I'm all for that."

"My crack research staff tells me that Lewis' theory of motive is that your client, a black man, became murderously jealous when his mistress, a black woman, dumped him for a Jewish man."

"You're doing your best to hype this, aren't you?"

"Wasn't me who invented the facts, so don't kill the messenger. My crack research staff also informs me that there was some postmortem mutilation of the body." In the style of a carnival barker, Rutherford warned, "Folks, if you have minors in the room, get them out of earshot." She gazed into the camera for seconds, as if watching youngsters being herded out, before saying, in undertone, "The killer cut off the rabbi's penis, presumably in ridicule of Jewish circumcision tradition." Rutherford's eyes did their thing, for effect.

"Since the indictment, all those particulars have appeared in print. Your crack research staff probably reads the Detroit newspapers." After that little putdown, Rose said, "Yes, there was a murder. Yes, there was mutilation. No, my client didn't commit them. Motives assigned to him are meaningless."

The space between Rutherford's eyebrows bunched, as though from confusion, as she asked, "If not your client, then who? Better yet, will you be pointing the finger at someone else?"

"I'm not going to show my hand before the trial."

"Albeit," continued Rutherford, "one might think there'd be no shortage of suspects, given the crime rate in Detroit."

"You can lose viewers with a comment like that."

"I wasn't bashing the city," claimed Rutherford. "Just stating the sad truth. I just as well could have mentioned the dismal closure rate on homicides."

Recognizing apophasis when she hears it, Rose responded, "You did mention it. Intentionally."

Back in the referenced city, Mary sat up, leaned forward, and then said, "That's right, Lisa. Call her out."

Cliff put a hand on Mary's shoulder and pulled her back. "Cheer for Rose, if you want, only don't forget that she represents the man you arrested for murder."

"I wasn't cheering and I haven't forgotten," Mary said, head turned, to hide the conflicted look on her face.

"Now, back to the righteous reverend," declared Rutherford. "You moved for a speedy trial, even though it's a first-degree murder case, didn't you?"

"True."

"Well, shades of that former, knife-wielding football star, whom we won't bother to name."

"Every day my client is in jail is a miscarriage of justice. The prosecutor's case is as weak as they come."

"And you want to make sure that he has the least amount of time to strengthen it."

"There's nothing out there with which to strengthen it."

Cliff glanced again at Mary, to see whether the lead investigator would voice a dissenting opinion. None.

"Isn't the trial date right around the corner?" asked Rutherford.

"A sharp corner."

Rutherford said, "Well, we courtroom observers have something to look forward to, because there's always some pyrotechnics with a Lisa Rose trial. I would wish you success, Sweetie, but that sentiment is reserved for justice, whichever way it falls. All I want is for the guilty to be punished and the innocent to go free."

"That's what justice is all about," cosigned Rose.

Rutherford shook her head in disagreement and said, "Don't give me that. Defense attorneys want the guilty to go free, too, if that person is a client."

Rose, smiling, heaved a sigh of tolerance and said, "Clarice. Clarice. Defense attorneys don't win cases. Prosecutors lose them. Prosecutors have the resources of government at their disposal. Furthermore, they aren't supposed to spend taxpayers' dollars on a trial unless they feel certain that their case is strong."

"Nice little speech," complimented Rutherford. "Does it explain why, as a prosecutor, you resigned from those first charges brought against Mueller? You never went on record with your reasons."

"Back to him, are you? Am I detecting a crush?"

"I have a segment to fill, Lisa Rose."

"I practice civil law, also. That's something you can ask about."

"I'd almost forgotten," claimed Rutherford. "Defense, civil, a little corporate on the side. I swear, you wear more hats than all my church-going aunts, put together."

"For example, I'm representing a woman with Stage IV breast cancer, the victim of gross medical malpractice. A mother, mind you."

At the Cunningham abode, Mary became rigid with attention. Cliff focused on the screen, awaiting the follow-up.

"Interesting, I'm sure it is," said Rutherford, "but my producer is giving me the signal to wrap up." She then said, "Folks, we've had the rare pleasure of hearing from one of the most brilliant and controversial attorneys out there, and a good friend of mine, I'm not ashamed to admit, Lisa Rose. As for you, Lisa, hurry back."

"Anytime, Clarice."

"In the meantime, keep doing your thing, which seems to be representing anybody who will pay you." Rutherford placed a finger to her temple, in fake contemplation, and added, "Sounds like a legal version of the world's oldest profession, if you ask me."

"Well, you did compare me to your aunts," was Rose's rejoinder.

"Ouch!" exclaimed Rutherford, who wet the tip of an index finger and pretended to mark an invisible scorecard in front of her face. "We're going to have to end this round with you one-up. Until the next bell, kissy-kissy, Lisa Rose."

Rose chuckled and signed off with, "Good night, Clarice."

Eager to escape before the channel was switched to Home and Garden, Cliff lingered long enough to ask, "So, what did you think?"

A simple enough question, but Mary didn't have a ready reply.

38.

Later on the day that young Lisa awoke to find Yetta missing, Lisa's head was bobbling, as time and again, she said, "Yes, Grandfather."

Motoring along, Bernie's sight was fixed on the road, except when he was looking in his rearview mirror at Lisa in the back seat. Each time that he remembered something else to add to the lecture, he would adjust the mirror, and via it, achieve eye contact. "And, another thing," he started, although his coming words would be almost a verbatim repeat, "you are to be seen and not heard."

Once more, it was, "Yes, Grandfather."

His point having been remade, Bernie readjusted the mirror back to where it could perform its designed purpose. Then he readjusted the volume on the radio back to a decibel suitable to his impaired hearing, a result of his military service in Europe during World War II.

The lecturing had begun at breakfast concerning how Lisa was to behave. It had been such a reading of the riot act that it sapped her appetite, although, out of fretfulness, she almost drank the entire carton of orange juice. She hadn't relaxed in the interim, her thoughts racing, captivated by the prospect of finally seeing where her grandfather worked, the place that, literally, puts food on their table, the place that, figuratively, he never leaves. It was the same place, that, throughout her short life, she'd constantly heard him allude to, praise, defend, and force-fit into any conversation that he could.

Bernie turned into the parking lot and steered his two-tone Cadillac to his reserved spot at the back of the building. After throwing the gear lever into park, he rested an outstretched right arm along the top of the front passenger seat and twisted his torso to address Lisa, face-to-face. Then, he cocked his right forearm, which allowed him to shake his index finger at her as he spoke. "And most of all, you will not speak about family matters," he directed. "Clear?"

Lisa's head bobbled in obeisance, faster than his finger shook. "Yes, Grandfather."

Bernie turned back around, then mumbled, "They're not above trying to pry information from a child because they're yentas," referring to the office gals as nosey busybodies.

Lisa sat in silent confusion about who "they" were, having not been told that she was to wait in the office, a cubbyhole crammed with three women who did bookkeeping, order-processing, and invoicing.

"Get out of the car," Bernie said, then did so himself. He stood erect and proud, as he gave rapid pats against his thigh, a gesture that told Lisa to stand next to him on that side. Their walking hand-in-hand would be beneficial to his image. He held out his palm but she didn't grab it.

Lisa was transfixed, shivering, her faculties pelted by a hailstorm of stimuli. There were the smells that imposed themselves individually, even as they combined for the most wretched stench she'd ever encountered. There were the entangled sounds: the wails of the condemned-in-waiting; the screeches of those being herded to their fate; and, the exclamations of those meeting their doom. Her besieged mind could not reconcile present conditions with what she'd long imaged. Nothing jibed in the least with the many crayon drawings she'd made. And despite what she'd heard from Bernie all of her life, how could anything humane and merciful be happening in that gray, brooding, low-slung building.

"What's the matter with you?" Bernie demanded, not knowing nor suspecting. The very things that were terrorizing Lisa, were second—make that first—nature to him. He never foresaw that she'd react as she was doing. If he'd had such a blind spot as a motorist, he'd have died on the highway long ago.

"I'm scared, Grandfather."

Harshly, Bernie assured, "There's nothing to be afraid of." The office was in the front of the building, and his plan to take her there through the back wasn't playing out well. He hadn't wanted to go through the trouble of temporarily parking in the front, taking her inside, and then parking in the back. He still could go through those gyrations, but that would be yielding to someone else's will—a child's, at that. So, he knelt on one knee in front of Lisa but in no way to beg. Stealthily, he untied both of her shoelaces and then began to slowly retie them, such that anyone watching would think that he was being solicitous of his granddaughter. Under that guise, he dictated, "You listen and listen well," the phony smile inconsistent with the threatening tone, "I'm not going to tolerate this nonsense."

"But, Grandfather—"

"No buts." He stood and pretended to brush something off her shoulders. He bowed to circumstances only enough to explain, "You won't be here long, only until Mrs. Cohen comes for you."

But a trembling Lisa said, "Let me wait for her in the car. Please, Grandfather."

Her request being out of the question, Bernie was through being the nice despot. He made a stabbing grab for her hand; she was faster in hiding it. He redirected his aim to her arm, successfully. Having snared her, he switched his hold to around her wrist and began the trek to the building.

Lisa resisted with her entire weight yet was pulled along as helplessly as a three-legged kitten on a chain. Even so, and despite her terror, she knew not to scream, acutely aware of her grandfather's intolerance for public spectacle. By the time they entered the door, she had submitted to his strength and had adopted the tactic of keeping pace but with arms wrapped around his waist and her face buried into his side.

From the sunlight streaming through the windows on the east wall and from the galaxy of overhead ceiling bulbs, the place was lit like a reading room for the far-sighted, causing a pink-orange screen to flicker behind Lisa's tightly-shut eyelids. Playing on that screen was a movie, projected by her imagination, of what might be transpiring around her, none of it good. It played to a horrific soundtrack and to smells that were more suited to a restroom than to a concession stand. Lisa quickened her blind steps, getting out of stride with Bernie, until she readjusted. And then, Bernie halted abruptly.

Lisa was certain that the sudden stop wasn't because they'd reached their destination. Not knowing why they'd come to a standstill and too fearful to open her eyes, she nuzzled deeper into Bernie.

He plucked her off, as he might a cockleburr. "Stay here. I'll be back soon."

Frantic, Lisa cried out, "No!" then found herself standing alone.

39.

"You'll be the third witness to take the stand," said Gerald Lewis, seated at his desk. "The medical examiner will go first to establish cause and method of death and then I'm calling the officer who went to the home and discovered the rabbi's body."

Mary, who'd made the short walk from Detroit Police Headquarters to the Frank Murphy Hall of Justice which houses the Wayne County Prosecutor's Offices, acknowledged with a nod.

"Coffee?"

"No."

"It's ice coffee." Lewis tried to entice by shaking the pot side-to-side, making the cubes rattle. "Better than ice water on a scorcher like this."

"No," Mary repeated, and not just because the room was comfortably air-conditioned. "I'm not a coffee-drinker."

Lewis filled his coffee mug and took a first swallow. "You're going to be seated at the prosecutor's table throughout the trial."

Mary, seated in a swivel chair, turned left, turned right, lowered her eyes, and then said, "I wonder why."

"I can do without the sarcasm."

Mary conspicuously looked at her watch and announced, "I have other things to do, so if it's all the same with you, let's get started."

"I want to get you out of here as soon as possible, believe me."

"I know you mean that in the nicest way," said Mary.

"But first, I want to get something out in the open." Lewis placed his right elbow on the armrest, hand raised, fingers folded, thumb straight, allowing him to punctuate with that hammering motion so popular with politicians. "I'm not accustomed to one of my witnesses having connections with the defense attorney."

The allusion obvious, Mary folded her arms, cocked her head, ready to react, as she asked, "Are you concerned that I've discussed the McArthur case with Lisa?"

"No, I give you more credit than that."

"What, then?"

"Well," said Lewis, "there was the Clarice Rutherford show, when Rose mentioned your mother's case, with some regard, I might add." Then he went more direct. "If you feel some kind of camaraderie with Rose, it can reduce your effectiveness as a prosecution witness."

Mary swiveled the chair to full-frontal and looked him squarely in the eyes. "See here, Gerald, this is a new one for me, too. But I'll handle it professionally."

Lewis raised the coffee mug to his lips, delaying, contemplating about whether he'd made his point. He decided that he had. "As I said, you'll sit at the prosecutor's table during trial."

"I heard you the first time."

"Rose is going to exploit your contentious history with McArthur and portray you as vindictive."

"I'm expecting that," said Mary.

"And there's the epithet."

"The what?"

"That nickname. I'm not saying that it's earned, but it is what it is, and Rose is going to play it up."

"So to counter that, you want me on display in front of the jury."

With some impatience, Lewis said, "Sorry, if you feel objectified, but I have a case to win and I have to play the hand I was dealt."

"I don't have any hurt feelings, and if I did, it would be up to me to deal with them."

"Good. So let's get down to what matters. When she cross-examines you, expect her to attack the investigation."

"And the entire homicide unit," added Mary.

"You bet. When she does, show her that you have a pair."

Feistily, Mary asked, "A pair of what?"

"Just an expression, that's all. No need to get all worked up." Then Lewis smiled slyly and said, "Though I'm glad to see a flash of that famous assertiveness of yours. Save some of it for trial."

Mary, suspecting that she'd been manipulated, asked, "Whatever happened to getting me out of here as soon as possible?"

"There's that assertiveness, again." He stood, to conduct business on his feet. He always moved about while prepping a witness. It got him into character. Practice the same way you play. He had never worked a case with Mary, at least not this directly. Back when he was just another prosecutor and before she made lieutenant, he'd worked a couple of her cases, but called the lead investigator to the stand, not her. "You're an old hand at this, Mary. This prep session shouldn't take long." He made a fist and slapped the other palm around it, in warm-up. However, he digressed to say, "Mind if I ask how your mother is doing?"

"She's doing badly."

40.

The reason that young Lisa suddenly found herself standing alone, frozen in fear, was that Bernie had dashed away to prevent something intolerable.

A cow, tan except for white down its front, was suspended upside down, its hind leg chain-shackled to a hoist. A minute earlier, a shochet had waited as his assistant clamped tongs inside the cow's nostrils to pull its neck taut. The assistant didn't get a chance to exert control, because the cow, terrified from being dangled and in pain from a broken leg, whipped its huge head sideways. To avoid being struck, the shochet jumped a step backward, accidentally dropping his chalef, which he instantly picked up, and then stepped forward to perform his job.

Bernie, face flush with anger, arrived in time to grab the shochet's wrist and bellowed, "What do you think you're doing, for God's sake!"

The shochet, although stocky, stammered, "Mr. Rosenberg, please," in pleading for relief from the painful grip. When it was granted, he said, "I'm afraid that I don't understand what you mean." He was younger than Bernie, even younger than Bernie had been upon becoming a shochet.

Bernie, who resented the fair-haired, recent hire, of whom he felt hadn't paid his dues, loudly proclaimed, "You dropped your chalef. Could it be nicked? You don't know, because you didn't inspect it."

Now the younger shochet understood his transgression. Shame registered in his eyes and his head dropped, as though from a hypnotist's command. Eyes still lowered, the shochet said, "You're right, Mr. Rosenberg. What could I have been thinking?"

"You weren't, obviously. Unless, you haven't learned Sh'chitah," Bernie said, referring to the laws of kosher slaughter.

"I know them, Mr. Rosenberg."

"You have a peculiar way of showing it," Bernie accused, loudly, so that everyone nearby could hear. "Sh'chitah requires a chalef that's razor sharp, hard, and smooth. It has to be inspected before each use. An imperfect chalef can't cut cleanly. The animal suffers, needlessly."

"It'll never happen again, Mr. Rosenberg," promised the younger shochet, aware of his probationary status and that the incident could result in his dismissal.

Bernie, also aware of the dismissal possibility, continued the dress-down, trying to disguise his agenda and counting on by-standers to report the incident to the Fleischman family, owners of the facility. "You were not given this job to produce n'veilah," he reminded, referring to botched kills that can't be sold as kosher. "Have some regard for your employer."

"I do, Mr. Rosenberg."

Bernie's stare was unrelenting as he irritably announced, "Well, I'm waiting."

The intimidated and confused shochet asked, "Waiting for what, Mr. Rosenberg?"

"For you to examine your chalef."

There are different chalefs for different animals. This one being for cattle, was about 16 inches long and 2 1/4 inches wide, with a hard, wavy handle for a secure grip.

"Right away, Sir." Struggling to keep nervousness from affecting his hands, the young shochet cradled the handle in his left hand and examined the blade by slowly running the fingernail of his right index finger along the top of the cutting edge, back and forth, then again. Next, the fingernail ran along one side of the blade then the other. "It seems to be fine, Mr. Rosenberg."

"Seems?"

"It is fine."

Bernie allowed seconds to tick away before he said, "And now, your chalef is fit for a kosher kill."

The younger shochet, who'd been holding his breath, exhaled and said, "Thank you, Mr. Rosenberg. For everything."

Both men had maintained a safe distance from the thrashings of the still suspended cow. The reason for inverting an animal is exsanguination, the draining of blood that otherwise could deteriorate and putrefy within the animal. Additionally, Sh'chitah requires that the animal be conscious at the time of slaughter. Death is to be quick, achieved by a swift, uninterrupted incision, severing the jugular, carotid, and windpipe, the belief being that the animal immediately and mercifully loses consciousness and never feels a thing.

As for Lisa, she was able to hear the exchanges but understood little. Throughout, she'd stood motionless—not counting the trembling—eyelids glued, but other faculties working overtime, bombarding her with scary stimuli. As if she needed something else to contend with, her bladder was begging relief from the orange juice that she'd drunk at breakfast.

She squeezed her thighs bloodless, the urge growing ever stronger. To pee on herself in public would be mortifying. She braved opening her eyes into slits, hoping to glimpse Bernie and be rescued. A desperate sweep and her vision locked on him.

Bernie was standing near the younger shochet, evaluating, waiting. For what, was soon to become evident.

Before Lisa knew to look away, she saw the younger shochet, under Bernie's scrutiny, slash the cow's throat, ending in mid-utterance a plaintive moo.

Lisa's eyelids flew so wide open that she felt strain in the eye sockets. The cow's blood gushed in a half-circular torrent. Lisa's own gush was vertical. It felt warm down her legs then cold and slushy in her socks.

Lisa jerked her head and saw daylight through the wire-reinforced glass in a distant door, unknown to her, the same door through which she'd entered. It represented a definite way out of this hellish place. And although a mystery door was closer, it contained no glass through which to give indication of what awaited on the other side. She chose the sure thing.

Lisa sprinted, pee sloshing between her toes. Once outdoors, maybe by some miracle, she'll find the car unlocked, allowing her to curl up on the rear floor and conveniently die. She raced toward the door, not hearing Bernie's shouts for her to halt, not that she would have heeded.

A worker, farther away, sized up the situation and intercepted Lisa, lifting her off her feet, just before she would have burst through the door. The worker's cooing words did nothing to calm the hysterical child, who was twisting and resisting so violently that there was danger of her dislocating a joint.

The crisis defused, Bernie began a quick, dignified walk toward his granddaughter. He shouldn't have been planning how he was going to give the impression of being consoling and understanding. He shouldn't have been planning his words. Shouldn't have been doing anything other than paying attention to his path.

Had he, he would have noticed that farther down the slaughter line another cow was about to be hoisted. The motor droned, the chain rattled then snapped tight, and the cow's shackled leg cleared the floor. The animal, white, patched with black, was prime slaughter weight. Its front hoofs barely yet in contact with the floor, the cow struggled, causing its body to rotate, as it unleashed a vicious kick with its free hind leg—no planned timing—just as Bernie was passing.

Bernie landed nine feet away, his right side pelvis, hip socket, and elbow shattered, downed not by the disease but by no less a mad cow.

Lisa, still being held by the worker who'd thwarted her escape, fought for a backward look to see whether Bernie was coming. When she gained it, she saw Bernie writhing on the floor, at least some of him, because most of the view was obstructed by the surrounding crowd.

41.

Gerald Lewis, standing, asked, "Is it true that a .357 Magnum revolver can fire .38 caliber ammunition?"

"Objection," said Lisa Rose, seated. "The witness has not been qualified by the Court as a ballistics expert."

"The question doesn't require such expertise, Your Honor," responded Lewis. "I'm not asking about trajectory, barrel markings, or the like. As a career police officer, the witness either knows the answer or not."

Judge Boyce Ellington, addressing the witness, asked, "Do you know the answer?"

"Yes, Your Honor," replied Mary.

"Objection overruled," said Ellington, in his third elected term, his stately courtroom persona so opposite his other, that of the flamboyant man-about-town bachelor. "The witness may answer."

"A .357 Magnum revolver can fire .38 caliber ammunition." Mary was dressed in pastels: a pink skirt of below-the-knee length with matching jacket and a blue blouse. Her earrings were simple plastic loops, also pink. The shoes were conservative, black pumps. The dainty white purse strung on her shoulder wasn't remindful of a holster. A couple of times, already, she'd brought her left hand to her face, ostensibly in thought, but in reality for the jurors to see her wedding ring. Just an everyday wife and mother who happened to work homicide.

"And was it .38 caliber bullets that killed Rabbi Winkler?"

"Yes."

"Lieutenant Cunningham," said Lewis, "did there come a time when you associated the ownership of a .357 Magnum revolver with the defendant?"

"Yes."

"Tell the jury how that came about."

Mary turned toward the jury, served a smile so pleasant that it only lacked a curtsey, then answered, "I'd been told by Ms. Alison Petrocelli—"

"Objection, hearsay," spoke Rose. "The state should produce Ms. Petrocelli to speak for herself."

"Your Honor, the witness was about to relate an exchange stemming from her investigation of this murder case. In that limited capacity, it is an exception to hearsay. Furthermore, Ms. Petrocelli will be called to the stand later."

"Overruled."

"You were about to relate something that Ms. Petrocelli told you, Lieutenant," reminded Lewis.

"Ms. Petrocelli told me that Reverend Jeeter McArthur owned a .357 Magnum revolver."

"Did she tell you how she came by that knowledge or belief?"

"Yes. She said that he had shown it to her and that he'd called it a .357 Magnum."

"Lieutenant, as you sit here today, has Ms. Petrocelli's statement been your sole reliance regarding such gun ownership by the defendant?"

"No. I ran a records check, which revealed that the defendant owned a registered .357 Magnum revolver."

"Did you interview the defendant about such ownership?"

"Yes. He said that the gun was missing and that he did not know how that came to be."

"Since the defendant is not the only owner of a .357 Magnum, registered or not, how did the defendant become a person of interest in your investigation?"

"Ms. Petrocelli told me the defendant made threats about giving Rabbi Winkler a circumcision."

"And what associations and interpretations did you make with that comment?"

"Mutilation."

"Of the type committed on the rabbi?"

"Yes."

"At the time that Ms. Petrocelli told you about the circumcision comment, had the mutilation been made public?"

"No."

"So, Ms. Petrocelli would have had no way of knowing about the mutilation?"

"Objection," said Rose. "Beyond the knowledge of this witness."

The judge, agreeing, said, "Sustained."

Lewis next asked, "Was a search warrant ever served on the defendant?"

"Yes."

"Were you present at the time of serving?"

"Yes."

"What, if anything, resulted, as far as evidence?"

"A crime technician discovered a red speck in the defendant's vehicle."

"Located where in the vehicle?"

"The ignition switch, on the edge facing away from the driver." "For clarification," said Lewis, "was the ignition located on the steering column?"

"Objection. Counselor is leading the witness," Rose calmly noted.

"Sustained," said the judge.

So Lewis reworded. "Where was the ignition switch located?"

"On the steering column."

"Was the speck visible by someone seated in the driver's seat?"

"No."

"How do you know?"

"I sat in the seat to test whether I could see the speck from that position."

"Then it's possible that the defendant did not know of its presence, correct?"

"Objection," said Rose. "Calls for speculation."

"Sustained."

Lewis went on to his next question. "Was the speck subjected to laboratory testing?"

"Objection," said Rose. "Unless the witness performed the testing or directly witnessed it, she has no direct knowledge to base an answer."

"That's ridiculous, Your Honor," returned Lewis. "Such collaborating and communicating between investigators and technicians are routine. I won't ask the lieutenant to explain testing procedures. I'll reserve such questions for when the lab technician takes the stand."

"Overruled."

Knowing she'd been cleared to answer, Mary said, "Yes, the speck was subjected to laboratory testing."

"Were the results reported to you?"

"Yes."

"Share them with the Court."

"The speck was human blood."

"Was the blood successfully tested for DNA?"

"Yes."

"And those results also reported to you?"

"Yes."

After an intentional pause, Lewis slowly asked, "Whose blood was it?"

"Rabbi Allan Winkler."

Lewis took a few steps closer to the jury box. From there he asked, "Any other significant evidence resulting from that search?"

"Yes. Also on the ignition switch, same side, was a spot of flour."

To prevent confusion, Lewis asked, "By that, you mean the baking variety and not the plant, correct?"

"Correct."

"Why was flour significant, Lieutenant Cunningham?"

"At the crime scene, on a kitchen counter, there was flour, like someone had been rolling dough, baking, maybe from the night before."

"Okay," said Lewis. "Is there a further significance?"

"Yes. Next to that area was a set of knives in a butcher block holder, except one was missing."

"Did you find that missing knife?"

"Yes. Next to the body, with blood on it that testing showed came from Rabbi Winkler."

"As the lead detective, Lieutenant Cunningham, do you have a theory of how the blood of Rabbi Winkler, as well as the flour, got on the ignition switch of the defendant's vehicle?"

"Yes." *Okay, Mary. Look and speak like you don't have an ax to grind,* she told herself. "The killer contacted the flour from the counter upon grabbing the knife from the block and contacted blood upon committing the mutilation. The flour and blood got on the sleeve of the killer and made contact with the ignition switch when the killer started the vehicle."

In Lewis' opening statement to the jury, he had promised evidence of that sequence. Now, his eyebrows relaxed from their once held-high arch, reflecting his satisfaction with how Mary had answered the question. "When you first were assigned the case, did you immediately consider the defendant a suspect?"

"No."

"Was your investigation, in any way, influenced by a dislike of the defendant, held by you or the police department?"

"No."

"Do you hold a vendetta against the defendant?"

"No."

"Did you go about this investigation in your established way?"

"Yes."

"No further questions at this time, Your Honor. Thank you very much, Lieutenant Cunningham."

"You're welcome."

As Mary awaited cross-examination, she placed her hands on her lap. She began massaging her knuckles, the activity hidden by the witness box. She was stimulating circulation and easing a little arthritic stiffness, that, or symbolically readying for interrogatory fisticuffs, which she expected would be of the bare-knuckles variety.

42.

Lisa Rose, in a black knit dress accented with a silver broach, asked, "What brand of flour was allegedly discovered on the ignition switch of Reverend McArthur's vehicle?"

"I'm not sure I understand the question," Mary claimed, stalling.

With impatience, Rose said, "The brand, the label, the maker of the product."

"I don't know."

"What is it about the flour allegedly—"

"Objection to the repeated use of the word, allegedly, Your Honor," said Lewis.

"Give us a break, Counselor," said the judge, in a tone that made it clear that he would follow with, "Overruled."

"What is it about the flour allegedly," repeated Rose, emphasizing that word to vex Lewis, "discovered that differentiates it from other flour?"

"I don't know."

Following up, Rose said, "Whatever the brand, type, or variety of the flour, you're not claiming that the only place where it's used is the Winkler household, are you?"

"No."

With sharpness, Rose asked, "You can't state with any degree of reasonable certainty where that flour came from, can you?"

"No."

"And you can't say that it came from the crime scene, to the exclusion of all other possibilities, can you?"

"No."

Rose paused, as was her habit before switching topics, similar to a writer starting a new paragraph.

Mary used the pause to monitor the courtroom. She took note of the cameraman and a familiar face or two in the gallery. She made an inconspicuous study of the jury and bet herself which one would be appointed foreperson.

Rose resumed with, "An owner not knowing the whereabouts of his gun, is that unheard of?"

"No."

"Guns get stolen, don't they?"

"Some."

"You testified that a .357 Magnum revolver can fire .38 caliber ammunition, didn't you?"

"Yes."

"But isn't it true that a .357 Magnum revolver also can fire .357 caliber ammunition?"

"Yes."

"And isn't it true that a .38 Smith & Wesson revolver can fire both .38 caliber and .357 caliber ammunition?"

"Yes."

"Given those multiple possibilities," said Rose, "isn't it true that the only way to determine if a particular bullet was fired from a particular gun is to submit both to ballistics testing?"

"Yes."

"Which is what was done in this case, correct?"

"No."

Feigning confusion, Rose said, "No?!" She looked combatively at Mary and then asked, "Why not?"

"We never recovered the gun."

Rose looked at the jury and slowly said, "We never recovered the gun."

"Objection," said Lewis. "Ms. Rose is not a parrot. The jury doesn't need her repeating the witness' answers."

"Maybe not," said the judge, "but I'll allow for individual style." In compromise, he said, "Overruled, but don't overdo it, Ms. Rose."

"I won't, Your Honor." Rose returned her attention to the witness. "Lieutenant Cunningham, let's summarize. Reverend McArthur sits charged with murder and the police have no murder weapon, fair to say?"

"Yes."

"And before we leave the subject of weapons, isn't it your theory that the mutilation was performed with the knife that the police took from the crime scene?"

"Yes."

"That same knife had the rabbi's blood on it, didn't it?"

"Yes."

"But what it didn't have on it were Reverend McArthur's fingerprints, isn't that true?"

"Yes."

Rose took another transitional pause and then said, "I want to follow up on the discussion of blood. What was found on the knife is not the only sample that you have, true?"

"You'll have to clarify that for me," said Mary, appreciative of the opportunity to break the monopoly of one-word responses.

"Gladly. You, meaning the police department, have the victim's bloody clothing, don't you?"

"Yes."

"Additional blood was supplied to you from the autopsy, wasn't it?"

"Yes."

"So, when weeks after the murder, blood magically appears—"

"Objection to such characterization, Your Honor," said, Lewis.

"I doubt that anyone on the jury believes in magic," said the judge, which drew snickers. "Overruled."

Although she didn't have to, Rose reworded the question. Unfortunately for the other side, the revision could not have been more inflammatory. "Given that the police had blood in their possession, any blood allegedly discovered in the reverend's vehicle could have been planted. True or false?"

"Objection!" Lewis proclaimed, leaping to his feet and in the process banging his knee. Ignoring the pain, he said, "This is preposterous. Ms. Rose has no good-faith basis for posing that question. The witness should be instructed not to answer and the jury told to disregard the question."

"Your Honor," said Rose, "the question asks whether it's possible that the blood was planted. It's not the same as an accusation."

The judge waved a palm, indicating that he didn't need to hear further from either side, then ruled, "Mere possibility is too wide a latitude. The foundation for the question is inadequate. Objection sustained." Then he instructed, "The jury will disregard that last question."

Just as Rose had anticipated; nonetheless, the jury had heard the question, and the vigorous objection had stamped it on its collective mind. There might be a jury member given to conspiracy theories. It only takes one holdout to avoid a conviction. "Thank you, Your Honor," she said, as amiably as if he had ruled in her favor.

"Proceed," said the judge.

Obeying, Rose stated, "You were asked by the prosecutor whether you went about this investigation in your established way and you answered in the affirmative. Remember that?"

"Yes."

"That doesn't hold for the arrest and booking, since both were videotaped, does it?"

"It wasn't the first time we've videotaped somebody."

Harshly, Rose said, "My question dealt with established procedure. Do you usually videotape arrests and bookings?"

"No."

"So why this time?"

"Orders."

"From whom?"

"Objection," said Lewis. "Such videotaping is legal. Who gave the order is irrelevant."

"It's relevant, Your Honor," argued Rose. "This witness gave the false impression that Reverend McArthur was treated routinely. To the contrary, police procedure was unconventional, and I should be allowed to explore why."

"If anything," said Lewis, "the defendant received preferential treatment and was treated more than fairly."

"Unlike incidences of police brutality that don't get videotaped, you mean?" asked Rose.

"Reframe from such comments, Ms. Rose," chided the judge. "Plus, you know better than to directly engage Mr. Lewis."

"I apologize, Your Honor."

The judge then said, "No privilege protects the decision to videotape. Objection overruled."

"Who gave the order to videotape the arrest and booking?" asked Rose, more sternly.

"Mr. Lewis."

"Mr. Lewis, the prosecutor?"

"Yes."

Lewis seemed unmoved. Back when he'd prepped Mary, he'd anticipated that Rose would bring up the videotaping. He'd instructed Mary to artfully dodge, but if cornered, to answer truthfully.

Rose asked, "You videotaped because Reverend McArthur was not the average arrestee, was he?"

"He was as far as I was concerned," claimed Mary.

"Oh, really?" asked Rose. "Are you familiar with the organization he heads, called the K-9's?"

"Yes."

"Isn't it a community watchdog organization?"

"Allegedly," said Mary, borrowing the term.

"And at times, hasn't that organization made public accusations against the Detroit police?"

"You'll have to be more specific."

"Okay. Various charges of police brutality, yes?"

"Yes."

"Various charges of police corruption, yes?"

"Yes."

"The organization even brought federal attention to the Detroit police practice of arresting and jailing reluctant witnesses didn't it?"

"Yes."

"And the practice was ruled unconstitutional and the police department was ordered to cease the practice, much to its embarrassment, true?"

"I don't know about the embarrassment part, but the rest is true."

"Isn't it a fact that the Detroit police department doesn't like Reverend McArthur?"

"Objection," said Lewis. "Lieutenant Cunningham doesn't speak for the entire police department."

Rose immediately said, "That wasn't the impression I got during direct." She flipped a page of her legal pad, scrolled her finger down to a section, tapped it hard, and recapped, "Mr. Lewis asked this witness, and I quote, 'Was your investigation, in any way, influenced by a dislike of the defendant, held by you or the police department?'"

The judge traced his mustache and goatee with his index and thumb and nodded receptively, indicative of how he was about to rule; yet, he asked, "Any further comment, Mr. Lewis?"

"Yes, if—"

"I withdraw the question," inserted Rose. "So that you can speak on your own behalf, my question to you now is, isn't it a fact that you, personally, don't like Reverend McArthur?"

"That is not a fact."

"To your knowledge, has Reverend McArthur ever referred to you as, Bloody Mary?"

"Yes."

"We'll get into specifics in a minute. But first, you dislike being called Bloody Mary, don't you?"

"Yes."

"Actually, you hate it, don't you?"

"I dislike it," was all Mary would admit. *Where'd they get this cheap-ass chair,* she thought, now aware that coils were pressing unevenly against her bottom; however, she chose not to shift, concerned that it might be regarded as squirming.

"But it wasn't Reverend McArthur who coined the name, because for years you've been called Bloody Mary within the police ranks, haven't you?"

"By a few," Mary said, charitably. *Ass-holes, each and every one,* she thought, less charitably. Mary knew that this part of the cross-examination would come, and Lewis had instructed her to refrain from any show of anger; still, she felt her jaw tighten, as she willed, *Don't let it get to you.*

"Tell us, Lieutenant, how many citizens have you shot and killed?"

"Objection, Your Honor. Has no relevance to this case," argued Lewis.

"Has to do with Lieutenant Cunningham's history with Reverend McArthur and his organization, who have heaped public criticism against her. Your Honor, I should have the right to explore whether dislike or prejudice by this witness played a part in her investigation, regardless of her denials."

"I'll allow the question," said the judge, "but tighten the connection, Counselor."

"Yes, Your Honor. How many citizens have you shot and killed, Lieutenant?"

But Lewis kept slugging, saying, "Objection to the use of the word, citizens. Is Ms. Rose distinguishing between citizens and foreigners, between citizens and the military? No. She's playing on the word, hoping the jury will interpret citizens to mean innocent people."

Judge Ellington smiled wearily, perhaps wondering if Solomon had had it as hard, and queried, "Would you be willing to rephrase the question, Ms. Rose?"

"Yes. Lieutenant Cunningham how many people have you killed?"

"Three, all of them ruled self-defense and justifiable."

"Through internal investigations," clarified Rose. "Police investigating police. Wasn't that the case each time?"

"Yes, that's established procedure."

"Isn't it true that the vast majority of police officers have never fired a weapon in the line of duty, let alone shot someone, let alone killed someone?"

"I don't know but I hope that would be the case."

"I'll come from another angle. How many officers do you personally know who have three notches on their gun handle?"

"Objection to the gunslinger characterization," interjected Lewis. "It's unprofessional and prejudicial."

"I withdraw the question. Maybe you've been unlucky, Lieutenant," Rose allowed, then insinuatingly added, "or maybe not, since the shootings didn't stop your promotions."

"Objection. Argumentative."

Sounding annoyed, the judge said, "Sustained."

"Reverend McArthur took particular exception to the third shooting, calling you an assassin with a badge, didn't he?"

"Yes."

"And didn't he and his organization lead demonstrations calling for you to be fired and prosecuted?"

"Yes."

"And yet, it's with a straight face that you tell this jury that you don't dislike him?"

"Objection, Your Honor," said Lewis. "Asked and answered. Counselor is badgering the witness."

The judge drew a breath, about to rule, when suddenly, he turned his head toward the witness stand and inquired, "Are you alright, Lieutenant Cunningham?"

Mary was bent forward in the chair, head bowed, a palm covering her eyes. Her shoulders heaved, keeping time with the sniffling. "I'm sorry, Your Honor. I'll try to compose myself."

"May I offer you some tissue?" asked the judge. "Water? Do you need to take a break?"

From the same broken posture, Mary said, "Thank you, but no. I think that I can hold up." She retrieved from her purse a hankie. She dangled it and it unfolded, revealing itself as laced linen. She dabbed her eyes, taking in snatches of breath though her mouth, the microphone amplifying to full effect. Whimpering, she nasally said, "The flashbacks are so easily brought on, Your Honor."

"Flashbacks, you say?" asked the judge.

"From having come so close to death those times, Your Honor."

An accommodating judge said, "Take whatever time you need."

"Thank you." Mary kept the hankie busy around her eyes, a tactic to hide the absence of tears. In between the dabbing, she stole a peek at Lewis, who wasn't a co-conspirator and who was observing helplessly, although hopingly. And, of course, she peeked at Rose.

Rose was not taken in by the performance; then again, she knew that she was not the targeted audience. She made a quick evaluation of the jury and read sympathy in the faces of several, the worse being a blue-haired senior who looked as if she wanted to sooth Mary with hugs and kisses, or maybe even cradle Mary's head in her ample bosom. Rose, sneering, strategically announced, "No further questions for this witness."

43.

Ross Brogan turned off the rider mower and dismounted. "No way," he assured. "You can go back the way you came."

Mary continued to approach from the driveway, a corrugated box tucked under an arm. "You can't go back on your word."

"You conned me."

"No, I didn't."

"That's your idea of a few photos and miscellaneous?"

"So I underestimated a tad," Mary admitted. "You want me to beg? Alright, I'm begging."

"I had it a lot better before you started confiding in me. Back then, you weren't intruding on my vacation days." Brogan shook his head in displeasure, but relented. "Come inside and let's see what you got."

Just before going through the door, Mary noted, "Your neighbor across the street apparently was never taught that it's impolite to stare."

Brogan gave a sharp salute to the guy who was standing on the porch, then confidentially told Mary, "It's the box. He's probably scared you're moving in."

"Same old Warrendale," Mary said, of that neighborhood of Detroit where many a white cop resides.

Inside, Brogan said, "Give it here," and then placed the box on the dining room table. "I can only offer you some water, if that's okay."

"I don't want anything."

Brogan laid down his safety goggles. "What am I supposed to look for?"

"I'm not sure."

"That narrows it."

"Will you let me finish? I need you to go through this stuff and group what seems related."

"Related how?"

Mary dug into the box and pulled out a handful of photos. She slid them around. Then she gave a studying gaze. A notion came to her and she made a grouping. "These, for example, seem to be from about the same time, judging from the clothes and hairstyles."

"That's the criteria you want me to use?"

"Or whatever makes sense to you. You're a detective."

"Something that you make me regret sometimes."

"Look, Ross, if you're just going to go through the motions, don't bother. I'll wait until I have the time and do it myself."

"What are you talking about? I don't do a half-ass job on anything." He began stirring his hand inside the box, watching the contents swirl, but not pulling anything out. "Some are group photos. Maybe they'll be some faces in common."

"There you go. And pay attention to the backgrounds. Maybe certain locations repeat."

"Some newspaper clippings mixed in there," noted Brogan. "I'll see whether they can be grouped by dates."

"Check out the subject matter too, for patterns."

"I would have done that, anyway, Cunningham."

"I swear, for such a tough guy, you can be so sensitive. And what's with the inside of this house looking like you're shacking with Martha Stewart?"

"You don't know what you're talking about. It's my Marines training. Barracks had to be spic and span, beds made so you could bounce a coin on them, shoes shined, uniforms pressed."

"Enough. Didn't mean to get you started."

"Back to business. You said on the phone that you have a theory about motive. You going to let me in on it?"

"Revenge. Maybe trying to right a wrong."

"How do you figure?"

"I sort of backed into it. Kent and Gibson both were up in age. So far, I haven't uncovered evidence that they had an enemy in common, at least not a recent one. That got me to thinking that maybe the killer's motive is buried in the past."

"How long ago?"

"Maybe decades, considering how long Gibson had been mentally-challenged."

"You figure that whatever the killer had against Gibson happened before Gibson became a retard."

"I wouldn't have used that word, but, yes, that's my theory."

"Same timeframe for Kent?"

"It would make sense. That's why I've only brought you Gibson's older mementos and not the later ones, like of his daughter and grandchildren."

"Thanks for small favors." Then Brogan asked, "You still think the killer might be some wacko dame?"

"Female."

"Female. And is this female an oldie like the victims?"

"I've thought about that but haven't made up my mind."

"I know you'll keep at it."

"I have to. In the meantime, I want you to know that I appreciate your help."

"Well, even without help you'd go it alone because you won't let it rest."

"Not with two murders and possibly more to come."

"If there is another victim," said Brogan, "do you assume it will be another male?"

"I don't want to assume."

"Could have something to do with sexual abuse," theorized Brogan. "Young girl victimized by older guys. Never got over it."

"Maybe. Maybe not. So many angles. And now I can't even work the cases part-time because of the McArthur trial."

"How's that going?"

"Hard to say. It's only been a couple of days. We had a half-day today because the judge had some personal business to attend to. I'm meeting with Gerald Lewis later this afternoon."

"You think McArthur is going down, Cunningham?"

"I never predict what a jury will do. But one thing's for sure, Gerald Lewis has to stay sharp, being up against Lisa Rose."

"Ain't that the truth."

44.

Rose stepped to the lectern while unbuttoning her jacket, white with black-trimmed lapels, paired with a solid-black skirt. She began the cross-examination with, "Good afternoon, Mrs. Winkler."

"Good afternoon."

"Please accept my condolences over the loss of your husband."

"Thank you."

Rose, arms hanging relaxed, facial expression pleasant, in a non-attacking voice asked, "Isn't it true that your husband was against Jews marrying Gentiles, that is to say, non-Jews?"

Winkler's mouth opened to answer but hung in that position. She hadn't anticipated the question.

"Objection, Your Honor," said Lewis, a little slow to the rescue. "Outside the scope of direct."

"It's within scope, Your Honor," said Rose. "Mr. Lewis asked this witness questions about the type of person the rabbi was. My question is along those lines."

"You opened the door, Mr. Lewis," said the judge. "Objection overruled."

"Objection on the grounds of relevance, then, Your Honor," said Lewis. "Regardless of whether the rabbi held such a belief, it has no bearing on these proceedings."

"Overruled."

"Do you need the question repeated, Mrs. Winkler?" asked Rose.

"No."

"Then please answer."

"I don't know whether he was against such marriages, not that I'm sure of what you mean by against."

"Then I'll reword the question. Mrs. Winkler, isn't it true that your husband refused to perform marriage ceremonies between Jews and non-Jews?"

"Yes, however—"

"Thank you."

"Objection. Counselor is not allowing the witness to complete her answer," complained Lewis.

"It was a yes-or-no question," said Rose. "And, Your Honor, it's only my first question and the prosecutor keeps objecting, even after being overruled. If he wants a narrative from this witness, he can get it on redirect. The jury is entitled to hear the cross-examination."

"Objection overruled."

Rose continued, "Although your husband was against marriage between Jews and non-Jews, he never told you that he was against sex between the two groups, did he?"

Winkler didn't answer immediately, hoping for Lewis' intervention but when it wasn't forthcoming, she said, "He... he..."

"Yes or no, Mrs. Winkler," reminded Rose.

"No."

"Is it fair to say, that, after your husband's death, you were shocked to find out that he'd had an affair?"

"Most certainly."

"Were you shocked because the woman is black?"

Winkler adopted an indignant tone. "The shock was over the affair, not race."

"So, it was the same shock you would have felt had she been Jewish?"

"Absolutely."

"By your standards, was the rabbi a hypocrite for refusing to perform marriages between Jews and non-Jews but at the same time having sex with a non-Jew?"

"Objection," said Lewis. "Rabbi Winkler is not on trial. This is nothing short of character assassination."

"Your Honor, with the Court's indulgence, I will tie this line of questioning together," promised Rose.

"Then get us to that point, quickly. Objection overruled."

"Do you remember my question, Ms. Winkler?"

"Please repeat it."

"Rose said, "Let's let the court reporter read it back."

The court reporter did.

Her memory refreshed, Winkler said, "Adultery, itself, is hypocrisy."

"It surely can be," conceded Rose. "Adultery unsanctioned by the other spouse is also betrayal, so aren't you angry, in retrospect?"

"Yes. What wife wouldn't be?"

"I say, in retrospect, because you became aware of the infidelity only after his death, correct?"

"Correct."

"In fact, you never suspected, did you?"

"Never."

"That's the same answer you gave in your deposition." At first, it seemed like Rose was making a sharp turn, when she asked, "Do you know a Mr. Charles Hearn?"

Winkler's expression was that of a deer caught in the headlights of an 18-wheeler.

Lewis started whispering to the assistant prosecutor about the unfamiliar name, without result, so he requested, "Sidebar, Your Honor."

The judge motioned the attorneys forward.

The court reporter's fingers stayed busy while the rest of the courtroom could only speculate about what was being said at sidebar. At its conclusion, the attorneys resumed their places, their facial expressions indicative of the ruling.

"I ask you again, Mrs. Winkler, do you know a Mr. Charles Hearn?"

Winkler gave a mousy, "Yes."

"Please tell the jury who he is."

Winkler adjusted herself in the chair. She ran the fingertips of her right hand along the pearl necklace that accentuated the black dress, an elegant uniform of mourning. "I believe Mr. Hearn is a private investigator."

"Believe? Didn't you hire him in that capacity?"

Winkler took in a long breath, needed to expel the answer. "Yes."

"Isn't it a fact that you hired Charles Hearn to trail your husband because you suspected that he was being unfaithful?"

Winkler didn't know how Rose had unearthed that information, didn't know what other information Rose held, didn't know...didn't know. To lie further might be akin to bluffing at poker when playing with an opponent's marked deck. Winkler decided that it was best to fold. "Yes, that's why I hired him."

"And Mr. Hearn reported his findings to you, didn't he?"

"Yes."

"Mr. Hearn told you about Alison Petrocelli, didn't he?"

"Yes."

"So," said Rose, "when you testified in your deposition and before this jury today that you learned of your husband's infidelity only after his death, you lied, didn't you?"

Winkler, wanting to get the flogging over with, gave a quick, "Yes."

It touched off reverberations that quickly died on their own accord, causing the judge to retract the hand that was reaching for the gavel.

Rose stepped to the side of the lectern, and with that change of position came a change of subject. "Mrs. Winkler, was your husband's life insured?"

"Yes."

"How many policies and in what amounts, please."

"Two policies. One paid for by the synagogue, another paid for by us. Each in the amount of one million dollars."

"Are you the beneficiary on both?"

"Yes."

"Both of those policies pay double in the event of accidental death, don't they?"

"Yes."

"Since murder falls under the accidental death clause, your payout was four million dollars, wasn't it?"

"Yes."

If, indeed, Rose had delivered on her promise to tie together this line of questioning, the big, bright bow became, "Mrs. Winkler, did you kill you husband because he cheated on you, or because of the insurance money, or because of both?"

Lewis, face instantly ruddy, sprang to his feet, like his seat had an ejector button. "Objection! The witness is a bereaved widow. Counselor's tactics are unconscionable and contemptuous."

Rose argued, "Your Honor, the proper foundation was laid and the defense is entitled to ask, especially in light of the witness' admitted perjury."

"I agree," said the judge, who didn't take kindly to lying under oath. "Objection overruled."

"Do you remember the question, Mrs. Winkler?"

Winkler rocked sideways twice and responded, "One's not likely to forget such a question." She marshaled her poise, turned toward the jury, made sequential eye-contact, and said, "I did not kill my husband." Then, she reset her sight on Rose.

"You lied to the jury earlier," began Rose, pleased to remind everyone present, "and now you want—"

"It's not a matter of believing me," preempted Winkler. "I was thoroughly investigated by the police and I was able to prove my whereabouts at the time of the murder."

Rose didn't challenge that claim, at least not frontally. "The investigator, your Mr. Charles Hearn, did you pay him out of the insurance proceeds?"

"I couldn't have. His services were rendered before my husband's death and before I received the insurance money."

"There's the possibility," said Rose, nonchalantly, "that he billed you and you paid him later. After all, his investigation, the rabbi's death, and the insurance payments all occurred within a month's time."

Winkler shot that scenario down, informing, "He was given an advance and was paid the balance immediately after he reported his findings."

"And I'm sure he appreciated the prompt payment. On the other hand, hypothetically speaking, of course, you could have hired someone to kill your husband, promising a cut of the insurance. Isn't that true?"

Lewis jumped to his feet and exclaimed, "Objection!" He was about to angrily state his grounds.

But Rose quickly said, "I withdraw the question. That's all I have for this witness." Then, she sat, leaving Lewis the tasks of rehabilitating the Mrs. and of un-ringing the bell still tolling in the ears of the jury.

45.

Grace Emanuel hummed to herself as she went back and forth in her antique rocking chair. All ten fingers were sweeping her thick, wavy, snowy locks upward in an arrangement; then, she began inserting the hair pins that she'd been holding between her pressed lips. She wasn't given to primping but every gal wants to look presentable, especially in front of company. After the last pin was in place and she could speak, she called towards her kitchen. "It sure smells good in there, Ms. Rose."

The sound of a knife chopping on a cutting board ceased and the reply came back, "What do I have to pay you for you to call me by my first name?"

"I won't forget again," Grace promised and in demonstration, said, "Lisa."

"Much better." Rose resumed with the knife, later using the edge to rake the ingredients into a pile that she scooped with both hands into a glass bowl. On the stove, olive oil and crushed garlic were being heated in a wok, into which she emptied the bowl. Steam shot upward, accompanied by hissing and sizzling, both quieted by dousings of rice wine, soy sauce, and hoisin sauce. Rose kept the spatula in constant motion, her objective being the right degree of al dente.

At the proper time, Rose hurriedly transferred the food into a wooden bowl, having factored into her calculations how much the food would continue to cook on its own. She took the bowl into the dining room and set it center-table. In sequence, she brought a bowl of brown rice, a kettle of egg drop soup, a pot of green tea, and a basket draped with a cloth.

Rose made a final evaluation. The place settings were perfect, down to the folded napkins. The slender vase holding a bunch of daisies added a nice touch. She untied the apron, used it to dab her moist brow, and then laid it across the arm of the chair in which she would be sitting. Tomorrow, she would resume her role as attorney at the McArthur trial; however, she was more than satisfied with what she'd done this evening as chef. She went into the living room and proclaimed, "Dinner is ready."

"I can manage," said Grace, declining Rose's gesture to help her stand; however, once on her feet, she did accept Rose's arm in escort.

At the table, Rose pulled out the chair, waited as Grace sat, and pushed the chair back into place. "There's a surprise for you in the basket." She pinched the cloth then snapped it upward, like a magician revealing a materialized dove. "Ta-da!"

Grace's cheeks sat high on a big smile and she said, "Oh, my goodness."

Half-laughing, Rose commented, "This might be the first time in history that Chinese is served with buttermilk biscuits, but I know how much you love them."

"Yes, I do. And these are so big and golden."

Rose took a seat. She opened her napkin and draped it across her lap.

Grace's brows bunched and her mouth arched downward as she frowned judgingly. Soon, the brows relaxed and the corners of the mouth turned up. "Looks like I have some serious competition."

"I don't know about all that," said Rose. "Your biscuits are the best there is."

The interior of Grace's house, what with its braided floor mats, shelves aligned with bric-a-brac, and period furniture, identified its occupant as hailing from a previous generation, or two. Totally absent, however, were visual cues of the occupant's international prominence. There were none of the photos taken with Presidents, for example; but, lovingly on display were several framed photos of her late husband. The childless couple had purchased the 3-bedroom bungalow shortly after relocating to Detroit, death threats having forced them to flee their southern roots.

Congressman Andrew Galliger gave Grace a job in his district office, where she worked for decades, until retirement. And it had been Galliger who retained Rose to represent Grace in a lawsuit involving the unauthorized use of Rose's image on the cover of a rap CD. It hadn't taken long for Rose to get the recording company to cease distribution, extend a public apology, and write a check.

Grace hadn't been keen on the lawsuit and gave the money to the foundation that bears her name. "I don't care that they used my image," she had said, "if it gets young folks to thinking about an era that many of them know little about."

And Rose had responded, "An era forever associated with you."

Now, before partaking of the spread in front of her, Grace asked, "Will you do the honors and give thanks for this lovely meal, Lisa?"

"I'm out of practice. Please, you do it."

"Alright." Grace closed her eyes, bowed her head, and brought her palms together. "Dear God, thank you for this food that is about to nourish our bodies and may your inspiration nourish our souls. And please bless and keep the preparer, my friend, Lisa, who visits me from time to time out of the goodness of her heart. Amen."

46.

It was Rose's second go at Alison Petrocelli, what's known as re-cross. "You've established that to everyone's satisfaction," Rose said of the last response, "but my question wasn't whether you and Rabbi Winkler were lovers."

Petrocelli, worn and weary, said, "Then, repeat the question."

"Sure. Were you in love with the rabbi?"

Petrocelli, in her mind's ear, heard the creak of a bear trap being pulled open and set. She tried to avoid stepping in. "I don't see what that has to do with—"

"Your Honor, please direct the witness to answer the question."

"Answer the question, Ms. Petrocelli."

"I thought I was in love with him."

"What does that mean?" asked Rose. "Are you saying that you now realize that you didn't love him?"

Petrocelli blew a tired sigh. "Perspectives can change."

"They can," agreed Rose. "So let me simplify matters. At the last time you were with the rabbi, shortly before his death, did you believe you were in love with him?"

"Yes."

"So you were not merely having an affair with a married man but with a married man that you loved, correct?"

"Objection, Your Honor. Asked and answered," said Lewis.

"Sustained."

"Did you want to marry the rabbi?"

"He was already married," dodged Petrocelli.

"Non-responsive, Your Honor," said Rose.

The judge instructed, "The witness will give a direct answer."

"Yes, if it were possible."

"But," said Rose, "you knew it wasn't possible, didn't you?"

"No."

"Really? A man who refused to perform marriage ceremonies between Jews and non-Jews? I mean no ridicule by this next question, just establishing a foundation. You are not Jewish, are you?"

Petrocelli did not appreciate the suppressed laughter from a couple of courtroom observers. "No, I'm not Jewish."

"Isn't it true that you knew that marrying the rabbi was not going to happen?"

"I suppose," Petrocelli admitted, then, to ward off being further pressed, said, "Yes, there came a point when I accepted that marriage was not in the cards."

"So you were in love with the married rabbi, who would never marry you, but was willing to use you sexually."

Lewis said, "Objection. Argumentative. Also, any insinuation that Ms. Petrocelli was anything other than a consenting partner is without foundation."

"Before you rule, Your Honor, I concede to both parties having been consenting. As for a question, I'm ready to pose one."

"Then do so."

"Consenting notwithstanding, you resented the rabbi's position concerning marriage between Jew and non-Jew, didn't you?"

"I didn't like it, no."

"And didn't the two of you have heated arguments over his position."

"Whenever we got together, we busied ourselves with other positions," said Petrocelli, triggering laughter.

"I'll get back to that," promised Rose, envious of the laughter. "My question to you now is, didn't you misrepresent your relationship with Reverend McArthur, in order to make the rabbi jealous?"

"Not at all."

"In fact, didn't you give the rabbi an ultimatum to marry you or else he would lose you to Reverend McArthur?"

"No."

"Isn't it true that Reverend McArthur was never the jealous, obsessed stalker you make him out to be, and that you invented the characterization, hoping to force the rabbi's hand?"

"Objection, Your Honor," spoke Lewis. "The question is compound."

"Overruled."

"I never lied on the reverend."

"Isn't it true that the rabbi rejected your ultimatum?"

"There wasn't one."

"And his willingness to have the affair end infuriated you, didn't it?"

"None of that's true."

"You knew where the reverend kept his gun, didn't you?"

"He might have moved it around, as far as I knew. Whatever the case, I never had possession of it."

"Did you ever have the means to take the gun when he wasn't around?"

"No."

"Now, back to your earlier reference to positions. Do you stand by your earlier testimony that you had sex with the rabbi the morning he was killed?"

"Yes."

"And that it explains why your DNA was on his underwear and severed penis?"

"Yes?"

"Are you familiar with the term, make-up sex?"

"No."

"Then, by whatever term, would you concede that sex is sometimes part of a reconciliation?"

"I've heard it said but can't speak from personal experience."

"On the morning the rabbi was killed, hadn't you used sex to remind him what he'd be missing if the affair ended?"

"No."

"He accepted the sex and still rejected you and it made you furious, didn't it?"

"No. And it was he who initiated the sex. I only came over to drop off some materials for the speech he was to give that day."

"Have you ever held the attitude that if you can't have something, or someone as the case may be, then no one else will?"

"No."

Rose switched direction. "Hasn't your appearance changed since, say, ten years ago?"

There was hesitation, then, "Yes."

"Back then, you were overweight weren't you?"

"Actually, I was obese."

"Okay, obese. And for the most part, not receiving attention from men?"

"Some men like larger women."

"True, but apparently not the ones you desired, since you lost the weight."

"I did it for myself, for health reasons."

"Commendable. But didn't you hope your days of being rejected were over, and when that turned out not to be the case with the rabbi, it made you furious?"

"No, and how many things are you going to claim made me furious?"

"However many, did they add up to a motive for murder, and afterward, did you become a self-styled Lorena Bobbitt?" asked Rose, invoking the name of the woman who infamously severed her husband's penis.

"Objection, Your Honor," said Lewis. "This entire re-cross has been nothing but groundless speculation and does not deserve the Court's further indulgence."

The judge, because Petrocelli was a key prosecution wit-ness, had granted Rose leeway. He would have done the same for the state with a key defense witness. But there were limits. "Start wrapping it up, Ms. Rose."

Rose flipped through some notes to give the impression that there was something she was contemplating. She'd accomplished what she'd set out to do with Petrocelli. The planned payoff was to be from other witnesses. "No further questions, Your Honor."

47.

Young Lisa Rosenberg was seated cross-legged on the floor, as flexibly as a yogi. In a flash, she unfolded, sprang to her feet, and rushed to an armchair a few feet away. "Grandmother!"

Bernie was seated nearby in the other armchair. He turned his head, such that, peripherally, he could still see the television. "What's the matter?"

"I don't know," admitted Lisa, with alarm, while shaking her grandmother by the shoulders. "She fell asleep with her eyes open."

Just minutes prior, all three had been laughing uproariously: Bernie genuinely, Yetta less so, and Lisa simply trying to curry favor. Laugher was a one-hour, weekly visitor. By Bernie's edit, every Sunday evening the television was tuned to the Ed Sullivan show. Bernie loved the comedians, especially the Jewish ones.

The futility of Lisa's attempts set in, and she stopped, covered her face, and peering through separated fingers, began to cry.

"Stop with the crying, already," demanded Bernie. "It does no good." His rise from the chair was slow and labored, accentuated by frowns and grunts. Since his injury at the slaughterhouse, he had convalesced to where he could hobble with the use of a cane. When he got to Yetta, he didn't speak to her, just pressed three fingers against her neck. His proclamation was dry and matter-of-fact. "She's dead."

"Noooo!" Lisa flung herself onto Yetta and wrapped arms around the grandmother's middle. She buried her face into the apron and wailed inconsolably.

Bernie pulled her off. "I thought I told you to stop the crying. It's not like it can bring her back."

Lisa was getting a taste of how life would be without Yetta, not that Bernie was behaving differently, just being who and what he is; however, going forward, she'd have to endure him alone, without intervention from Yetta.

Bernie shifted weight to relieve pain on his bad hip. Then he looked down at his wife and told her, "At least you didn't suffer."

Lisa, the back of her hand wet from wiping away tears, reached toward Yetta.

But Bernie grabbed that hand. "I don't want you touching her."

Lisa was beside herself with grief and frustration. She pressed her lips together to muffle the crying but it escaped as baleful sputters.

"And I'll tell you one last time to quit that racket." Bernie gimped to a lamp table where a telephone sat and then dialed three numbers.

"911. What's your emergency?"

"I have a dead person in my house."

"Who?"

"My wife."

"Are you sure she's dead?"

"I'm a World War II veteran," Bernie informed and then cynically added, "I ought to know it when I see a dead person."

"Sir, I only asked because maybe CPR—"

Bernie interjected, "I said she's dead."

"How did she die?"

"Just dropped dead."

"What's the address?"

"18449 LaSalle."

"I'll dispatch a unit."

Bernie was irked that the discourteous operator had not said good-bye. He lowered the receiver, letting it drop the last few inches onto the base.

Lisa felt faint, weak from the emotional toll and light-headed from trying to suppress the crying; yet, she dared not move without Bernie's permission.

Bernie waddled to his chair, flopped down, pointed his cane at a nearby area of the floor, and then said, "Sit."

Lisa ran to the spot and sat. She wanted to keep her back turned to Bernie, which meant she had to face the television, at the sacrifice of not being able to see Yetta. Although whimpering and in a stupor, she was aware of the man on the television screen, tall, stout, and carrying a violin. She'd seen him before, knew him to be a comedian, and knew that Bernie liked him. Lisa, however, didn't understand the act. Why was the comedian asking someone to take his wife and where? Why did the audience laugh when he said it?

Obviously, Bernie understood the punch-line, because he let out a one-note chuckle, even as Yetta sat still warm.

Not caring about any possible consequences stemming from not asking permission, Lisa sprang to her feet then fled out of the room.

48.

When the prosecutor rested his case, Rose, as any defense attorney would do, argued a motion for judgment of acquittal, claiming that the state had not met its burden of proof. Judge Ellington denied the motion, not wasting words as to his reasons. He did, however, adjourn for that day.

The next morning, Rose was conducting the direct-examination of the first defense witness. "Sir, what is your profession?"

"I am a congressman in the U.S. House of Representatives for Michigan's 14th District." Andrew Galliger's rich, baritone voice was the type that narrates nature films.

"And for how long?"

"Forty years."

"May I address you as, Congressman?"

"Yes."

Rose paused, so that the jury could study the urbane and sophisticated Galliger. In due course, she resumed. "Congressman, do you know Reverend Jeeter McArthur, and if so, please point him out."

"I know him. He's seated at the defense table, green suit, yellow tie."

Procedurally, Rose said, "May the record reflect that the witness has identified the defendant."

"So ordered," said the judge.

Earlier and outside the presence of the jury, the judge had heard arguments regarding whether Galliger should be allowed to testify. Lewis had argued that Galliger was not a fact witness nor an expert witness, but a character witness. Such witnesses, Lewis went on to argue, are only appropriate in the penalty phase of a trial. Lewis even had been so bold as to have argued that Galliger's presence was quid pro quo for Rose's having represented Grace Emanuel.

Rose had counter-argued that Lewis had opened the door by charging a hate crime and that he'd used Petrocelli's testimony to corroborate the charge. Galliger, according to Rose's winning argument, was being called to rebut the contention that Jeeter McArthur is anti-Semitic.

"How long have you known the Reverend Jeeter McArthur?" asked Rose.

"Decades. Give me a second and I'll calculate the exact number."

"That won't be necessary. Over those decades, in what capacity, if any, have you and the reverend interacted?"

"Community involvements."

"And have any of them involved Jews?"

"Objection. Vague, Your Honor," spoke Lewis. "Does Ms. Rose mean on the individual level or group level?"

"The congressman's response will be self-evident as to his interpretation," said the judge. "Overruled."

"Yes, with individuals and groups both," answered Galliger.

"Then, my question to you, Congressman, is, in all your involvements with the reverend, spanning decades, including interactions with Jews on the individual and group level, have any of his behaviors or words impressed you as anti-Semitic?"

"No."

"No?" repeated Rose, wanting the same answer to underscore the point.

But Galliger misinterpreted and believed that Rose wanted a stronger denial, so he elaborated. "Absolutely not. All his life, he has been a crusader for harmony among races and religions. And, I do mean all this life, because—"

Rose cut him off, saying, "No narrative required, Congressman." Then she announced, "That's all I have."

Lewis was surprised by the brevity, having expected a longer direct-examination, even though his own questioning would be short-and-sweet. He got up and stood before Galliger, maintaining respectful distance. "Good morning, Congressman Galliger."

"Good morning."

In an example of an aspiring politician paying homage to a dean, Lewis said, "First, I commend you on your long and distinguished public service."

"Thank you." Galliger's cordial demeanor gave no indication to the jury that outside their presence he'd taken umbrage, believing that Lewis had impeached his integrity.

"Congressman Galliger, isn't it true that you, personally, have no knowledge about the guilt or innocence of the defendant as it relates to this murder trial?"

"That would be true."

Feeling less the sting of having failed to keep Galliger off the stand, Lewis said, "Thank you, Congressman. No further questions."

49.

Bernie use to try to catch Yetta in the act. Certain that teachings that he didn't approve of were being conducted behind his back, he would eavesdrop at every opportunity, sometimes resorting to sneaking into the house and literally tiptoeing around. And whenever his efforts were successful, he would berate Yetta for filling Lisa's head with nonsense, just as Yetta had done with their daughter.

The threat of discovery kept Lisa on tenterhooks, and try as she might, she never was able to give her full attention to Yetta, distracted by thoughts of a preternatural Bernie, who could spy unperceived like a ghost or from a distance like a wizard.

Those thoughts didn't apply after Yetta's death because Bernie's whereabouts were seldom in question because he rarely left the house, preferring to sit around and brew, like stale tea. After all, it wasn't as if he had a job to go to, the accident having left him unable to be a shochet. His surgically-repaired right elbow would randomly and momentarily lock, no good for guaranteeing the swift, uninterrupted cut essential for a kosher kill. But whereas living on a disability check was humbling, it was more honorable than working a job that was beneath him, and compared to being a shochet, that included most. No wonder that he took his advocacy to new heights, or it might be said, to new lows, given that his captive audience was a child.

In the early going, Bernie would preface his remarks by invoking his dearly departed wife. "Your grandmother understood," he would say to Lisa.

"Yes, Grandfather," Lisa would say, knowing she was about to be lectured on something that she little understood, but that nonetheless carried traumatic associations.

"Up until her last breath, your grandmother was a defender of Sh'chitah and you will be too, understand?"

"Yes, Grandfather."

"Your grandmother told you about the evil Adolph Hitler. You need to know that one of the worst things he did was try to outlaw Sh'chitah. He knew that there was no tradition that was more Jewish."

Actually, Bernie had always resented the small, unsought celebrity Yetta received as a Holocaust survivor and had always been quick to remind her fawning admirers that he was among the forces that liberated the concentration camps. Throughout the marriage, he had tolerated Yetta's friends while being thankful that he didn't have to deal with in-laws; for, her immediate family perished in the camps and none of her other relatives were in the States.

Sometimes during the indoctrinations, Bernie would hold Lisa by the shoulders and lean forward until they almost were nose-to-nose. At least his breath didn't reek of alcohol. A teetotaler, he wasn't a mean drunk, just mean.

"Anybody who speaks against Sh'chitah is ignorant and anti-Semitic, or maybe even a self-hating Jew. You got that?"

"Yes, Grandfather."

"There is nothing inhumane about Sh'chitah. It's merciful. Without pain and suffering. Know that."

"Yes, Grandfather."

50.

The night before Jeeter McArthur was to take the stand, Rose was preparing in her office, her work table doubling as a dinner table. "So, what do you think?"

Kirk Rhodes chewed slowly and deliberately, not wanting to be hasty with his answer, finally saying, "Definitely can't say that it tastes like chicken." He contemplated other comparisons and then conceded defeat. "Actually, I can't say that it tastes like anything on its own. Sort of soaks up the flavor of the sauce, like a sponge."

"Tofu is an acquired taste," said Rose, who had provided the sample from her meal.

Rhodes wasn't in an acquiring state-of-mind. He patted his full belly and declared, "I'll stick with pepper steak."

"I wasn't trying to convert you."

"I'm thankful for that," said Rhodes, who'd been serving as second chair throughout the McArthur trial. He had a wife, a newborn, a dog, a mortgage, and was so nondescript, that were he to commit a crime in front of witnesses, they would be of no use to a police sketch artist.

With expert use of chop sticks, Rose ate a little more. Then, she closed the container and set it on the floor to avoid an accidental spill. A yellow marker now in hand, she took the last of several transcripts from previous trials in which Lewis cross-examined a defendant and started high-lighting, the objective being to identify Lewis' tendencies.

Rhodes watched, feeling even less useful than earlier, when, at least, he'd been sent twice to the copying machine, and—oh, yes—once to get take-out. So, it was mostly to be noticed, to have his presence acknowledged, that he asked, "What made you become a vegetarian?"

Rose stiffened, although not observably. She leaned against the backrest of the chair and used the bottom end of the marker to scratch her chin, deciding, and then trot-ted out one of her stock responses. "You have to be specific with that label. Some vegetarians don't eat anything that comes from an animal, including dairy and eggs."

"Vegans, right?"

"Vegans. Others eat fish and fowl and claim to be veg-etarians. I don't understand how, though."

"So, how do you describe yourself?"

"Someone who doesn't eat red meat."

"For how long?" asked Rhodes.

Simply by edit, Rose could have ended the questioning, which had gone beyond the conventional show of interest, beyond conversational filler. But she decided to indulge it further, wanting some catharsis, yet wary of the price. "Since I was six years old."

Rhodes' head pulled backward, like he was avoiding a punch. "Wow! Didn't expect that answer." Recovered, he guessed, "Your parents must have made the decision for you."

"No. I made the decision on my own."

"How does a six-year-old know about health?"

"I didn't and it had nothing to do with health. There just came a time when I hated meat."

Rhodes tactfully said, "Interesting."

"Weird, is the word you wanted to use."

"Rather than lie, can I substitute the word, unusual?"

"Accepted."

During Rhodes' entire tenure at the firm, this marked the first time that he'd had a conversation with Rose that could pass as personal. She had always been cordial, would ask about his family by names. In contrast, he knew zip about her personal life. Not wanting to spoil the rare occasion by one too many questions or by the wrong reaction to an answer, Rhodes chose to take his gains and be satisfied. "Do you expect a long cross from Lewis?"

It was as if Rose had not heard the question; for, she said, "I was living with my grandparents."

"Grandparents," repeated Rhodes.

"Earlier, you mentioned my parents. Just correcting the record, that's all." But, she still wasn't finished. "My grandfather worked in a slaughterhouse. Daily, he'd bring meat home." She stuck some fingers in the top of her blouse and rubbed, where cleavage would have started, were she busty. "Funny, how everything's relative. While other kids subsisted on hot dogs, I developed a hatred for choice cuts."

Spurred, Rhodes ventured to ask, "What did your grandparents say about the meat thing?"

"My grandmother tolerated it but it aggravated my grandfather to no end."

"Oh-kay," sang Rhodes, about to drop the subject.

Rose scowled. The discussion would end when she chose and not a syllable before. "Which is it, Kirk? Is my upbringing so boring or is your imagination so limited that you're out of questions?"

"Neither. It's just that I know that you're prepping for trial, and, well..."

"You were concerned about being a distraction."

"Correct."

"Leave such concerns to me."

"If you say so." He picked up where they'd left off. "Your grandfather was aggravated. What would he do?"

"Take it out on my grandmother, through criticism. Held her responsible for not bringing me to my senses. He mostly ignored me."

"Are your grandparents alive?"

"My grandmother died of a brain aneurism, the same year I stopped eating meat."

Rhodes' facial expression bespoke confusion. "And, in all the time you lived with your grandfather, he never could get you to eat meat?"

Rose gave a get-ready-for-this smile. "He gave up because I kept spoiling his appetite by vomiting at the table."

"Gross." Rhodes was quick to add, "I didn't mean you."

Rose gave a laugh but there was no merriment. "You'd think a man who worked in a slaughterhouse wouldn't be so disgusted by a kid's upchucking."

"Is your grandfather still alive?"

"Too much so." She slapped her forehead in chastisement and said, "I didn't mean it like it must have sounded. What I meant was that he's just as bull-strong and bull-headed as ever."

"I see."

It's easy to awaken memories that sleep with one eye open and the other twitching. The ones presently yawning and stretching in Rose's mind prompted her to suddenly gather the documents into a stack and then to decree, "No need to overdo the preparation. Be in court at seven. That'll give us time to go over last minute details with the reverend."

"I'll set my alarm." Rhodes didn't fasten the top button of his shirt before drawing his loosened necktie into place. He cleared his stuff off the table and made a successful underhand toss of his empty food container into the nearby wastebasket.

Rose went to her desk and stuffed the documents into her briefcase. *No need to swear Kirk to confidentiality. Didn't say anything that I can't own up to.*

Another question occurred to Rhodes and he mulled over the wisdom of asking. He decided to brave it. "Given all that you've said, do you love your grandfather?"

The response wasn't immediate, coming after the turning away of the head to hide the welling eyes. "With all my heart."

51.

"Reverend McArthur, did you kill Rabbi Winkler?"

McArthur smiled blissfully. "No. Killing is against the Ten Commandments."

"Objection as to relevance," spoke Gerald Lewis. "What matters is that killing is against Michigan law. I don't want this witness sermonizing every time he answers a question."

Rose threw up her hands, as if in disbelief. "Your Honor, was that comment so surprising, coming from a reverend? Mr. Lewis is being petty."

McArthur was spruced in a black silk suit—Rose's idea—that made him appear dapper and pastoral. "Mr. Lewis, why didn't you object to the so-help-you-God part, when I was being sworn in?"

"Your Honor, really," beseeched Lewis.

"Reverend, do not speak while an objection is pending. And, do not address the prosecutor unless when answering his questions."

McArthur, wedged into the witness chair, couldn't easily turn his torso, so he turned his head to the judge and said, "I apologize, Your Honor."

"And Reverend, you are to give secular answers to secular questions." With that, the judge said, "Objection sustained."

Rose picked a thread off her knitted dress and resumed. "Where were you the morning that the rabbi was killed?"

"At home, in bed, alone. I'm rarely up before nine."

"When did you learn of the murder?"

"On the news at noon. I was shocked and disgusted."

"Did there come a time when you discussed the murder with Alison Petrocelli?"

"Yes. She phoned me, distraught, asking if I'd heard."

"She phoned you?"

"She phoned me."

"Same day as the murder?"

"I can't say for sure. At most no more than a day or two after. I think we were playing phone-tag for a while, so I'm not sure what the phone records will show."

"What's the history between you and Ms. Petrocelli?"

"We met two years ago at a mayor's function. She introduced herself as someone who did public relations work. She gave me her card. So the relationship started out on a professional note."

"At some point, did it turn personal?"

"Yes. Months later. I hired her and we spent considerable time working together on projects. A mutual attraction developed. We became lovers."

"Did the two of you consider yourselves to be an exclusive couple?"

"No. Nothing that formal, at least not by my thinking. In fact, I ended the sexual part of our relationship. Told her I wanted us to be business associates and friends."

"What was her reaction?"

"Anger. She accused me of using her. She said she was in love with me. I broke off communications until she agreed to just be friends."

"You sat through Ms. Petrocelli's testimony, did you not?"

"I did."

"She testified that she ended the sexual relationship."

"Not true. I did."

"She testified that you refused to accept it and started harassing and stalking her."

"A lie. If anything, she pestered me to reconsider. She was always calling, demanding to know whether there was someone else in my life, and when she wasn't calling, she was coming by unannounced."

"And from that same witness chair, she testified that you were furious upon learning of her affair with Rabbi Winkler."

"Another lie. I didn't know of the affair until after his murder."

"So you never threatened to give the rabbi a circumcision or anything to that effect?"

"Nothing even close. And I repeat, I didn't know of the affair until after the murder."

"Affair aside, did you know that they knew one another?"

"Yes, because I introduced her to him. I introduced her to a number of people that I thought could use her services."

"What was your relationship with the rabbi?"

"Professional. We were members of an inter-faith outreach program devoted to reducing frictions and increasing understanding between religious groups in the metropolitan-Detroit area. And not just between Jews and Christians, but among Muslims and others, as well. I liked and respected Rabbi Winkler."

"Did you hear the prosecutor say in his opening remarks that he will prove you guilty on all counts, including that of a hate crime?"

"Yes."

"Bear with me Reverend, for some common-sense logic. You've denied killing the rabbi, am I correct?"

"Yes."

"This might seem an unnecessary question, but I have to ask. If you didn't kill him, period, you couldn't have killed him for any hate reason, yes?"

"Objection," said Lewis. "Leading and argumentative."

"Overruled," said the judge.

"You can answer, Reverend," instructed Rose.

"I didn't kill him, therefore, reasons don't apply. Like you said, common-sense."

"Good old common-sense," said Rose, about to embark on a different line of questioning.

But, McArthur quickly volunteered, "I've been a life-long crusader against hate and bigotry of all forms. My history—"

"Excuse me, Reverend," interrupted Rose, not wanting her witness to go off script. "There's no question before you." She returned to the defendant's table and took a sip of water, a tactic that she had worked out with Kirk Rhodes, who discreetly placed a finger to show where she was on the list of questions. All the preceding questions bore his checkmark; hence, she had not missed a one in her attempt to give the jury the impression that she was conducting a direct-examination that was as informal as a living room chat. Her eyes inconspicuously swept over the rest of the list. She returned and faced the witness. "Are you a registered owner of a .357 magnum revolver?"

"Yes."

"Do you know its whereabouts?"

"No."

"Why?"

"I discovered it missing from my bedroom closet, where I kept it."

"When?"

"When the police executed a search warrant."

"Who else, if anyone, knew where you kept the gun?"

McArthur gave a weighted sigh and said, "Alison Petrocelli."

"And how did she come by that knowledge?"

"Once, not long into our relationship, she was at my house and saw me take it off my person."

"You routinely carried a gun, Reverend McArthur?"

"My ministry sometimes requires me to go into high-crime areas of the city. I drive a nice vehicle, am fond of jewelry, and sometimes carry moderate amounts of cash. Before we ask God to protect us, we must do our best to protect ourselves."

"Objection, non-responsive," said Lewis. "And he's sermonizing, again."

"Sustained." The judge then said, "You're violating my instructions to you, Reverend McArthur."

"Not intentionally, I assure you, Your Honor. It's difficult overturning what comes naturally." Then McArthur saved Rose the trouble of repeating the question. "I didn't routinely carry a gun. Only under certain circumstances."

Rose then asked, "Did any discussion ensue between you and Ms. Petrocelli regarding the gun?"

"Yes. She asked to hold it. I handed it to her after removing the bullets. I explained what type of gun it was but don't remember all I said. What I do recall with clarity is taking it from her, reloading it, and returning it to its box in the closet, all the while with her watching."

"How long prior to the rabbi's murder did this occur?"

"Let's see… six months, maybe. I can't pin it down better than that. Sorry."

Rose cut a conferring glance at Rhodes, his eyes telling her that she hadn't skipped anything. She decided to forego another trip to the table. "Did Ms. Petrocelli ever drive your vehicle?"

"Yes. One time she had it for the weekend while I was out of town at a conference."

"Even though you were out of town, why leave your vehicle with her?"

"She'd been planning to take hers in for mechanical work and this was a convenient way for her to do so and still have transportation."

"Can you place this in a time context?"

"It definitely was after we'd resolved our differences about the nature of our relationship. Yes, shortly after she'd said that she'd gotten over her anger at me for ending our sexual relationship."

"That would mean that she had your vehicle after having seen the gun, true?"

"True."

"When you gave her your car keys, were your house keys on the same ring?"

"Yes. We were running late for the airport. When we arrived, I jumped out and rushed in. It didn't occur to me to take the rest of my keys."

"So, Ms. Petrocelli had your car keys and house keys for a weekend?"

"Correct."

"And while they were in her possession, she could have had duplicates made without your knowledge, true?"

"Objection!" injected Lewis. "Calls for speculation on the part of the witness. He doesn't know what Ms. Petrocelli could have done, by whatever restraints. This is another bad-faith stunt by Ms. Rose."

"Sustained," said the judge.

But Rose went backdoor with, "Were your car and house keys imprinted with the message, do not duplicate, as are some keys?"

"No."

"Nothing of that sort to prohibit duplication, true?"

"True."

"I want you to look at something, Reverend." So saying, Rose retrieved a document from the defendant's table. She first showed it to Lewis, who returned it without comment. "Permission to approach the witness, Your Honor."

"Granted."

Rose handed the document to McArthur and asked, "Can you identify what I just handed you?"

"Yes. It's the hotel bill for when I was out of town and left my car and keys with Ms. Petrocelli."

"Please read aloud the name of the hotel, the city, the dates, and the amount." After McArthur complied, Rose said, "Your Honor, I request that this document be marked as Defense Exhibit 1 and entered into evidence."

"So ruled."

Rose repeated the sequence with another document, which would become Defense Exhibit 2, the registration of McArthur's vehicle, having him twice recite the license plate number. Then, she proceeded to ask, "Do you remember your car's location the night before the murder?"

"Yes. I parked it in my driveway and didn't move it until the following afternoon."

"Since you've testified that you were asleep at home, would it be fair to say that you don't know for a fact, whether at the time of the murder, your car was still in your driveway?"

The implication was as subtle as a car bomb, but the wording afforded Lewis scant grounds for an objection. On his legal pad, he scratched out how he would attack it on cross-examination.

McArthur pinched the bridge of his nose in contemplation before saying, "I can only assume—"

"Don't," admonished Rose. "No one's asking you to assume."

"In that case, I'm forced to admit that I don't know for a fact that my car was in the driveway the morning of the murder."

"Your Honor, with the Court's indulgence, I request to interrupt my direct-examination of the reverend to call another witness, whose availability is limited to today."

"Availability aside," began the judge, "your witness doesn't have to be sandwiched in between the reverend's testimony."

"True," agreed Rose. "But, I assure you, Your Honor, that my request, if granted, will assist the jury in making tie-ins with other testimony."

"Sounds cryptic to me," said the judge, "but before I rule, I'll give the state an opportunity to respond. Any response, Mr. Lewis?"

Since Rose had framed her rationale in terms of its benefits to the jury, Lewis decided it best to say, "No objections, Your Honor."

So the judge said, "We'll take a fifteen minute recess, then you'll call your next witness, Ms. Rose."

52.

"Is it true, Sir, that you were served with a subpoena, ordering your appearance and ordering you to bring a certain document?" asked Rose of the witness who was the middle of the McArthur testimony sandwich.

Zachery York shook his head in affirmation.

"You must give a verbal response," instructed Rose, "for the benefit of the court reporter typing the transcript."

"I know," claimed York. "I forgot because I'm a bit nervous. First time testifying. The answer to your question is, yes."

"Thank you." She infused her voice with interest and said, "Tell the Court what you do for a living."

"I'm the sales and leasing manager at Progressive View Townhouses, in Detroit." The mousse and dye had his hair resembling wet crow feathers, the navy blazer, open collar shirt, jeans, and sneakers being further evidence of a Baby Boomer in denial of the aging process.

"Is Alison Petrocelli a resident?"

"Yes."

"Please identify what you are holding."

"It's called a guard station log."

"And its purpose?"

"To record visitors to the grounds. Name of visitor, name of resident, date, time, and license plate number."

"Is the guard station log kept in your regular course of business?"

"Yes."

"And your office has maintained continuous custody of the log?"

"Yes."

"I'm going to show you what's been marked as Defense Exhibit 1, a hotel bill." After allowing a generous review time, Rose asked, "Do you see the check-in date?"

"Yes."

After taking back the exhibit, Rose said, "Please turn to that date in your log. Tell me when you've done so."

The efficient York soon said, "Done."

"Now, I'm going to show you what's been marked as Defense Exhibit 2, a vehicle registration." After allowing for ample study, Rose asked, "Do you see the license plate number of that registration?"

"Yes, I do."

"Does that license plate number appear in your log on the date that I asked you to turn to?"

York ran his finger down one page, then a second, occasionally referring back to Defense Exhibit 2, until he said, "Yes, it does."

"Please read aloud the name associated with that entry."

"Alison Petrocelli."

Rose said, "But didn't you testify that the log was for visitors?"

"It is, most of the time, but when a resident is parking a vehicle on the property other than the one registered with the office, that resident has to register with the guard station, otherwise the vehicle might get towed."

"Tell me if I understand, Mr. York. Your guard station log says that Alison Petrocelli registered a vehicle, other than the vehicle assigned to her parking space. Is that correct?"

"Correct."

"Do you agree that the date in the log coincides with the check-in date on Defense Exhibit 1?"

"Yes."

"And that the license plate number listed on the log is the same as the one listed on Defense Exhibit 2?"

"Yes."

"Thank you. That's all I have. I pass the witness."

Lewis saw no upside in keeping York on the stand any longer. York had no ax to grind and to treat him as if he did might be taken by the jury as a diversionary tactic. "Nothing for this witness, Your Honor."

53.

The front doorbell rang thrice, full-throated and reverberating, easily heard from the deck in back of the house. Seconds later came another set of three.

"That's probably Izetta," said Sophie, of her fellow church member who had phoned earlier. Sophie was stretched out in a patio lounge chair, the adjustable back angled to support her head. Loosely draped over her otherwise bare torso was a mesh poncho, a special garment that allowed aeration with minimal friction.

"She's going to run up our electric bill, leaning on the bell like that," Joe said, seated on a teak garden bench. He stood, in bent position, and straightened by bracing his lower back with his hands.

"Your disc acting up, again, Joe?"

"I'm fine." Joe sucked in his gut to appear more elongated. His doctor had recommended surgery more than a year ago. Reluctant from the onset to go under the knife, it was out of the question now because no way would he jeopardize his role as devoted caregiver. Upon saying, "I'll go let Izetta in," he went back into the house.

Meanwhile, the doorbell rang—four times, this round.

Alone, Sophie took advantage and let loose a coughing spell. It was dry, hacking, and prolonged enough to wind her, as did the least exertions of late. In a rush to recover, she drew a long breath through her mouth and it sounded like the honk of a goose. Her lungs didn't fully inflate, only capable of shallow, uneven functioning. Even if her doctors at the Jonas Cancer Center had not told her that the disease had metastasized to her lungs, she would have concluded it herself.

Sophie, spent, lay limp, her eyes closed, sunshine playing colorfully on the insides of her lids. Sophie didn't want to be caught in that repose, didn't want the obvious to appear so obvious; so, she listened for the unmistakable clomping of Izetta's heels against the kitchen tiles.

Izetta Bright, she of feet of lead and heart of gold, mustn't be given reason to fret. A goodwill ambassador in the truest sense, Izetta had her own health problems, but she didn't let them prevent her from making her rounds, visiting the sick and the shut-ins.

Don't forget to tell Izetta that you love her, Sophie reminded herself. Ever since her fateful diagnosis, she had made it a point to tell loved ones how she felt about them, friends as well as family. Furthermore, those who hang around for any period are likely to be told more than once. To overcome distances, she used phone calls, letters, and even had learned to e-mail. It was of utmost importance not to leave anyone wondering, after she dies. As for death, she was in acceptance of its imminence. She had a living will and one of its provisions was that there be no resuscitation.

More recently, Sophie had decided to forego further chemotherapy. Over the months, she had been administered a variety of drugs that attack fast-dividing cancer cells; regrettably, they also attack cells that are naturally fast-dividing, resulting in side effects. At one time or another, for varying durations, she had suffered not only hair loss, but mouth sores, skin discoloration, and digestive distress, not to mention chronic fatigue. Nonetheless, it hadn't been a matter of intolerance that prompted her decision, rather one of practicality: why endure such battering when the cancer had progressed beyond any drug's ability to slow it.

At least now, that constant metallic taste in her mouth had disappeared and her taste buds had returned to normal. It was a little thing, but Sophie had become so appreciative of the little things. If only her appetite weren't so absent. At any second, Izetta would walk onto the deck, no doubt toting something hot and wholesome. Sophie readied herself to nibble just enough to keep her friend from worrying. Then again, it was yet morning, and Sophie even might be able to sell Izetta on the excuse that it was too soon after breakfast to eat.

It was concern for others that kept Sophie from sharing all her tribulations; otherwise, she would have confided that the morphine patch was not doing the job and that she needed something stronger. It was all she could do not to groan with every step taken with her walker, the means of her remaining mobility. The pain was sharpest throughout her ribs, pelvis, and legs. In addition to her lungs, the cancer had spread to her bones.

Sophie continued to recline with her eyes closed. There came a soft thump, which she recognized as a walnut falling to the ground. The tree in her back yard was as tall as the roof and bore a heavy yield of nuts on alternate years, such as the current one. The feasting squirrels will be bushy-tailed fur balls way before they typically fatten for the winter. It all made her think about nature and its cycles, its seasons, its times, and that there is one for every purpose, including a time to die.

Abruptly, Sophie's eyes flew open and she struggled into an upright seated position. The effort was painful and her breathing became short and quick. Her sudden state of alarm had been triggered by loud, angry noises.

Joe was cursing, and Joe—ex-cop though he is—seldom cursed. Something, rather someone, had caused him to explode and his profanities were flying like shrapnel.

For sure, the visitor wasn't dear ol' Izetta Bright.

54.

"I remind you, Reverend McArthur, that you are still under oath," said the judge.

"I know, Your Honor." Having retaken the witness stand after York's testimony, McArthur looked out upon the courtroom and saw that there still were no unoccupied seats. A county deputy still was posted at the door to turn away latecomers.

Since his arrest, McArthur had been housed in the county jail, charged with first-degree murder, felonious use of a firearm, mutilation of a corpse, and commission of a hate crime. None of that had deterred Rose from citing lack of priors, strong community ties, and not being a flight risk as reasons to release him on his own cognizance. That didn't fly with the judge nor did her backup request that McArthur be released on bail. Still, she had made a point, namely, that there was no limit to the lengths that she was willing to go for a client.

"In your earlier testimony," resumed Rose, "you said that you don't know for a fact that your car was in the driveway the morning of the murder. Do you recall having said that?"

"Yes."

"Before that, you stated that you did not murder Rabbi Winkler. Do you recall that?"

"Objection," complained Lewis. "She's leading the witness. Also, the witness' prior responses are matters of record, given less than a few hours ago. No need for refreshing his memory."

Rose read agreement in the judge's face and quickly said, "That's not my purpose, Your Honor. I'm laying a foundation and this is my last question toward that aim."

"Make sure that it is, Counselor. Objection overruled."

"Thank you, Your Honor." Rose next asked, "Reverend, since you deny murdering the rabbi, do you have any explanation for the blood and flour discovered in your car, forensic evidence that the prosecutor says ties you to the murder?"

McArthur gave the sigh of the burdened righteous and then said, "What I know is that the blood and flour didn't come off me, and could not have come off me, because I had nothing to do with the murder."

"Was your car impounded by the police?"

"Yes."

"Was the forensic evidence discovered after or before the impounding?"

"After."

"During the interim between the rabbi's murder and the impounding of your car, did you perform any cleanup of the interior or have it done by someone else?"

"No. When it was impounded, it was no dirtier, no cleaner, than normal."

"How would you describe your relationship with the Detroit Police Department?"

"Contentious."

"And why, in your opinion?"

"Objection," said Lewis. "The defendant is a fact witness and not an expert witness. Let him keep his opinions to himself."

The judge said, "Overruled," and then cast a look of annoyance at Lewis.

After a staged pause, McArthur said, "The relationship is contentious because I crusade against police brutality." His tone turned apologetic as he added, "A good part of that calls for singling out certain officers."

"Is there an officer in this courtroom that you would cite as an example?"

Lewis had anticipated the question, would have bet his life that it would be asked, so he was ready with an impassioned, "Objection! No officer is on trial here."

The judge immediately ordered a sidebar.

Out of earshot of the jury, Rose argued, "I'm willing to accept that it's mere coincidence that Lieutenant Cunningham ended up being the lead investigator. What I'm not willing to do is to pretend that there's no history between her and my client and that it couldn't have influenced her investigation."

The judge agreed in principal, told Rose that her leeway would be tight, and ended the sidebar.

Mary guessed the judge's decision from Lewis' sour countenance. Each day of the trial, she had brought the investigation case file, pulling from it as Lewis needed, at times whispering to him and passing him notes. Except for her time on the witness stand, her courtroom presence had been low-key. Now she was about to become a defense exhibit.

"Yes," said McArthur, after Rose repeated the question. With a dart-throwing motion, he pointed and said, "She's sitting at the prosecutor's table, wearing blue."

At least name the designer, asshole. This is the most expensive suit that I own. Mary also was wearing the unflustered facial expression that she'd practiced in the mirror for days for just this occasion. It proved to have been time well spent because McArthur had directed all eyes upon her. Even a cameraman scurried to the side to capture her better.

"You've pointed to Lieutenant Mary Cunningham, correct?"

"That's correct."

"And what's been your complaint against Lieutenant Cunningham?"

"She's trigger-happy. Killed three people, unnecessarily. After the third, I organized a protest at police headquarters, demanding that she be removed from the force or at least assigned permanently to a desk. She's had it in for me ever since."

"Objection!" Lewis punctuated by slapping his palm on the table. "The witness is not qualified to comment on the lieutenant's mind."

"Sustained."

"Has she ever threatened you?"

"Not directly."

"Meaning?"

"Meaning that if looks could kill I'd be her fourth victim."

The response touched off suppressed laughter from a few, reminding Rose that laughter can inject itself into any setting, no matter how inappropriate. It didn't, however, distract her from her mental checklist of the points that she planned to hammer home with pile-driver force when the trial moved to closing arguments.

Point one: she had drawn testimony that Petrocelli once had possession of McArthur's car and house keys and that Petrocelli knew where he kept his gun—fuel for a somebody-else-did-it argument.

Point two: she had used the second part of McArthur's testimony to allege a bad-blood relationship between him and the police in general, and between him and the lead investigator in particular—fuel for a police frame-up argument.

There would be a point three. Rose didn't want to leave herself vulnerable to any theory that McArthur and the widow were in league—not that it was Lewis' style to make a bad-faith allegation. She also wanted to guard against jurors that have overactive imaginations. "Reverend McArthur, do you know the rabbi's widow, Debra Winkler?"

"I met her at a function in the presence of her husband but she and I have never interacted on any level."

Rose had conducted the direct-examination with the objective of supplying Lewis with a barebones scope under which to conduct his cross-examination. Beyond that, she'd be on the watch for possible missteps by him that she can exploit on redirect. Prosecutors rarely get a shot at cross-examining defendants because most defendants, wisely, don't take the stand. As a former prosecutor, Rose knew that it takes discipline not to be the ravenous wolf, tearing indiscriminately into the prey, perhaps accidentally biting oneself.

Rose announced, "I pass the witness, Your Honor."

55.

Joe Kingsley answered his house phone. "Hello." To the first question, he responded, "She's not here," and to the next, "No comment." He said, "Goodbye," and hung up.

Cliff wearily asked, "Who was it this time?"

"A Channel 7 news reporter."

That phone rang again, joined by others throughout the house, in harassing stereo.

"Don't answer it, Daddy." Mary was standing, hands in pockets, back resting against the wall. She closed her red, dry eyes and arched her neck backward, her head contacting the wall. She felt like repeatedly butting it, but didn't, as she thought about the events of the previous hours. She snarled and then beefed, "That bastard. That scrawny, ballsy bastard."

"I meant for you to call after court was over for the day," spoke Joe, who had left a voicemail to that effect, knowing that Mary would have her cell phone turned off. He rested a supportive hand on her shoulder. "I feel responsible."

"You needn't feel that way, Daddy. I'm the one who insisted that you tell me, although you kept saying it should wait."

At the conclusion of McArthur's direct-examination, the judge declared a short recess. It was during that time that Mary checked her phone and saw that Joe had left a voicemail. Concerned that it might have something to do with her mother, Mary immediately returned the call. That's how it came to be that, in the hall of the courthouse, people crisscrossing, Mary learned that Fritz Mueller had come to the Kingsley home, wanting to speak with Sophie.

The news transported Mary to somewhere else. It was a momentary trip; too bad that she returned without her better judgment. Not remembering that Joe was still on the line, she snapped the phone shut with spring-loaded force but resisted the urge to throw it. Joe, therefore, was spared from hearing the forthcoming profanity, but not people nearby, including some jurors, who heard every syllable, as Mary, almost cross-eyed with anger, blurted, "I'll kill that motherfucker!"

Proving that timing is everything, Lisa Rose came out of the courtroom, as though pushed by an invisible, conspiratorial hand.

With the quickness that typically precedes a flying tackle, Mary was in Rose's face, stridently demanding, "You need to control that goddamn Mueller and keep him the fuck away from my mother." Mary took a long blink, her upper lip rising, teeth showing; then, her eyes reopened, wider than normal, from the surprise that Rose had done a disappearing act, or so it seemed.

In reality, someone taller and wider had stepped in front. "You don't want to say anything else, Mary," advised

Gerald Lewis in a low-volume sternness that penetrated her fog. "Let's go." He grabbed her elbow and steered an escape to the stairs.

Several reporters pursued, while others rushed to Rose for comments.

Rose told them, "I don't know what that was about," which was true, technically, but she'd heard enough to have a good suspicion.

Shortly thereafter, with both attorneys in chambers, Lewis requested a recess, which the judge, angry as a hornet with its stinger jammed inward, granted. TGIF: thank goodness it's Friday. The court proceedings would have the weekend to regain the decorum lost in the spectacle of the prosecutor's lead investigator confronting the defense attorney about another of that attorney's clients.

Mary was spending the beginning of that weekend holed up at her parents' house, the two most important men in her life trying to shield her from public fallout. She went into the living room and flopped down onto the sofa. "How could I have been so stupid?"

"You'll survive it, Honey," said Cliff, who had followed her into the room. He revised it to, "We'll survive it, together."

Mary gave a weak smile and said, "Remind me to marry you in my next life, too."

"Mary? You in there? That you, Cliff?" came a voice from the downstairs bedroom.

"Yes, Mama."

"Yes, Mrs. Kingsley."

"Well, you two coming in here to see me or not?" asked Sophie, with playful authority.

Mary winked roguishly at Cliff and answered, "We're still deciding."

"Girl, don't you have me—" Sophie's threat was interrupted by a coughing spell, after which, she said, "take a switch to your behind."

Admitting under her breath, "It would be embarrassing for my husband to see me get a whipping," Mary sprang from the sofa, but because she was hungry and stressed, the sudden rise made her lightheaded. "We'll be in there shortly, Mama."

The downstairs was redolent with the fragrance from flowers. They were Sophie's idea, along with the plug-in air-fresheners, meant to cover the smell of decaying tumors. Mary vacillated over whether she preferred stench or stems. Flowers reminded her of funerals and graves; but, the unmasked odors reminded her of the dead.

Mary wasn't in denial of her mother's impending death but she damn sure wasn't going to allow Mueller any role in the inevitable. Even so, there were better ways to have reacted to his interloping. Enraged at Mueller, she'd lashed out at Rose in proxy.

Forget six degrees of separation. With Mary, Rose, Mueller, and McArthur, it had become more like six-tenths. Mary had told herself and others that she could keep perspectives separate, compartmentalized, like eggs in a carton. This day, she had dropped that carton, making a scrambled mess.

56.

Lewis centered himself behind the lectern and rested his notes, indications that he would not be his usual nomadic self. "Your alibi that you were at home alone, asleep, at the time of the murder is uncorroborated, isn't it?"

Unaffected, McArthur pointed out, "When someone is alone, that, in itself, means that there's no one around to corroborate the fact."

Not the most auspicious of beginnings, but Lewis didn't waste time sulking; instead, he launched into a rapid-fire series of questions. "You claim uncertainty about whether your car was in your driveway the morning of the murder, but that's a lie, isn't it?"

"No. It's the truth."

"It's a lie, because you drove your car when you went to kill Rabbi Winkler, didn't you?"

"No."

"You want this jury to believe that Alison Petrocelli had your car and that the blood and flour evidence came off her, don't you?"

"I want the jury to believe the truth, which is that I didn't kill the rabbi."

"You claim that you didn't know that Petrocelli and the rabbi were having an affair, but you did know, didn't you?"

"I did not."

"You knew because she told you."

"Not so."

"And when she told you, you went into a jealous rage, true?"

"Not true."

"From then on, you threatened and harassed her. Isn't that true?"

"No."

"You took to stalking her, didn't you?"

"No."

"When you couldn't get her to end her affair with the rabbi, you ended it by murdering him, didn't you?"

"Absolutely not."

"Tell the Court and jury the truth, Reverend. On the morning of the murder, were you at the Winkler home because you'd followed Ms. Petrocelli or because you'd come there on your own to kill the rabbi?"

"Neither."

"And the motive was as old as the stars. Jealousy. Admit it."

"That's not true."

"It was Ms. Petrocelli who ended the sex, not you. You would not have, because you were obsessed with her, weren't you?"

"No."

"From the early going, didn't you tell her you loved her, spent lots of money on her?"

"She begged me to tell her that I loved her, so I did to satisfy her. I came to regret it because she became clinging and smothering. As for money, I wasn't trying to buy her, just spending what I could afford."

"You're a bachelor, aren't you Reverend?"

"Yes."

"And you've never married?"

"Never."

"Would you call yourself a lifelong bachelor?"

Rose said, "Objection, Your Honor. Beyond the scope of direct, which did not delve into the reverend's marital status."

"Within the scope of his claim that Ms. Petrocelli stalked him, Your Honor. The tie-in will be evident with my next few questions."

"Objection overruled. Be direct, Mr. Lewis. The Court will indulge you only to a point."

Lewis nodded and said, "Thank you, Your Honor." Then he said, "The question, Reverend McArthur, was would you call yourself a lifelong bachelor?"

"Yes."

"Someone with the reputation of playing the field?"

"I've never liked that phrase. But I enjoy the company of women."

"Women," repeated Lewis. "Plural. So why were you so frequently in public with Ms. Petrocelli, if you only wanted a platonic relationship?"

"What do you mean?"

"Reverend, do you want me to go over, one-by-one, the documented social events you've attended with Ms. Petrocelli?"

"That won't be necessary."

"Then explain why Ms. Petrocelli, and not others, if not for your desire to give the public the impression that the two of you were a couple."

"I...well...I enjoyed her company, yes. And she knew how to conduct herself in public. In addition, we both had professional ties with some of the public functions we attended together."

"Surely, she wasn't the only woman you knew who could conduct herself in public and who had professional ties. You were parading her as your woman. And when she dumped you, it had the potential of being publicly embarrassing, yes?"

"I wasn't dumped."

"Even more embarrassing would be if it became known that she dumped you for a married man, what, with you the eligible bachelor, and all. Isn't that true?"

"You've yet to say anything that is true, Mr. Lewis."

"And isn't it true that it infuriated you that you'd been dumped for a Jew?"

McArthur rolled his eyes, shook his head slowly in pity, and then said, "I repeat, I wasn't dumped. But hypothetically speaking, what does religion and ethnicity have to do with any of this?"

Lewis' eager response was, "You tell me, Reverend. If they weren't factors, why the circumcision threat?"

"I made no such threat."

"You repeatedly demanded to know what the rabbi could give her that you couldn't." Raising his voice in hopes of amplifying the embarrassment, Lewis said, "She told you that he was the better lover, and when you continued to press, she told you he had the larger penis, didn't she?"

"That's perverted and under other circumstances I wouldn't dignify it with an answer." McArthur folded his arms—as much as his girth would allow—and said, "But, since I'm under oath, the answer is, no."

"That's the connection with circumcision. That's why you mutilated the man, isn't it?"

"I did no such thing."

A trial can be a slow, lulling ride to the 100th floor, testimony the bland elevator music. The jury appreciates the intermittent bump. The rarity of a murder defendant on the witness stand is enlivening, in and of itself; nonetheless, interest can be notched up by certain words, penis being among them. Now operating before a perked jury, Lewis transitioned into the next phase of his cross-examination.

"Let's delve into this alleged vendetta that the police department has against you. You want this jury to believe that you were framed by the police, that they planted the evidence. Or would you prefer they believe that the evidence came from Petrocelli. Most likely, you don't care which lie they believe, as long as they acquit, true?"

"I can't answer from personal knowledge what the police or Ms. Petrocelli did or didn't do. What I do know is that I didn't kill the rabbi."

"Specific as to the police, you want the jury to believe that Lieutenant Cunningham has a personal motive to get you tried and convicted because you have attacked her through your K-9 organization, am I right?"

"I never said that."

"You certainly implied it, wouldn't you say?"

"I'm on trial for a murder that I didn't commit, confronted with so-called evidence I had nothing to do with. Someone is out to get me. That's not paranoia. That's logic."

Lewis thumbed through some notes, retrieving a sheet, and placing it on top. "I'm going to read off some names." After finishing, he asked, "Was there any name unfamiliar to you?"

"No."

"Who are those individuals?"

"Police officers."

"Homicide detectives, to be precise," said Lewis. "Each has been the subject of K-9 attacks, whether in your public meetings, newsletter, or website, true?"

"They deserved it."

"Isn't it a fact that you've even attacked Inspector Warren Newberry, over how he runs the homicide unit?"

"And justifiably so. He tolerates rogue officers and rogue practices."

"So even if Lieutenant Cunningham were not involved, you still could play the revenge card with another lead investigator, couldn't you?"

"This is no card game."

Lewis detected weakness in the response. He hadn't harbored any illusions that McArthur would deconstruct and confess, no matter how withering the questioning. But witnesses do wear down, become less assertive, less attentive. If a confession wasn't forthcoming, a concession would be better than nothing. The moment seemed ripe for removing a liability. He turned sideways and extended his arm in Mary's direction, palm open, much the way an emcee introduces a performer taking the stage. "You have no evidence, no knowledge, that Lieutenant Cunningham has ever been in the revenge business, or that the use of force has been her first choice. Isn't that true?" Lewis dropped this arm and awaited the concession.

McArthur immediately, confidently, challengingly, said, "That's not true at all, Mr. Lewis."

Lewis caught himself in time not to do a double-take. He thought he hadn't violated the rule of never asking a question to which one doesn't know the answer; but, had he? He had no choice but to ask the follow-up question, before an awaiting jury and courtroom. Filtering reluctance out of his voice, he asked, "And why isn't that true?"

McArthur licked his lips, not from dryness, but in preparation for the tasty treat that had been set before him. "Just last Friday, Lieutenant Cunningham, using salty language that I won't repeat, shouted out that she was going to kill someone. I wasn't there, of course, but it's my understanding that it set off quite a commotion. However, you know all that, since you were there, along with some of the jurors."

Lewis had practiced the cross-examination for days, down to every pause, and had been almost slaphappy in anticipation of conducting it. He had prepared so unvaryingly on case matters that he failed to factor in recent events, proving that it's a fine line between focus and myopia.

Lewis' thoughts raced for a way to undo the blunder, maybe by having the response stricken, but his mind's ear vibrated with Rose's sure response: *He opened the door, Your Honor.* Lewis, the doorman, was only missing cap, buttoned jacket, and gloves. He knew that any attempts to explain the extenuating circumstances would be risky, drawing additional attention to Mary, without assurances of rehabilitating her. And that's assuming that he could get such attempts past Rose's objections, highly unlikely.

Rose had recounted Mary's meltdown to McArthur and told him to stay alert for an opening. The way things turned out, she'd been spared from having to use a redirect to finesse it out of him. Even her decision to remain silent during the cross-examination, with the exception of that single objection, was purposeful; for, it allowed Lewis to get into overdrive, making him less aware that a trap was lying in wait.

McArthur would be the last witness called by the defense, and barring any rebuttal witnesses called by the prosecutor, the trial would proceed to closing arguments, jury instructions, and, finally, jury deliberations.

Rose silently conceded that some parts of Lewis' cross-examination might have resonated with one or more jurors. There would be time, soon enough, to devote herself to such concerns, like in closing arguments. For now, she savored Lewis' pie-in-the-face predicament.

57.

The McArthur jury was in its third day of deliberations. That fact might presage a hung jury; conversely, there have been juries, out that time and longer, who have emerged with a guilty verdict, others with acquittal. As such, protracted deliberations aren't a reliable indication of whether the jury is divided or just being methodical.

No one knew that better than Lisa Rose, but it never helped her cope productively with the intestine-twisting effects of verdict watch, her coping mechanism being to squander time in trivial distractions, only able to revert to her proficient self after the verdict. She had frittered away the first day in her office rewriting documents that had nothing wrong with them and ignoring calls from the media. On the second day, she had stayed home and watched a week's worth of rented movies. Now, on the third day, she was out-and-about, watching something of a personal nature.

Two movers in the final stage of unloading their van were carrying a long, purple sofa down the ramp. The one who was slight-of-build was in as much control of his end as was his jumbo partner. When they reached level ground, they took the sofa into the house formerly owned by Bernie and Yetta Rosenberg.

Lisa Rose, on the advice of the realtor, had spruced up the property: not only landscaping but new windows and doors. The added curbside appeal plus a below-market asking price resulted in a quick sale. That is to say, once she decided to list the house, months after it became vacant. During that time, she'd occasionally performed solitary walkthroughs, her temperament that of a former inmate returning to a closed-down prison. She had sent the warden to Florida, an easy banishment compared to the memories imbedded in the woodwork like termites.

Rose was parked several houses down and on the opposite side of the street, undecided on whether to sit through the entire unloading. It wasn't the most exhilarating use of time, but better than watching paint dry or grass grow.

Her attention shifted up to her once bedroom window, through which she used to gaze down at children romping about, wishing that she could join them or even invite them up. There was a time when Lisa knew what it was like to have visitors, girls her age with whom to play, share secrets, and argue about matters that only could concern the innocent. But that ended when Yetta died. Bernie had made it clear that he had no stomach for bratty intruders, bad enough that he was stuck with raising a granddaughter who had caused him irrecoverable loss.

Lisa became quite bookish, a common refuge for an isolated child, although her subject of interest was uncommon. On the other hand, Bernie's incessant diatribes against the legal system and how it had failed his family was bound to exert an influence—one way or the other—on her attitudes about law. By the age of nine, she had made a secret career choice.

When she turned sweet sixteen, the momentous day was spent at a lawyer's office, but not in any type of intern capacity. She was there seeking representation for filing for emancipation. She'd boned up on the subject while counting down the years. She was a few months from an early graduation from high school, having been double-promoted. And she'd received a full scholarship to an Ivy League university, where she would earn both her under-graduate and law degrees. The lawyer accepted her case pro bono, impressed by her plans for college, law school, and career, and in equal measure, sympathetic with her narrative about her home life.

Good riddance was Bernie's outward reaction after a judge awarded Lisa emancipation. He never contested the case; yet, the disrespect and ingratitude that he felt Lisa had shown wedged a boulder-size spur up his butt that never dislodged.

One of the new owners of the house, the wife, came outside. The woman, black, short, late-thirties, and wearing sweats, sneakers, and bandana, would appear whenever the movers were handling something fragile. This time, it was something in a carton, that from its size and shape, could have been a painting or a wall mirror. An office manager accustomed to overseeing, the woman circled the movers, seeking the best position from which to call out cautions,

if needed. The somewhat older husband, a computer pro-
grammer, remained inside, trusting that the movers knew
their job. Completing the household was a spirited nine-
year-old daughter.

Hey Lisa, Rose telepathically called to her childhood
self, *just our rotten luck that a playmate shows up a lifetime too
late, huh?*

The Lisa who materialized at the bedroom window was
the same age as the couple's daughter; then again, whenever summoned, the imagined Lisa always would adopt an
age consistent with the circumstances. Being a figment of
the mind, Lisa didn't have one of her own; otherwise, she
might have wondered why Rose wasn't below, in front of the
house, why Rose was communicating from an undisclosed
location.

*Look across the street, Lisa. I'm parked in front of where the
Kramers used to live. I'm in the new black Jaguar.* In the wake
of that thought, Rose, feeling foolish, struck a fist against
the steering wheel. Hell, Lisa hadn't cared about material
trappings; they hadn't been the motivation that had kept
the youngster's nose buried in books.

*Okay, Little Miss Idealistic, don't think I don't know that if
you'd had the money for that doll house, the one in the Sears cata-
log, you would have sprung for it in a heartbeat. So what if I have
a few big-girl toys now. Doesn't mean that I sold out.*

Rose unwrapped a stick of gum, popped it in, and
attacked it with quick, teeth-knocking chomps, as a defensive mood settled in. *Before you get too judgmental about how I
turned out, don't forget that you had more than a little to do with*

*it. Childhood is short, for sure, but a person can spend the rest of
her life trying to recover from its effects.*

Rose's thoughts were interrupted by a car approaching
from the opposite direction that had slowed to a crawl. It
was a classic Chevy, pimped, with oversized tires and spinning rims. The occupants were a couple of young males,
one black, one white. After taking in their fill of the Jag,
they flashed admiring smiles and nodded to Rose, before
cruising off. She tracked them in her rearview mirror, not
convinced of their good intentions.

Similarly, for years, Rose had been concerned for
Bernie's safety, not that there had been a particular incident. In fact, neighbors kept a watchful, protective eye
on the old cuss, while knowing better than to visit. And
although Rose had the house equipped with an elaborate
security system, it didn't resolve other issues stemming
from Bernie's age and health. What if, while climbing or
descending the stairs, his hip gives out, and he tumbles and
breaks his fool neck? Then there are the joint-stiffening
winters and the possibility of a slip-and-fall. If Bernie's
uneven walk meets the wrong patch of ice, the result could
be disastrous.

Yet, over the years, Rose's every entreaty that Bernie
bow to reason and move to safer and warmer surroundings
drew mulish refusal, even though she made it clear that she
would foot the expenses. He delighted in her worrying and
hoped that it contained a heaping portion of guilt. Bernie
was so much about the guilt thing.

It was that aspect of his character that made Rose change tactics and she wanted to kick herself for not having thought of it sooner. She employed reverse psychology. Bernie had regarded moving out of his house as something done for her benefit, which automatically hardened him to the idea. Rose repackaged it as an obligation on her part, one she'd rather not shoulder but nonetheless owed him, and guilt was eating her for not delivering what was owed. Bernie, blinded by ego and pettiness, fell for it; besides, it was to Florida that many of the haughty, who'd fared better than he had in life, had resettled. He deserved no less. He was owed.

Once given that green light, Rose didn't tarry and in short order had everything in place for Bernie's relocation. She told him that she would arrange to have his household belongings trucked. All he had to do was throw a couple of day's worth of clothes into a carry-on suitcase. On the day that she came to whisk him to the airport, however, they had a little spat; well, not little, since he threatened not to go. He conceded, but only after she told him that his last-minute addition to his suitcase would not pass airport security and would be confiscated, likely permanently. To Bernie, that was unthinkable.

As for the present-day movers, they had completed the delivery and were buckled in their seats, the muscled one behind the wheel. They drove away, unaware that they'd been watched from a distance.

Well, Lisa, this'll be the last time I visit you at the old home-stead. It's only right that we let the new occupants enjoy the place without us around. You shouldn't mind, anyway. Of all your haunts, this is your least favorite.

Rose turned the ignition. *Come on, Lisa, time to go. Maybe we'll hang out in front of our grade school and dredge up memories. That should be good for a half-hour.*

At that time, her phone sounded, announcing a text message. She pulled the phone out of her purse and took a look. The message, saving her from having to find another trivial pursuit, was from Kirk Rhodes.

It read: Verdict in.

58.

The testing officer led the way to the counter, where he laid down the evaluation form. "Got another one for you, Eddie."

The cadet bookmarked the training manual he'd been reading, rose from his desk, and came forward. He slid the form along the counter, down to the computer, where he would input the information.

The testing officer, about to leave, said, "That was a mighty fine bit of shooting."

"Thanks," said Mary, "but you already told me that. A couple of times, in fact."

"What, you put off by a compliment?" asked the testing officer, his tone more accusing than apologetic.

"It just sounds like you're talking to Annie Oakley."

A now testy testing officer, having started for the door, responded, "Annie probably would have been able to take an innocent compliment."

"Hold up a second," requested Mary, and after he turned around, admitted, "You didn't do anything wrong. Sorry that I reacted like I did."

"Accepted," said the testing officer who then exited.

The cadet, fingers busy at the keyboard, said, "Almost through."

"Take your time." Mary wanted him to know that he was in no danger of her snapping at him.

The cadet, reading the screen, made the observation, "You cut it kind of close. In a few days you would've been decertified."

"I know," said Mary, reaching for her ringing cell phone. The ensuing conversation only took seconds.

The cadet pressed one last key and then said, "The printer is in the other room. I'll be back shortly with your paperwork and you can be on your way."

But Mary said, "Send it through department mail." And with that, she hurried out, headed for court, having been notified that the McArthur verdict was in.

59.

Throughout their marriage, Bernie and Yetta seldom argued but only because she rarely challenged him on anything. But there was one instance that was the mother of all exceptions. It even involved a physical tug-of-war over her faux-alligator leather suitcase, as she somehow found the strength to wrest it from him when he tried to stop her from packing.

The suitcase did a single bounce as Yetta threw it on Lisa's bed. Yetta unlocked the brass hardware and pushed the top open as much as the hinges allowed, making the suitcase resemble a gaping maw awaiting to be fed. And that's what she began to do, first with some clothes from the closet.

Bernie, rankled almost beyond containment, thought about slamming the suitcase shut, but wasn't confident that such a show of force would serve the intended purpose, not against whatever body-snatcher had taken over Yetta. Still, this was his house, where he reigned supreme, and he would not be a silent spectator to this revolt. "Have you taken leave of your senses?" he loudly asked. "You're not going anywhere."

"I'm leaving you," Yetta said, as she slipped some clothes off their hangers.

The smile was meant to demean and to intimidate. "And why would you even think of doing something so patently absurd?"

"For Lisa's sake."

Bernie put two and two together and said, "I have no tolerance for foolhardy questions."

In a room with Mother Goose wallpaper and a Raggedy Ann doll that was slumped face-down on the bed from having toppled when the suitcase landed, Yetta pleadingly reminded, "She is but a child. Even too young for kindergarten."

"But old enough to know that I am her grandfather, not her father."

"Lisa does not understand that you can't be both. She plays with Selma Cohen's granddaughter who speaks of her own parents. Lisa needs to have things explained."

"That's why I set her straight."

Notching up her voice, Yetta responded, "Not in a way proper for any child. Least of all your grandchild."

"You have the easier part to explain," said Bernie, speaking along gender lines, "were she to come to you with similar nonsense."

"Lisa knows that I am only her grandmother. This, I have explained to her."

"And I repeat. You have it easier. How am I to talk about someone who I know nothing about, including his name?"

"And for that you blame Lisa?"

"Don't be silly. I just don't want to be reminded that I don't know who he is." Bernie paused, then in a particularly insinuating tone, said, "Or what he is."

Suspecting his drift, Yetta boldly said, "Out with it. Say what you mean."

"Let's just say that her hair is a tad too crinkly for my liking. I'll leave it at that."

"What you imply is not true, but even if it were—"

"Don't you dare!" demanded Bernie. "Don't you dare say that it makes no difference. I have standing in this community. I have an important job."

"But no heart. And I must leave you."

"No heart, you say?" Bernie's boastful rebuttal was, "I brought you back with me to this country when I could have left you over there, pregnant. I didn't have to accept my responsibility."

That it sounded like charity was not lost on Yetta, but she overlooked it. "That is true. And in return, I always have tried to do my very best toward you, while asking for virtually nothing."

"Then you prove it now, by ending this ridiculous charade."

"It is no charade," Yetta said, and pressed down on the clothes to make more room.

"That suitcase won't even hold all her clothes," observed Bernie. "There won't be room for a single stitch of yours."

Yetta looked down at the modest dress she was wearing and said, "I don't care if this schmata is the only thing of mine that I leave with."

Having a dickens of a time coping with his wife's resolve, Bernie sought to receive that which he wasn't known for giving: sympathy. Even so, it was a harsh, staccato way that he said, "Look, I admit that it's difficult for me. Lisa reminds me of things I'd rather not be reminded of."

"And I see her differently. As a gift of life. Someone through whom I will live after my days are done. It is the natural order of things."

Defiantly, Bernie asked, "Are you ordering me to think the same way?"

"I don't have that power, as you well know." Even while making that concession, she stood erect and determined. "But I do have the power to leave."

"Ha! Where would you go? How will you support yourself?"

"No need to try to scare me. I'm already scared. And maybe you should be too, Bernard Simon Rosenberg, if only a little. Scared that people will wonder what conditions would cause a woman with no means of livelihood to leave a good provider, even taking a child with her."

Now it was all too evident to Bernie what the body-snatcher had done: turned a docile wife into a masterful negotiator, one who wasn't above putting into play that which meant most to him—his reputation, manufactured though it was. He was standing in the middle of the room, but nonetheless, he had been backed into a corner. With each word burning his ears, he said, "I'd hate to see you and her having to fend for yourselves. What understanding can we reach to prevent that?"

Her tone hopeful, Yetta answered, "Show our grand-daughter patience and kindness." She intentionally didn't include the L-word, not wanting to go for too much.

"So be it," was his terse reply but the simultaneous, dismissive wave of the hand said a lot more. Returning to form, he decreed, "Now, I'd appreciate some damn supper," and started for the door.

Lisa had an ear pressed against the other side of that door and had heard the entire exchange. By the time Bernie gripped the knob, she had twirled and rushed downstairs.

60.

With golden oldies playing over indistinguishable conversations and the frequent clap of swinging kitchen doors, the waitress placed two bowls on the table, one of pretzels, the other of potato chips. "What can I get you folks?"

"A pitcher of beer, to start," said Gerald Lewis. "And tell Joey I'll be crying in it, so no need to water it down."

"I'll be sure to tell him," said the waitress, writing the order while walking away.

Barbara Phillips, the assistant prosecutor who'd sat second chair during the McArthur trial helped herself to a pretzel and said, "If you're going to cry in your own mug, fine. Just don't cry in the pitcher until after I've poured mine."

"I'm not making promises," said Lewis.

Mingles Bar & Grill, popular with the legal eagles who practice in the downtown courts, wasn't Mary's type of place, but neither was she a habitué of any of the haunts of her fellow cops. "You two work it out between yourselves," she said. "I don't drink."

Lewis, the good host, suggested, "Try the lemonade. It's excellent." He craned his neck, searching. "Where did our waitress go?"

"Don't bother," said Mary. "I can't stay long. I'm going to look in on my mother this evening."

Phillips, a cycling enthusiast, was lithe as a sapling and wore her auburn tresses shoulder-length. Her marriage to her job was in its ninth year. "Tell her she's in my thoughts and prayers."

"Same here," said Lewis.

"Mary didn't want to be the focus of attention. It wasn't her crying party. She was merely attending, a reluctant invitee. "I'll tell her."

"Ah, here comes the beer," announced Lewis.

The waitress sat the pitcher in the middle of the table and a mug in front of each of the party of three. "Can I get you anything else?"

"Lemonade for my friend, here," said Lewis, ignoring Mary's objecting frown.

"Wing-dings for me," said Phillips.

A hand placed on Lewis' shoulder caused him to look up.

"You tried a good case," said Judge Boyce Ellington, drink in hand. He patted Lewis on the back and consoled, "But, like they say, you can't win 'em all."

"Unless your name is Lisa Rose," Lewis carped. "Care to join us, Judge?"

"Thanks," said Ellington, his attire living up to his reputation as one of the area's best-dressed, "but, I'm going to circulate."

Mary's eyes took on a mischievous twinkle and then narrowed into shifty slits. Like a character out of a bad spy movie, she looked down and away, put her hand over her mouth, and spoke in undertones. "Judge Ellington, don't look yet, and when you do, be subtle," she instructed. "Standing at the bar, blue dress with a killer weave, eyeing you like you're dessert."

Ellington slyly looked in that direction. It turned out that he knew the long-legged lovely, who looked so comely in the subdued lighting. He lifted his glass in salute and held up one finger, letting her know that the wait wouldn't be long. He bade adieu to the table with, "See you around."

Mary never doubted what Ellington's reaction would be. She had engineered his departure, surrounded by enough law school graduates, as it was.

The waitress brought the lemonade in a big frosted mug.

Having done the courteous thing and waited until all drinks were at the table, Lewis raised the pitcher of beer, filled Phillips' mug, and then his own. He raised his mug and said, "I propose a toast. Here's to the pursuit of justice. Whatever the result, may we always agree that the system works."

"Here, here," said Phillips.

"I'll drink to that," said Mary.

A round of clinks and they took their first sips.

"You didn't cry in your beer, after all," observed Phillips.

"I'll save the crying for my pillow."

Mary dropped her head guiltily, lifted it, and said, "I'm still sick about my meltdown."

Lewis waved away the comment, like he was clearing cigarette smoke, and said, "We can't blame it on that. Not one juror mentioned it when I interviewed them after the verdict."

"Still, I was unprofessional."

"Well," said Lewis, "I know better than most that Mueller is a master at pushing people's buttons."

"The entire Prosecutor's Office can attest to that," said Phillips.

Lewis set down his mug and said, "Besides, my bone-headed cross-examination of McArthur trumps you, Mary."

"Since we're baring our souls," said Phillips, "we could have done without the hate crime count. The jury might have seen it as overcharging and political."

"Barbara Phillips," began Lewis, who always called her by both names whenever they sparred, "I'll grant you just one I-told-you-so."

"Do I get one, too?" asked Mary. "I told you from the beginning that there were holes in the case."

Lewis huffed and said, "That's right, kick a man when he's down."

The conversation shifted to other topics, the time passing, as the contents of the pitcher were reduced to suds and Mary finished a second lemonade. Her evaluation: full-bodied and pulpy, but a bit too sweet. "I have to get going."

"Sure," said Lewis. "Thanks for joining us."

Phillips let the wing-ding that she was holding drop to her plate. Because her mouth was full, she communicated by patting the tabletop with one hand, while with the other, pointing to an overhead flat-screen television, one of a number throughout the place.

On the screen was video replay of Lisa Rose, post-verdict, in the court hallway, answering questions from the media. Standing next to her was the freed Reverend Jeeter McArthur. In back of them was a gaggle of McArthur supporters. There also were the usual camera hounds, waving and gesturing.

After the verdict, Mary, Lewis, and Phillips had made a beeline out the courtroom ahead of Rose, with Lewis stopping only long enough to tell the media that he was disappointed but would not second-guess the jury.

"Wonder whether she's crowing," said Phillips. "I can't read the closed-caption from here."

Mary stood and said, "You two might want to move closer, but I'm leaving."

On her way to the door, Mary strung together glimpses from the various screens that she passed. She stopped cold, however, upon noticing that someone in the courthouse crowd was muscling toward the front, causing others to glance backward in annoyance over being bumped and jostled. The culprit emerged to the left and rear of Rose, who kept speaking into the microphone, oblivious to his presence. Mary recognized him, as did the cameraman who zoomed in.

Fritz Mueller gave a hamming smile into the camera and squarely into Mary's face, taunting and threatening—or, at least that's how it seemed to Mary.

61.

Bernie slammed the refrigerator door. Beer can in hand, he peg-legged to the patio glass door to check the weather. Bumpy clouds, with flat, gray bottoms patched an otherwise blue sky. The past few days had been rainy, aggravating his hip. He pulled the ring tab, the can hissed, and a whiff of carbonation drifted to his nostrils, the smell sour, like his mood.

Rose, left eye twitching, arms folded, watched her grandfather's antics from across the room. If she were a smoker—of anything—she would be lighting up about now, as a means of dealing with the vexation. "Can't you settle for being just one of the most ornery men alive instead of the undisputed champion?"

"Save your breath. I'm not listening." Bernie began emptying the can in loud, rude swigs. When he finished, he said, "Be useful and dispose of this," and then made an overhand toss.

Rose snared the can sure-handedly then deposited it into the kitchen garbage pail. "You're impossible."

Bernie slid open the patio door and stepped outside. Bernie knew that Rose would follow. When she did, he let loose. "The chutzpah! Coming down here, like I'm a child in trouble."

Rose would have appreciated more time to decompress after the McArthur trial, instead of having to jet to Florida to defuse a situation. "The administration was ready to kick you out."

"So let them. I never asked to be here. I don't need any damn assisted living. I can look after myself."

"If you get kicked out, then what?"

"I'll move back into my house."

"What is it about the word, sold, that's not filtering through to you?"

Bernie made a fist, and as though against an invisible desktop, made a pounding motion with each word, as he alleged, "You had no authority to sell my home from under me."

"Come off it, will you. I had every authority, as you well know." Rose had paid Bernie double the fair market value in return for a quit claim deed. Even though she later willingly took a bath on the sale to the present owners, she gave those proceeds to him also. And, a decade prior, she established a trust that secured his financial well-being for life, however torturously long it turns out to be. "Can we return the discussion to assault and battery?" she pleaded.

"Is that what you're calling it, Ms. Fancy Lawyer? I call it self-defense."

"The man you punched in the face wasn't attacking you."

"So say you. He attacked my honor."

In a tone that was not a testimonial, Rose said, "And all the world knows you are a man of honor."

"You with the sarcasm."

"The man is older than you an half your size."

"There's nothing small about his mouth, though." An unrepentant Bernie said, "No one calls me a liar."

"He said he didn't believe you'd been a shochet."

"Like I said, no one calls me a liar."

"I doubt that he's the only nonbeliever. Just the only one who voiced it."

"And the only one who got punched."

Rose, fighting exasperation, massaged her eye socket with the heel of her palm and then slid the palm down her face. "Look, what would it take to satisfy you?" She was serious when she asked, "You want a plaque signed by the Fleishmans and hung in the lobby that says you were a shochet? If that'll keep you from going around kicking ass, I'll arrange it."

If she had to make good on the offer, she'd consider it a tack-on to the dual objectives behind this visit: to dissuade the aggrieved from pressing charges against Bernie; and, to persuade the administration not to boot Bernie from the complex. The first was achieved by writing a check and the second by giving her personal guarantee that there would be no recurrence.

"My word should suffice. The fool probably believes that only a rabbi can be a shochet these days."

"Not necessarily." Rose placed her shoulder purse on the round glass-top of the wrought iron table, which along with two chairs, furnished the patio. "Maybe he knows that a person can become a shochet through apprenticeship. Maybe he simply can't believe that you passed the character requirements."

Blind to the possibility that she could be serious, Bernie said with disdain, "Another one of your poor attempts at humor?"

"I wish it were. The fact is that you are mean and ornery."

"You don't know what you're talking about," Bernie said, while looking down and away. He had spotted a tiny lizard that was hiding against a table leg, frozen in alertness, waiting for instinct to instruct it. He balanced himself on his bad leg and raised the other, in preparation for stomping the reptile. He slapped the tabletop, causing the spooked critter to perform some nifty, broken-field scampering that ended in a flying leap into the safety of the grass. Bernie's reflexes never stood a prayer.

I rest my case, thought Rose, regarding his being mean and ornery. What she spoke, however, was, "This visit has been a hoot, as always, but I have a plane to catch." She dithered over whether to attempt physical contact in departing—nothing too familial, nothing too awkward, nothing too risky, maybe a tepid hug or a peck on the cheek; but, there was no guarantee against rejection. She ended up blowing him a kiss. Wearing pants, she considered going over the railing but dismissed it as unseemly. Instead, she grabbed her purse then walked back inside, so that she could leave out of the front door.

Bernie followed, willing to endure the discomfort of a brisk pace, in order to not have to talk to Rose's back. "Oh, sure, go catch your bleeping plane. You think they only fly when you're a passenger? I can catch one, too. You can't keep me here if I don't want to stay."

Rose stopped abruptly and spun to face her tormentor. Glaring, she invited, "Do as you please."

"Easy for you to talk so big, now that you've sold my home."

"I'll buy the damn thing back. No matter what the asking price."

"Good," replied Bernie, except his voice lacked conviction.

Rose combatively said, "If you could move back today, you wouldn't. You'd be there by yourself, with no one to punish." She turned to the door and undid the deadbolt.

Bernie clamped his palm against the door, preventing her from exiting. "So, now it comes out. You believe I kept the house to punish you."

"I know you did. You watched contently as the neighborhood changed. You delighted when I became one of a few Jewish kids in school."

He removed his hand from the door, and said, "I was a disabled man who had to give up his livelihood, as if I have to remind you. How was I to afford the suburbs?"

Rose pursed her lips and shook her head, not buying the defense. "Others of equal or lesser means did it. You stayed out of hatefulness and spite. All those years, you allowed me to be picked on and excluded, because you blamed me for your injury. Do you know the meaning of accident, old man?"

"You're talking out your head."

"Let's face it, you blame me for being born. But it gets richer. You blame me for my mother's decision. She wouldn't have made the decision had I been important enough to her, right? You're one twisted individual."

"I don't care about your ridiculous charges. This is no court room and I won't be put on trial by the likes of you."

Rose raised her hands, shook them in hallelujah-fashion, and exclaimed, "The likes of me?!" Too accustomed to the abuse to actually be incredulous, she went on to say, "Listen to yourself. You talk like I'm a goddamn thing. I'm your flesh and blood. Practically all my life, you've been my only family."

At least Bernie didn't make a disowning response, just grunted.

"And the guilt you laid on Grandmother was inhumane. How do you live with yourself?"

"Quite well. Thanks for asking."

"I believe it. You can live with yourself but not by yourself. You need somebody to make miserable."

"So say you, but I got along just fine those years that you were out East," Bernie said, of when she attended college and then law school. "No one asked that you return to Michigan. At least I didn't."

"That's true. But I believe that you always knew that I'd come back. I'd like to think that I returned to look after you in your old age, but maybe the reason was much darker. Maybe I'm a masochist. God knows, you're a sadist."

There was a silent face-off for tense seconds, during which Rose stood ready to call any bluff that he would return to Detroit. It didn't come.

"If I'm so evil, why do you foot the bill for me to stay here?"

"You mean in this concentration camp, as you've referred to it?"

"Whatever. Could it be guilt on your part?"

"So, now you're Sigmund Freud? You needn't concern yourself with my motives. Just continue playing it for all it's worth."

Bernie sneered and then said, "Just as I thought. It's more about you than about me."

"No," snapped Rose, "it's about you. It's about your inability to see the obvious, because you question how can it possibly be true? But, it is true. I've said it many times and I'll say it to you now. I love you." Succumbing to tears would have been of little catharsis, absent a shoulder to cry on, or even a sympathetic pat on the head, comfort that Bernie never doled out. The last person to sooth her that way had been Yetta. So, before her mistiness could overcome her, she swung open the door and hurried out.

Bernie called out after her, "And another thing, I'm tired of waiting for you to send me my chalefs. Tired of your excuses." He cupped his hands at the sides of his mouth, not to yodel, but to compensate for the increasing distance, and shouted, "You better send me my chalefs."

62.

Inspector Warren Newberry, without looking up from the memo he was reading at his desk, said, "It's on top of my out-box."

Mary, there because she'd been summoned, picked up the two-page stapled report, but remained.

Newberry's eyes cast upward, and he said, "That'll be all."

"I was hoping for some feedback."

In less than an encouraging tone, Newberry said, "Feedback, like what?"

"Never mind." Mary took two backward steps, in preparation for turning toward the door.

"Wait. Here's your feedback. You wrote it. I read it. Case officially closed." Newberry made a sharp motion with his wrist, and the memo that had been hanging limp in his hand acquired a spine, but he didn't immediately resume reading; instead, he gave the qualifier, "That is, unless you're expecting someone to waltz in and confess to having killed Rabbi Winkler, murder weapon in hand. A video and eye witnesses also would be nice to have."

Newberry wasn't overstating by much, since double jeopardy protects the acquitted from being tried again on the same charges. And once a suspect is acquitted, nailing someone else is made all the more difficult. The first claim the defense attorney will make is that the authorities have charged another innocent person.

Mary's lingering wasn't because she wanted to lament over the verdict; she was too familiar with the vagaries of jury trials for that. She was fishing for compliments. "I thought it was one of my better reports."

Newberry swallowed, the lubrication needed because praise was known to get stuck in his throat. "Good writing job."

Mary grinned and said, "Thank you."

Newberry gave a weary stare before claiming, "Sometimes I wonder whether I'm running a nursery or a homicide unit."

"You're calling me a baby?"

"If the bootie fits, wear it." Newberry's eyes returned to the memo, finishing the remaining lines.

Mary figured that if she remained any longer there would be nothing to salvage of the already tattered compliment, so, she gave a salute, and said, "Have a nice day, Inspector."

But Newberry said, "You might as well stay. Got something to tell you."

Wondering about the sudden turnaround, Mary readied herself and then asked, "What is it?"

Newberry twisted one end of his mustache. "Have a seat."

"I'll stand, if it's alright with you."

"Suit yourself." Newberry proceeded to say, "The latest brain-fart from up high is this so-called cold case squad. You might have heard rumors."

"Three, by last count."

"Save the wit for someone who admires it."

"Will do."

"Well, the squad is a go. That's what this memo is about." Newberry let the document drop from his hand onto the desk. He paused, looking her in the eyes, before announcing, "I'm going to give them your slashed throat cases."

"Kent and Gibson?"

"You have others?"

"No."

"Then those must be the slashed throat cases I'm talking about."

"I didn't mean to sound dense. It's just that I'm taken by surprise."

Newberry responded, "If that's the biggest surprise of your life, then you've led one damn boring life. And we both know that that's not true."

"You're the definition of sensitivity. You know that, don't you?" Having allowed herself that bit of sarcasm, she went on to ask, "When did you make the decision?"

"Just now."

Mary silently rehearsed, her mind's ear evaluating the words to assure that their tone wouldn't sound as if she were challenging him. "So, why my cases?"

"Politics. The Mayor and City Council are backing the squad. I've been around long enough to know that they want some early success so that they can look good."

"I still don't see the tie-in."

Newberry slowly tapped knuckles on the armrest, tugged between further explanations and having it seem as if he needs her approval. "First, those cases are not as cold as some of the others I could throw at them. And, second, your files are better organized than most."

Underwhelmed, Mary said, "Oh."

"That's your reaction? Shortly ago, you were deep-diving for compliments and now I can't force one on you. What's that about?"

"Nothing." In support of that answer, she tried to move the conversation along. "Who's going to be on this squad?"

"FBI, State Police, Sheriff's Office, and our unit."

"Seems to me, that the focus is being put on the wrong end. If the homicide unit weren't so understaffed, there'd be fewer cold cases to begin with."

"I agree. All the more reason for you to give up those cases. I want you on current ones." Newberry wagged a finger in preemption. "I know what you're about to say, that you've been working those cases in addition to current ones."

"I have."

"And part-time is better than no time, but that's not the point. The squad can give it its full attention, supposedly."

By right, Mary should have welcomed being two cases lighter, especially since the cases would continue to be worked, and by a squad, at that. The problem was her devotion to seeing matters to the end. None of her smoke-screens had worked, the one about understaffing had even backfired, and now she stood resigned to the loss.

Newberry adjusted his posture then fidgeted with a cuf-flink, tell-tale indications of discomfort, since he was about to show compassion. "You're going to run yourself in the ground if you don't let up. Plus, you can use more free time for your mother."

"Thanks for considering her."

"Sure. Now that the trial is over, you might want to take some days off. Attend to personal matters."

"I'll think about it."

"You're damn good, true enough," began Newberry, as if in preamble to a compliment, a misconception immedi-ately exposed when he said, "but it's not like the homicide unit will fold without you. Get real."

Mary's smile was one of exasperation. "Why use a criti-cism, when a compliment can serve the same purpose, huh, Inspector?"

"Call it energy conservation. My way of going green."

"Who from homicide will be on the squad?"

"Brogan. He's a decent investigator. And, who would get more of a kick out of working with those other agen-cies?"

"Nobody. He'll play it up in his mind like it's a military special operations something or other."

"That's Brogan, alright."

"When do I turn over the files?"

"They want me to tell them ASAP which cases will be transferred."

"You want me to stop working the cases immediately?"

"Might as well." Newberry thought to ask, "You haven't caught any breaks with either, have you?"

Her facial expression deadpan, Mary answered, "Not unless you count my head, from crashing into one dead-end after another."

"Like I told you before…"

"I know, save the wit."

63.

The dark, tinted driver's side window began to lower, revealing strip-by-strip that it was Jeeter McArthur behind the wheel. He grabbed the stapled papers that were lying on the front passenger's seat and handed them through the opening. "Here you go."

Lisa Rose, standing alongside the vehicle, took the offering, folded it lengthwise, and shoved it into her trusty shoulder purse. "Anything else?"

"At least look at it," urged McArthur.

"I will, later. Anyway, you gave me the gist over the phone."

"As best that I understood it, but I might be off the mark."

"You understood well enough to know that you need legal representation," said Rose, but retrieved the papers from her purse. "If it'll make you happy, I'll review it now."

"I'd appreciate it."

Rose flipped through the papers in rapid succession, not bothering with boilerplate. She refolded them and slapped them across an open palm. "Your understanding was spot-on. At this rate, you might want to consider legally changing your name to Defendant."

"Will you take the case?" Not receiving an immediate answer, McArthur said, "Get in and let's negotiate." The door latch sounded a click as it popped up, toaster-like.

"Can't. I'm running late." She'd suggested the meeting site, claiming that it was in the path of another appointment; still, she dallied to say, "I saw that she retained Sandy Bulger. That means that our bereaved widow is going after big bucks."

McArthur thought that he recognized a ploy, so he said, "If this is your way of upping the ante, it's unnecessary. Just name your price. Now, do we have a deal?"

"I don't remember you this worried over the criminal charges."

"It's not a matter of being worried," assured McArthur. "But, I wouldn't be the first person acquitted of a crime, only to be found liable in a civil suit." Giving credit where it was due, he admitted, "You warned me that Debra Winkler would sue."

"No clairvoyance, there. More like warning that night would follow day."

"I can write a check for your retainer right now."

Coyly, Rose said, "I don't know. You might do better with someone else. Juries can tire of the same pair. Hell, the pair can tire of each other."

"That hasn't been your attitude with Dr. Deceased," griped McArthur, like someone resentful of a favored sibling.

"Silly me. I thought we were talking about you." Rose made fanning motions with the papers, and said, "I wish you luck, but it's best that we—"

"Wait," pleaded McArthur. "I was out of line. I'm sorry." Spreading it thicker, he asked, "Can you blame me for wanting the best attorney there is?"

Rose's mouth twisted in cynicism. She moved away from the vehicle, exaggeratingly raising and replanting one foot, then the other, as though trying to avoid stepping in something. "Don't lay down the horseshit too deep," she requested. "I'm not wearing high boots."

Unaccustomed to begging, McArthur took another approach. "This is so topsy-turvy. You popped up at my booking, like a jack-in-the-box, surprising the be-Jesus out of me, and named yourself my attorney. Now, when I'm trying to retain you, you play hard-to-get. What am I missing?"

"Personality and charm?" Rose was immediately apologetic. "Sorry. I'm a frustrated comic, a bad one, most of the time."

McArthur's nose wrinkled in cast-off as he shook his head, saying, "I'm not easily offended. But, returning to the matter at hand, will you represent me?"

"I won't commit one way or the other at this time. I'll think about it and get back to you." She returned the papers to her purse but didn't fasten the flap.

"When?"

"Tomorrow."

"Good enough."

"And I'm going to invoice you for time I spend making the decision, whatever the decision turns out to be."

"Agreed."

"That's that," said Rose, in wrap-up. "I have to be on my way."

"Me too." McArthur pushed the window control button.

The window hadn't risen all the way up, however, before Rose started tapping against it. When she had McArthur's attention, she pointed downward with a crooked index finger, signaling him to lower the window again.

McArthur did. "Forgot something?"

Rose removed a white bag from the vehicle's roof. She dangled the bag and said, "You were about to drive away without this."

"What is it?"

"Chinese."

McArthur had seen her approach with the bag but it hadn't retained his attention, his mind having been on weightier matters. "Same kind that I had in your office?" he asked, in reference to the celebration meal the day of his acquittal.

"The same. You said you liked it."

In truth, McArthur wasn't fond of Chinese, but having subsisted for months on jail food, he'd downed the meal with gusto, and now, not wanting to offend—especially since he was seeking a favor—he grinned broadly and reached for the offering. "Thanks."

"Don't mention it. Containers sometimes leak, so you ought to set it on the floor."

McArthur didn't question the advice. To comply, he had to unfasten his seatbelt. His size made it a task to lean to the side and forward so that he could place the bag on the front passenger's floor mat.

As he was straightening, Rose was reaching through the opened window. She made a quick swipe across his throat and the resulting scraping sound flooded her brain with panic. *Fuck!* The blade had scraped across a thick chain, the one that held the platinum, diamond-studded cross that he loved to sport.

Her arms flew around his neck in a desperate attempt to pull him into position for another swipe; however, not only couldn't she budge his bulk, she was lifted off her tiptoes and farther into the vehicle's interior, as he lurched to the side and away, all the while fumbling to turn the ignition key.

Given the conditions, a man of the cloth should be relieved of the expectation of clean, civil language. "Get the fuck away from me, you goddamn psycho bitch!"

Rose knew that it would be ruinous for her were she not to finish the attack, ruinous if he were to drive off. Past desperate, she wiggled even farther into the interior, wishing that her arms could stretch like rubber. She ended up draped across his back. Her own arms were blocking her vision, such that the second swipe across his neck was made blindly; nonetheless, it traveled smoothly and continuously. Rose quickly pushed against his shoulder to send herself back through the window and to regain her footing.

McArthur was trapped. He didn't dare sit up, for fear of getting slashed again. His feet, positioned at an angle, kept slipping, as he attempted to push off toward the passenger side and escape through that door. The struggling made his heart beat faster, pump more. His throat gurgled like a fountain. In seconds, blood had wet his front torso, pooled onto the leather seats, and spilled onto the floor. Shortly, he lay motionless.

Rose shifted into programmed mode, about to perform what she'd planned and memorized. With slight-of-hand swiftness, she pulled the driving gloves out of her purse and put them on. She raced around to the other side and opened the door to retrieve the bag, but when she lifted it, the container dropped through the blood-soaked bottom and into a puddle of blood.

Her original plan to drive away with the bagged contents was not plausible now. To transport the bag or container, blood-soaked as they were, would risk transferring evidence to her vehicle. But, she had the presence of mind to know that her fingerprints only were on the bag and that she had not handled the container.

An improvisation was in order. She lifted the bag with thumb and index, careful to avoid the blood. She let it drop to the pavement. In a flash, she was digging in her purse for the cigarette lighter, kept for heating her eyeliner pencil. In seconds, the bag was set aflame, and she watched, as the white paper turned black and wizened, and a stir of wind scattered the pieces, leaving just a few straps that hadn't burned because they were wet with blood. No problem, though, because she hadn't handled the bag's bottom.

The burning of the legal papers would be done under more relaxed circumstances, in her fireplace.

64.

"Can I get to him, now?" Mary asked.

"In a second," responded the crime scene technician, who was stooped, videotaping.

Mary rubbed her forehead impatiently and thought, *It's the inside of a vehicle, not the inside of a cave.*

The technician snapped the viewing screen closed and declared, "Finished. He's all yours."

The driver's door was open and Mary poked her head inside. McArthur's shirt was plastered against his front torso in wet, sticky folds, the blood copious enough to have come from multiple wounds, but Mary could see the lone source. Wearing gloves, she turned his neck variously, and the gash opened and closed, like the mouth of a sock puppet. She pulled back from the vehicle and stood erect. "Get him out," she told the EMS team.

There had been no need for medical assistance, since McArthur was irretrievably dead when the police arrived. Typically, a meat wagon—as it's known—from the Medical Examiner's Office transports a body to the morgue, but one wasn't immediately available. EMS had been called, in substitution.

The location was northwest Detroit, in the parking lot of a home improvement warehouse store that had pulled up stakes, acres of concrete, open, yet secluded. Cops and flashing squad cars confined the media and the onlookers to the outskirts, where they were resorting to long-range lenses and stretched necks.

"Got anything to shield the body from view while you remove it?" Mary asked the EMS guys.

"Some sheets, if they'll do," said the younger one.

"Grab one out of there," Mary told Chuck Smith, a homicide cop who possessed the longest wingspan in the group.

Smith took a sheet out of the ambulance, unfolded it with a snap, and held it between outstretched arms, providing a privacy curtain while the EMS guys got McArthur out of the vehicle and onto a gurney. Then Smith draped the sheet over McArthur.

The EMS team loaded the gurney into their vehicle.

Mary climbed into the ambulance through the rear and sat on a bench toward McArthur's head. She called out, "Hop in, Ross."

Brogan did, taking a seat on the opposite bench. He closed the door, knowing Mary had called him for private discussions. To prove that he was worthy, that his powers of deduction were up to par, he said, "This was an agreed-to meeting."

"Yes," said Mary, "and the back of the building was chosen because it's the most secluded part of the property." For months, she'd had the word out that she was to be notified of all cases involving slashed throats. Four cases had been reported but none involved a fatality. In each, the perpetrator was nabbed and the case proved unrelated to Kent and Gibson. But, she knew shortly after arrival that McArthur was the killer's third victim.

"I'm not going to be a hypocrite and pretend that I didn't dislike him," said Brogan, "but I never dreamed I'd see him like this."

"Me neither, but I never disliked him, personally."

"The conspiracy-minded are going to have a field day," predicted Brogan, "claiming that the police had a part in it, or even a so-called Jewish mafia."

"Likely, but that's not my concern right now."

"Still think that the killer might be female?"

"I do, and I said so in my write-up to the cold case squad. But now, I get the cases back."

"Because McArthur is a current case and Kent and Gibson are tied to it."

"That's right."

"But, come on, Cunningham. Kent and Gibson were seniors. McArthur was younger, stronger, twice the size. What could a female do against him? The man was six feet, thirteen inches."

"Not when seated."

"Shot down, again," said Brogan, although not begrudgingly.

"Don't look at it that way. You do me a favor when you have me defend my theories." She gave a studying look at the draped McArthur, blood having soaked through the sheet. She pulled the sheet down to his shoulders. Head cocked, she leaned in for a close examination of the wound, and mused, "Un huh."

"What?"

Mary didn't answer nor move her head, but pointed up, and said, "Turn on the light."

Brogan flicked the switch for the roof light, adding to the natural lighting coming through the windshield and rear windows. His curiosity increasing, his patience decreasing, he said, "How about cluing me in."

"Look above his left ear." Directing his gaze, she said, "Right here."

"Some dried blood, so what? In case you hadn't noticed, he's a bloody mess."

Mary allowed the flippancy and again pointing to the left, said, "And here, on his collar, at the top, a smear."

Brogan admitted, "I still don't see any significance."

"The slash on his throat is below the ear and collar and McArthur was found slumped forward and to the right. Blood doesn't run uphill, doesn't defy gravity."

"You're wondering about how the blood got there."

"And whether it's his." She pulled her cell phone out of her jacket so quickly that it flew out of her hand and she snared it in midair. It hints at one's occupation to have the medical examiner on speed dial.

The ME answered.

"Hello, Doctor. Mary Cunningham. You'll be receiving the body of Reverend Jeeter McArthur." She paused, interrupted by a question, to which she answered, "One and the same," and to the next, "Murdered." Returning to the reason for the call, she said, "The killer's blood might be on the body." There was a comment on the other end of the line, to which she replied, "That's exactly what I want. Thanks. Good-bye."

Brogan asked, "So, what's it gonna be?"

"He's going to wait for us to get there before he cleans the body."

Brogan put on gloves and turned McArthur's head, like he was about to shave him. "The slash is deep and straight. But look below it and to the right. You have to lean in close."

And, that's what Mary did, and after seconds of examination, said, "Looks like a slight cut."

Controlling his excitement, Brogan used a clean corner of the sheet to wipe away blood from the area, and after a quick reexamination, declared, "That's what it is."

Mary had a theory; however, she thought it only fair to give first dibs to Brogan, since it had been his discovery. "What do you make of it, Mister Eagle-eye?"

"A failed attempt. It's close to the big-ass chain around his neck. That's probably what interfered."

"I think you're right. The lethal cut was the second attempt."

"Put the chain under an electronic microscope and I betcha you find tool marks."

"For sure," agreed Mary, "but, we'll need to match tool marks with the weapon that made them."

"And we don't have the weapon," conceded Brogan.

"And might not ever have it."

Someone began pounding at the door.

Mary called out, "What do you want?"

"Need you to see something," said Chuck Smith.

"Okay." Mary exited, followed by Brogan. She motioned with her arm to tell the EMS guys to get in and leave. To Smith, she asked, "What do you have, Chuck?"

Smith went to the driver's side of McArthur's vehicle, white Lincoln Navigator, chrome trim, showroom clean. "There're some dings in the door and red smudges. They look fresh."

Mary stooped for a better look at the door. She remained there a while, scenarios playing in her head. Ready to stand, but with knees complaining, she swallowed her pride, extended an arm, and said, "Help me up, Chuck."

Smith grabbed Mary by her wrist, pulled her up, and asked, "Think it means anything?"

"Maybe," she said, not willing to disclose her theory that the dings and smudges were made by the killer's shoe striking the door, while the killer was reaching into or being pulled through the window.

A flash-flood of thoughts came to her. A tall killer would have been able to remain flatfooted. Judging from how high up the dings and smudges were, the killer was about her height, maybe shorter. Then, there were the sizes and shapes of the dings: small, round, as though made by something pointed, more pointed than the typical man's shoe—discounting cowboy boots—pointed, like a female's shoe. And, there was the color: red. Had Dorothy again arrived by tornado, this time as a killer? If not, someone else out there owned ruby slippers. Not that men never wear red shoes, but, Mary, the Wizard of Odds, was convinced that the odds pointed to a female.

Mary's eyes glinted with determination. Her skin tingled, like that of the hunter who senses that the quarry lurks nearby. *You're out there, somewhere, Sister, and I'm going to get you.*

65.

Behind a locked front entry door, Lisa Rose, voice laced with anger and disbelief, bellowed, "You got to be kidding me!"

"Should I have called first?"

"Get off my porch. Crawl back into that pathetic excuse for a vehicle and drive it off a cliff."

Fritz Mueller endured the abuse in saintly fashion. If he'd had a third cheek, he would have turned it, too. "May I come in?"

"You...you may go to hell, is what you may do."

Having not budged from his spot, Mueller said, "Whatever is eating you, why can't we discuss it, like the friends that we are."

The comment reminded Rose that she was trapped between two crusty, oldsters, one who wanted to be in her life, one who didn't, both with the perverse ability to infuriate and perplex her. She peered through the peephole and thought that its distorting, funhouse-mirror effect actually improved Mueller's features.

Mueller, correctly interpreting the lull and realizing he was being watched, raised a hand ear-level and then fluttered his fingers in greeting.

Rose regarded the gesture as effrontery and threatened, "If you don't get your ass out of here now, I'll call the police. I kid you not."

"No need for that." Mueller leaned his head close to the door, like someone about to give the password at a speakeasy, and said, "Give me a chance to explain. If I can't change your mind, I'll leave. I promise."

Rose considered it the height of arrogance that he was attempting to negotiate the terms of his departure from her own property. Under more normal circumstances, she would have told him so, in no uncertain terms; except, the circumstances were far from normal. Even before his arrival, she'd been unraveling, beside herself, more up in the air than he ever had sent her. Compared to what she'd been contending with, Mueller was a distraction that she needed to dismiss, so she called out through the door, "I'll give you one minute, after you hide that rolling eyesore. Pull up to the garage."

"Right away." Mueller hopped into his van and started the engine. He inched the vehicle forward to the garage door, which hummed in low-key as it opened. He drove in and the garage door closed.

It was an attached garage and could be entered through the kitchen door. Soon Rose was standing there, intent on maintaining the distance between herself and Mueller, and wearing a facial expression that would give an invading army pause. "That minute I promised you is the New York type."

Mueller gave thumbs-up. He opened the van's door and it creaked like the hinges on an exhumed coffin. He exited, wearing his signature mohair sweater, as bare in areas as if it had mange. "Such intrigue," he said of her actions. "Almost as if you're ashamed of me."

"Go ahead and waste time with asinine remarks," Rose warned. "You're down to about fifteen seconds."

"Alright then. First, I apologize for coming here unannounced, but what was I to do? You never returned my calls."

"My subtle way of saying, get lost."

"But why?" Mueller asked with a straight face.

"Those last antics were over the top, even for you."

"What antics?"

Rose jerked her gaze about, like she was looking for something to throw, but it returned to Mueller. "You went to the Kingsley's house, you damn fiend."

"Oh, that." Mueller hunched his shoulders as he was prone to do, held his palms up, and claimed, "It was just a humanitarian visit. I wanted to let her know that I empathized with her suffering."

Insulted by what she considered to be bullshit, she declared, "Time up. Get the hell—"

"It's the truth," he was quick to say. "I watched some of the coverage of the trial of that reverend fellow. Every time the camera showed the prosecutor's table, there was the daughter. Seeing her reminded me of the mother. Compassion and maybe a little curiosity got the better of me."

"Compassion? Merely speaking that word should tie your tongue in a knot."

"I don't see why," said, Mueller. "But if you don't buy compassion, how about camaraderie? Mrs. Kingsley and I being fellow clients of yours."

Rose's patience shrank a full size and she said, "Makes no difference what off-the-wall rationale you come up with, I told you more than once to stay clear of Mrs. Kingsley."

"I took it that you were referring to offering her my services. Which I didn't do. Couldn't do, even had that been my intent, because Mr. Kingsley wouldn't let me in. He misunderstood. And that daughter of theirs totally overacted. I heard that she threatened to kill me."

"You wouldn't be her first. Something you should keep in mind, in case you have plans to come a-knocking again."

Mueller licked a finger, ran it along a mark on the hood of the van, and upon discovering what the mark was, said, "I wonder what caused that scratch," as if it made a difference in the appearance of the clunker.

"The nonchalance attitude is supposed to impress me?"

"No. I'm simply not moved by threats of death. Dying is not necessarily the worst thing that can happen to a person. But if it'll restore me in your good graces, I promise to never initiate any contact with Mrs. Kingsley again."

"Initiate," Rose distrustfully repeated. "Sounds straight out of a weasel clause."

"How so? You said yourself that she would never initiate anything, therefore, my promise is solid." Then he asked, "Anything else eating you?"

Willing to get it off her chest, Rose said, "And you crashed my post-trial interview."

"Congratulations on the acquittal, I should mention. But I didn't crash anything."

"You had no right to be there."

"I certainly did. The courthouse is open to the public."

So Rose changed it to, "Then, you had no reason, other than to leech off my publicity."

"Careful," cautioned Mueller. "What you're implying is that we are linked in the public's mind. If that weren't so, you would have considered me another face in the crowd."

Rose couldn't refute the logic; all the same, she had a response. "All the more reason to sever ties. Keep away. I mean it. If I have to, I'll get a restraining order."

Mueller shifted to one foot, then the other, trying to see past Rose. "May I just stick my head inside? To see how the other half lives?"

Rose didn't budge from her guard post. She hardened her body language by folding her arms. "Out of the question. You shouldn't even be in my garage."

"Quite all right. I'm not impressed by material possessions, anyway."

"No? Well, perhaps I can impress you with some electronic wizardry." Rose, who all the while had been holding the garage door opener, pointed it. "The door is going to open like magic. Then you back out of here and drive out of my life."

"You don't mean that."

"The hell if I don't."

Like a smug suitor, Mueller said, "You simply need a cooling-down period. You'll come to your senses."

"I find that patronizing and offensive."

"I didn't mean it that way. I just want you to keep in mind that those other clients come and go, but I've been the one who has kept you in the spotlight."

"If your ego could be surgically removed, you wouldn't weigh enough to move the dial on a scale. If anything, you are indebted to me."

Mueller, happy that they agreed on something, grinned and said, "Indeed, I do owe you. And I'll always be ready to help you in any way I can. All you have to do is call."

"Fine. Wait on that call. Until then, we're kaput."

"Fate's a funny thing, Ms. Rose. I'm confident that our paths will cross."

"I've said it before, you're delusional."

"Hardly, because I know that you are against hapless suffering, as am I."

The comment caused her to tug at her earlobe as she paused to sooth the nerve he had touched. "I am, and I used to believe that you were too, and that it was your only motivation, but no longer. As I've said, the cause is better served by someone else leading it."

Mueller calmly insisted, "No one else is as qualified."

Rose stuck the garage door opener into her pants pocket. Hands free, she slapped her palms, slidingly, several times, symbolically cleaning her hands of something unwanted, and said, "Say whatever you want, but I'll never represent you again." To give him something further to think about, she threw in, "Incidentally, I've heard that Gerald Lewis will lobby for legislation that will make assisted suicide a felony. One of these times, he could have the law on his side, and at your age, even thirty days can be a life sentence."

"We'll cross that bridge when they build it," paraphrased Mueller.

"We," said Rose, emphasizing that pronoun, "won't be doing a damn thing. And speaking of bridges, you've burned yours with me." She retrieved the garage door opener and aimed, both hands, straight-armed, about to activate.

It gave Mueller a view, enabling him to note, "You have a stain on your sleeve. Looks like blood."

Now reminded of what had her in an apoplectic state prior to Mueller's arrival at her doorstep, she felt that state returning and she started forcefully pressing the garage door opener, repeatedly, even while the garage door was retracting.

66.

Lisa Rose, standing in her conference room, continued clicking through a PowerPoint presentation while responding to questions. "The last time that I saw him was at the courthouse, the day of the acquittal."

"And you've had no contact since," interpreted Mary, who'd said that she didn't mind if Rose worked and answered questions at the same time.

"I didn't say that. There were phone conversations. He wanted me to represent him in the civil suit filed by Debra Winkler."

"Were you going to?"

"Hadn't made up my mind."

"Why not?"

Her eyes on the projector screen, a wireless mouse in hand, Rose clicked, then said, "I was taking my time deciding, that's all. Didn't see any rush. I was leaning toward turning him down, though."

"Because?"

"You ask, as if you don't know by now that I don't take every case offered."

Mary, not sounding indebted, said, "I've thanked you for taking my mother's case."

"I wasn't referring to that."

"And I was just making a point." Mary sent her glance around the room, remembering visits—that first one with her parents, a later one for the press conference, others later still. The room looked unchanged, except for a tall rubber plant standing sentry in a corner. Refocusing, she said, "Since McArthur is dead and this is a murder investigation, I hope that you and I don't butt heads over lawyer-client privilege."

"Depends on what you ask."

"Well, let's start with whether he ever spoke of threats or a concern for his safety?"

"No. But my conversations with him dealt with the case and I know next to nothing about what might have been happening with him outside of that sphere."

The disclaimer didn't deter Mary from asking, "Did he ever mention the names Matthew Kent or Raymond Gibson?"

Rose's heart began thumping, any more so, it would have been audible. "Let me think," she requested," as she willed herself to calm down. After some seconds, she said, "No, he never did." Careful to use the present tense, she asked, "Who are they?"

"You needn't concern yourself."

For all of Rose's expertise in interrogation, she couldn't think of a way to pursue a discussion of Kent and Gibson without arousing suspicion. What she decided was to continue the conversation along related lines and to stay alert for useful information. First, she sat the wireless mouse on the table. "Roles have changed, wouldn't you say? You've gone from investigating McArthur the murder suspect to investigating McArthur the murder victim."

"I never would have anticipated it."

But there was something that Rose had anticipated, namely, that the investigation of McArthur's murder would wind to her. How could it not? McArthur had been her client and there was a phone record of recent communications; however, she was confident that the civil suit explanation would deflect suspicion. What she hadn't anticipated was the mentioning of Kent and Gibson but was satisfied that she had masked her reaction.

The wireless mouse still lay on the table and the same slide had been on the screen for a while. It finally caught Mary's attention. "I recognize that graphic. You used it in your closing in the McArthur trial."

"I use it in all my criminal trial closings." The graphic depicted a triangle, the three vertices labeled victim, crime scene, and suspect. In her closing argument to the jury, she had argued that the prosecution had failed to complete the triangle, had failed to show a connection among the three factors, and at best, only had established a case against McArthur's vehicle.

"Sort of your trademark."

"You might say that."

By now, Mary had concluded that the visit had been a bust. She had no more questions, at least not of an official nature. "I'm done, but I'd like to ask you something unrelated."

Unrelated sounded good to Rose's ears and she said, "Fire away," not implying anything by that choice of words.

Mary didn't like the phrasing, too remindful of how she'd been characterized as trigger-happy by Rose during the trial. But that had been business. Holding a grudge wouldn't be professional. "Like you said, you don't take every case offered, but it didn't seem that McArthur had come to you. At his booking, he was as surprised to see you as I was."

"What's your point?"

"Just wondering what attracted you to the case, that's all."

Rose smiled, gears turning. "More than money, more than fame, I'm motivated by the pursuit of justice. When I learned that Gerald Lewis was trying the case, it smacked of politics. And politics and justice make a bad mix."

It was good enough for Mary. "I'm outta here. Thanks for your time."

67.

Mary turned one knob, igniting a ring of blue flame. She repeated the test on three other knobs, with the same result. "The stovetop works," she said of the vintage appliance. She turned the remaining knob and in a few seconds came the confirming swoosh. "Oven, too. And if a pilot light goes out, there's a box of matches in the overhead cabinet." Dispirited, she admitted, "I don't know if I'm doing this in logical order. I feel disorganized."

Gloria Crockett nodded her understanding and said, "Don't fret." She was early-senior, tall and hefty, with large cradling hands. Crockett launched into action, moving as nimbly as someone half her size, inspecting cabinets, drawers, countertops, broom closet, pantry, and lastly, refrigerator. As she reached, bent, and stooped, her dread locks flopped about her head like grey ropes. When she came to a standstill, she said, "This is a well-stocked kitchen. I'll manage just fine."

"Good." Mary knew every square inch of the kitchen, having grown up in the house, yet, her eyes roamed, as if the surroundings were unfamiliar. She was purposely stretching out this interview. The day before, she had interviewed and approved the other members of the team. That the last one now was on board forced the recognition that time was short, perhaps very short.

Sophie wanted to die at home. She had accepted her physician's opinion that the only thing that medical science could offer her was pain management. Last week, she signed the forms, becoming a hospice patient.

With inputs from Sophie and the family, the hospice agency assembled a team and assigned each member a schedule of visits. In addition to Crockett, the cook, there was a nurse, therapist, housekeeper, and a sitter whose job would be to give Joe breaks.

"Anything else?" asked Crockett.

Reluctantly, Mary said, "No."

68.

Rose offered a handshake and with the other hand patted the visitor to her office on the back. "Thanks for coming. Good to see you." Amenities out of the way, Rose asked, "What's the latest on your mother's condition?"

"She's under the care of a hospice team now."

"Oh. How long has that been the case?"

"Couple of weeks."

"A good choice. Being at home and around family might not alleviate the physical suffering, but it can be good for the emotions."

Not wanting to dwell on the subject, Mary said, "You said you had something to show me."

Rose took a seat at her desk, then invited, "Take a load off your feet."

Mary would just as well have remained standing but did as asked.

"They made a settlement offer," announced Rose.

Apprehensively, Mary repeated, "A settlement offer."

"That's what I said." Rose grabbed a legal pad and a pen. "Could have been that the McArthur verdict gave them second thoughts about going to trial."

"And maybe that had nothing to do with it," countered Mary, conflicted.

Rose, not interested in a back-and-forth, wrote the offer in big strokes, making a single slash through the dollar sign. Without comment, she slid the pad forward.

Mary stared at the number, expecting that there might be a mistake: digits transposed, misplaced commas, too many zero's—something. "I tried not to think about an offer and how much it might be, but, this...well, it..."

"Exceeds your expectations?"

"By more than a little."

"Get's better," said Rose. "No installments. No annuity. It would be a lump-sum payment. So, do I tell them that you accept?"

Mary answered, "Yes," although she was thinking, *Hell yeah!* She caught herself about to break out in a broad grin and nipped it, after which, she chastised herself. *How could I even think about being glad about a settlement, knowing that it comes at the expense of Mama's life.*

"I'll let them know that their offer is accepted." Rose, after reflection, said, "If my reference to Reverend McArthur came off as insensitive, it was unintentional and I apologize."

"Don't worry about it."

Rose saw an opening. "Speaking of my former client, how's the murder investigation going? Having once represented the man, I can't help but being interested."

"No one is in custody. That sums it up."

Rose tried a different tactic. "I wish I could have been of more help. Maybe I still can. Feel free to contact me about anything."

"Will do."

Rose stood and said, "I'll walk you to the elevator."

Mary stood too, said, "Not necessary. I know my way around the place by now," and headed toward the door.

Kirk Rhodes entered. Seeing Mary on the approach, he held the door. "Good to see you, Lieutenant Cunningham."

"Good seeing you, too."

Still holding the door, Rhodes raised a white bag and told Rose, "I'm back with your Chinese."

Mary was slammed with a flash recall. She now remembered having seen take-out containers in Rose's wastebasket, only at that time, she had no reason to give it a second thought. "Good with the chopsticks, are you Lisa?"

"I like Chinese food, if that's what you're asking. But so do millions of other people."

"You're right, and that gives me an idea for lunch. I'll try your place. Where is it?"

Rose, by no means math-challenged, had put two and two together and offered, "Take mine. I don't have much of an appetite, anyway."

"You needn't."

"I insist."

Mary cheerily said, "Then I insist on paying." She walked to the desk, took money from her purse and laid it down. The spot she had chosen allowed a good look at Rose's shoes. Black patent leather. Had they been red, with scuffed toes, Mary—with that type of luck—would have sprinted out and bought a lottery ticket. Actually, she couldn't remember ever seeing Rose in red shoes; then again, she'd never before paid attention to Rose's feet.

Rose didn't deign to pick up the money, but maintained unblinking eye contact with Mary, while telling Rhodes, "Give her the bag."

69.

Cliff lay on his back in bed, staring at the ceiling fan, which was rotating slowly, unlike his whirling thoughts. Nudging the words out of his mouth slowly and haltingly, he muttered, "Lisa Rose, a triple murderer."

Mary, lying on her side, head resting on Cliff's bare chest and an arm across his waist, softly admonished, "Don't go putting words in my mouth."

"You suspect," rephrased Cliff, stressing that verb, "that Lisa Rose is a triple murderer."

"I do."

"Does she know?"

"If she is the murderer, then she knows I suspect her."

"Because of the interest you showed in the Chinese."

"Right, although she kept her cool. I'll give her that much."

After Mary had been given the food, she didn't press Rose further about from where it had come, wanting to preserve some pretences, just in case. So she left with the food, supposedly headed to some place where she would eat it. Of course, she had other intentions, namely to try to assign evidentiary value to it.

The container that had been taken from McArthur's vehicle was in an evidence freezer, but Mary remembered that the meal was rice noodles. The meal she'd been given was Chinese vegetables. More disappointing, she was told by a laboratory technician that, even if the two meals had been of the same ingredients, it would be impossible to prove that they came from the same source.

The two containers looked identical, a worthless observation, because her sleuthing by phone revealed that a single distributor supplied area restaurants. There was nothing proprietary about either the one from the crime scene or the one taken from Rose's office, nothing that could tie either to a particular restaurant.

Mary went back to the phonebook, checked listings of Chinese restaurants and wasn't encouraged by the multiple listings in the downtown area and in the pricey area of Detroit where Rose lived. Mary was assuming first that Rose was fond of a particular restaurant and second that it was close to work or home; but, she knew that those assumptions might be empty. It didn't crimp her dogged style, however. From the website for the law firm of Rose, Miller, and Greene, she printed two photos of the senior partner. Then, photo in hand, she made the rounds of downtown restaurants, inquiring whether any employee remembered Rose, as Ross Brogan did the same at restaurants near Rose's home. Mary came up with zilch, Brogan with zip.

But even if they had gotten a hit—better yet, even if that restaurant's video camera had captured Rose on the day of the murder—such wouldn't prove what Rose had bought nor that she had taken it to the crime scene. Furthermore, the container found at the crime scene wouldn't be traceable to that restaurant, being free of employee's fingerprints, for example. Mary reasoned that the absence of such fingerprints was due to food-service gloves, although she couldn't explain why McArthur's fingerprints were absent—not knowing about the bag that Rose destroyed. As for the absence of the killer's prints, Mary assigned that to careful execution, no pun intended.

Mary didn't need to have her arm twisted to concede that expanding the restaurant search was patently impractical. Additionally, she had considered ways to factor in Kirk Rhodes, but his photo wasn't on the website, and interviewing him about Rose's take-out habits carried more chances of alerting Rose than it did of yielding something probative. No, Mary didn't have anything with which to take to the prosecutor, but she did have something that she'd been floundering about in search of, dating back to the Kent murder: a suspect.

Cliff began rubbing Mary's back. "Boy, oh boy. Who would have ever thought? Especially since she'd been his defense attorney."

"If she killed him, she took the case with that in mind," said Mary, in retrospect. "She didn't want to trust another lawyer with his freedom because, if he got convicted and sent to prison, he'd be out of her reach."

"Makes sense. But I wonder whether she thought he was innocent."

"She might not have had an opinion either way. Might not have cared."

Thinking aloud, Cliff pondered, "Why would she turn murderer? And why those three victims?"

"I asked myself those questions more than a few times." Then Mary said, "Cliff?"

"Yes?"

"Thanks for not saying that I should have suspected her earlier."

"You didn't have reason. It's to your credit that you made the Chinese connection. Not every detective would have."

"And thanks for not asking whether I'll give her some slack."

"Because of your mother?"

"Yeah."

"Never crossed my mind." Cliff pulled her closer and said, "I know what you're made of."

Lampooning a bro'-to-bro' confession, she faked a sniffle then gave a light punch to his shoulder. "Dude, I love you."

Cliff kissed her on the forehead. "Love you, too. Goodnight."

Instead of returning his sign-off, Mary threw a leg across him and sent a searching hand under the covers. She said, "I ate late tonight," which she had upon arriving home. "If I go to sleep on this full stomach, I'll awake five pounds heavier."

Cliff, knowing where the conversation was going, smiled and said, "I see."

"So make me burn some calories."

70.

Dennis Sloan, carrying a briefcase, stopped in the doorway of his office, concern in his eyes. His gaze burrowed into the back of the head of the seated visitor. "Good morning, Lieutenant Cunningham."

Mary turned, smiled disarmingly, and said, "Good morning."

"Please, you needn't rise," said Sloan, when he saw her about to do just that. He strolled to the window. He set down the briefcase. "What brings you back?"

Mary crossed her legs, rested a palm on a knee, then as casually as one inquires about the time of day, asked, "What's your relationship with Lisa Rose?"

Sloan's immediate, reverberating thought was, *What?!* The lawyer in him wanted to say that the question lacked foundation: first ask whether there is a relationship; if there is, then ask its nature. He had the sneaky suspicion, however, that her phrasing had been intentional, purposeful, meant to convey that she knew things and that he shouldn't get cute. He chose to be direct and short. "She referred us some cases."

Mary's spirits sank, not her usual reaction when she received support for a theory. "How did the referrals come about?"

Sloan sighed, sat on the window sill, and attempted to assert some authority. "What does any of this have to do with your previous visit?"

"No disrespect," she said cordially, "but I'm here on official police business. Let me ask the questions. You supply the answers."

Sloan, lawyer and therefore an officer of the court, didn't want it alleged that he obstructed a police investigation, especially since neither he nor a client was a target. "She phoned and asked whether I'd be interested in handling some civil cases that she didn't have the time for. I told her yes."

"Before that, had you sought business from her?"

"No."

"Did you ask why she'd picked you?"

With umbrage, Sloan said, "You make it sound like charity."

"I didn't mean it that way," said Mary, who by her steady gaze demanded an answer.

"I was happy to get the business and too busy thanking her to give her the third degree. Like I told you, my firm is diversifying away from worker's comp. Besides, she has a reputation for helping minority firms."

"How many times has she been here?"

"Two. On the first, I gave her the nickel tour, meant to convince her that she could refer business to us with confidence. The second time, she dropped off some case files."

"You have dates and times?"

"Neither time was by appointment." There was insinuation in his voice, as he said, "Not that she dropped by unannounced, mind you."

"Of course not," said Mary, absorbing the dig.

"Although they were by short notice, calling and saying that she was available and asking whether I could fit her in."

"I asked dates and times."

"All I remember is that they were on consecutive days and in the morning."

Mary let silence reign, maintaining eye contact the entire while before she spoke. She raised her eyebrows and said, "Details might come to you later, so I'll keep dropping by."

Sloan got the message and went to his desk where his calendar lay. He licked a thumb then flipped some pages. Soon, he placed a finger and said, "Here's something."

Mary stood, looked, and asked, "What do we have?"

"This particular day is marked. As you can see, I had to be in court that afternoon."

"What's the connection with Lisa Rose?"

"She'd dropped off the files earlier that day. I remember, because I mentioned it to a friend at the courthouse. We left the courthouse together and went to a bar where he bought me a drink in celebration."

"That would have been the second visit, correct?"

"Yes. The first would have been the day before. I'm fairly sure, but it might have been a couple of days before."

Mary now knew that Rose's visits and Gibson's murder occurred within the same week. "I need to know whether Lisa Rose ever had your office key to the public restroom."

Sloan now knew—without having been told outright—that Rose was a murder suspect. The possibility had presented itself from Mary's opening question but he had held out for other possibilities. "I have no personal knowledge, one way or the other, concerning the key."

"How long did each visit last?"

"An hour, give or take."

"Those weren't in-and-out visits. You don't remember if she went to the bathroom? I don't mean to sound crass, but, I've been here for less time, and I could use a pit stop."

"Too much information, Lieutenant, if you don't mind my saying."

"Then disregard that last comment. All the same, did she excuse herself to go to the restroom during either visit?"

"I have a vague recall that she went to the restroom. Can't say which visit, though." Eagerly, he added, "But, I directed her to the office restroom."

"Did you watch her go in the direction of the office restroom?"

"No, just as I wouldn't watch you, if you were to go off on that pit stop you mentioned."

"How long was she gone?"

Sloan's posture drooped, indicative of the weight being applied, and he said, "Really, Lieutenant, was I supposed to have clocked her?"

"I had to ask."

"She wasn't gone long enough for me to think that she'd gotten lost, that's for sure."

"Have you heard from her since the last time she was here?"

"I haven't."

Mary wasn't going to be able to put the restroom key in Rose's hand through Sloan. She might not be able to do it through any means. "That's all the questions I have. And I ask that you not discuss my visits with anyone."

Sloan gave a nod-of-sorts that didn't convey promise, just that he'd heard her. As he watched her leave, he said, "If you still feel the urge, Lieutenant, the office restroom is down the hall, to your left."

71.

"I know of her," said Myron Shuster, at the receiving dock of his warehouse. "Who doesn't throughout this area? But I don't know her personally."

"And never had any contact with her?" asked Mary.

"Define contact."

"Spoken, written, sign language, smoke signals. Contact of any sort."

Shuster paused to watch an employee cut the box away from a refrigerator and then said, "As best I can recall, I saw her once in a courthouse. Recognized her from a distance but didn't approach. I suppose that doesn't qualify."

"No, it doesn't."

"That's the best I can offer you. Any more questions?" Shuster didn't stand still waiting for the answer. He walked to the now freed refrigerator. He circled it once. He opened the refrigerator door, closed it with a flick of the wrist, did the same with the freezer door, and by the sounds concluded that the appliance was solidly built.

Mary went to Shuster. "I like stainless steel appliances," she said, in reference to the type that had undergone inspection.

"Own any?"

"No, but my kitchen is overdue for a makeover." That little digression over, Mary said, "Yes, I do have more questions." Her next one was, "Do you know of any contact between Matthew Kent and her?"

"You're still talking about Lisa Rose, right?"

"That's right."

"You certainly can't ask Matt. But why not ask Lisa Rose, herself?"

"I happen to be interviewing you at the moment," Mary said, without rancor. "Need I repeat the question?"

"I have no knowledge about any contact between them."

"He never mentioned her to you?"

"How many ways can I say the same thing, Lieutenant Cunningham?" Shuster placed thumb and middle finger to his mouth and made a loud, shrill whistle that drew the attention of the forklift driver, and then by gesture, gave the order to unload the rest of the refrigerators. Next, he returned his attention to Mary. "I'll be candid with you, Lieutenant. This conversation is making me uncomfortable."

"And why might that be?"

"Follow me." Shuster led the way to the opposite end of the dock, where there was no activity and he could continue the conversation without concern of being overheard. Even so, he spoke in low tones. "You're investigating Matt's murder. You requested a second interview. But it's all been about Lisa Rose. The only conclusion that makes sense is that you suspect her of being involved. If that's the case, I have the right to know whether—"

Mary didn't let him finish. "What you have is the right to answer or not answer my questions. But you don't have the right to privileged information."

"Well, you certainly set me straight on that," said Shuster. "Matt never mentioned her to me."

"You told me that Mr. Kent was a coordinator with the Jewish Elves."

"He was."

"Could volunteers sign up through Mr. Kent?"

"Yes. Or through any other coordinator."

"Was that encouraged?"

"Oh, yes. That's a big part of what coordinators do."

"Therefore," said Mary, "the identities of your coordinators and the means to contact them are public information."

"Correct."

I've gotten about all there is to get from this stop. "Mr. Shuster, I won't guarantee it, but I don't think you'll be seeing me again."

"I'll see you to the front." Once underway, Shuster switched to pitchman, saying, "When you said I wouldn't be seeing you again, I hope you meant in an official capacity and wasn't ruling out the possibility of coming back for that kitchen makeover."

"I won't guarantee that, either."

"Ever bought from one of my stores?"

"No."

"Then you've been paying too much."

"So I understand from your commercials."

"Where do you buy?"

"I'm loyal to a particular store. It's a family thing. Got it from my mother."

72.

Mary rested her fingers on the keyboard, waiting, as Brogan came into the room. "You get lost on the way?"

"I started not to come. Every time you say you have something to show me, I get suckered into more work."

Mary made no promises that this time would be different, but asked, "You do recall my theory that the link between Kent and Gibson lies in the distant past, don't you?"

"How can I forget, for all the time I spent going through Gibson's box of mementos."

"You did a good job, too."

"That's what I'm known for."

"Yeah, yeah," said Mary, in a tone that conveyed that she wasn't going to indulge his ego further. "But since McArthur was a generation younger than the other two, I had doubts that he fitted my theory."

"Until?" Brogan asked, smirking and suspecting that she hadn't abandoned the theory.

"Until I remembered two incidents that happened during the trial. Twice, Lisa Rose interrupted comments about

McArthur's past. Once with Congressman Galliger, once with McArthur."

Brogan had no reason to think that Mary was intimating that the interruptions hid ulterior motives. His correct conclusion, reached incorrectly, was, "Remembering those incidents have got you thinking that you need to dig as far back as you can into McArthur's past, age difference be damned."

"Right," said Mary, without corrections.

"And you're using this thing," continued Brogan, referring to the computer as though it were some newfangled, yet-to-be-named contraption, "to do that digging."

"Right again." Having toiled for years with tortoise-speed dial-up, Mary was thankful when the city sprang for broadband for the police department. Still, the hardware could use some upgrading by way of sleek towers and flat-screen monitors, although that likely wouldn't reduce the times when hardware is out-of-service, fried because some-one spilled a drink. Pointing at the monitor, she said, "I've been looking at McArthur's personal website, which hasn't been taken down."

Brogan thought that he was about to be asked to do something at the computer, so to sidestep that, he said, "Don't ask me to take your seat."

"I'm not." She scrolled up to the top of the page and clicked on a navigation tab. The screen changed to another page of the website. "Read this."

Brogan began, eyes moving back and forth over a nar-rative about a boy, so precocious that he'd been ordained at the age of eight, a child-preacher, who, at that same age became a member of a particular group. Eye movement stopped and Brogan did that thing of his, grabbing his waistband and twisting it back and forth, before saying, "Hey, I recognize the name of that group."

"I knew you would."

"The, uh, newspaper clippings from Gibson's box."

"Yep."

The website also showed a photo of a preteen boy, whose size presaged the man-mountain he would become. The youngster was sporting an exploded afro and was posing with some adults. From the background, it was apparent that the group was at a travel stop. The photo was oval, cropped, and feathered around the edges, but otherwise not retouched.

Brogan squinted at the photo, hard, as if he could magnify it and sharpen its resolution. "I'm looking to see if I can pick out Kent or Gibson."

"Rest your eyes. You should know better than to be that optimistic."

"Don't look at me like I'm some kind of Pollyanna," protested Brogan. "None of Gibson's group photos showed Kent or a young McArthur. I figured we're owed."

"We are. Too bad that it's not the type of debt that pays interest."

73.

Mary was at the main branch of the Detroit Public Library, having come there straight from her internet searches at Police Headquarters. She was working a microfiche machine, and vice-versa. Placing a sheet of microfiche in the tray was the easy part. It was the moving around of the tray—the turning of knobs to rotate, zoom in, and focus—that was causing her fits. As a result, the images were zipping about the projector screen, like cats avoiding herding. But until all archives are digitized, people researching decades-old newspaper articles will continue to undergo such frustration.

The internet searches that she had conducted at Police Headquarters had not filled in all of the blanks. The search on Matthew Kent had turned up numerous entries, but the ones about her guy appeared several pages in, and even then, they mostly were about his rise through the ranks of the United Automobile Workers, from which he retired as a vice-president. The search on Raymond Gibson turned up many a sundry person, but not the ill-fated janitor.

Mary changed tactics. For the search words, she typed the names of both men and the name of the group, and voila! Up came entries of the right coverage and vintage, entries that not only spoke of both men, but also of an unnamed minor. More than that, in each entry, the major coverage was on a fourth person.

The information about the fourth person had been short on biography—understandable, given the person's age at the time—although one detail, in particular, was why Mary had expanded her research to the library.

74.

It was during an ugly era. The driver of the DeSoto shifted his gaze upward to the rearview mirror, again, although he'd done so seconds earlier, and seconds before that. Nervously, he reached up and adjusted the mirror, but it didn't change what the mirror was reflecting: two headlights, drilling twin holes in a night as black as onyx. Throughout a long stretch of road, those headlights had remained at a constant distance, as if the DeSoto were towing the trialing vehicle by a long chain. Of late, that distance had been closing.

All the windows of the DeSoto were down, the night hot and muggy, the country air equal parts fresh and pungent. Sounds entered unblocked, unfiltered: chirps, croaks, trills, and the occasional scampering of feet or hooves among the trees. The gravel road crunched like it was paved with peanut shells, as the DeSoto's whitewall tires barreled along. All at once, however, the din was overpowered by the growl of the gunning engine of the approaching vehicle.

Rebecca, in the backseat of the DeSoto, also had been monitoring via the rearview mirror and was apprehensive over developing conditions. She considered saying something to the driver, but was undecided about what to say.

There hadn't been much gabbing inside the DeSoto, its occupants tired, hungry, drowsy. Their bus ride had taken seventeen hours, including rest stops. Practically upon arrival, they were given their posts and assignments. At the end of this first day, they were given the use of the DeSoto, several years old, yet still reliable transportation, although its trunk wouldn't open, which was why the luggage was stacked on the front seat and the three passengers were shoulder-to-shoulder across the back seat. Now, the group was on their way to a safe house, one of many dotting the area, where volunteers could eat, bathe, and hunker down.

Rebecca kept watching the rearview mirror, a miniature movie screen that was becoming increasingly brighter from the nearing headlights, which were too high up from the road to be those of a car and had to be those of a truck, a pickup, to be exact. Meanwhile, there came no flick of high-beams from the pickup, no blare of its horn, nothing to indicate a desire to pass the DeSoto.

Rebecca entertained a forced hope that the vehicles were on the same road by happenstance and that the driver of the pickup simply was under no urgency to pass. She alternatively hoped that if the pickup was following them, it wasn't for ominous reasons; maybe both vehicles were bound for the same destination, the driver of the pickup in possession of a hand-sketched map similar to the one that had been given to her driver. But as occupying as such hopes were, they didn't crowd out thoughts about home and the conditions under which she'd left.

"You are not going down there," her father had decreed. "I absolutely forbid it."

"I've made up my mind, Dad."

"It's not our fight. Not our cause."

"But, it is."

"That's your mother's nonsense you're talking."

"You're always blaming Mom for everything. I reached this decision on my own."

"You can't pack up whenever you please and go roaming around the country. You have a baby, for God's sake. Practically a newborn."

"And I want my child to grow up in a better world. Mom will baby-sit while I'm gone. I'll be back in a week, Dad. Cool out."

"Is that an expression you picked up from them? By the time you return, you'll be scatting and carrying a switchblade."

"And maybe I'll come back addicted to watermelon. They're plentiful down there."

"You watch your sass, young lady."

"I apologize, Dad. I don't want to disrespect you. Don't want to hurt you."

"A bit late for that, wouldn't you say?"

"Referring to my being an unwed mother turned college dropout, right, Dad?"

"I've said my peace."

"Yes, you certainly have. And I'll make you a promise, Dad. The first thing I'll do when I return is move out."

From the pickup came a quick succession of horn blasts.

Almost simultaneously, Rebecca and the other rear-seat passengers jerked and looked through the back window, then, one-by-one, turned to the front to see what their driver was going to do. Their driver was gripping the steering wheel so tightly that his fingernails were digging into his palms. Desperately wishing that the other driver wanted to pass, he slowed a notch. Passing would have been easy, in fact, there had been no oncoming traffic for miles on end. Instead of passing, however, the pickup began tailgating.

The driver of the pickup leaned on the horn differently this time, a series of blasts, each as long as a train's whistle. It was the latest rudeness in a day scarred by such behavior.

Starting with their stepping off the bus, the volunteers had been pelted with jeers, taunts, and derision. The harrassers—men, women, and brainwashed children—were dressed in every fashion, from suits to overalls, from Sunday dresses to maternity tops, from school uniforms to knickers, self-described good, wholesome Americans.

The behavior became more boisterous and demonstrative where the volunteers set up shop. Local residents seeking their constitutional rights endured shouted threats to their persons, families, and properties, as they marched into and later out of voter registration sites.

There to protect registrants and volunteers was a phalanx of armed U.S. Marshals, postures regimented, eyes busy behind dark glasses, communicating by walkie-talkie. Unfortunately, that protection did not extend beyond city limits and certainly didn't include patrols of the isolated roads traveled by the threatened.

The pickup pulled alongside the car and it became evident that there were two occupants in the cab and three more standing in the bed. Each of the three standing buffoons was pushing and jockeying, vying for position, so that his particular obscenities and insults might be heard over those being spewed by the others.

Meanwhile, Rebecca and her companions were engaged in their own competition, frantically shouting conflicting advice to their driver. "Pull over." "Speed up." "Slow down." But, their driver had his course of action decided for him when the passenger in the cab pointed a rifle, motioning with it, to convey that the driver had two choices, only one of which did not involve getting his brains blown out. The car's driver brought it to a stop, along the side of the road.

The pickup stopped behind the car. The rifleman stayed put, his weapon aimed, while the other terrorists rushed to the car and began pulling out the occupants. Rebecca tried to resist with slaps and kicks and was unceremoniously extracted by the hair.

"She's a hellion, she is," said the rifleman, who had thick, hairy forearms and was the most city-looking of the group.

The youngest nightrider had a hyper quality about himself, bouncing on his soles, rubbing his grimy hands like he was lathering them. He stuck out a coated tongue and rapidly flicked it from side to side. His mouth curled lewdly as he said, "I bet she could fuck a man an inch within his life."

The rifleman, descending from the cab, said, "Can't you see you ain't her type? From the looks of it, she prefers dark meat. Hell, boy, these coons likely got her so stretched that your little ding-dong wouldn't even tickle her."

The driver of the car quickly said, "None of us touched her," and was dropped to his knees by the rifle butt rammed into his midsection.

"That'll teach you to keep your yap closed unless you're asked something." The rifleman issued the warning, "The next one who flaps his big lips out of turn gets his kneecap blown off."

"We best clear these vehicles from sight less somebody comes along," said the pickup driver, wearing a cap advertising a feed store, his belly hanging inches past the waistline of his oily mechanic's pants. "You sure we're in the right parts, George?"

"Yeah. These fields used to belong to old man Lowery. Not far infield, there's this big tree with low, strong limbs." George was long and boney.

"First," said the rifleman to his male captives, "you boys hand over your wallets and valuables. You won't be needing them." He looked at George and said, "Collect them."

George did and then asked, "What about her?"

"Check her I.D.," said the rifleman.

George snatched the drawstring purse and rummaged through its contents. Reading her driver's license, he reported, "Seems we got us a Rebecca Rosenberg."

"A goddamn Jew," slammed the rifleman. "No wonder she's a nigger-lover. She's half one, herself."

"Y'all came down here by bus," accused George. "The one with the sign in the windshield." Faking that he didn't know, he requested, "Somebody remind me what that sign said."

Answering for the captives, the rifleman gloated and then responded, "Detroit Freedom Riders."

"You don't say!" mocked the youngest. "I bet they could use a little freedom of their own right about now."

The rifleman, showing himself to be a man of action, asked his buddies, "Are we going to stand around and jaw-bone all night?"

"I'm ready," claimed the pickup driver.

"Y'all jungle bunnies gonna do some stepping," informed the rifleman.

"And smile, so we can see y'all in the dark," wisecracked George.

"You're coming too, bagel girl," said the rifleman. "And if any of y'all think you can outrun a bullet, go for it." To the pickup driver, he said, "Follow us in the truck." And to the youngest, he said, "You bring their car."

The fifth goon was heavy-set, with infected acne. He hadn't spoken up to that point, but was now whispering to the pickup driver, and by his facial contortions and mouth spasms, he was a stutterer.

Next, the pickup driver summarized the conversation, telling the rifleman, "Jimmy here wants to have a little backseat fun with the girl and I don't see nothing wrong with it."

"I wouldn't mind some, myself," said the youngest.

His voice resolute, the rifleman said, "There won't be any of that."

"What's the harm?" asked the youngest. He chortled and said, "Shit, man, let her go out with a little pleasure."

"Little is about all you have to offer," said the rifleman.

Red-faced, the youngest said, "That's the second time you put me down like that."

"You can count. I'm impressed." The rifleman reasserted, "Nobody touches the girl."

The field, overrun with weeds, brush, and crop stubs, was uneven, requiring those on foot to walk carefully to avoid twisted ankles; but, the vehicles rolled bumpily along. When everyone was at the tree, the headlights were killed, and darkness enveloped the gathering, shielding it from roadside detection.

Then, without announcement, the youngest leaned across the front seat and pushed open the passenger's door. Jimmy snatched Rebecca off her feet, threw her in, and dove on top of her. Then the youngest sped away—passenger door slapping on its hinges—completing a plan that had been hastily devised behind the rifleman's back.

The pickup driver, surprised by events, nonetheless removed his cap and with it slapped his leg, gleefully exclaiming, "Hot damn! Them boys got spunk."

Fury in his eyes, the rifleman cursed, "Those stupid-ass shitheads."

"No need for that kind of talk," guaranteed the pickup driver. "They'll bring her back. She might just be wearing a smile when they do. 'Til then, we got enough to keep us busy. Like stringing us up some meddling niggers."

75.

"This can be tricky," said Warren Newberry, and he wasn't talking about a putt.

As if I need to be told, thought Mary.

Newberry, now having been briefed, said, "The least little misstep and she walks. She knows the law, the Prosecutor's Office, and police procedures."

"I'm open to your suggestions, Inspector."

Newberry, who was given to idiosyncratic rituals when in deep thought, pressed a thumb against pursed lips and sent the air inside his mouth back and forth, from one cheek to the other, causing them to inflate then deflate, as if he were rolling one of his beloved golf balls in his yap. Then he relaxed and said, "It's a strong circumstantial case, but that's all. You'll need more than that to nail her."

"What I wouldn't give for the murder weapon covered with her prints and a victim's blood," wished Mary.

"What I wouldn't give to be tall, handsome, and hung. And guess what, I like my odds better than yours."

"You really know how to shine a positive light on things."

"Just keeping it real, as the kids say, nowadays."

"Do you think I should swear out a search warrant?"

"For the house, office, car, what?"

"Any or all."

"Listing the murder weapon as the object?"

"Yeah, among other things."

"Such as?"

"Blood, trace evidence. You know that the game is to only be specific enough to get the warrant. C'mon, Inspector. Give me a break."

"My breaks won't do you any good, since I don't sign search warrants. It's a judge you have to satisfy."

"And you doubt that I have enough for probable cause."

Newberry snorted dismissively and said, "We both know who the judges are who sign whatever is placed in front of them. It's like they're in love with their own handwriting. That's not your biggest hurdle." He paused to read her face. "She knows that she's in your crosshairs?"

"I believe so."

"So what are the chances that she's discarded the weapon or at least has it somewhere other than home, office, or vehicle?"

"One-hundred percent."

"And that's low-balling it."

"Right. I was thinking pretty much the same thing but wanted to get your viewpoint."

"Stealth is your best friend. No jumping the gun. Once you execute a warrant, everything's out in the open. There'll be no keeping a lid on it. The media will be on it like rabid dogs."

"Speaking of the media, I thought about using them to alert black seniors that there was a killer out there targeting them."

"Before you found out that she was only interested in three, one who wasn't a senior, anyway."

"Yes, so it probably wouldn't have done Jeeter McArthur any good," reasoned Mary.

"We'll never know, will we?"

Mary declined to answer but did ask, "Mind if I keep this from Gerald Lewis for the time being?"

"Hold off until you have something he can run with."

"But there is someone I want to bring into the loop."

"I'm guessing that it's Ross Brogan."

"Not bad. Can you also guess my weight?"

Newberry studied for a second, and then responded.

Mary's eyes bespoke indignation, and she said, "I beg your pardon."

"That'll teach you to stick to the subject," lectured Newberry, who intentionally had guessed too high. "I have no problem with Ross. He's not going to go shooting his mouth off. How will you use him?"

"Not all together sure. But he's been a help in a number of ways, already."

"Does he know that she's your suspect?"

"Not yet."

"Any idea why a blade?"

"None whatsoever. Luckily, I don't have to know, to nab her. "

"Just wondering," said Newberry. "Carry on. Go out there and gather the goods."

"Meaning forensics," translated Mary.

"And the kind that Rose won't be able to explain away."

"Like she can with trace evidence, by claiming the transfer happened when she and McArthur were together discussing legal matters."

"I'm going to take a seat," said Newberry. "Tired. My daughter and her baby are visiting. The rascal kept the house up all night."

Mary followed his lead and sat. "I'm sure you know what I'm placing all my chips on."

Newberry flashed a wry smile. "The DNA results."

"You know it. I've been bugging the hell out of the State Police laboratory, but basically they tell me to wait my turn."

"You're betting that the results show a second blood source."

"And if they do, I'll know just where to get the comparison sample." Mary folded her arms and declared, "And that's what I call something worthy of a search warrant."

76.

Mary didn't completely remove the certified check, just pulled it up from the envelope enough to read the amount. She pushed the check back down then placed the envelope inside her jacket.

"Lastly, I need your signature on some documents," Rose said, and flipped open the folder lying on her desk. "The first one is for receipt of the check."

Following a perfunctory review, Mary signed.

"And this one ends the attorney-client relationship," Rose said, of the longer document.

The language of the document was straight forward; yet, Mary took more time than might have been predicted. She reread sentences, paused in mid-sentence, distracted by the surrealism of conducting her dying mother's business with a suspected murderer.

"Need anything explained?" asked Rose, dedicated attorney to the end.

"No," Mary said, and signed.

"Excuse me while I make copies." Rose swiveled to her computer station located at her back and used the laser copier. She put the copies, unfolded, into a large envelope, which she handed to Mary.

"Thank you, Lisa."

"My pleasure, I assure you."

Mary uncrossed her legs and stood.

Rose stood, too, and extended her right hand.

Not automatically, not immediately, Mary shook hands.

"No more reasons for me to ask you to drop by," declared Rose. She trapped her bottom lip in an overbite, released it, and then said, "I'm sure that, from now on, you will rely on your own reasons."

Mary welcomed the insinuation; for, pretense by a cop is not effective if the suspect recognizes it for what it is. Mary wanted to be sure that the jig truly was up before being straightforward. "Why do you say that?"

With an index finger, Rose doodled on the desk, the invisible line ending at the edge. Then, she looked up. "For starters, you're going around asking about me in connection with Kent and Gibson."

Mary was not all that surprised that either Sloan or Shuster, maybe both, had blabbed about the interviews. She always knew that she had no power to force anyone's silence. It therefore didn't matter by what means Rose had come by the information. "And you take that to mean what?"

Rose laid it out. "You think that I killed them."

Now liberated, Mary, head held high, corrected the wording. "Not just them. McArthur, too."

Rose didn't flinch, although she said, "Wow!" She followed with, "Back when I was representing your mother and McArthur, you and I agreed to be allies and adversaries, remember?"

"In this very room."

"Regrettably, it's come down to just adversaries."

"Regrettably for you or for me?"

"My record speaks for itself," said Rose.

"I have a record, too."

"A record, yes. Evidence, no."

Mary knew that she was being baited and she faked a nibble. "Only circumstantial."

"And it won't get any better. McArthur, of course I knew. But I didn't know Kent and Gibson."

"True, but there was someone who knew all three, from a lifetime ago. Rebecca Rosenberg, who had a daughter named Lisa."

Again, Rose showed no outward reaction, but her churning stomach could have turned milk into butter. She stepped to the window and looked out onto the street, her back to Mary. Sounding incredulous, she asked, "That's your theory of motive?"

"Yes. Plus, it says a lot that you're not pretending that you don't know who Rebecca Rosenberg was."

Rose sharply turned away from the window. "Why should I stoop to antics. After all, there's a difference between gamesmanship and playing games. You're a good detective, for sure, and you've obviously uncovered certain facts." But that's where Rose's concessions ended. "Still, all you have is a circumstantial case. I chew them up and spit them out. Or didn't you learn anything from the McArthur case?"

"I did. That's why I didn't prance in here with an arrest warrant."

"Smart."

"I learned something else from the McArthur case, by the way." Mary pointed at items on the desk. "May I borrow pen and paper?"

"As much as you like."

Mary made a quick sketch and then asked, "Recognize this?"

"I should hope so," said Rose, of her trademark triangle, labeled at the vertexes with victim, crime scene, and suspect.

"Good, because I'm nobody's artist. Imagine a prosecutor using it as a visual aid in the opening statement and closing argument, just as you've done so many times."

"I can imagine that easily enough. What I'm having trouble with is imagining what it has to do with me."

"In this imagined scenario, the prosecutor argues that you are the suspect that's linked by evidence to the victim and to the crime scene." Mary began to slowly send the pen over the triangle several times, thickening the lines, underlining the words at the vertices, not saying anything.

Uneasiness reared, which Rose concealed with, "You plan on signing and framing your artwork?"

"No." Mary tore the page from the pad and laid the pen on top, as a paperweight. "But I'll leave it here, if you admire it that much."

"It's you that I admire, Mary Cunningham. Have for a while. But you're way over your head. Three murders?"

"Oh, I might not be able to get you on all three, but one will do. Same life sentence."

"Big talk from someone who doesn't have enough for an arrest warrant."

"You're fixated on that arrest warrant, aren't you?" Mary closed the distance with a step forward. "What you ought to be concerned about is a search warrant."

Rose instantly understood the allusion and said nothing. She tried to will a smile, but it traveled only to one side, involuntarily stretching and relaxing, making her mouth twitch. But even that reaction was more controlled than might have been expected, given the dark irony.

For, McArthur had been the exception, with Kent and Gibson having been disposed of swiftly, cleanly, with one lethal swipe; then again, after the botched first swipe on McArthur, Rose certainly couldn't have aborted the attack, nor could she have paused it to evaluate her blade. There had been nothing else that she could have done, except to bull forward. Now, what threatened to undo her was the McArthur murder: the one among the three that hadn't been a kosher kill.

During those frantic moments that had followed the unsuccessful swipe across McArthur's throat, her arms flailing, repositioning for another swipe, she accidentally cut herself, a slight puncture, but enough to draw blood. Running on adrenaline, she hadn't felt a thing. It was only on the drive home that she noticed the blood on her left sleeve. In reaction, she veered out of her lane, almost sideswiping a car, before correcting her steering.

For days thereafter, she obsessed over whether she'd left blood at the scene, and if so, whether it would be distinguishable from McArthur's. Ultimately, she'd convinced herself that even if her blood were discovered, the cops would have no reason for obtaining a matching sample from her.

Now, the long-healed wound on her arm suddenly seemed to itch and throb.

77.

The rifleman had waited until George and the pickup driver were standing close enough together. In a lightening motion, he cocked his weapon and aimed at their heads, shifting the barrel back and forth, ready to drop whoever failed to heed his command. "Hands up!"

George's arms shot up, like he was a football referee signaling a field goal, his facial expression a welter of fear, surprise, and confusion. When he realized he was still holding the rope that he was about to throw over a branch, he let it slide from his fingers.

The pickup driver's hands inched up to shoulder level.

"Higher!" demanded the rifleman.

"Okay!" agreed the pickup driver. "Don't get a twitch in that trigger finger." Trying to sound unconvinced as well as persuasive, he said, "What's got you so riled, fella, 'cause I know this can't be about that Jew heifer."

The rifleman didn't answer, but Rebecca had been on his mind since her abduction. The most he could do was hope for her return, because he had no idea where she'd been taken. To receive the returning degenerates in the way he wanted, he had to work fast. "Get your asses down from there," he said to the three Detroiters standing on the pickup bed, under the tree.

One after the other, they jumped to the ground, their hands still tied behind their backs. The last one landed ungainly, stumbled forward, and fell face-down. Considering his previous predicament, grit and scratches were nothing.

Loud and impatiently, the rifleman said, "Get over here," to the apparently oldest of the three. "Turn around." With one hand, he kept his weapon trained on the would-be lynchers, and with the other, tugged and clawed, until he untied the would-be lynchee.

The Detroiter didn't quite know what to do next, unable to interpret the whirlwind events; however, in short order, it was decided for him.

"Can't you see that I'm busy?" the rifleman derisively asked. "Untie the others."

The pickup driver, the lids of his beady eyes batting like they were sending Morse Code, contemptuously asked, "Hey, you some kinda lawman?"

"U.S. Marshal, asshole."

The infiltration hadn't been difficult, the formula simple. Express the right opinions around the right people and get received into the ranks, being new in town not mattering. Eagerly accept when recruited for night rides. Volunteer to ride shotgun, or whatever the rifle equivalent.

"I always had a sneaky suspicion about you," claimed George.

"You didn't suspect a damn thing, bright boy." The
rifleman ordered, "You morons hug the tree. From opposite sides."

"Say what?" responded the pickup driver.

"You deaf? Hug the tree. Like you're fucking a knot-
hole."

The pickup driver and George wrapped arms around
the trunk.

The rifleman was not satisfied. "Space yourselves so
that you can reach around and grab one another's wrists."

The pickup driver's reach, because of his ample belly,
went less than halfway around the tree. To compensate,
Jimmy had to press the side of his face against the tree
and blindly grope until he lashed on to the pickup driver's
wrists. The end result made for a ridiculous pose, the purpose of which would soon be made clear.

The rifleman reached under his shirttails and produced
a pair of handcuffs, which he dropped to the ground. His
hand disappeared again and out came his spare pair, with
which he did the same thing. He told the oldest Detroiter,
"Cuff them in that position."

Only after the rifleman checked and found that the
cuffs had been applied correctly did he lay down the
weapon long enough to gag both men with strips torn from
George's funky shirt.

The rifleman was improvising, just as he'd been doing
the entire evening. He had gone along with blasting the
horn and tailgating, after which he'd told the pickup
driver that they'd put a good scare into the Yankees and

that that was good enough. When the pickup driver took the words as a joke, the rifleman had to continue playing the role, waiting for the right opportunity. But how would the drama unfold for Rebecca? He hated that she'd been snatched from under his nose.

The tree huggers weren't going anywhere and the rifleman didn't have to worry about their shouting a warning; however, he had no more handcuffs and he hadn't decided how he was going to restrain the other two when they returned with Rebecca. He'd just have to improvise some more.

He slapped the back of his neck, smashing a mosquito. The bloodsucker felt as large as a grain of rice, as he slid it across and away.

From his shirt pocket, he withdrew a pack of Chesterfields, then inverted it and tapped one cigarette loose, which he extracted with his mouth. From a pants pocket came a lighter that he ended up having to flick several times. The flame flared tall and then bent toward him, as he took a long drag. His exhalation was even longer, his bottom lip jutting to direct the smoke upward. There, in the inkiness, the grey stream wafted spookily, like a dissolving ghost. A few more drags and he felt his frayed nerves start to relax.

Then, he began his wait.

78.

Grace Emanuel, typically asleep by ten p.m., could not have been more wide-eyed had she been hooked to a caffeine I.V., despite a wall clock ticking toward midnight. It wasn't insomnia keeping Grace awake but conversation and companionship, and she was enjoying both. In her faithful chair, she rocked and reminisced. That her eyes, as well as her mouth, were smiling suggested pleasant thoughts, but to know their specific nature required questioning.

And questioning was what Rose, seated at the end of a sofa that had a wavy top, crowned in mahogany, continued doing. "So, why didn't your father like him?"

Grace, wearing a button-down-the-front dress, open collar, said, "I was his only daughter and he called himself protecting me." With an index finger, she girlishly twirled a strand of hair. "You know how fathers can be."

"I never knew mine."

Sensing that the conversation might have hit a snag, Grace said, "I hope that I didn't stir up bad memories."

Rose reached and patted Grace's hand, said, "Not at all. Facts are facts," then quickly steered the conversation back on track. "You were saying that your father didn't approve."

"Right. But I kept seeing Jerome, anyway. I was fresh out of high school. Young and spry. You might say headstrong."

"And your mother?"

"She liked Jerome."

A three-socket pole lamp bathed the room in pale yellow, the color and wattage not too imposing on Grace's sensitive retinas. The only television in the house was a low-slung cabinet model and its screen reflected the room like an opaque mirror.

"How long were you and Mr. Emanuel married?"

"Fifty-four years."

"Quite an accomplishment."

"Don't misunderstand," Grace cautioned. "We had our spats and all. Never a time, though, that I didn't love him something fierce. I wouldn't trade that part of my life for anything." She stopped rocking and asked, "Have you ever been married, Lisa?"

Rose looked down, where underneath her bare feet lay an area rug, braided-rope type, coiled into an oval. Along its edge was a raised area that resembled a corn on a toe, which Rose flattened with her left sole. She slid that foot to the side and looked to see whether the area would spring back. After it didn't, she found herself out of delaying tactics and answered the question. "No. The only walking down the aisle in my future probably involves a movie theater."

Grace frowned, although not in disapproval. "I'm surprised. A smart, pretty girl, like yourself."

"Very kind of you to say that."

Pressing with the kind of nosiness that only seniors can get away with, Grace asked, "Ever come close?"

"No."

"I see."

"And I'm a klutz when it comes to dating. I started college having never been on one." Rose was going to leave it there, but asked, "Can I thrust you with a secret, just between the two of us gals?"

"You sure can."

"The first time I accepted a date, I hide in my dorm room, like I wasn't there, when the guy came for me." Rose tugged down on the tails of her oversized shirt. "Can I get you anything from the kitchen?"

"No, but you can slide that foot stool over here. I need to elevate my feet from time to time. Helps circulation."

"Coming right up."

Grace lifted one foot and then the other onto the stool. She shifted from side to side then sat higher, comfort showing in her face; but, what wasn't showing were signs of sleepiness.

After some mental rehearsal, Rose said, "May I ask you about that day?"

Grace, not requiring additional specificity, simply said, "Go ahead."

"First of all, what kind of day had it been?"

Grace had been asked that question innumerous times over the decades, including some through translators. One would think that it would grow tedious, but Grace never gave such indication, nor would she now, especially since the questioner was her trusted friend, Lisa Rose. "The day started with Jerome and me arguing. I went to work in a bad mood."

"You worked in a machine shop, if I remember correctly."

"Yes. In the packaging department, manually packing boxes, standing the whole while. Throughout the shift, things had been happening. Not big things. Just enough to try my patience. So, when I clocked out, I was in a worse mood than I'd been in when I arrived." After pausing to switch the order of her crossed ankles, Grace said, "On my way home, that man just happened to catch me on a bad day."

"What if it had been a good day?"

"Might have made all the difference. I might have done what I was told, like the other times." Adding perspective, Grace said, "Then maybe not, because folks had grown tired of that treatment."

"It was true bravery."

Grace, present weight and size close to what they had been back then, recounted, "I refused him before I thought about what I was doing. Can that be called bravery?"

"Absolutely."

Sounding amused, Grace said, "His eyes got as big as saucers and his ears turned red." Then her voice turned serious. "I was wearing a dress that came to the calf, and my knees were knocking underneath it. It crossed my mind to apologize and do as told, but something inside wouldn't let me."

"Bravery."

"So, the police came and hauled me off. It was the first time I ever saw the inside of a jail."

"Were you scared in that jail?"

"No," said Grace, shaking her head slowly from side to side. "I was through being scared, even though I didn't know what they were going to do to me. Sitting on that hard bench, I prayed. Told God that whatever he had in store for me, I would endure it in his name. Are you religious, Lisa?"

Rose wanted to maintain appearances of a conversation and not an interview; therefore, although she could have done without the question, she chose not to dodge it, at least not fully. "My grandmother was very religious and I learned a lot from her. I'm Jewish, but not observant in all traditions. I do, however, keep kosher."

"I don't know of any other two religions that have more in common than Judaism and Christianity, starting with the Old Testament."

"True," agreed Rose.

And as if to tie in with the main topic of discussion, Grace added, "Many Jews were active in the Movement. Came from all around the nation."

"They certainly did." Again, Rose kept the conversation on course, reminding, "You left off with you in jail."

"I wasn't there long. They hurried me to the courthouse, where the judge fined me."

"For?"

"Violating a city ordinance. Oh, yes. It was on the books."

Rose leaned forward on the sofa, hands on knees. "This is what I want to know most. Did you have any idea, whatsoever, what you had set into motion?"

Grace gave a thin, demurring smile. "You give me too much credit."

"Not possible," Rose said, in respectful disagreement.

"The times being what they were, if it hadn't been me, it would have been someone else."

"Would-have's don't count. You were the someone. The credit goes to you."

"Then it's only right that credit be given to the many others who played roles just as important as anything I did. Take for example the ones who organized the protests and boycotts. I didn't have the skills for that."

"Nonetheless, you were the face of the Movement."

"So it turned out," said Grace, stoically. Next, her facial expression turned sheepish. "I'll tell you something else. I was way more scared speaking to the crowds than I ever was getting arrested. Sometimes, that megaphone felt like twenty pounds, my hand shook so bad."

Rose gazed into Grace's eyes and said, "You're a treasure."

"It's you who's the treasure. I so enjoy your visits."

"As do I. It's an honor being in the presence of a legend."

"Thanks, but I shy from being called that. I'm more concerned that the sacrifices others made not be forgotten."

Grace recognized the approach of stiffness in a shoulder and tried to ward it off by flexing forward then backward. It didn't work. She grimaced as she reached around and clutched that shoulder.

"Something the matter?"

"Just some stiffness."

Rose stood and with palms smoothed that oversized shirt of hers. It hung loose and long, concealing her jean's waistband and pockets. Then she stepped behind the rocking chair. She gently removed Grace's hand, said, "Allow me," and began to apply massage.

Having learned the futility of trying to decline Rose's considerateness, Grace submitted, closing her eyes and rotating her shoulder to test the effectiveness of the massage.

Knowing that her talents were being evaluated, Rose asked, "Better?"

"Yes, but the stiffness is creeping up." Grace touched herself and said, "I forgot. What do you call this?"

"That's your clavicle, your collarbone."

"The stiffness is trying to settle there, now. Like it's chased from one place and goes to another."

"Then I'll keep after it until it leaves altogether."

"You're so giving, Lisa."

With schoolteacher sternness, but smiling, Rose said, "Don't try to butter me up, thinking that I'll let you off the hook."

Rose would have turned to look up and around if not for the stiffness. "Whatever are you talking about?"

"The fact will forever be that it was you, on that particular day, who set everything in motion." Then Rose pledged, "If it takes me all night, I'm going to get you to admit that."

"You are one somebody who knows how to get her way, Lisa. If it's that important to you, I admit it. Satisfied?"

Rose halted the massage long enough to say, "You have no idea."

"Good." Grace lowered her chin and rubbed it in short pendulum arcs against the front of her chest, a test that revealed no stiffness.

Rose kept busy, kneading with all fingers, intermittently pressing down with the thumbs, working along the clavicles and inward toward the base of the neck, saying of one side, "I feel a knot, here. Are you tense?"

"Not at all. And I don't feel a knot." Grace sent a hand in search.

But Rose intercepted the hand and guided it back down. "I must be mistaken. Imagination running wild. Next thing you know, I'll be detecting a fetus' heartbeat and declaring you pregnant."

"Oh, Lisa, don't be so naughty."

"Just one more area to attend to." Rose held Grace by the shoulders and bent down to say into her ear, "Hold your head back, so I can get to the front of your neck."

79.

Mary was battling the steering wheel, turning the corner with rapid, hand-over-hand grabs, tires squealing. Centrifugal force pulled her toward the passenger's door, like she was a robot reacting to an electromagnet. She pressed the gas pedal too soon out of the turn and the rear of the unmarked police car fishtailed, side to side, a few times. She yanked the wheel sharply in one direction, and as quickly, reversed it, totally having forgotten whether one steers in the direction of a skid or against. High-speed driving wasn't her long suit.

Minutes prior, she'd been driving more sanely while talking on the phone. "I got a recording saying that the number has been changed to an unlisted one."

"That's the only number in police records," Brogan had said. "Want me to go through the phone company?"

"Don't bother. I can be at the address shortly."

"Unless the address on record is wrong, too."

"Gotta go."

"Before you hang up, want me to send backup?"

"No. This might be nothing, but if something, I still won't need backup." She instantly second-guessed her wording and how it might be interpreted. Had she implied that the perpetrator—if there is one—likely had fled, or, that she wanted to handle the perpetrator alone?

Now, as Mary sped along, she hoped that her screaming siren and flashing lights would be sufficient warning, because the car likely would flip if she had to suddenly avoid something in her path. Danica Patrick, she wasn't.

Before Mary started burning rubber, she'd been on her way back to Headquarters, ironically from having interviewed a witness to a vehicular homicide. Not sparked by anything in particular, the recall struck with pile driver force. *Grace Emanuel! In the office of Lisa Rose! A client!*

Just as Jeeter McArthur had been.

No, Grace had not been with the Freedom Riders; however, the bus trip was one of many events that could be traced directly or indirectly to her courage. Was Rose's hit list longer than Kent, Gibson, and McArthur? Willing to error on the side of caution, Mary needed to get to Grace quickly. Besides, how could Mary make any assumptions about Grace's safety when Rose's whereabouts were unknown and had been for days. During that time, the DNA test results came in, verifying a second blood source. Mary swore out a search warrant, the justifying affidavit citing those test results and saying that there was reasonable cause to test Rose as that second source.

Only, Mary can't serve such a search warrant on someone who has evaporated. Just like Allison Petrocelli had done, Lisa Rose had performed a disappearing act. As songstress, Carole King, might ask, doesn't anybody stay in one place anymore?

Mary turned onto Grace's street and killed the siren and lights. She reduced her speed so that she could read addresses and determined that the address she sought should be on the next block, on the left. She arrived just as an automatic garage door was lifting. But Mary knew that Grace no longer drove. Mary pulled into the driveway, blocking the exiting vehicle. Both drivers slammed on the breaks, stopping feet apart from one another, but it was a type of head-on collision, nonetheless.

Mary and Rose locked eyes, like cobra and mongoose.

Mary unfastened her seat belt as fast as she ever had. Within seconds, she'd gotten out, having unholstered her gun in the process. She aimed squarely and shouted, "Get out the car! Now!"

Rose threw the transmission into reverse, sped backwards, slammed the breaks, and then flattened the accelerator. In whizzing past the patrol car, she unintentionally smashed its headlamp. She drove the lawn and the car sounded twin thuds, as first the front tires and then the rear dropped over the curb and onto the street.

Mary gave chase on foot. She halted and aimed, had a clear view of the back of Rose's head, and there was still time to demonstrate the skill she'd shown at the shooting range and in her recertification. The trigger finger tightened but not all the way. Too many unknowns to fire on a fleeing suspect. She reholstered.

Mary turned and sprinted to the house. The angle of approach took her first in front of a picture window, the blinds of which were open, so she stopped to look inside. What she saw made her breath leave in a single heave. Grace was in the rocking chair, slumped, head down, chin against neck, motionless.

80.

Mary pressed her fist against her mouth but that didn't prevent the escape of a lone, anguished moan. She backed away from the picture window, having seen through the blinds a deathly-still Grace Emanuel. Mary rushed to the front security door.

Maybe it would be unlocked.

It wasn't.

Mary violently pulled and pushed at the knob, as though trying to rip the door off its hinges. All the while, she wanted to hang herself for being so late in connecting the dots between Grace and Rose. Her anger and frustration led her to give the door a few stiff kicks.

Her mind clearing, she realized that she should call Headquarters to request a crime scene unit as well as to put out an all-points-bulletin on Rose's vehicle. She would only be able to give make and color, having not memorized the plate. She reached into her pocket for her phone, flipped it open, and started tapping digits. She was just about to press the talk icon, but suddenly halted.

"Who's out there?" came an apprehensive voice from inside the house.

Mary had to swallow hard then wet her lips to ask, "Mrs. Emanuel, is that you?"

"Yes."

"Thank you, God," Mary softly intoned, and louder said, "I'm a police officer, Mrs. Emanuel. Please open the door."

Grace opened the wood slats that covered the lookout window of the inside door. She peeked and saw Mary's I.D. badge held up for close inspection. "What do you want?"

Mary spoke fast. "It's about Lisa Rose. I met you in her office. Mary Cunningham. Remember me?"

First the sound of locks turning, followed by the inside door swinging open. "Yes, I do remember you."

Mary quickly stepped inside, wrapped Grace in an embrace, and planted a kiss on both cheeks before releasing her.

"Land sakes, child," declared Grace. "What's gotten into you?"

"Are you all right?" asked Mary, elated and almost tearful. "Are you really all right?"

"As best I know."

"I saw you in your chair—"

"Dozing, like I do sometimes after a good meal. Lisa made lunch." Grace bounced a searching gaze around the room. "She must have left without waking me."

"Has she been staying here?"

"For most of this week. Why?"

Before Mary could respond, her cell phone rang. She didn't recognize the number. For that very reason, she all but knew who it was. "Excuse me while I take this call, Mrs. Emanuel."

"Sure thing, child. I need to be off my feet, anyway. I'm going back to my chair."

Actually, it was Mary who had intended to step away, but having gained privacy by other means, she answered the phone. "Hello?"

"Hello, Lieutenant Mary Cunningham." Rose, before going into hiding, had smashed her subscriber cell phone, knowing that to use it, or even have it on her person, would make her whereabouts traceable. Now, she was talking on a disposable cell phone, like the one she used when she called Kent for their impromptu meeting and like yet another that she used when she set the last meeting with McArthur, claiming that she was using a client's phone.

"Turn yourself in, Lisa."

"Sorry, but that's not the reason I've called. However, I do have something to tell you."

"Speak."

"I was surprised to see you, I admit. But, now that I've thought about it, I know what brought you there. I'm insulted that you think I would hurt Grace. She's the mother of the Movement. And I revere mothers."

81.

A pacing Gerald Lewis paused and vowed, "If the DNA is a match, I'll prosecute. That's a given." Even so, he again asked, "You're sure about what she said, right?"

Mary, this time said, "As sure as I'm standing here." And she, indeed, was on her feet, ready to leave, after having sat through more than an hour of discussions.

But Lewis, allowing for no misunderstanding, specified, "That she hadn't seen McArthur after his acquittal."

"That's what the woman said."

"My brain is overheating here, trying to predict her defense. Even if she denies what she told you, how would she explain the DNA?" Lewis, referring to findings issued from the medical examiner's office, revised the question to, "How would she explain that both blood types showed the same degree of deterioration?"

"Makes it difficult to claim that there weren't two people bleeding at the same time, that's for sure."

"All the more my question." Lewis hooked a finger down his collar and pulled, loosening his tie; however, his neck muscles remained taut as he thought aloud, "How would she explain it?"

"Maybe she can't. Could be the simple reason that she disappeared."

From experience, Lewis didn't trust simple. "There's no law against disappearing. There's no law against hiding from a search warrant, either, if that's what's she's doing." Then, he logically asked, "But how would she know that a warrant was coming?"

Mary, reluctance in her voice, said, "Might have something to do with the last time I was in her office, when she was riding me about not having enough for an arrest warrant." Embarrassment crept in as she admitted, "I told her that she ought to be concerned about a search warrant, not to tip her off, but to give her something to think about."

Preceded by a look of incredulity, Lewis' response was, "Aww, give me a break, Mary."

Mary speedily tried to redeem herself. "Look at it this way, though. I said nothing about DNA testing, so if Lisa concluded that that's what the warrant would be about, it points to her guilt. Also, she would have anticipated that an arrest warrant would follow if she went missing, so she's hiding from arrest, too. She's guilty. I know it."

"Then I'd appreciate it if you grab some Q-tips and go find her."

Mary put on a puzzled facial expression and said, "Hell, Gerald, why didn't you say so? I'll leave here and go straight to her hideout."

Lewis smiled, in recent times having become more accepting of Mary's occasional impertinence. He risked more by adding, "Bring back the murder weapon, too. I know, first-hand, how she can exploit the absence of one."

"I've added it to the list. Anything else, my Captain?"

Lewis walked to his desk, where he sent the swivel chair into a full rotation and then sat. "A motive that I could defend would be nice, and I'm dead serious. I've listened to your theory about how the murders are connected to what happened to her mother. But, if that's the motive, why now, after all these years?"

"What was the trigger, the stressor?" Mary, shoulders drooped, flat-out admitted, "I have no idea."

"Try to scare one up," requested Lewis, "because a jury likes to know little details like that." He leaned back in the chair and drummed fingertips against the desk top. "Meanwhile, I'm holding my breath over how long we can keep the arrest warrant under wraps. When the media gets wind of it, there's going to be a circus."

"Yeah, the three-ring kind." Reciting why, Mary said, "Famous attorney a serial killer."

Actually, the media would have had grounds to suspect a serial connection had it not been for the police policy of withholding from the public specifics that only the killer would know—useful for separating the killer from the pathological confessors.

And there was another reason why the media didn't know that there had been a trio of victims with slashed throats. The Detroit Police Crime Incident Record, which the media relies on, utilizes a small number of standardized descriptors for homicides, among them: shooting, beating, strangulation—and, yes, knifing, which, by default, was assigned to each of Rose's victims. The notoriety surrounding the McArthur murder prompted the media to delve further, leading to the discovery that his throat had been slashed; but, that didn't send newshounds sniffing along a branching trail.

"If there's a trial, it'll be high-profile to the max," said Lewis.

"Are you looking forward to trying the case?"

"I've tried my last case. Here out, it's back to assigning. But even if I were to try the case, I wouldn't look forward to it. It would be a sad day in so many respects."

"I feel the same way."

"I meant to ask you earlier," began Lewis, "whether, before your investigations, you knew of Rebecca Rosenberg."

"No. Didn't know about her. Never learned about her in school, either."

"Same here."

Mary, in a tone that didn't sound as if she was exempting herself, said, "In my research, I saw that the media reported on it back when it happened. However, society conveniently forgets a lot about those times."

Lewis tilted his head in reflection and said, "That shouldn't be. Rebecca Rosenberg deserves to be remembered."

"She certainly will be if this plays out like I think it will." Mary gave a leaden sigh and then said, "But at such a cost."

"Tragic." Lewis stood. "I got your signal that you were ready to leave when you got out of the chair," he said, walking past her to the door. He chivalrously opened it and held it for her.

Mary, walking through, commented, "She can't stay underground forever."

"True, but that's of limited consolation because I'm sure that when she resurfaces, she'll spring on us something that we haven't thought of."

82.

Not to imply that any car ride involving Rose and Bernie could be pleasant, but the one in which she drove him to the airport for his relocation to Florida was thirty-two miles of nonstop complaining and demanding—his complaining about not being allowed to pack his chalefs in his carry-on and his demanding that she send them to him by overnight delivery.

It wasn't that Rose had never heard of checking a piece of luggage, but a claim ticket wasn't the simple solution that one might think.

Bernie, who hadn't flown in decades, was as unwilling to entrust luggage to airlines as some Depression survivors were unwilling to entrust savings to banks; and, to risk lost luggage containing his chalefs would be like playing Russian roulette with multiple loaded chambers.

In between his obsessions over the chalefs, Bernie yammered about the wheelchair awaiting him at the airport, that he was to be pushed in it, his disability on display. Never mind that she'd explained that she'd ordered the wheelchair because the distance through the terminal and to the gate would have been tiring; his emphasis was on how he didn't deserve to be disabled, that it wasn't his fault, that he was not to blame. The implication, obviously, was that the fault and blame lie with someone else; however, rather than say with whom, he found it more fulfilling to let it go unspoken, to have it linger throughout the car, like a stench.

So even before she rolled to a curbside stop at the airport, popped the trunk, got out, and retrieved the carry-on, she knew that for them there would be no hugs, kisses, well-wishes, or other gestures of affection commonly exchanged at partings. She pulled up the handle on the carry-on and was about to roll it to the entrance doors, but he grabbed it, bumping her in the process, and brusquely told her to be on her way and to send him his chalefs.

She was long-accustomed to the emotional pain, but that didn't mean she felt it less. From the car, she watched as he plodded through the doors. Soon, her view of him was obstructed by the surrounding crowd and she strained for any glimpse, no matter how partial, just as she'd done that fateful day at the slaughterhouse. When he had completely disappeared she slowly drove off.

His instructions to her could not have been more stamped on her mind had they been encoded on a microchip implanted in her brain. She got on the freeway, first stop: back to the house to get his chalefs. Then, it'll be off to the nearest FedEx, UPS—whatever—to arrange overnight delivery of those chalefs, those infernal chalefs.

83.

The rifleman's name was Floyd
Harmon, and a year later, he was the federal government's
chief witness in the trial of the two who had sped off with
Rebecca Rosenberg. On the stand, Harmon was unshak-
able. Dispassionately, graphically, he testified to the abduction, but couldn't, from personal knowledge, testify to what
happened afterward, especially since the abductors didn't
return to the scene.

Matthew Kent and Raymond Gibson testified after Harmon, but also had no personal knowledge about what the
defendants did after whisking away Rebecca. Even less, neither Detroiter had witnessed Rebecca's being thrown into
the car—preoccupied and distracted as they had been at
the time.

Jeeter McArthur didn't testify, wasn't summoned by
either side. The Feds didn't want to risk having the youngster confused by the defense attorneys, and the defense
attorneys didn't want to risk having the youngster receive
sympathy from the jury, even though that was a long shot.
McArthur became part of the trial record only in reference—as the unnamed minor—not that his family would
have allowed his return, especially his father, who had:

ridden the Freedom Riders bus with his son; suffered
appendicitis upon arrival; and, given permission for his
son to carry forth.

Kent, the driver that night, testified to being forced off
the road, taken out of the vehicle, and almost lynched. But
the defense attorneys got him to admit that the most physical harm he suffered was a blow to the gut with a rifle butt,
delivered by none other than Harmon.

Gibson, on the other hand, could not claim any physical harm, although the federal attorneys tried mightily to
emphasize the realness of the mental and emotional harm
endured. Countering, the defense attorneys got Gibson to
admit that those reactions had been caused, in some measure—again—by Harmon.

Earlier, the federal attorney attempted to show that
Harmon had been role-playing, by asking Kent hadn't it
been Harmon who had rescued the three Detroiters. But,
the judge sustained objections that such testimony was
irrelevant, since these defendants were not facing charges
related to attempted lynching. Besides, by the government's own account, these defendants were not present
when the nooses were placed around the necks of the ter-
rorized three. More than that, the two who the government claimed had been present, namely the pickup driver
and George, already had been tried and acquitted of such
charges.

Both Kent and Gibson, however, were allowed to testify that these defendants wanted to rape Rebecca and

that Harmon quashed the notion. Of course, the defense labeled both those contentions as lies.

The presiding federal judge was known to be in support of separate-but-equal laws, seeing no inherent contradiction in them. Even so, the draw could have been worse for the government because there were other federal judges whose closets contained white robes, in addition to their black ones.

The courtroom was packed tighter than jumbo sardines. The whites who were reputed to be integrationists sat in groups, availing themselves of whatever safety there might be in their modest numbers. Fewer yet, were the Negroes—as they were politely called back then— some of whom defiantly sat up front.

The majority of the attendees, however, were white segregationists; therefore, it was not surprising that the ruling sentiment was that Harmon was the outsider, the carpetbagger, who also had been the masquerader, the deceiver. He had been the Yankee infiltrator and a symbol of federal trampling of states' rights. But if the glares directed at Harmon were icy, those directed at Kent and Gibson lowered the room's temperature by degrees.

84.

Jimmy and the youngest night-rider were James Polk and Beau Ralston, respectively, and had agreed to be tried together, although each had his own attorney. When it became the defense's turn to put on its case, each would take the stand.

Ralston, a tenth-grade dropout with two misdemeanor arrests but no convictions went first. He wore an ill-fitting suit borrowed from an uncle, and the borrowed white shirt, although washed, showed vestiges of a dirt ring at the top of the collar. His direct-examination started with some creampuff questions meant to present him as a wholesome Dixie dude. Later, he testified, "I was sure that Mr. Harmon was going to kill the girl. Same with them colored fellows." After saying, "None of us knew he was a U.S. Marshal," Ralston's mouth hung open for a moment, as if to convey that he still found that fact incredible. "He sure didn't act like one, for all that I saw."

Ralston's lawyer possessed a booming, baritone voice, in such contrast with his puny frame that it seemed the product of ventriloquism. Part of his courtroom style was to hold onto his lapels, now and then releasing a hand to turn a page of his notes. "Why were you out there that night, in the first place? Explain that to the jury, Son."

Ralston wrung his hands for effect and said, "I had me a few beers and I was buzzing. I admit that. I was up to having some fun at the expense of the Northerners. I know now that it was the wrong thing to do, but I swear, the plan was to honk at them, shout some insults, maybe even moon 'em, but all from the road."

"So how was it that the vehicles ended up stopped?"

"That was all Mr. Harmon's doing."

"How so?"

"All of a sudden, he points his rifle and makes the colored driver pull over. Then he tells our driver to do the same."

"Was Mr. Harmon the only one in the truck with a weapon?"

"Yes. Plus he was all take-charge, is how I would put it. So we wasn't in the best position to challenge him."

"Did you feel intimidated by Mr. Harmon?"

"Most certainly."

And so the lying continued unabated, with the questioning eventually focusing on Rebecca.

"Let's return momentarily," said the lawyer, "to your earlier testimony that, far from being a kidnapping, taking Miss Rosenberg away was a rescue. Explain that further."

"Well, me and Jimmy wasn't for killing nobody. The thing of it was that we couldn't save all of them, so we came up with a plan to get the girl out of there."

A few questions later, the lawyer asked, "What happened once you had Miss Rosenberg safely away?"

"I told her she ought to go back into town and tell the sheriff about the coloreds we had to leave behind. Since it wasn't my car, I let her get behind the wheel. I went over directions with her on how to get back to town. I asked her to drop me and Jimmy off on the way."

"Wouldn't it have been the gentlemanly thing to do to have escorted the young lady into town?"

"I agree." But Ralston tacked on, "Except that I knew that lots of folks saw the Northerners as trouble-makers and I didn't want to be seen as a sympathizer. I still wasn't for violence, though. So that she wouldn't have to get off the main road, me and Jimmy got out about a mile from my house and walked the rest of the way. That's how her and us parted company. And that's the gospel truth."

James Polk's lawyer each day wore a three-piece white suit. Beyond dress, he resembled Colonel Harland Sanders, of KFC fame, down to the chalky goatee. "I know you stutter, Jimmy," is how he began. "These good folks on the jury are patient and understanding, so you just relax and take your time answering truthfully." Then, for more than an hour, the lawyer led Polk through a litany of denials and narratives, sometimes finishing a word when Polk seemed hopelessly stuck mid-syllable.

An interesting part of Polk's testimony was that after he lifted Rebecca and flung her into the car, he dove on top to shield her, because he expected Harmon to open fire. It was heroism, like when a soldier throws himself on a live grenade. And from the way Polk was straining the seams on a cheap seersucker suit, it was easy to see that he had a lot of body to hurl in sacrifice.

Late in the examination, the lawyer said, "Jimmy, you saw the photos of Miss Rosenberg that the government introduced into evidence, didn't you?"

"Yes."

"I'm not going to ask that they be shown again, because that would only serve to assault the sensibilities of all present in the courtroom. And you aren't keen on looking at them again yourself, are you?"

"No."

"But you do recall the suffering that those photos depict, don't you?"

"Yes."

The lawyer began a question, but said, "Strike that. First I want to ask, on the night in question, were you in possession of a knife, blade, or any type of cutting instrument?"

"No."

"It could be said that your earlier answers make my next question unnecessary," said the lawyer, loving the sound of his own voice, "but let's not leave the jury anything to have to wonder about." After that set-up, he asked the earlier began question. "So Jimmy, I don't know how to pose it any simpler, any more direct than this. Did you have any involvement, whatsoever, with what happened to Miss Rebecca Rosenberg?"

Polk's reply took twice the time, but although delivered in stammers, was emphatic. "Sir, no way am I capable of doing something like that."

85.

Lisa Rose never took the chalefs to a delivery service. She did, however, take them to her house. She laid them on her dining room table. And there they remained throughout the several times she left the room to battle her thoughts. And there they remained on each return, despite her illogical hope that she'd find them gone, that they would have sprouted legs and have walked out on her and her newly-devised murderous plans.

They were handsome, custom-made instruments, those chalefs. Their blades were forged from stainless steel, especially formulated for overall strength and for maintaining a sharp cutting edge. Their handles were made of mammoth ivory, from the tusks of that extinct pachyderm. The set was contained in a velvet, foldout holder which had a compartment for each chalef. Those chalefs—collector's items in every sense of the term—were not made to slash the throat of any animal, let alone any human.

No, those chalefs were a gift from the Fleischman Meat Packing Company to Bernard Simon Rosenberg, as reflected in the initials, *BSR*, etched in calligraphy on each handle. They were a retirement gift— make that a forced-retirement gift—to an employee who'd been permanently disabled, no longer capable of being a shochet, but had been too loyal to sue his employer.

In her latest return, Rose found herself begrudgingly admiring the hard beauty of the set. It was a rarity to see it out of its glass display case which Bernie kept in the living room, on a wall table, impossible for anyone in the room to miss. But Bernie was not a gambling man, willing to rely on someone else's powers of observation, and Yetta's visitors regularly became captives when Bernie went show-and-tell. After Yetta died, visitors became as scarce as hen's dentures, and there were many occasions when young Lisa watched from around a corner, as Bernie, sitting in his armchair, cleaned non-existent dust and smudges from his precious chalefs, using a jeweler's polishing cloth, while complaining to himself.

Now, decades later, Rose lowered a hand, fingers hovering above the chalefs but not touching. She wiggled the fingers, as if testing whether they still did her bidding. The hand, shaking, lowered farther, stopping just short of contact. The hand swept back and forth, but since her palm wasn't magnetic, no chalef slapped up against it. The choice would have to be hers and she chose the one that was about the size of a kitchen knife—smaller than what was used on the cow that traumatic day—but big enough, and concealable.

It was the first time that she ever held a chalef, first time that she had extracted one from its compartment. She raised it to eye-level and rotated it, horizontally, vertically, diagonally, the ceiling light gleaming off the blade. Next, in ritual fashion, operating from patched-together recall, she sent the fingers of her free hand along the sides and the edge, evaluating.

It still was early in the day. Hell, Bernie's plane was still winging its way to the land of oranges and alligators. There was still time, plenty of time, to put the chalef back into its compartment, fold up the set, and get it off for overnight delivery. It would have been the sane thing to do.

But she had seen the photographs.

They'd been in a brown envelope, the type with a top flap that closes with a metal clasp. Bernie had placed the envelope in his carry-on, on top of the chalefs. After saying that the chalefs couldn't be taken on the plane, Rose removed them from the carry on, after first removing the envelope and placing it on the edge of the bed. Bernie promptly snatched the chalefs from her, not noticing that he'd brushed against the envelope, causing it to fall to the floor. After setting the terms under which he would leave his chalefs behind, Bernie resentfully zipped the carry-on, grabbed it by the handle, and stomped out of the room. Rose hurried behind him, she too, unmindful that the envelope was being left behind.

Having gone straight from the airport back to Bernie's house, she bounded up the stairs to get the chalefs and was on her way out of the room when—curse peripheral vision—she noticed the envelope. No problem, she'd just send it to him along with the chalefs. But when she had the envelope in hand, curiosity caused her to look inside.

Immediate wooziness made her drop into a seated position on the bed.

Back when she was in law school, by her own research, she read the transcripts of the trials of James Polk and Beau Ralston and learned that there were photos that had been entered into evidence, although copies of them were not attached to the transcripts as exhibits. What she hadn't known throughout the decades that followed was that Bernie possessed copies. They were aged, black and white, but as graphic as if they'd been rendered in blazing color.

From the time that she was a young prosecutor, she'd used investigators in an official capacity, as she'd done in unearthing the snooping of Debra Winkler. Equally long, in an unofficial as well as anonymous capacity, she'd used other investigators for keeping tabs on the four nightriders. George had died of kidney failure after suffering for years on dialysis. The truck driver was still alive but suffering as a quadriplegic, trapped in a shell of a body courtesy of a shotgun blast to the spine delivered by his irate Mrs. But what of the two who had been most responsible? James Polk was dead, the victim of a farm equipment accident that ripped off an arm and caused him to bleed to death, and in the process, suffer greatly.

There came a time when the only one not dead or suffering was Beau Ralston, who had been the youngest. There also came a time when Rose traveled south to seek him out. She tracked him one night to a rowdy bar where the smell of sweat hung heavily, like it was being pumped in.

In the dim light cast by red bulbs, a twanging guitar playing on the jukebox, she was approached by Ralston, eighteen years her senior, his intent being to work his charm on the new skirt in the joint.

Rose, sporting a Vampirella wig, used a finger to part her black bangs and arranged her facial expression to communicate interest. As Ralston invaded her space she stood her ground, enduring his dog breath, as she inconspicuously dropped a capsule into the glass of draft beer that he was holding. She hadn't packed the capsule full, not enough potassium cyanide to be instantly fatal, because she would need time to leave the scene of the crime, time to put distance between herself and Ralston. When she tried to walk away, he grabbed her wrist and asked what her hurry was. She pleasantly wrested her wrist free and explained that her husband was waiting for her in the parking lot.

On the flight back to Michigan, Rose delighted over how Ralston must have suffered, imagining his writhing in convulsions and ultimately succumbing to cardiac arrest. In her lap lay the hick newspaper that she'd brought onboard, which announced that local resident, Beau Ralston, had collided head-on with a semi-truck after leaving a bar. Highway patrol ruled it an obvious case of drunk driving. She reclined her seat and rested her head, an I-know-what-really-happened smile playing on her lips

That had been more than ten years ago, and throughout the interim, Rose, no subscriber to karma, nonetheless felt that accounts had been balanced, if not perfectly, at least enough to allow her to cope. But when she was sitting on Bernie's bed, struggling to hold down the contents of her stomach, she felt that something else was owed to her mother. But from whom would the debt be extracted?

She was all too familiar with Bernie's rants about how the legal system had failed in the prosecutions of James Polk and Beau Ralston and that had Rebecca been black, the Feds would have made a better effort, aware of world attention to the Civil Rights Movement. He never entertained the possibility that the Feds had done their best before a jury that was comprised of people who were too pissed about the Civil War to give a piss about civil rights, even though he often fumed over how the jury stood and took a bow when the courtroom broke out in applause upon the announcement of the not-guilty verdicts.

When on his soapbox, at some point he would transition into cursing the other occupants of the DeSoto for having been with Rebecca, exposing her to danger by their very presence. He seldom ended without condemning the unfairness that it was the schvartzes who survived. If the Movement were so righteous, it should have been they who gave the full measure. In the past, Rose had dismissed his remarks as the illogical squawks that they were, dismissals made easier by remembrances of lectures by Yetta that one people's injustice is everyone's injustice and that thousands of non-Jews died in the liberation of the concentration camps.

The photographs, however, opened a window, through which a cold, infectious wind blew through. Now, what was passing as logic was the recognition that whatever could be blamed on the Detroiters was not as monstrous as what could be blamed on the nightriders. No, all things considered, the Detroiters—though they owed—didn't deserve to suffer.

86.

Bernie wasn't certain whether he'd been awakened by a full bladder or by an ache in his bad hip, the latter aggravated by the rain storm that was buffeting southern Florida. No matter, he could kill two birds with one trip. He threw back the covers and rolled out of bed.

Standing at the toilet awaiting the stream, he popped two pills—sans chaser—that he'd taken from the medicine cabinet. His mouth was pasty and dry, and the pills raked across his tongue, leaving a white trail of bitterness. Upon finishing his business, he flushed. The water swished powerfully and then disappeared in several gulps. Then he headed back to bed, sliding his feet along, one in front of the other, like slow, lazy cross-country skiing on carpet.

Fat raindrops slatted against the bedroom window and wind gusts flattened them into cascading sheets. A bolt of lightning momentarily turned the room into a photo negative. The ensuing thunder drowned out the first telephone ring, but the others seemed to grow successively louder, a psychological phenomenon, reflecting that mostly bad news comes in the middle of the night.

It wasn't just the hour that was inauspicious, however, but that the phone was ringing, period; for, Bernie received few calls, and mostly, they were from a particular caller. The phone kept ringing, not having a voicemail feature, as he stood there, staring down at it. When he became good and ready, he raised the receiver and gave a standoffish, "Hello."

"Hello, Grandfather."

He'd been expecting her call, had tried to call her, but she'd gone incommunicado. Instead of returning the greeting, he waded straight into troubled waters. "I got a call from Detroit homicide. A woman."

"That would have been my good friend, Lieutenant Mary Cunningham."

"That's the one. Tight-lipped she was, but I'm not senile, and I figure this has something to do with McArthur's death. I told her that I didn't know your whereabouts, which was true." Then Bernie asked, "Aren't you concerned that my phone might be tapped?"

"Interstate wiretaps is what the Feds do, and no one has any indication that I've crossed state lines. Besides, it takes a little time between an order and its execution."

"Or so you say. Still, why are you calling me? It's not like there's anything I can do for you."

"Spoken like the warm-hearted, giving, softy that you are, Grandfather."

"Even now with the smart mouth," Bernie scolded, reaching to turn on the nightstand lamp, "when they're after you about that McArthur character, not that I would ever mourn him."

"And why are you speaking ill of the dead?"

"He's a rabbi-killer, or was."

"I've heard that from you before. That's the only association that you make with McArthur?"

"What other association is there?"

"Well, let me throw a few names at you," said Rose. "Mathew Kent. Raymond Gibson."

"Those names mean nothing to me. What are you getting at?"

"Let's try Beau Ralston and James Polk."

"Enough already with the name game. Either get to the point or change the topic, like why the cops are looking for you." He proved that he didn't understand the nature of her plight, by saying, "I'm guessing McArthur was killed doing something criminal, you know about it, and are trying to protect his reputation."

"Nothing like that."

"Then what?"

"The less you know, the less time you need spend on the phone if Mary calls you back." Then Rose said, "But back to those names. The first two, along with McArthur, were in the car with my mother the night she was killed. The last two were the ones who killed her."

Bernie didn't immediately respond, feeling that he was being judged, but eventually said, "That was a lifetime ago. Your lifetime, in fact. So what if I don't remember names. As far as I'm concerned, they all share the same name, and that's bastard."

Rose then flatly reported, "Each bastard, to use your term, is dead."

The question was posed almost like a challenge. "And how, not counting McArthur, do you know that?"

"Because it's important enough to me to know."

The answer, oblique as it was, didn't sit well with Bernie. He believed that something was being implied, something uncomplimentary. "What good would it have done me to fixate on them? Wouldn't have brought back Rebecca. The less they crossed my mind the better."

"So why did you keep those pictures?"

"Pictures?" he repeated, knowing full well to what she was referring. "You said that you didn't look in the envelope before sending it."

"I lied."

"So in addition to being a liar, you're a prier."

"So, now it's insults in rhyme. Go the next step and compose a poem about how I disgust you."

Bernie was feeling the pills starting to numb the throbbing in his hip, but it didn't mellow his mood. "I don't like this conversation," he declared. "I like it even less than our usual conversations. And I still don't know why you called."

"I don't either. I thought I did. Some crazy notion about healing. An even crazier notion about setting things right. Now nothing makes sense. Go back to sleep, Grandfather."

"I'm no child. I'll sleep when I choose," Bernie said, then sat in a bedroom chair. To emphasize his point, he extended the conversation, returning to the last topic of discussion. "You asked about the pictures. I kept them as a reminder of what had been done to me."

"To you?!"

"That's right. It was as if those bastards who killed Rebecca knew that I was a shochet and cut her throat that way just to mock me. Raggedly. Opposite of a kosher kill."

Rose, stunned by what she'd just heard, recovered to say, "Unbelievable, even by your standards. All this time, you were seeing yourself as the victim of some kind of twisted-ass irony." She paused, harnessing her resentment, emboldening herself, in order to say, "You arrogant, cold-hearted, egomaniacal old man. You're a disgrace to my mother's memory."

Bernie, incensed, spoke loudly into the phone. "You mean unlike you, who, despite your fame and fortune, have never publicly acknowledged that she was your mother. Hell, you were too ashamed to share the same name with her."

"The name change was a symbolic break with you, not Mom." Then, suddenly, as though the weight of denial had become unbearable, Rose caved, saying, "I was wrong to have called you a disgrace to my mother's memory without admitting that I've disgraced her memory, too. And, of the two of us, dear Grandfather, it's I who's been the greater disgrace, for reasons that, I fear, will come to light all too soon."

Bernie hadn't expected such an admission but nonetheless resented his inclusion. In reference to the last part of her statement, he said, "Now, you come with the riddles, do you?"

"Better than my jokes, I suppose." Next, it might have seemed like a questionable changing of the subject, but Rose had her reasons for saying, "I can't believe that we've talked this long and not once have you mentioned your chalefs."

Bernie was as helpless against the bait as a famished trout is against a fat, wiggling nightcrawler. His focus became singular. "What's your latest excuse?"

"The time for excuses is past. Forget the chalefs. No chalefs for you."

Bernie launched to his feet and his bad hip threw him off balance, so he steadied himself with a hand on the chair's armrest. Anger coursing like a contagion, his breathing audible, he demanded, "You tell me where they are, and I mean right now!"

In a most matter-of-fact tone, Rose said, "Somewhere at the bottom of the Detroit River."

The wind had relented, such that the rain was tapping a steady rhythm against the patio door, a quiet storm, now. But had there been a script, and thunder knew how to read, it would have known that Rose's confession was the cue to boom. Thunder, however, made nary a whimper.

Instead, silence roared briefly, until broken by, "I'll never forgive you! I mean it. Not ever!"

"I expected as much. I know you don't give a rat's ass about my reasons, but I didn't do it to spite you. But they're gone and that's that. Now, you know."

"You're dead to me, from this moment on."

"It'll be difficult to notice the difference."

"You will notice," Bernie threatened once, then again, stronger. "You will notice."

Rose pooh-poohed the threat, saying, "Oh, lighten up, for once. You're risking hypertension. Your arteries will have more pressure than most ocean depths."

"Hardy, har, har."

"That wasn't meant as a joke. But, as a matter of fact, I do have one. Care to hear it?"

Bernie was seething too much over the question to give a response.

"Why did Bernie Rosenberg cross the road?" Rose asked, and then supplied the answer. "Because his nature is to cross anybody and anything."

Rose had no difficulty imagining steam shooting out of Bernie's ears, but that didn't deter her from delivering her material. "Boy, rough crowd, tonight. Didn't care for that one? No problem. I have another version." Again, she asked, "Why did Bernie Rosenberg cross the road?" Then, she dejectedly gave the answer, "Anything to get away from his granddaughter."

87.

The Kingsley abode had four bedrooms, all upstairs, that is, before a downstairs room was converted into a fifth. It was the latest of the purposes that room had served over the years. When Mary was a little girl, it was a playroom and the object of many a territorial squabble between her and her brother, Junior. Later, it served a stint as Sophie's sewing room. Later still, Joc converted it into a television room. Now, it was Sophie's bedroom, albeit only in the technical sense: it had a bed and Sophie slept there. More accurately, it was a waiting room, as in purgatory.

Sophie's speech now was given to sudden, sharp transitions—faint, moderate, high-pitched—as if a volume dial were being randomly turned from side-to-side. Attempts at conversation often zapped her energy and breath, leaving her drained and gasping. None of that, however, deterred her from continuing with her plea. "I'm tired," she repeated. "And I'm ready."

Mary was standing at the head of the hospital bed that had been acquired for Sophie. Mary pressed the control, raising Sophie's head a little more. Mary then lowered the side rail so that she could more easily hold Sophie's hand. "Mama, I can't do it."

Sophie clinched her eyes, the pain emotional. Physical pain was controlled by intravenously-fed morphine. Her request already had been refused by the hospice caregiver, as well as by husband, Joe. "If I could do it for myself, I would. I hate being a bother."

"No one considers you a bother. Least of all me."

Sophie fell silent, yielding to the toll, but her eyes did the imploring until she could speak again. "I can't get out this bed. Can't get around anymore, even with a walker." Speaking brokenly, trying to conserve energy, she said, "Bring me something. Aspirin. Sleeping pills. It don't matter. And water. I'll do the rest."

It wasn't supposed to get to that. When Sophie was diagnosed as Stage IV, she, naturally, figured that the time she had remaining would be short, although she never conceptualized it in terms of months. Now, she thought that the time had come and gone; now, keeping death at bay only was resulting in monumental suffering. The sand in her hourglass of life had emptied, except for a small, stubborn amount that had become caked. She wanted the hourglass shaken, the last grains to flow.

"Please," begged Mary. "Ask me for anything except that."

"People talk about the will to live. What about the will to die? Why won't it work for me?" Sophie required around-the-clock care. She considered the diapers an affront on her dignity. And if there was delay in replacing the morphine drip, she soon was groaning in agony. She craved permanent relief. She gave a deep, sorrowful sigh, wishing that it was her dying breath. Her breathing, however, did become more shallow, only capable of supporting a raspy whisper, so she motioned for Mary to lean closer. Then, Sophie, mouth inches from Mary's ear, said, "Call that man, Fritz Mueller."

Mary recoiled like she had suffered a busted eardrum. She had been warned by Joe about the request for pills and had arrived with a rehearsed refusal, her stumbling delivery notwithstanding. The mentioning of Mueller, though, was complete ambush. "I don't...know...I mean." She wiped her palm down her face and wearily beseeched, "God, have mercy."

"I heard Joe cursing him that time he came over," confessed Sophie, voice a little stronger. "I even heard you talking when you came over that day, after you had confronted Lisa Rose about it. It wasn't her fault."

"No, it wasn't." Mary had not told Sophie that Rose was a triple-murder suspect on the lam.

The arrest warrant for Rose still wasn't public knowledge. Had it been, it might have served Sophie's purpose; for, the shock, disappointment, and grief likely would have killed Sophie.

"Because of Lisa Rose, I'll die knowing my family is financially secure."

"We'd rather have you than the money, Mama."

"I know that, but I should be gone by now. Mueller. Have him come back."

Needing to retreat and organize her thoughts, Mary announced, "I'm going to go get Daddy. He should be part of this discussion."

Before Mary could turn, Sophie grabbed her wrist, vise-like, and it scared Mary, who was all too familiar with the phenomenon of a death grip. In this case, Sophie was holding to prevent Mary from leaving. "Joe won't do it. You're the only one I can turn to. Get me Mueller."

Mary's head was in a whirl as she struggled to reconcile her thoughts. Maybe she hadn't been as blindsided by the mentioning of Mueller as her reaction had suggested. Maybe the present moment had been foretold by her interview of him at the hospital, by her blowup at the courthouse, by her harried reaction to seeing news footage of him. On some level, subconscious or otherwise; had she been in denial that this moment, this damnable moment, would come?

Sophie's next entreaties were interspersed with coughs. "I'm already a corpse, the way I look. Soon, I won't be fit for an open casket. Help your mama, Mary. Promise me Mueller."

Shaking, choking back tears, Mary feebly said, "I promise."

88.

Late evening, on the day that Sophie had begged for him, Mueller unrolled a poster and then held it as might a town crier about to blare an announcement. He smiled smugly upon seeing what it depicted: a drawing of two perched vultures, one advising the other, "The hell with waiting, let's kill something." He glanced at the mailing tube. There was no return address but the postmark was out of state.

Mueller received mail from around the world and had for years. Aside from a smattering routed in care of Lisa Rose's office, his mail came to his home. He'd always made his address public record, foregoing the impersonal safety of, say, a post office box.

Friend and foe knew where he lived or could easily find out—remarkable, when one considers how impassioned the debate over assisted suicide can get. Regardless, he was an incurably high-profile type of guy, and when he wasn't busy administering to clients, defending himself in court, or creating clay figurines, he took long, brisk walks that accounted for his wiry physique. He delighted in being recognized, being pointed at, and being the object of whispers, jeers, or cheers.

So it was that Mueller took no offence over the poster. If the sender's intent was to call him a buzzard, the good doctor had been called worse. He, however, did not rule out the possibility that the poster came from a supporter, one who sympathized with him over the lean times that had descended. He blamed religious nuts, ethicists, and other such hypocrites. Their right-to-life argument was sucking the oxygen from the right-to-die argument. Matters had reached an extreme, an example being a national debate over the rights of a vegetative woman on life support to stay plugged-in, while the rights of conscious, rational people to end their own suffering go ignored.

Dying hadn't gone out of style, neither had suffering; hence, there was a need for his services. There's a difference, unfortunately, between need and demand. The dwindling amount of mail, along with a too silent telephone, suggested that he needed to drum up demand.

Recent attempts had fallen short, the unrequited overtures to the media a case-in-point. He'd further been disappointed in how quickly the Thomas Duval matter lost the public's interest. But, resilient as a sapling, he always sprung back from whatever temporarily had him bent out of shape. To do so again would require a revamping of strategy, one that reflected the times.

He'd decided to repackage the cause as the right to choose instead of the right to die. Label it a freedom, a liberty, something that the founding fathers had meant to include in the Constitution, except that they ran out of space and ink.

And, while at it, why not widen the market. The right to choose would not be limited to the terminally ill, but would be extended to whoever, after due reflection, decides to answer in the negative, Hamlet's query, "To be or not to be." Duval, not having been terminal, was a start.

The challenge was how to market the new strategy, not only to attract clients but to stay top-of-the-mind with the public. Breathing life into suicide might seem a contradiction but not to Mueller. He envisioned a carousel of appearances on all the talk shows—radio and television—and the print media clamoring for interviews and quotes. And, although he'd never owned a computer, he'd decided to hire someone to design him a website. He even decided that he would join Facebook and Twitter—might as well do it right. He would need a theme and he'd come up with: The rebirth of dying with dignity.

A higher profile makes for a bigger target, but Mueller never shied away from controversy, and, although he never bowed to critics, he lamented that Lisa Rose seemed to have joined their ranks. At least she hadn't made her defection public; as far as the world knew, they were still ideological soul-mates. Then again, it wasn't out of the question that she would return to the fold. Until then, what's an occasional tirade. "But words can never hurt me," is how the saying ends.

The, "Sticks and stones may break my bones," part he never had to contend with literally, prior, that is, to Mary's vow to kill him. There's a first time for everything. Then again, he, too, had committed a first by visiting the Kingsley's home when he knew that Mary was in court. In retrospect, he regretted it, made him look too much like an ambulance-chasing attorney. But, that was the past; his new, promotion-driven strategy was a cinch to funnel clients to him.

Mueller affixed the poster on his wall, but the cellophane tape—dollar store variety—relented against the poster's curl, and the poster fell to the floor. He put it up again, this time with masking tape, and achieved functionality at the expense of aesthetics. Upon review, the poster wasn't level but close enough.

The doorbell rang, rather the buzzer grunted.

"Who is it?" Mueller asked into the intercom. The response caused him to briefly suspend blinking, an index finger tracing up and down his Adam's apple, as he thought, *I doubt that she just happened to be in the neighborhood and decided to drop by.* Yet, without inquiring on the nature of the visit, he pushed the buzzer then listened, as rickety stairs complained during the climb.

89.

Mary hurriedly swallowed a spoonful of ice cream, clearing her mouth to say, "No. It was in the summer."

"You sure?" asked Cliff, next to her on their living room love seat.

"Positive." Fighting laughter, she added, "Because you didn't teach summer semester, remember?"

Cliff made a face, looked toward the ceiling, and said, "Right." He chuckled in embarrassment and then admitted, "It took me a month before I could face your mother."

Mary scooped another spoonful of decadence—chocolate mint with pistachios—but couldn't get it to her mouth, seized by laughter. When it subsided, she said, "I bet you first did one of these numbers," and placed a cupped hand at the side of her mouth, like some people do when they are about to call out. Then, adopting a husky voice in imitation of her husband and wearing a macho scowl, she delivered the first of his infamous lines.

Still, after all the years, Cliff dropped his head, shamed by the time he'd said, in explicit, lustful terms, how much he'd been thinking about a certain part of Mary's anatomy, what he was going to do to it, and how she was to disrobe on the way up the stairs. "You're never going to let me live it down."

Mary was too busy convulsing to deny it. She collected herself long enough to deliver more of his lines.

Cliff gave a good-natured groan and repeated, "Never."

Mary mirthfully recalled, "Mama was looking all serious at me." She folded her arms, imitating Sophie this time. "What kind of English professor talks like that?"

"When I heard your mother's voice and realized that she had come into the house with you, I thought about climbing out the window."

"From the second floor?"

"I could have tied some sheets together. Then, I could have come in through the front door, like I was just arriving." Then, Cliff placed the blame where he believed it rightfully belonged. "I hold you responsible."

With wide-eyed theatrics, Mary pointed both thumbs at herself and asked, "Moi? I didn't put those words in your mouth."

"Might as well have. You'd told me that kind of talk excited you."

"Yeah, because it contrasts with your prim-and-proper side." She threw in, "But I love both sides."

"You still should have warned me that your mother was with you."

Mary gave the same defense she'd always given. "I didn't have time. You started as soon as I came in the house."

"You could have said something as soon as I blurted out. I would have ended up only embarrassed instead of mortified."

"My mind was on saving my own reputation. I'm all looking at Mama, like, we must be in the wrong house. But she gave me her own look. You know the one I'm talking about."

"The one that says she's not fooled for a second?"

"That's the one. So I knew I was busted, right along with you."

"What a way to meet a future mother-in-law."

Mary picked up the spoon that rested atop the mound of ice cream, licked it clean, and then shook it scoldingly at Cliff. "You knew better than to bring ice cream into the house. Don't you dare say a word, no matter how much weight I gain."

"I won't," promised Cliff, who'd supplied her favorite comfort food. Getting back on topic, he recalled, "Your mother could have made me feel worse, but she cut me some slack."

"Because from everything that I'd told her, she knew I loved you. And soon, she grew to love you, too," Mary said of Sophie, whose body lay in the funeral home, one day after Mary had promised her that she would contact Fritz Mueller.

Reliving the day that Cliff met Sophie had brought tears of laughter to Mary's eyes, which remained red and swollen from earlier crying spells. On the coffee table was a mixing bowl that contained a face cloth immersed in ice water. She took out the cloth, folded it lengthwise, and pressed it against her eyes for about a half minute.

Meanwhile, Cliff tried to keep the conversation positive. "It'll be nice to have the kids back home for a while," he said, in reference to the funeral.

"I better get the guestroom ready, too. Most likely, Aunt Lucille will stay with us."

Lucille would be among the later arrivals, her philosophy being that if God had meant for her to fly, he would have made her a pilot. The bus was fast enough and more comfortable than a car.

Mary ate the rest of the ice cream, polishing off the pint single-handedly. She shivered, in part due to the frozen delight but mostly from contemplation of her loss. She leaned into Cliff, wrapped his arm around herself, and felt warmly cocooned. "Can I ask you something?"

He kissed her forehead and drew her closer. "What?"

"How should I feel?"

"No one can say, Honey," advised Cliff, who'd lost both his parents. "You'll feel different emotions at different times."

"I mean about Mueller."

"Grateful that things turned out as they did."

"I'm more than grateful. But what if things had turned out differently."

"Don't torture yourself with such wonderings."

"I promised her, but I never could have gone through with it. I never could have gone to Mueller."

"And you didn't have to. It's best to leave it at that."

But Mary wouldn't. "Maybe, because Mama believed that relief was on its way, she relaxed so much that she slipped into God's arms." With hope resonating in her voice, she asked, "What do you think?"

"I think that's exactly what happened. Your mother was suffering something awful. She's at rest now. Rest that she deserves."

Mary snuggled like she wanted to burrow inside him. "Don't ever leave me."

"You know better." Throughout the day, Cliff had been answering the phone, accepting condolences on Mary's behalf. It rang again. He picked up the cordless unit from where it sat at his side. "Hello."

"Hi, Cliff. Ross Brogan, here. How is Mary?"

"She's holding it together."

"With your help, I'm sure. Can I talk to her?"

"I'll take a message."

"Well, uh, it's business. I apologize. I know the timing stinks but I think she'd want to hear this. I'll make it short."

"Hold on." Cliff covered the mouthpiece and told Mary, "Ross says you would want to take this."

Mary took the phone. "Yes, Ross."

"First of all, my condolences."

"Thanks."

Brogan said, "Lisa Rose was dropped off at a hospital by Fritz Mueller."

"Is she sick or hurt?" asked Mary, thinking in the traditional mode.

"Listen again. Dropped off. By Mueller. You know he doesn't care about Miranda rights, so he's been talking. Claims that Rose wanted to end her suffering."

The understanding now there, Mary let the phone slowly slide down the side of her face.

90.

Mary was seated between Joe and Cliff inside the stretch limo which maintained a slow, dignified speed, second in line behind the hearse. Her cheeks showed flecks of lipstick from pecks and kisses from funeral attendees. No fan of high heels, her ankles were hurting. She stared straight ahead, her vision blurry from tears and further compromised by dark glasses and a black veil. The other occupants were her children and three of Sophie's siblings.

The funeral had been somber, but also rousing, the pastor's eulogy and the choir's selections especially stirring. Mary had been the last to deliver remarks, her words unscripted but cohesive and moving.

Cousin Suzette, as she did at every family funeral, put on her copyrighted performance: attempting to climb into the casket when the lid was being lowered, act two to be performed at the cemetery, with her attempting to jump into the grave with the casket. Family, no matter how quirky, is a source of strength in such times.

Mary clutched a purse stuffed with leftover programs. The picture that graced the front had been taken several years prior: Sophie, the smiling sophisticate, in full Easter regalia. Mary would not keep all of them but would send some to family members who weren't able to attend. The remainder would be her treasured keepsakes.

Mary had looked upon her mother for the last time, no more solace in knowing there'll be another glance, as had been the case at the funeral home. The finality now was a fact, of which no two individuals acknowledge on the same schedule.

There had been another funeral days prior, under the glare of national media and before overflowing attendance, and Mary directed a thought to it. The courtesy was unavoidable, since that other deceased had been a constant presence throughout Sophie's end-of-life.

At that other funeral had sat Bernie, the devastated, bereaved grandfather, or at least that was the performance he gave.

Lisa Rose, in accordance with a provision in her will made years and years ago, was buried next to her mother.

91.

Mary's body had aged years over the past hour, or so it felt from the assortment of current complaints. Her stride was jerky, all semblance of form had deserted her miles back. She kept going, though. The sun in the cloudless sky added to the drudgery, such that she wished she could rip her shadow off the pavement and carry it overhead for shade, but where would she find the arm strength?

The ten-mile run/walk was an annual fundraiser for breast cancer research and this was the first since Sophie died. Mary had trained for months, but adrenaline had made her take the early miles at too fast a pace and she was paying for it. She'd been reduced to having to take breaths in snatches. But she kept going.

Her sweat-drenched jersey was stained with Gatorade, from inexperience with running and drinking—multitasking more challenging than walking and chewing gum. If she would only pull her pink head band lower it would do a better job of keeping sweat out of her stinging eyes. Down her face, body salts and minerals had given her white, grainy sideburns. And she kept going.

Mary and Cliff initially placed their share of the out-of-court settlement in a savings account, while they weighed options. Ultimately, they decided that they didn't want to use the money to elevate their standard of living. Instead, after making a donation to breast cancer research in the name of Sophie Kingsley, they gave generously to their children, and then put the remainder in a trust fund for future grandchildren.

Mary was hoofing close along the sidelines, a strategic choice providing easier access to refreshment stands. She was closing in on one, where outstretched hands were holding a variety of offerings. She slowed and accepted a cup of water from one volunteer and a piece of banana from another who was wearing food service gloves.

The entire route was aligned with spectators, many of them boisterously shouting encouragement, particularly to those runners who seemed to be laboring on the brink. "C'mon, c'mon. You're going to make it. One foot in front of the other." Additionally, mile-markers silently informed how much farther there was to go, which had varying effects on the psyche, depending on how a runner was fairing at that time.

What Mary didn't know was her position relative to other runners, how many ahead, how many behind. There were those so far ahead that they were, literally, out of sight, and she'd abandoned the occasional look over the shoulder to see who was behind because it cramped her neck muscles as well as threw her further off stride. What mattered was not position but finishing. So she kept going.

There were spectators who'd come in support of Mary and were bouncing, waving, and calling her name. Less demonstrative was Ross Brogan, who'd helped Mary train and was there to evaluate her performance. Gerald Lewis was there, too, now officially the Republican candidate for State Attorney General. Pinned to his shirt was a big campaign button, reflecting the sunlight so splendidly that it seemed battery-powered.

Seeing Lewis always reminded Mary of Lisa Rose, not that Mary didn't think of Rose often, anyway. Their relationship had been so entangled and fateful, that she still was haunted by its tragic ending.

By homicide unit standards, the murders committed by Rose were solved and the cases closed. Not so, by court standards, however, which don't permit posthumous convictions. When Rose died, so did the opportunity to stamp her as a convicted killer. Regardless, Mary contacted the survivors of the victims, laid out the entire investigation, and assured them that the killer had been correctly identified.

Another character in the tragedy, however, was facing conviction on murder charges: Fritz Mueller. It wasn't for the death of Lisa Rose, though. Not long after the Michigan legislature, in an emergency session, passed a bill making assisted suicide a felony, Mueller performed one, in intentional defiance. Mueller, presently free on bond, was milking the sensationalism and media circus like a champion dairy farmer with six fingers on each hand. Plus, a number of big-name attorneys were vying to represent him.

The cheering from the spectators was becoming more frantic. Along both sides of the street, some were gesturing wildly, pointing at something ahead. Whatever it was, it was on the other side of the rise. Could it be the finish line? It must be the finish line. It better be the finish line.

A person has got to be sick in the head to lay out a course that has a hill before the finish, thought Mary. *Truly sick.*

Pounding the pavement had become akin to running in quicksand. Mary's heart was thumping like it might fracture ribs. Could she keep in the stable the charley horse that was threatening to break free and gallop through her left calf? As long as the tank isn't completely empty, even fumes will get you farther. She kept going.

She made it to the top, and although the foreground waved eerily in the heat, she knew that the banner strung between lamp posts was no mirage.

It read: FINISH.

And there, as always, was Cliff. He was holding one of those capes—given to each finisher to manage body temperature during cool down—made of that shiny, metallic-looking film used for gift balloons. After she crossed, he raced to her, draped the cape around her, and held her tightly around the shoulders as he slowly walked her to the registrar's table. They resembled the iconic routine of the late Soul Brother Number One, James Brown, but there would be no sudden castoff of the cape, no sudden infusion of energy, no sliding on one leg back to center stage. Mary was completely spent and she wasn't making any pretenses to the contrary.

"You did it," said Cliff. "You went the distance."

Mary gave a half-smile, the most she could manage at the time, appreciating that his words didn't apply only to the race.

ABOUT THE AUTHOR

STERLING ANTHONY is a management consultant, living in Detroit. He has resolved to devote more time to writing fiction.

CPSIA information can be obtained at www.ICGtesting.com
Printed in the USA
LVOW101420290212

270993LV00005B/17/P